The last letter before Ausch.

Haya Ravinsky-Mandelbaum

Producer & International Distributor
eBookPro Publishing
www.ebook-pro.com

The Last Letter Before Auschwitz
Haya Ravinsky-Mandelbaum
Copyright © 2025 Haya Ravinsky-Mandelbaum

All rights reserved; No parts of this book may be reproduced or transmitted in any form or by any means, electronic or mechanical, including photocopying, recording, taping, or by any information retrieval system, without the permission, in writing, of the author.

ISBN 9798316960446

The Last Letter Before Auschwitz

Haya Ravinsky-Mandelbaum

Editing and historical research: Jan Torringa

Dedicated to my three daughters

Efrat
Noa
Tamar

Introduction

When Ilse Birnbaum stepped off the boat in Haifa in 1946, she possessed little more than a stack of 105 letters written by her lover Erco. He was murdered in Auschwitz in 1944. Those letters are the heart and soul of this book. Ilse and Erco wrote to each other in German. Ilse's daughter Haya later translated the letters into Dutch.

Ilse Birnbaum and Ernst (Erco) Cosmann had much in common. They both came from affluent, assimilated Jewish backgrounds in Germany, had to leave their country, and ended up in the Netherlands. Ilse, born in 1921, and Ernst, a year older, grew up under very different circumstances than their parents. In 1933, the Nazis gained power in Germany, and it quickly became clear to the young generation that there was no future for them in their motherland. As a result, they were drawn to Zionism. Given the ever-increasing hatred of the Jews, there was no other solution: establish a Jewish country of their own.

They never heard anything at home about Palestine as their future Jewish home. Their parents were a part of the group of people who felt more German than Jewish and who were well-placed in society. For the younger generation in Germany, ever-increasing anti-Semitism and, from 1933 onwards, a government that took more and more anti-Jewish measures was the reality they grew up in.

Ilse and Ernst met in Amsterdam at the Jewish youth movement Maccabi Hatzair, of which many young people like them were members: children of affluent, assimilated families hearing about Palestine and Jewish culture for the first time. They shared a grand ideal: transforming the Palestinian desert into fertile land and establishing their new Jewish home there. In preparation for their aliyah – emigration to Palestine – they sought to learn the trades they would need in that new country.

Erco wanted to become a farmer and took up an apprenticeship with a farmer in a village called Wilp, situated between Deventer and Apeldoorn. He later became an educator at a new agricultural school for Jewish youth living at Huize Voorburg in Elden, close to the city of Arnhem.

Ilse had a strict and conservative upbringing, which made it difficult to see Erco on a regular basis. The Birnbaums felt that Erco was not the right match for their daughter and especially objected to his Zionist ideals. They had a very different future in mind for their daughter than being a farmer's wife in a distant, unknown country. Ilse initially shared her parents' objections, and she and Erco discussed them vehemently, even in their letters. Nevertheless, Ilse traveled to Wilp regularly and later also to Elden. Although initially chaperoned by her younger sister Margot, Ilse and Erco, with much trickery and deceit, succeeded in seeing each other in private. Their correspondence, of which only Ernst's letters to Ilse have survived, traces the course of their love.

Huize Voorburg in Elden in 1930

Early in the morning on October 3, 1942, the Germans surrounded Huize Voorburg. All 38 Palestine pioneers who lived there were captured and taken to Camp Westerbork. From Westerbork, Ernst wrote Ilse about 30 more letters. They managed to meet on two occasions. Ernst made himself indispensable in the camp and stayed there for almost a year. Regardless, on September 14, 1943, he was deported and taken to Auschwitz-Monowitz, where he died of hunger and exhaustion on January 17, 1944. His last words to Ilse were, 'Stay strong, believe in our love and our shared future.'

Ilse survived the war and emigrated to Israel, where she married and had a daughter, Haya. She returned to Amsterdam in the 1950s and passed away in 1999. Shlomo Samson, Erco's friend and fellow pioneer, was the first to recognize the historical importance of the letters. He translated the letters into Hebrew and used them for his book *Between Darkness and Light: 60 years after 'Kristallnacht.'*

During the COVID-19 lockdown in 2020, Ilse's daughter Haya finally decided to read the letters. That led her to discover her mother's secret. The family she grew up in always focussed solely on her father's suffering – he had survived many camps, including Auschwitz. They never spoke about her mother's traumatic war experiences.

> Montag 5. Oct. 1942
>
> Mein geliebter Ernst,
>
> Die ganze Tragik und Hoffnungslosigkeit unserer Sache kommt mir jetzt erst völlig zum Bewußtsein. Bisher war betäubt, all die Menschen um mich herum haben mich nicht zum Bewußtsein kommen lassen. Erst jetzt wo ich ganz allein bin, allein ohne Dich, in einer trostlosen Bahnhofshalle in Zwolle, erst jetzt begreife ich's gänzlich. Du bist nicht mehr erreichbar für mich. Meine Energie und Lebenswille ist schon gebrochen, ich bin so ein unfähiges Mädchen. Da mein Geliebter warst die Kraft in meinem Hintergrund. Alle Handlungen und Gedanken waren durch Dich angetrieben. Ich weiß, ich bin nervlich schon lange ein Schwächling, aber jetzt kann ich nichts mehr daran ändern. Du, mein Alles bist nicht mehr da!
>
> Ich weiß, daß dieser Brief Dich nie erreichen wird, aber er beruhigt mich. Mein Gewissen kann kein Mensch beruhigen. Ich wollte Dich Freitag abend haben, ich habe mich gehen lassen und war zu bequem, Liebchen, das ist nie wieder gut zu machen. Was denkst Du jetzt mein Blondes? Wenn ich mit bei Dir wäre. – Wozu hat man sich einen Kameraden fürs Leben ausgesucht wenn in seinen schwersten Stunden er nicht bei ihm ist. Oh, Liebes, ich weiß nichts mehr, ich bin leer wie eine schlechte Nuss. Mein Licht ist weg – Deine Ilse

> Diesen Brief schrieb Ilse, als sie hörte, daß Elden nach Westerbork geschickt wurde. Sie hat den Brief nicht abgeschickt - darum blieb er erhalten.

Shlomo Samson in Kibboets Schluchot, Israel, 2021. Above is a letter from Ilse to Ernst in Samson's handwriting. He transcribed all the letters first before translating them into hebrew.

PART I

Ernst and Ilse

Ilse

On July 26, 1921, a long, beautiful summer day, the long-awaited baby, a girl, Ilse, opens her eyes and sees a beautiful world. Innsbrucker Strasse 12, Schönberg, Berlin.

Nanny, nursery, pram, white starched lace, and a little white fur cape. Everything is crisp, beautiful and clean.

After two years, another girl is born. Ilse now has a little sister; her name is Margot. Babies, nursery, pram, white starched lace, and two white fur capes.

Kaethe with Ilse in 1921

Berlin 1925: Ilse and Margot

Life in Berlin is beautiful, especially for assimilated German Jews like the Birnbaums, who are proud Germans, German Jews second. World War I, in which Rudolf Birnbaum had fought fiercely on all fronts, from Saarland to Silesia, is over. He returns from the front, tired but happy. Life with his beloved Kaethe is finally underway.

Former soldier Rudolf Birnbaum becomes a cunning stockbroker on the Berlin stock exchange. He is successful and enjoys the good life with his family. The family moves into a posh apartment on Hewaldstraße 9, Schönberg, full of beautiful Biedermeier furniture and artifacts. Every summer, they travel to a different seaside resort. They go to Arendsee, Norderney, Warren, and Binz. In 1928, they even go to Sicily in the summer and Sankt Moritz in the winter. They travel from one seaside resort to another, all four branches of the family accompanying them. Vati Rudolf has two brothers and a sister: Uncle Benno, Uncle Willy, and Auntie Else. Mother Kaethe has a sister, Aunt Dora. All the uncles, Aunts, and their children travel together, happy and cozy, to their wonderfully well-organized vacations. Their suitcases are packed with the finest clothes, and the latest jewelry adorns their necks, fingers, and arms. All the nannies (*Kindermädchen*) go with them, and the families are happy. *La dolce vita*, the world is beautiful. Berlin is the best place to live.

Rudolf Birnbaum, Ilse's father, in 1915.

Vacation in Binz in 1925, everybody was dressed in white, as was customary when vacationing at the seaside

1924, the Birnbaums on holiday in Arendsee

In 1930, after the world economic crisis of 1929 started, the value of the German currency drops significantly, and the unemployment rate is high and increasing by the day. Elections are held in September 1930. Adolf Hitler's NSDAP becomes the second-largest party in Germany, after the Socialists and before the Communists. The great age of the Nazi party commences. The November 1932 elections were the last democratic elections in Germany. In January of the following year, Hitler becomes chancellor. Within a year, he transforms Germany into a national-socialist, totalitarian state. Opponents are arrested, political parties banned, and the whole society is thoroughly Nazified. Economic recovery and the new national consciousness lead to widespread popular support.

1927, Ilse at home on Hewald Strasse 9, Berlin, 'beautiful Biedermeier furniture'

The world is changing, and decisions have to be made. One day, Ilse comes home from school crying. The teacher had said: *'In deinem Haus ist wahrscheinlich der Kamm in der Butter!* (In your house, the comb is probably in the butter. Meaning: the place must be a mess).

The situation becomes more difficult by the day. Vati Rudolf makes his first decision, and thus Ilse is sent to England so that she no longer has to attend her German school. Ilse leaves her parental home at the tender age of 12.

Ilse at boarding school in Hazlemere, England, 1936

Many Jewish children from families that can afford it send their children to English boarding schools. Ilse ended up at a boarding school in Haslemere, the Stoatley Rough School, which many Jewish children from Germany attended. It doesn't take long for her to become very happy there. She has a wonderful time in Haslemere. Many years later, she would still speak of these years with a smile and a great sense of happiness.

Margot, who is two years younger, stays at home. Communication with her family at home can now only happen by mail. In 1935, Ilse comes home for winter break.

In the summer of 1936, many of Ilse's friends from school go back to Germany for the summer vacation, and so does Ilse. She attends a Haboniem (youth group) summer camp in Hamburg with her schoolmates from Haslemere.[1] This experience will play a significant role in her future life; here, the seeds of Zionism are planted. At the youth club, she hears about Palestine and Zionism, ideals that are never discussed in her assimilated family.

Rudolf Birnbaum is determined and decides that the whole family must leave Berlin; there is no more room for Jews. He arranges certificates for all of them. Uncle Benno, his wife, Aunt Selma (born Lewinsky), and the children leave Germany and go to Buenos Aires. Aunt Else (born Birnbaum), with her husband Adolf Ebstein and their daughter Lilo, do not leave Breslau until 1940 and then go to Santiago de Chile. Their daughter Ruth moves to Montevideo in Uruguay, and their third, the youngest daughter, Steffi (Ora), emigrates to Palestine in 1939 with a group from the youth club.

A cheerful Ilse (left), Haboniem summer camp in Hamburg, 1936

---

1   Haboniem is an international socialist-Zionist youth movement and has existed since 1928. The Dutch branch was founded in 1950. Ilse's daughter would later become an enthusiastic member.

Uncle Willy marries Helene Feder, a non-Jewish woman. Helene, a clever and extraordinarily courageous woman, manages to stay in Berlin with her family throughout the war. After saving her entire family, the youngest members of the Birnbaum family do not leave Germany until the war is over – they move to Akko in Palestine. Aunt Dora and her husband, Adolf Liebeskind, go to New York. Rudolf Birnbaum leaves Berlin in 1934 and goes to Amsterdam. Kaethe and Margot stay behind. Kaethe, although raised Orthodox, now takes advantage of her non-Jewish heritage. She handles all the necessary arrangements and closes all outstanding accounts in Berlin. In 1936, a truck is loaded with all the beautiful Biedermeier furniture and art. Kaethe and Margot depart from Hewaldstr. 9, Berlin to Stadionweg 117, Amsterdam. They will never return to their homeland.

Ilse, still in England, 1937

The family, who was always together and intimately shared their joys and sorrows, was now scattered over three continents. They would never see each other again and never see Berlin again! Yet all the siblings and their children survived the war. A miracle!

In 1938, Ilse completes her final exams in Haslemere and returns home, which is no longer Berlin but Amsterdam. Ilse is given a lovely spacious room with a sink and two windows on the street side. Tramway 24 whizzes by until 11 p.m., street lamps illuminate Stadionweg all night, and rays of light sneak into the room through large glass windows as shadows dance across the wooden floor. A bustling city, very different from the Haslemere countryside!

Tramway 24 on Stadionweg

Ernst

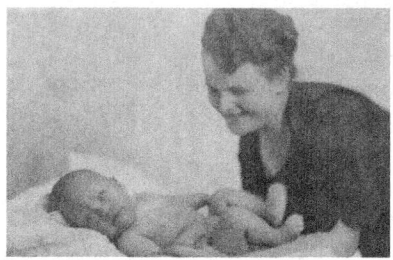

Ernst and his mother, 1920

1915, Fritz Cosmann, World War I

Ernst Cosmann is born on May 22, 1920 in Wuppertal. Like many Jews in Germany at that time, the Cosmann family is detached from religion and tradition. Because there is no Jewish school in Bielefeld, Ernst attends public school. He comes from a wealthy family – dignitaries of the city – his grandfather owned a department store in Recklinghausen. Fritz, his father, who returned from World War I as a German hero, decorated with the Iron Cross, builds a successful practice as a lawyer. Fifteen years later, he is suddenly no longer a hero; as a Jew, the German people now consider him a traitor. In 1933, he is forbidden to practice his profession and had to support his family on a meager salary of 200 Reichsmark as secretary of the Jewish community. After a prolonged illness, he dies in 1937. His wife Thekla and their son Werner, Ernst's brother who is two years younger, go to Palestine. Ernst had already left home.

During his high school years, Ernst realizes that he has no future in Nazi Germany.

He discovers Zionism and has heated discussions about it with his father, who is against it. He leaves school at the age of 16, very much against the wishes of his parents. His parents have an entirely different future in mind for him than becoming a farmer, but Ernst says: 'In Israel, they need farmers, not academics.'

In 1936, Ernst is 16 years old and goes to the Hachshara farm, 'Halbe' near Berlin. He stays there for two years, then goes to Bremen, where he becomes a trainer (madrich) in the youth movement Maccabi Hatzair. During this time, he works as a gardener to earn a living.

May 22, 1921. Ernst, with his father on his first birthday.

1936, Ernst Cosmann in
Halbe, 16 years old, Knows
exactly what he wants to be
one day.

Ernst in Halbe, around 1936.
Photo: Kenneth. Renberg,
Jüdisches Museum, Berlin.

After Kristallnacht in November 1938, the night in which Jews were beaten and murdered on a large scale, their possessions destroyed, and their synagogues set on fire, Ernst returns to Bielefeld and, together with his younger brother Heinz, tries to find a way to leave Germany.

Brothers Heinz, Werner and Ernst together for the last time, Passover 1938

On December 19, 1938, the two brothers arrive in the Netherlands. They are welcomed at Riverhuis De Steeg in Rheden, a shelter for child refugees run by nuns. They do not stay there long. Ernst pursues his Zionist ideals and, after spending several months in Amsterdam, begins his 'individual training.' This individual training to become a farmer and schooling in language, culture, and history is believed to be the best training for farmers who 'have to build Erez' in the future. He goes to work for farmer Oldenboom in Wilp, Gelderland. His little brother Heinz ends up at the Pavilion Loosdrechtse Rade in Loosdrecht, a training center intended for children who fled to the Netherlands without their parents. This training also focuses on emigration to Palestine. Loosdrecht is home to about fifty students who receive their training from farmers in the area during the daytime.

Heinz (left, second row from the top) in Loosdrecht, 1941

Ernst's driver's license, which he obtained in Bremen in 1938

The Palestine Pioneers

Ilse and Ernst's generation, born around 1920, became infatuated with Zionism out of necessity: the idea that the future of the Jewish people lay in Israel turned into reality when German authorities made it clear that there is no future for them in their homeland. As teenagers, they witnessed firsthand how Jews were demoted to second-class citizens and excluded from the 'people's community' in a short period of time. Jews were bullied out of their homeland.

Even though less than 1 percent of the population was of Jewish origin, the Nazis saw them as the main threat to the Germans, and they were blamed for the Germans losing World War I. It was alleged that a 'Jewish-Bolshevik conspiracy' existed that was a threat to the German people. Immediately after Hitler seized power in 1933, all sorts of anti-Jewish measures were introduced. A general Jew boycott (Judenboykott) was declared against Jewish shopkeepers, and all Jewish officials were fired. In 1935, the Nuremberg Race Laws were passed, which stipulated that Jews were to be stripped of their citizenship and were no longer allowed to marry people with 'German blood.' The extent of the hatred towards Jews became evident during Kristallnacht on November 9, 1938, when riled-up crowds across Germany attacked and destroyed Jewish homes, stores and synagogues. About 26,000 Jews were detained and imprisoned in concentration camps, and hundreds were murdered. Hitler's rise to power in Germany had changed the meaning of the Zionist dream. For the young generation, it was no longer a dream but the only possible future.

Zionism

In 1886, Theodor Herzl's book Der Judenstaat was published. In it, he drew the conclusion that the anti-Semitism that had led to the persecution and massacres of Jews under the increasingly strong nationalism of the nineteenth century, especially in Eastern Europe, was unsolvable. The Jews needed to leave Europe and establish their own nation.

In 1899, a Dutch Zionist Association is established in the Netherlands. However, the Zionist ideal by no means appeals to everyone. Many people felt a bigger connection to the country where they live than to their Jewish background. Socialists and communists believe that if class differences disappear after the revolution, so will anti-Semitism, and religious Jews want to wait for the coming of the messiah before they can return to Palestine. Still others wanted to emigrate, but then preferably to America. Many Jews want to avoid promoting themselves too much as a group because they fear it will only fuel anti-Semitism.

Nevertheless, some boldly began to prepare for their aliyah, their crossing to Palestine: the *Chalutzim*, the forerunners who would return to Palestine as pioneers. This Hechalutz movement arises in Russia and Ukraine after violent pogroms at the end of the nineteenth century.

There weren't many Jewish farmers in Europe because Jews were often prohibited from owning land. Most Jews were small- and medium-sized independent entrepreneurs or intellectuals who were not apt for farming. A Jewish agricultural community had to be created; Jewish immigrants had to 'conquer labor' in Palestine. Therefore, young people had to be trained before their aliyah to become accomplished farmers. This training, called hachsjara, was organized by Jewish youth movements. These young people called themselves chalutzim or Palestine pioneers. The majority of these chalutzim came from Germany and Eastern Europe. Young Dutch Jews showed little interest. They had not experienced the ever-increasing anti-Semitism that threatened their lives and futures, like their peers from the East, and considered themselves well-integrated into society. They had no desire to move to a barren desert. There was widespread opposition to Jews in the Netherlands, but not from the government and not comparable to what was happening in Poland and Germany.

The pogroms in Eastern Europe caused many Jews to flee at the beginning of the century. For many of them, America was the promised land, and they subsequently traveled to the ports of Amsterdam and Rotterdam. From there, they continued their journey by boat. Border Societies were established along the Dutch border to help the destitute Jewish refugees who often arrived in the country on cattle wagons. The Border Association for Emigrants in Deventer had been in operation since 1902, after World War I, followed by the Deventer Association for the Vocational Training of Palestine Pioneers, founded by furniture merchant Ru Cohen and his wife, Eva Cohen-Köningsberger. This 'Deventer Association' aimed to train refugees in the trades that would be needed in Palestine. They tried to find farmers in Gelderland and Overijssel who were willing to take in the mostly immigrant boys and girls and teach them to milk cows and harvest hay and potatoes. Often, these young people had never performed any kind of manual labor before. The pioneers did not live together: hence, it was referred to as Einzelhachshara – individual training. Ernst also joined the Deventer Society. An apprenticeship was arranged for him with farmer Oldenboom in Wilp, which was not far from Deventer.

The Beth Chaluz house, where the young Palestine pioneers could spend their free weekends learning Jewish history and modern Hebrew (the language that would become the language of the Jewish state) and where lectures were held, was located in Deventer. In 1941, the Deventer Association opened a youth aliyah home in Elden, near Arnhem, where young pioneers lived together. Here, Ernst became a madrich – youth leader.

Hachshara homes, such as in Gouda (1937), Amsterdam (1939), and Loosdrecht (1939), had previously been established due to the large number of Jewish refugees arriving in the Netherlands. Religious Jews had their own hachshara organizations and had established several kibbutzim (collective farms), including in Franeker, Beverwijk, and Enschede. In the hachshara homes intended for the younger pioneers, such as those in Gouda, Elden and Loosdrecht, religious and non-religious youth and children lived together.

In addition, after Hitler's rise to power in 1933, a large Working Village was set up in the newly drained Wieringermeer for Jewish refugees from Germany and Poland. The Wieringermeer Working Village housed more than 300 residents, mostly single young people aged 18 to 24. There, they learned a trade or how to farm. The intention was for them to then emigrate to Palestine or another country because the Dutch government feared that they would flood the job market in times of crisis and high unemployment. The Working Village differed from the other programs because it did not focus on emigration to Palestine only but also to other countries. Two-thirds of the residents were not Zionist and wanted to emigrate, but not necessarily to Palestine. To many, America was more attractive. When Germany invaded in May 1940, three hundred people were living in the Working Village. The other hachshara centers in the Netherlands had more than five hundred young people who did not manage to get out in time.

On the roof of Beth Chaluz in Deventer, 1940.
Ernst is sitting in the front row, far right.

After World War I, Palestine was governed by the British. In 1917, British Foreign Secretary Lord Balfour declared that Jews have a right to own land, and British administrators are instructed by the League of Nations to facilitate a 'National Home for the Jewish people.' That dis not mean that everyone was allowed to settle there. The Jewish Agency for Palestine, which represented the Jews in Palestine, issued certificates entitling them to settle in the country, but the British authorities had stipulated a maximum of 7,500 per year. Those who had completed their education were eligible for a Palestine certificate – permission for immigration – but the British administrators of Palestine were concerned about conflicts with the Arab population, so they only allowed a limited number of Jewish immigrants. As the number of refugees increased, it became more difficult to obtain entry visas to other safe countries. Even America was refusing to grant Jews entry.

Due to the German invasion, emigration was no longer an option. Young people who had completed their education and had received a Palestine pass could not leave. They thus remained at the various hachshara centers, which, since 1940, fell under the Jewish Central Vocational Training Board (JCB). For the time being, these young people felt safe there. After all, they contributed to the food supply and therefore assumed that they would not be considered for Arbeitseinsatz and deportation. Initially, the German occupiers left the various training programs in peace, but when the Jewish Working Village in Wieringermeer was evacuated by the Germans in March 1941, it came as a great shock. A few months later, many of the residents were rounded up and murdered in the Mauthausen concentration camp.

March 20, 1941: Jewish Working Village in the Wieringermeer is rounded up. The young village workers are waiting for their transport.

Amsterdam-Zuid

In Amsterdam, Ilse soon joins the Jewish youth movement Maccabi Hatzair.[2] 'The movement' becomes her joy and her life. Ilse is a cheerful, nice, sociable, and pretty curly-haired girl, and she immediately becomes the center of attention among all the new friends she has just met. A lot of those new friends have the same background. German Jews who are wealthy and could afford to leave Germany. They also all live in the same neighborhood ... So wie es sich gehört (as it should be)... all of them in South Amsterdam.

The Pintus family, very wealthy Berliners, assimilated German Jews, are among those new residents in Amsterdam-Zuid (Amsterdam-South). The father was the director of Shell in Germany. They lived in a fourteen-room palace in one of the most beautiful districts of Berlin and had the kind of life wealthy people were accustomed to. They had many parties, wore beautiful dresses, had lots of champagne, and were very happy.

In 1936, the Pintus family's luxury lifestyle in Berlin also ends. They leave Berlin with their twins, Lore and Heini, who just turned sixteen, and move to Amsterdam, where they rent a six-room house on Minervalaan.

---

2   Zionist youth movement founded in Prague in 1929. Resembles scouting.

Heini (Bad Godesberg 1921- Mauthausen 1941) and Lore Pintus (Bad Godesberg 1921- Israel 1989)

Heini looks like the Aryan ideal, blond with big, beautiful blue eyes. Lore has a beautiful classic Jewish face, with black curls, jet-black eyes, olive-colored skin and snow-white teeth. She looks more like the oriental princess Scheherazade from the story *One Thousand and One Nights* than a Jewish girl from Berlin. Heini and Lore Pintus, the twins from Minerva Square, live in a friendly house where anything goes as long as the children are having fun.

Heini Pintus is a calm, reserved boy, absolutely the opposite of his lively sister Lore. Heini and Lore, like Ilse, join the Maccabi Hatzair youth movement. All these assimilated children who have nothing to do with Judaism or Zionism are now learning Jewish subjects and Jewish history for the first time, and about Palestine and what is needed in Palestine. They realize more and more that their future lies in Palestine, and so they begin to dream of a new ideal.

In the Netherlands, they are no longer allowed to attend university – after the German invasion, Jews are prohibited from attending – and so many boys choose agriculture. There is separate training for girls. At Gerzon, the chic fashion store on Kalverstraat, Ilse learns to sew. Lore learns to be a kindergarten teacher. These are trades that are needed in Palestine.

Ilse, learning to sew at Gerzon

The meetings in Maccabi Hatzair are tremendously enjoyable; everyone attends, is cheerful and upbeat, and no one ever misses a meeting. Young children, fresh love stories, eighteen-year-olds. Hormones are also running wild. Heini meets Lea Mikulinsky and immediately falls in love with this cheerful girl. Lea, unlike the others, is still at the Vossius Gymnasium and has yet to take her final exams. Heini is so infatuated that he does not notice Lea's strange Russian accent.

Lea was born in Charkov, Ukraine, in 1920. Ukrainian Jews suffered pogroms and increasing anti-Semitism during the civil war that followed the revolution in Russia. Several armies fought against each other, and they all massacred Jews. Between 50,000 and 100,000 people were murdered during these years. The situation was getting worse by the day; it was clear that they had to get away from there.

The Mikulinsky family, three brothers and a sister, all married with children, leave Ukraine in 1925 bound for Palestine. They settle in G'eula Street in Tel Aviv, on the coast, with a view of the sea, a pleasant afternoon breeze, no frost, no rain, but sand, lots of sand, southern desert winds, lots of dust, few trees, and no shade. There are low white houses with red roof tiles, Theodor Herzl's dream, no more than three stories high in the first Hebrew

G'eula Street, Tel Aviv, 1925

town outside the walls of Jaffo. All the nephews and nieces – Lowa, Shura, Masha, Lea, Munia, Aharontshik, Lania, Sacha, Bashinka and Ariele – adapt quickly, learn Hebrew, go to school and replant the trees that the Turks uprooted in the Ottoman period to build rail lines throughout Palestine. The children are given small, young eucalyptus trees and hoes and plant trees non-stop. Bare streets gradually turn green. To this day, the streets of Tel Aviv are decorated with these trees, which the Baron de Rothschild brought from Australia in order to dry up the marshlands.

However, happy, rosy-cheeked children do not necessarily mean happy parents. Salomon Mikulinsky opens a shoe store and is doing very well. Kula Mikulinsky opens a textile business, but it fails. He goes bankrupt and flees to Amsterdam with his wife Itta and son Lowa in 1932. Sasha Mikulinsky has no luck either; a hot and dusty life in Tel Aviv simply doesn't work for him. He follows his brother Kula to Amsterdam in 1933 with his wife Polina and their four children. In the meantime, their sister, Batya Mikulinsky, married Moshe Ravinsky. They open a men's store in Tel Aviv and their business is doing well.

Lea, who just recently celebrated her bat mitzvah with all her cousins in Tel Aviv, is now in Amsterdam with her little brother Mark, her sister Haya and their youngest brother Yizchak, who just turned ten. Life in Amsterdam is impoverished and difficult. The two families live in a two-room apartment on Jodenbreestraat and operate clothing carts on Waterlooplein. The families are as poor as church mice, but the children lack nothing; they learn Dutch and are outstanding students. Lea goes to the Vossius Gymnasium and simultaneously studies the piano and singing at the Amsterdam Conservatory.

More and more German Jews leave their beloved Heimat, and many choose the Netherlands, the land of infinite agricultural plains and an endless horizon. In December 1938, a cute eighteen-year-old boy, Ernst Cosmann, arrives in the Netherlands with his little brother. Ernst, called Erco by his friends, has a dream: to learn agriculture in the Netherlands, the most important thing needed in Palestine, or so he believes. He spends his first months in Amsterdam, where he joins the Maccabi Hatzair youth movement. Soon, Ernst finds himself
staring at the blond, curly-haired girl with her loud laugh that can be heard from miles away. This does not go unnoticed by the blond girl, who is flattered by his attention. It not only excites her but is the beginning of a beautiful, touching, true love story. The first letters are sent back and forth.

Ernst in 1939

Fifteen-year-old Esther Singer – people call her Eshu – leaves Berlin and comes to the Netherlands alone. Eshu's mother was killed in a car accident three years earlier. She has two older brothers who have emigrated to Palestine before. Their father remains in Berlin; he is confident that he has saved all his children from Hitler's clutches. Eshu, although very young, joins Maccabi Hatzair. She meets her boyfriend,

Dudi Rosenbaum, at the Pavilion in Loosdrecht. They spend every spare minute together and fall madly in love. They have no family, but they have each other.

Meanwhile, at the Pintus family on Minervalaan, the party continues. The Pintus family permits everything that is forbidden by the all-serious youth movement. Dozens of bikes are parked out front, blocking the sidewalk for passers-by. Pedestrians complain, and rightly so ... but who cares?

It is summer 1939, with long, beautiful summer days; it stays light until late. The Pintus family home empties; couples scatter by bicycle or on foot. Hand in hand, Heini accompanies his girlfriend, Lea, back home. They walk from Minervaplein to Jodenbreestraat, and before they realize it, they arrive at the Mikulinsky family's doorstep. One more hug, a loving kiss on the stairs, quickly, before someone disturbs these beautiful young children's naive, pure intimacy.

Ilze on Minervaplein, Amsterdam 1941

It is only a short walk for Erco and Ilse from Minerva Square to 117 Stadionweg. On the way, they immerse themselves in Zionist philosophies, discussing its profound principles. When they stop at the bottom of the stairs at number 117, they realize that they have walked around the block three times already. They say goodbye with a friendly embrace.

Erco does not waste any time; he has a plan. He wants to work for Dutch farmers to earn a living. The most important thing is learning the farming trade. That will come in handy when he goes to Palestine on aliyah. That's the plan.

After spending a few months with his little brother Heinz in Amsterdam, Erco first goes to Dieren to learn the farming trade in practice. Later, he lands an apprenticeship with farmer Oldenboom in a village called Wilp, not far from Deventer.

In 1941, he attends the agricultural school in Elden. Sixteen-year-old Heinz ends up in the Loosdrechtse Rade pavilion, where over 50 children live. There, they learn farming skills from farmers in Loosdrecht and the surrounding area.

Erco busy plowing in Dieren, 1939 (from Ilse's photo album)

By now, their mother, Thekla Cosmann, and their brother, Werner, have settled in a kibbutz in Palestine; their father had previously passed away in Germany. Erco looks out for his little brother and takes good care of him; they have much contact, although they do not live together. Erco is also active in the Maccabi Hatzair movement in the east of the Netherlands. It means everything to these young people growing up. A lot of ideals, a lot of ideology, mixed with good sex among wonderful eighteen and nineteen-year-old youngsters with raging hormones. They still feel safe and are focusing on the future, which, as far as they are concerned, is bright with a red-colored rim of passion.

On September 1, 1939, Germany invades Poland without having declared war.
Poland is conquered within six days. The war has begun.

*Ernst, reading between farming chores,
Dieren 1939*

War breaks out

On May 9, 1940, the twins Lore and Heini celebrate their nineteenth birthday. The party lasts until the early morning hours. They are unaware of the fact that these are their last moments of freedom, their youth, innocence and happiness. Early in the morning, they hear the sound of airplanes and many loud bangs. The twins are absolutely thrilled with this surprise from their parents – even though they know that the impossible is possible with the Pintus family, they certainly did not expect this... Fireworks across Amsterdam... No, it is not a surprise for their birthday; it is war. The Germans are invading the Netherlands. For the group of teenagers, as for millions in Europe, reality is changing forever. The German octopus hurls its terrifying arms effectively in all directions, sowing fear and destruction throughout Europe.

Black clouds above Amsterdam, May 1940

The joyful, curly-haired Ilse is no longer that joyful. A rigid German mentality prevails at Ilse's home: a protective home with strict conservative views on parenting. The days are getting harder and more dangerous, but when you are in love, you don't see the danger; you just want to be with your boyfriend.

Meanwhile, Erco is in Wilp at a farm. Once in a while, Ilse has a bit of luck and is allowed to travel to Erco, accompanied by her little sister Margot, who acts as her chaperone. They manage to 'lose' the annoying little sister, their pesky guard, and go their own way. Lots of tenderness, lots of love, good cuddling, swimming in the IJssel River in the moonlight and, what Ilse needs most, lots of encouraging words.

Ilse is very insecure; Erco has to confirm his love for her over and over again and repeatedly encourage and reassure her that their future together lies in Palestine. All these sweet, loving words give her hope until she is no longer with him, at which point Ilse once again falls into despair. From June 1940, Ilse and Erco correspond with each other, often via ordinary daily letters, but sometimes also with passionate love letters. Ilse kept Erco's letters her entire life.

The group of teenagers from South Amsterdam grew up overnight but are still keeping it together; they are still alive...for now. Maccabi Hatzair is still organizing meetings, an agricultural school is being established in Elden, and they are still allowed to travel.

However, it has become more difficult for Ilse to travel. The situation at home causes her to lie; she learns to lie well, and she reinvents herself over and over. She demands that her entire environment lies for her, is taken aback by herself, and does not believe in her own willpower. Yet, a love that keeps growing stronger makes the impossible possible. This is how she manages to see her lover, Erco. The Birnbaums are not in favor of this relationship. It's not good enough for their gifted daughter. Ernst is an unrealistic dreamer who left his parental home at sixteen, which most certainly cannot have been a good *'Elternhaus und Kinderstube.'* This Cosmann family is not suited to their well-brought-up Ilse.

On June 11, 1941, there is a second major raid in Amsterdam. The Nazis arrest roughly three hundred young Jewish men. One of them is Heini Pintus. On June 26, 1941, these boys are deported via Schoorl to the Mauthausen concentration camp. Three weeks later, the obituaries arrive in Amsterdam. Heini has been murdered. It is rumored that they were killed with poison gas.

Lore no longer has a brother, no longer has her friend. Lea no longer has a fiancé, no longer has her friend either. Father and mother Pintus no longer have a son. Maccabi Hatzair has lost a member. The world collapses; the pain is unbearable.

Erco and Ilse write increasingly more and more to each other. It keeps Ilse going; it gives her a strength she was never aware of. Yet Ilse succumbs to depression often, and Erco speaks to her with hope and encouragement. Jewish Amsterdam is being depleted, and deportations are in full swing, but at least Elden remains an island of common sense for these young twenty-somethings for a while. They enjoy the farm work and everything around it. They have incessant disagreements about anything and everything. In Elden, they can still be young for a while and discuss the silliest subjects, argue, make fun of each other, laugh at each other, gossip about each other, and, if it is convenient, make tender love and enjoy sweet love.

What a difference from dreary Amsterdam, where Ilse still lives. Once every two or three weeks, she is given permission to travel to Elden, where she meets Eshu and Dudi, as well as all her other friends. The love between Ilse and Erco intensifies. It is an intimate, gentle love; they belong to each other and support each other. In these dark times, such moments of deep emotion are the main theme in both Erco and Ilse's lives. They are floating on clouds and seem oblivious to the black clouds filling the sky. They still have rosy cheeks, a frightened look is replaced by a loving one, and they still get to touch each other's bodies.

Margot and Ilse at home in Amsterdam, 1941

At home on Stadionweg in Amsterdam, Ilse's situation is only getting worse. She is hardly allowed to leave the house. It is understandable – her parents are apprehensive, restless and worried. The word 'Nein' is then the easiest solution. These uncertain times are hard for Vati and Mutti Birnbaum; dealing with a young woman in love is beyond their emotional capacity, and it's hard for them to understand.

The Pintus family goes into hiding. Lore translates enemy documents from German into Dutch for the Dutch resistance. After two years, the family is betrayed. Father and mother Pintus are deported to Theresienstadt, and Lore disappears to Westerbork.

1. Kulla Mikulinsky died on February 9, 1942, in Amsterdam and is buried in Amsterdam.
2. Itta Mikulinsky, Kulla's wife, murdered in Auschwitz on October 1, 1942, aged 62.
3. Mark Mikulinsky, the son of Kulla and Itta, murdered in Auschwitz on December 31, 1943, aged 23.
4. Sasha Mikulinsky, murdered in Auschwitz on September 21, 1942, aged 52.

5. Polina Mikulinsky, Sasha's wife, murdered in Auschwitz on September 21, 1942, aged 41.
6. Lowa Mikulinsky, son of Sasha and Polina, murdered in Auschwitz on January 31, 1943, aged 20.
7. Chaja Mikulinsky, daughter of Sasha and Polina, murdered in Auschwitz on September 21, 1942, aged 15.
8. Yitzhak Mikulinsky, son of Sasha and Polina, murdered in Auschwitz on September 21, 1942, aged 12.

 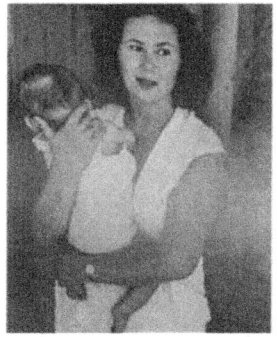

From left to right: Chaja, Mark, Lea, and Yizchak Mikulinsky, Amsterdam 1933. Lea survives Auschwitz. The rest of her family is killed in the war.

Lea Mikulinsky – Milstein holding her baby and with Auschwitz number 20264 on her arm, 1950.

Only Leah, at Auschwitz since 1942, survives this hell on earth, perhaps because of her beautiful voice. Dr Mengele, the monster, has her sing his beloved German arias for hours every day.

In September 1942, Ilse and Erco announce their engagement. After the engagement, the relationship with Ilse's parents improves. They are more accepting of both Ilse and Erco.

Ilse does not have to wear a Jewish star and has Aryan papers because her mother is listed as non-Jewish. She joins the Dutch resistance and does a lot of illegal work. She travels the country on her bicycle, sometimes disguised as a German nun, and is regularly in Elden, Deventer, Zutphen and Arnhem. Her depression is replaced by incredible courage, which is essential in these dark times. By then, the German occupiers have already taken Erco away from her.

The letters

(21)

Wilp, 5. Juni 1940

Liebe Ilse!
Schönen Dank für Deinen Brief, der grade rechtzeitig ankam, ich
hatte mir nämlich vorgenommen, Dir heute zu schreiben. Er war ja
wirklich nicht sehr lustig, aber ich kann Dich schon verstehen.
Mir war in den letzten Tagen auch sehr mies, aber es hat sich schon
wieder gelegt, und jetzt habe ich eine "strahlende" Laune, wenn man
es "strahlend" nennen kann.
Zuerst will ich mal wieder alles beantworten.
Was Du da von dem Jungen mit dem Finger schreibst, ist wirklich
ein typisches Beispiel für manche unserer Unterhaltungen. Ich bin
auch immer "bange", dass mir mal sowas passiert, darum sehe ich mich
auch sehr vor. Aber man kann niemals jeder Gefahr bei der Arbeit
ausweichen, meistens sind die Maschinen ungenügend gesichert, die
Bauern sind ziemlich leichtsinnig.
Auf Deine Frage, ob es noch Sinn hat zu leben, will ich mal lieber
nicht antworten. Du behauptest sonst noch, ich sei zynisch. Aber ich
empfehle Dir, über diese Frage die nächsten siebzig Jahre nicht nach-
zudenken, später ist immer noch Zeit dazu.
Prima ist das, wenn Du mich mal besuchen kommst. Schreib mir vorher,
wann das so ungefähr sein kann, damit ich mir entsprechend freinehmen
kann und Dich gemütlich unterbringe. Mach's aber auch wahr, ich freu'
mich schon!!
Ich finde es fein, dass Sommer ist. Ich geniesse ihn sehr, die Arbeit
macht grossen Spass. Ich bin schon ganz braun, Du würdest vor Neid
grün werden. Bloss für die Landwirtschaft wäre ein tüchtiger Regen
sehr nötig. Ich bin dieses Jahr noch garnicht schwimmen gewesen. In
der IJssel ist es verboten (wegen der Leichen).

Prima, dass Ausländer nicht mehr nach Amsterdam dürfen. Da brauch ich
garnicht mehr zu diskutieren. Ich hatte mich nämlich entschlossen,
nicht hinzugehen. Es wäre ja Quatsch. Hier ist es viel besser.

Viel Erlebnisse habe ich in der letzten Zeit nicht gehabt. Hier ist
es wunderbar ruhig. Von Korrespondenz habe ich wenig Lust, ein bisschen
bisschen nach Deutschland, ein wenig in Holland, das ist alles. Wenn
Du willst, kann ich Dir mal öfter schreiben. Ich lese etwas mehr.
Jetzt habe ich grade von Alfred Döblin "Babylonische Wandrung", ich
werde nicht ganz klug draus, habe erst ein paar Kapitel gelesen, es
scheint sehr satirisch zu sein. Dann habe ich mir noch "Heilung
durch den Geist" geliehen. Wenn ich nich nicht irre, hattest Du es
mir auch empfohlen. Ferner habe ich noch "Fabian" von Erich Kästner
gelesen, teilweise gut. Ausserdem pumpe ich mir noch alle möglichen
Kriminalromane zusammen, das ist gut für die Mittagspause.
Ich habe auch ein paar gute Filme gesehen, hier gehe ich auch ins

The first letter

Wilp, June 5, 1940 (Letter no. 1 from Wilp)

Dear Ilse,

Thank you very much for your letter; it arrived at exactly the right moment. I was planning on writing you today. Your letter was not very upbeat, but I understand why. I, too, have been in a very bad mood the last few days, but things are better now, as far as you can use the word better.

First, I want to answer all your questions:

What you describe about the boy with his finger is typical of the issues we mentioned in our conversations. I am always afraid that something like that could happen to me too, so I am really careful. However, it is impossible to escape all the dangers while working. The machines are usually not sufficiently protected, and the farmers are quite frivolous. As for your question of whether there is still reason to continue living, I would rather not answer; otherwise, you might call me cynical. I suggest you stop thinking about this matter for the next seventy years; you will have plenty of time for it then. It would be great if you could visit me. Write me when approximately, so I can ask for a vacation and tidy up the house. I am really looking forward to it.

It is so wonderful that summer is here; I am enjoying it, and it also makes the work enjoyable. I am wonderfully tanned, and I am sure you will be jealous when you see me. The farms desperately need rain now, good rain. I have not yet swum in the IJssel River this year. It is forbidden to swim because of the corpses in it.

It is very good that foreigners are no longer allowed to come to Amsterdam; I do not have to participate in debates then. Anyway, I decided a long time ago not to participate. These debates are aimless and nonsensical; it is much better here.

There haven't been many nice things happening here lately; it is wonderfully quiet here. Only a few letters to write, some to Germany, some to the Netherlands, that's all. I am currently reading *Babylonische Wandrung* by Alfred Döblin, but I have only read a few chapters. It is supposedly very satirical, but I am struggling to get into it, and I don't understand it very well. I borrowed *Die Heilung durch den Geist*. If I'm not mistaken, you recommended it to me. Besides that, I also read Fabian by Erich Kästner; I kind of liked it. Apart from that, I devour all kinds of detective books, a nice read at lunchtime. I also saw a few good movies. I visit the cinema here, but not with such nice company as in Amsterdam… One of the movies was very nonsensical but still funny; we seriously laughed.

My job here is getting harder by the day. The 'Old Man' is very impatient with me and has many comments that do not really make sense; not a nice situation. Besides, the worst thing that can happen to you here has already happened. We have a new employee, and now I have to share my little room with him, worse, we would have to sleep together in the same bed (the farmer has said that he is a very neat man), but I immediately refused, this is absolutely out of the question and impossible! If he insists, I will leave; it is miserable enough here without having to deal with that as well. The last 'place' where I could be myself and do what I please is also gone now. And then with a guy like that! – nothing I can do about it. I don't think I'll be here for long. One of us has to end this episode. In time, he will not be able to keep two employees on a permanent basis, and as I am 'the less gifted one,' I will have to leave; my co-worker is a 25-year-old farmer's son. But he is no match to me when it comes to milking; besides, he is a chatterbox who spends days telling me about his wretched war experiences.

Well, my dear Ilse, I have to finish this letter. The idiots are insisting again; I have to work tomorrow. It's 10 p.m., and I can't even read in bed anymore. I got a new bed, but it is uncomfortable to sleep on. I have more things I would actually like to write to you about now, but I am in an impossible position in my little room, which makes writing difficult. The sun is already setting, and there is not enough daylight left to continue writing. One thing I want you to know is that I enjoyed my time with you immensely. I remember those days with affection. No, I am not saying it out of politeness; for me, it was a period during which I could truly unwind.

Next week, I plan on visiting my brother in Loosdrecht. I haven't seen him since January.

Give your parents and your sister, Margot, my warmest regards, and tell your mother the cigarettes are very good and I enjoy smoking them. (Please be sure to do it; it doesn't cost anything.)

Warm, heartfelt regards, write back soon.

Erco

Erco working with a sawing machine in Wilp.

Wilp, June 17, 1940 (Letter no. 2 from Wilp)

Dear Ilse,

It's already late, and I have to sleep, but I will start this letter. I don't know when I will be able to finish it. Thank you for the letter you wrote in stages.

Why do we have to get our 'alia plans' for the next twenty years out of our heads or forget them? Do me a favor, and don't throw yourself into the psychosis of 'immigrant politicians' who always view everything negatively. Despite everything (and despite the developments of this war so far), I remain a great optimist and look forward to a bright future. Pessimism based on nothing is just pointless.

Thus far, we can see that everything is changing very rapidly. Of course, we have to take all possibilities into account, yet I firmly believe that we will get over it, please don't let the environment influence you, I would find that terrible.

Your thought that you cannot get on hakhshara because you have to learn and earn money is both objectively and subjectively complete nonsense. If the war drags on for a long time, no one will need your professional services; the same applies if the war lasts for only a short while. After the war, there will probably be a severe economic depression; everyone will be content just to have something to eat, and we know this from the last war. If you want to earn a living as a seamstress, you will need a lot of luck and the right connections. And on top of that, you also want to help or support your parents? How could you even think that possible?

It is incomprehensible (to me) how a human being could be walking around with such future plans. Of course, the best option, the most certain way to make money, lies in agriculture. At least, if 'certainty' is still something worth talking about. A seamstress in the city????? Think again, and if you agree with me, try to make it clear to your parents as well. If you're on hakhshara, they won't have to spend another penny on you. Be happy with anything your mother buys for you; considering all the rationing, it is very little anyway.

The topic of 'working in the MOVEMENT' is definitely closed for me. Decided today not to drive to Dieren for a group Hadracha.[3] I have had quite enough of the whole Dutch youth association; one cannot do much with their snobbery, idiots (excuse me for being this rude, but that is honestly what I think). I have no desire to try again.
Should there be a merger with Haboniem (we, over here, very much insist on it), in which case, I am willing to try again. Do you understand my position? That you want to lead a group again is beyond me; that is yet more proof of your inconsistency. In any case, I wish you 'good luck'.
Loosdrecht was wonderful; it is ungraspable that there is still a place where people can live so happily and contentedly. They celebrated a Shavuot party[4], fun games, lots of hora and POLKA dancing (do you know the POLKA?). The children are great, and the whole group gave me a wonderful impression. I do not like the teachers – snobbish, etc. Go there sometime, maybe with Uri. Uri can help you transfer from train to train just fine. That would be fantastic.
You ask if I like sitting on the balcony in light summer clothes? NO, I don't like sitting in the sun, but miraculously, I don't suffer in the sun. I am able to work all day under the blazing sun without any protection.

---

3 training

4 Shavuot, often called Jewish Pentecost, is the Feast of Weeks celebrated seven weeks after Passover.

A few days ago, I was visiting my Hebrew teacher and his wife. He and his wife are both exactly 25 years old. Their baby boy was born on Whit Monday. Suddenly, I realized that my 'anti' towards babies has significantly subsided, probably because I am getting older. I see grandparents who always love their grandchildren. The little baby is really cute.

My lunch break is almost over (I failed to finish this letter yesterday). I want to send this letter when I go to Hebrew class tonight, so I have to end it now. Except for that, there is nothing further to tell. May I point out to you that you write ISRAEL with the Hebrew letter ALEF and not with an AJIEN. I also noticed that you wrote my name correctly for the first time with double NN, probably a 'hasty mistake??'

I hope to hear from you soon.

Many kind regards (also to your friend)

Good luck,

Erco

Wilp, July 24, 1940 (Letter no. 3 from Wilp)

Hi Ilse,

You probably think I'm going to forget your birthday, no, I'm not that stupid. So, first, best wishes (that's always so tough). I wish that all the struggles that plague you in your private life and give you so many headaches will soon disappear and that you can finally look into the future safely and cheerfully.

Furthermore, I wish you good health, that you may always be cheerful and happy... etc. That is always the usual text, of course, but I mean everything with all my heart. I am not good at expressing 'best wishes,' as opposed to condolences... The 'home pharmacy' enclosed herein will certainly be useful when you lose your temper again. (Honestly, without any ironic intent.)

Do you feel more mature now? Finally exiting your 'guppy' years.

I arrived here at noon on Sunday without any problems. I was a little tired, but the next day, it was all over, and I was able to harvest the rye. (Rye is harvested manually with a scythe.) Yesterday, we worked from 05.30 in the morning until 21.00 in the evening with a break of just under an hour for dinner, oh well. This is what farming work looks like!

Are you better feeling better again? I hope you are feeling better and can return to work with renewed strength.

The visit with you was very pleasant and enjoyable. I still think about it with pleasure, and it was well worth the long bike ride. Please give your parents my warmest regards.

Back to our conversation about the youth movement, I want to formally inform you that I decided to leave Maccabi Hatzair today.

Ernst with the scythe, August 1940

I must finish now; the farmer's wife has already served the porridge on our plates. Please do not think I am just telling you a story; it is already 01.30 a.m. I darkened the window in my room (here, it's not the same as with poor people...).
I wish you lots of fun on your birthday, lots of fond regards.

Erco

Wilp, August 13, 1940 (Letter no. 4 from Wilp)

Hello Ilse,

Today, I plowed until late and could not drive to Deventer as usual, so I have time to start writing a letter to you. I received your letter of July 30. Thank you very much.

I fear that your good recovery has taken a turn for the worse again; after all, I know everything that is going on there.

I really had to laugh about what happened to you on Sunday night. It's true what they say; young girls should not be left alone for even a moment.

Since the beginning, I have attended Hebrew lessons maybe three times; I already foresee that you will have to teach me Hebrew.

In my free time, when the weather is nice, I enjoy swimming, and then I write many letters for the Hechalutz.[55] I read a lot while traveling to Deventer.

The Agricultural Committee occasionally has a meeting. What do you think of the article on Maccabi Hatzair in *Het Joodse Weekblad*? It's amusing, isn't it? We had a good laugh about it. One hears little of the consolidation here. I suppose it has 'gone to sleep,' so to speak, for the time being. I don't see anything changing soon.

I don't know what else to write about. It is silly season. Next week, we will finally see each other, and then we can gossip about everything, so why should I worry about this writing

---

5   Hechalutz (The Pioneer) was an international Jewish Zionist youth movement that trained young people for settlement in Palestine. In 1939, the organization had about 100,000 members in Europe, North Africa, the Middle East and North America, including 16,000 members in training centers and 60,000 immigrants in Palestine.

business now? It would be great if I could sleep over at your place; you just need to let me know whether or not it is possible. We are scheduled to arrive Saturday afternoon.

Have you ever seen a nest of young hares? We found such a nest in our meadow yesterday. The little critters were apparently just born; they were still wet, so cute, so sweet.
My lunch break is over.
Best regards, also to your parents,

Erco

Erco behind the plow at the Oldenbooms in Wilp,
Summer 1940

Wilp, September 11, 1940 (Letter no. 5 from Wilp)

Hello Ilse,

Many thanks for your nice letter from Wolfheze. It's wonderful that you were able to have such a vacation. Now work is twice as 'nice' again. That's how I feel after the vacation. As for your weight being the same as the standard weight at the hakhshara, I think you might be exaggerating, given how slim you are.
You know, I hope to also have a short vacation soon, FINALLY.
I think my time in Wilp will be ending soon. From October, my salary will drop considerably, which is absolutely reasonable from a farmer's point of view; he really doesn't need me during the winter months. There are four workers here, while three are more than enough now. The farmer knows there is little work during winter months but does not want to fire me, which is very decent; not a single farm in the whole area is looking for workers right now. A few chawerim have been fired by their farmers because the farmers fear there won't be enough to eat. I think that is a terrible attitude; you cannot be any more selfish than that. My boss gave me freedom of choice; should I find another workplace, he is willing to terminate our contract. On the one hand, I have no worries in the winter months; on the other hand, I don't like being the fifth wheel. Besides, it's hard to work like this. It's not a complete thing, and it's not half a thing; it's just not pleasant to work based on sympathy.
I have several projects to continue my work. With a little luck, I can learn different agricultural disciplines in Groningen. Eager to learn to work with horses and grain farming, and with exceptional luck, I will learn to drive a tractor!!!!!!! This week,

we are looking for jobs there, and I assume I will soon hear what I can learn there. Even there, the hachshara is very hard work and not at all enjoyable. Moreover, you are far from the cultural world like Deventer and Amsterdam. Yet, despite all that, hachshara is hachshara.

David P. does not like it at all; he believes that I should come to Amsterdam to work with the youth movements and with Hechalutz. To me, it seems impossible because of the fact that I cannot get a work permit in Amsterdam (i.e., the Shushu case).

I suppose there are other possibilities.

I am not okay with this if it blocks the possibility of specialization. Of course, you understand that, as you know my position on this.

Should Groningen not happen, I still want to spend the winter with my farmer in Wilp. I don't miss anything here.

The work at the center in the youth movement is much needed. However, everything depends on many issues, such as a work permit, money, etc.

We are now busy with the potato harvest. If you do this work next year, you will appreciate your spine a lot more... Although, mine doesn't hurt at all.

Other than that, I have nothing more to say. I am tremendously busy with a job, etc., and the porridge is on the table. I must finish this letter.

I hope to hear from you soon. I don't know when I will be able to be in Amsterdam again. Many warm regards, also to your parents and your sister, of course.

Erco

Planting trees in Wilp, 1940

Wilp, October 23, 1940 (Letter no. 6 from Wilp)

Hello Ilse,

So, after having just written a few letters for Hechalutz, I can finally start writing a letter to you. While I don't think I'll get it done today, I'm sure I will by Friday because I'll probably have time again then.
You must have wondered about my long silence, but believe me, I had very little free time. I had a stack of letters to answer, in addition to many other things that took up a lot of time. I will try to describe the events of the past few weeks in order. Right after my last stay in Amsterdam, all the members of the

hachshara had a meeting during Rosh Hashanah.[6] We put an enormous amount of effort into the preparations, and in the end, we were very satisfied with the result. Everyone was convinced that this meeting was the most successful, best-organized meeting there has ever been. A decisive contribution to the success was the fact that the meeting was not held in the terrible Beth Chaluz but in a nice youth hostel near Deventer. The atmosphere was very pleasant, and everyone got along very well.

The agenda included a talk on the history of Zionism, Bible study and reading groups. All of these talks were held in two stages. In addition, we heard a very mediocre lecture by Sam de Wolf and a very good lecture by Kurt Reilinger, which led to a heavy debate.

In the evening there was a big party ... all in all, there was a lot of free time planned, to my great surprise everything was carefully organized, it was a great success.

I had four vacation days, and after the meeting, I spent two of those days reading and talking in Deventer.

I spent the last two days with my brother in Loosdrecht during Yom Kippur. That was also very pleasant; I even slept in until 9:30 in the morning – a pure and rare pleasure.

And... unfortunately, the holidays are over (nothing better than a few beautiful days like that), and work starts again with the inevitable tensions, but still, work is going quite well. We are harvesting beets now, which I assume are beets for cattle feed. You should have seen my hands, black and wounded; I am almost unable to write.

At present, we are working hard on the Hechalutz. The debate on whether or not to establish an 'elderly kibbutz' is becoming heated; I suppose you have heard about it. Although

---

6   Jewish New Year.

I am not a pessimist, I really don't see this poor idea coming to fruition. There are so many technical problems involved, as well as many other problems to overcome. If you think about it realistically, the chances that it succeeds are very slim.

I can't come to Amsterdam on Sunday; I have to stay here with the youth group, as I haven't been here for a long time. Saturday (Sabbath), there will be a general meeting here, and I can hardly ask for vacation again because then I risk being fired.

And ... how are you, madam? Can I call you madame seamstress already? Or did you fail the exam? What are you doing now? Write back to me soon. The stupid country folk are tired again, so I must end.

Many warm regards,

Erco

PS: Do you like the photo? You look a little dreamy!

Wilp, November 18, 1940 (Letter no. 7 from Wilp)

Hello Ilse,

I started writing to you eight days ago but didn't get beyond the first paragraph. It's too bad I couldn't visit you last Sunday. Abraham dragged me back to Deventer early in the morning because of the Agriculture Committee that took place here. It is important for the kibbutz because we had to present our suggestions regarding the veteran members of the kibbutz. I do not believe such a center will ever develop or be established; the practical difficulties are probably too great.

For example: We must find at least twenty workplaces in a very small area. Places with permanent jobs where one also has the opportunity to learn something ... and where one does not sleep at home at night, etc. ... finding all this in one place is close to impossible. Yet, despite that, many dream of this. They can see themselves living in the kibbutz in the spring as if everything has already been arranged perfectly. I can't remember whether or not I told you that I am not joining this group; after all, I have already completed a professional hakhshara. I can still learn from the farmers; I am not 'farmer tired,' so to speak. I prefer to do my internship with a farmer. I do not plan on attending the Maccabi Hatzair meeting on Sunday; I can't take a vacation every time, except I don't feel like being part of the minority. If I appear in favor of merging with Haboniem, I will alienate everyone against me because most of them do not agree with me. I categorically demand and claim pioneering as a must, and no one agrees with me on this either. If I am not mistaken, Ilse Birnbaum is among my opponents! My presence in the youth movement is useless since I no longer have any connections there at all.

What do you think? What is your opinion? The decision

will not be easy for me; it will affect my whole life. Both 'yes' and 'no' can spoil life for me or, on the other hand, potentially open up doors.
Other than that, I don't have much new (as always). My work suits me fine at the moment, and I am satisfied. At the moment, there is a lot of activity in the Hechalutz, and we are quite successful in Deventer. I hope we can talk to each other again soon; it is much easier to talk about all this in person. Just like for you, writing letters is becoming more and more difficult; I almost can't manage it anymore.
Do you remember... you once told me you have adhesive tape at the store that I can use to repair my raincoat; it's very torn now. Could you send 1 or 2 such adhesive tapes with Abraham? I can't repair this raincoat here, and also write me what it costs.

I hope to hear from you soon, from now on we may not have such long breaks. I have to stop again – porridge etc.
Warm regards, (are you already freezing?)
I am still walking with a sleeveless sweater – but it's very wet here.

Lots of fond regards, also to your parents,

Erco

Wilp, February 4, 1941 (Letter no. 8 from Wilp)

Dear Ilse,

You should have received this letter ages ago, but I had the flu. Last week, I was in bed almost the whole week and could not work. Now I am all well again. I was the third person in our group to become ill; the farmer and his son were also sick in bed.

In the last few days, I have been busy again with the publication of a newsletter; we are currently doing a literary supplement with selected excerpts of good books, conversations about books, translations, and articles about all kinds of art. This is important for the individual hachshara. People here do not know much about good literature and read many bad books. I hope this is the right way for us to help with that.

Did you get home safely after the seminar? Was it a big problem that you arrived late? Because of the bad weather, we stayed in Utrecht for a while and, of course, spent 'some' money ... then we got on the train and headed back home. After the seminar, I had no money left; I even had to borrow money, and thus, I could use my 100 points allowance to buy some clothes. But in the meantime, everything is back to normal again.

It's too bad we didn't have to quarantine; we could have spent wonderful weeks together. At the moment, it is very nasty here; since my return, I have only gone out once. I couldn't go to Deventer either; the temporary boat bridge[7] was yanked out of place. Currently, there is no work here; we are wasting time doing

---

7   A temporary bridge was placed on floating barges to replace the permanent bridge that was blown up during the invasion. The bridge was removed because of the large chunks of ice in the river.

nothing, and the internship is not amounting to much either. I spoke with my confidant here from the organization, a great guy by the way, who completely confirmed my concerns. He, too, believes it is a mess to be alone somewhere during times like these. I also do not know whether I want to be a madrich in a kibbutz near Arnhem (Elden); I'm not even sure about that yet. Meanwhile, I'm looking at various options and will have to wait and see whether anyone needs my services.

I think they urgently and desperately need me; I imagine a thousand arguments in my favor, but to my regret, I know as always that a closed door awaits me. It is important for me now to leave the farmer; at some point, my studies must come to an end. After five years of hakhshara, I have had enough of it.

You know, it was really great that we talked to each other this time. I think things are clearer now, even though some of the things we discussed were not so important and serious. I am sending you a little gift because you deserve it for different reasons; I hope it arrives in one piece.

I think this letter will be somewhat difficult for you to decipher; there is something wrong with the typewriter at the moment.

Lots of fond regards, also to your parents,

Write back soon…

Erco

The start of Jewish persecution

After the German invasion of the Netherlands, the Palestine pioneers were initially left in peace. Gradually, more and more anti-Jewish measures were taken, slowly creating a more threatening atmosphere. Debates grew among the pioneers: did they have to go into hiding, flee, or was it possible to live their lives under German occupation? For a short while, there was hope. The Dominican Republic had expressed its willingness, in return for a hefty payment, to accept a large number of Jewish refugees. Some chalutzim immediately began to learn Spanish. Others just wanted to emigrate to Palestine. In the end, nothing came of this plan.

In February 1941, more than four hundred young Jewish men were gathered on Amsterdam's Waterlooplein, mistreated and taken to Buchenwald concentration camp and later to Mauthausen. All but one were murdered. In the same month, the Germans shut down the Working Village in Wieringermeer. In June, 60 pioneers from the Working Village were sent to Mauthausen along with 240 Amsterdam Jews. News about their deaths also soon arrived at the chalutzim in the Netherlands. A place had to be found for the others.

At the beginning of 1941, violence against Jews in Amsterdam, especially from the NSB (the Dutch National Socialist Movement) and with the approval of the German occupier, continued to increase. People were harassed in the streets, and Jewish stores were vandalized. Fighting ensued between squads of Jews and non-Jews and the NSB. After a brawl, where an NSB member was killed, and a German patrol at a Jewish ice cream parlor was sprayed with ammonia gas, the Germans held a raid in the Jewish neighborhood in retaliation, detaining 427 people. Thousands of non-Jewish witnesses saw it happen. The people of Amsterdam were deeply shocked by the raids in their city. The illegal Communist Party (CPN) called for a protest strike. On Feb. 25, public transport and various factory sites in Amsterdam and other places went on strike: the so-called 'February Strike.' Ernst refers only indirectly to these events in Ilse's hometown and calls them 'difficult days.'

The Germans established the 'Jewish Council for Amsterdam,' which from now on was held responsible for any disturbances. Abraham Asscher and Prof. David Cohen, the brother of Ru Cohen of the Deventer Association, became the chairpersons. The Jewish Council, composed of Jewish dignitaries, soon gained authority over all Jewish affairs in the Netherlands and became a tool the Germans used to remove Jews from Dutch society. The occupying forces thus allowed, through the Council, the Jewish community itself to organize anti-Jewish measures.

Wilp, February 25, 1941 (Letter no. 9 from Wilp)

Hello Ilse,

I was so pleased with your letter (finally a fairly sensible letter again), a letter I wanted to answer immediately. However, for the last few weeks, I have been busy preparing for the lecture about the philosopher A.D. Gordon[8] that I was giving on behalf of the Youth Federation here in this region. The preparation took a little longer than expected, and thus, I did not get around to writing. The 'success' resulted in quite a delay, and now I have a stack of letters to reply to.

From what I hear, you have had some difficult times; I understand that things are a little better now. I hope all is well and normal at your home. You write about your thoughts on our conversation and relate them to human relationships. I have yet to answer you about that; our discussion about it is not finished. It is clear and inevitable that we still need to talk some things through. In any case, I think we understand each other well and hope we will see each other again soon to continue talking about it; I don't like to write about such things. As far as the uninvited intrusion into the soul of another – we see eye to eye on that – it is unpleasant (there are many examples in our circle), but there are also examples of too little interest in people. (I promise, I'm not talking about you.) In any case, it is possible to show interest in other people and in their private affairs if they are not complete strangers to you. (How far you take it is a question of tact.)

Also, I haven't told you yet that shortly before the seminar, I encountered a group of people (you asked about it in your

---

8 A Jewish philosopher from Ukraine, 1856-1922, often called the 'righteous secular.

letter), but I didn't think it would interest you very much, so I didn't write about it. After all, you emphatically write about the fact that I do not easily share my personal problems.

The decision to join this group was actually not that difficult. I have already had close relationships with a few of these people for some time, but these relationships are growing stronger now. Those connected to me are, in my opinion, the most important and the best friends of this group. We spent quite a few nice evenings talking, and I really feel connected to these people.

I know the thought of living here with these people is almost inconceivable for you. What I can tell you is that you really don't know these people because you have never met them. They are mostly Dutch (Jews) and really the best of the Dutch chalutzim.

You know, your comment in your last letter that I don't like to give gifts was very insulting and really not true. I do have to admit that I don't have very creative ideas, but I eventually find something appropriate, even if it's only after our date.

And if the things you wrote about the little picture (that I sent you) weren't merely polite words, it proves me right.

I started writing this letter on Tuesday. On Wednesday, Abraham came to tell me that there will be a Central Committee meeting today (Friday) in the evening. I did not continue writing this letter because I intended to visit you on Saturday or Sunday. Much to my regret, I couldn't. I should have asked for three days off. I hope to come to Amsterdam again soon. Abraham tells me that you are doing well.

still don't know what will happen to me. Jewish fate doesn't even reveal anything about the near future. I really want to quit working here, but the farmer very much wants me to stay with him, although he doesn't really need me, as he says. He also says it is impossible to pay me more this coming summer than he did last summer.

I don't feel like staying here for longer than a year because I don't get to do professional trades and jobs here, so I don't learn enough. I will stay here for as long as I have nothing better.

I hope to get the job as madrich in Elden; my odds are looking good. I really do not want to stay with the farmer as there is not much more I can learn from him. I want to have a bit more freedom and want to be less dependent on him so I can then do more for myself. All I can do now is to wait and hope. When you receive this letter, celebrate with me in thought. On March 1, I will have been on hakhshara for 5 years, but I won't celebrate this day in any special way.

I would like to see if something can be done to improve theoretical vocational training and Dutch training. I feel that the years for chawerim pass without
proper training; speaking in professional terms, there is actually very little progress. This significantly decreases the value of the hachshara, which has been good overall. I will write to the training committee to explain my position and add my practical suggestions for implementation. Moreover, it is extremely difficult to arouse the chawerim's interest in these matters. I really hope that it succeeds, because this is very, very important.

Other than that, there is not much more I can tell you, at least nothing worth mentioning specifically in a letter. Except that I am rather tired today because the day before yesterday, I had to look after a mother piglet that went into labor. Last night, we chatted with some friends until 4 a.m. I fell asleep by 5 and slept until 6:30… terrific, right?

I also received a letter from my brother in Eretz[9] via The Red Cross. It's two months old already, meaning it had been sent two months ago!

So, I would like to end this letter now; otherwise, it will never be mailed. I won't manage to write another letter before Tuesday.

Many kind regards, also to your parents, and goodbye.

Erco

---

9   Traditional name of Israel.

Wilp, March 13-14, 1941 (Letter no. 10 from Wilp)

Hello, dearest Ilse,

Thank you very much for your letter, which I am going to answer immediately before another two to three weeks pass (and then I will have to apologize for it again).
Your observation that I am not bored on the 'lonely farm' (as you call the farm next to the main road to Deventer) is absolutely correct. I have spent many wonderful hours with good friends lately. (We often chat all night long.) I am very glad I got to know these people. My relationship with these people is totally different from my previous friends, which was more 'political' than anything else. Other than that, there is plenty of work to fill up my free time. Refreshing discussions with Abraham, the Snief and all the other activities I have told you about many times. Unfortunately, I hardly get around to reading; I try to read only good books. Right now, I am reading Joseph Kerkhoven's Dritte Existenz. The author is Jakob Wasserman (if you haven't read the book, I highly recommend it, but first, you should read his books Der Fall Maurizius and Etzel Andergast).
Do you know how much free time I have per day? I work until about 7:30 p.m. At 9:30 p.m., we get porridge for supper. I spend the two hours in between washing, dressing, glancing at the newspaper, preparing the barn and stable for the night, and often having a chat with the farmer.
This lack of free time is precisely what makes me want to leave the farmer. Unfortunately, this has put me in a predicament – you have probably heard by now that they want me for the organization's secretariat. I have tried very hard to resist because I don't think I am fit for the job, but it didn't do any good. Anyway, as a precondition for my joining the secretari-

at, I have made it clear that a merger is required. If that fails, I have no interest in working in the pioneer organization, but I believe it could succeed this time. Are you going to vote for it? I completely understand that things aren't that easy for you at home. I hope your parents are finally easing up a bit. Don't give up, and try to get out of the house more often. I hope to talk to you soon, just the two of us, in private. Good thing you weren't here last Sunday. It would have been a waste of money if you had been here.

Many thanks for the invitation to Passover; I don't know yet if I will be able to come. We don't know yet when the big meeting will take place. If it takes place, I will certainly have the honor of a seat on the Board; I won't be able to avoid that obligation. Should this meeting not take place, then I can celebrate the holidays with you. In any case, it is not yet clear what my vacations will be during Passover since Passover falls at the same time as Easter, but I will let you know. I look forward to coming, despite the fact that you think I will be bored with you.

Purim[10] was nothing special. I was at the Apeldoornsche Bosch, the Jewish psychiatric hospital, where a few friends were working in the garden and with the patients. We chatted a bit, snacked, and ate delicious chocolate custard.

Well, I have now completed this letter and actually managed to write it rather quickly, considering the limited time I have. I have to mail the letter on Friday; otherwise, it will be a long time before it can be sent.

hope you will be able to decipher my letter. I will tell you later in person why I wrote it by hand.

---

10 Jewish holiday in early spring, often called Jewish carnival. Commemorates the rescue of the Jews in Persian exile, as described in the Bible book of Esther.

i hope you will answer me as quickly as last week. I am also quite punctual this time; I only received your letter six days ago.

Warm regards (also to your parents),

Erco

Spring is starting again here. Do you remember what I wrote about it a year ago? If not, I will have to tell you again.

Kaethe and Rudolf Birnbaum, Amsterdam 1941

Wilp, March 28, 1941 (Letter no. 11 from Wilp)

Hello Ilse,

Well, now you can see that I, too, can respond quickly. I am replying to you tonight, just twelve hours after having received your letter. I actually have to write to a friend in Denmark, but he also made me wait a long time for his letter....
Many thanks for all the pictures. I like the photo where your face is more serious better. Your smile in the second photo is a bit silly (you look very different when you smile).

Of course I have heard about the Working Village. It is very difficult to find a place for all those people; I can understand their frustrations. As far as I have heard, there are no concrete evacuation plans yet, and we will probably accommodate some of those people (if we receive permission).
You shouldn't worry about me remaining unemployed when I leave here. I'm probably going to announce my resignation. The farmer has hired another new worker, so I will be the 'second' worker again, and I don't want that. At least there is work for me in the organization – so... NO WORRIES!
Your letter utterly annoyed me – no, not you! Rather, with all those who complain about me and my behavior. It shows the spiritual level of this gang, which calls itself 'Center.' I was criticized for being too critical of Abraham, with whom I had a heated discussion.
I was dumb enough to opt for silence for the sake of peace,

but now they are doing the same to me. I am enraged! You should have seen how Rulle and his peers turned on us. There are considerable reservations about Abraham here, and we haven't done anything about it. Abraham blew everything out of proportion as if all the agriculture was no good and in complete chaos. Several friends and I have been accused of this. They were not ashamed to tell lies and hash up old lies (yes, really!) to substantiate their lies, such as that I allegedly neglected the connection to the Center and a few other things. I promised to take care of everything, and at this point, I thought things were settled.

No, absolutely not, apparently. Not only that, but now they want to bench me!

Since the dissolution of the Working Village, I have not heard a word from Amsterdam except a general newsletter. After all, it directly concerns things that I am involved in and that I care about. Things are being proposed that are directly related to the individual hakhshara that I am doing, but I then hear it from the immigrant group... can you understand that something like this could drive a person to a point where he just wants to give up? It is good that the Union will be formed soon; the Center is merely a 'nice little clique.' I'm sorry to write to you about this whole mess. Sometimes, I just need to get it off my chest. Do you understand how I feel when I think about all this?

You are honest with them and try to do everything you can, and then they do everything they can to humiliate you and render you useless. Anyway, I'm not married to them, and if I want to, I can turn around and leave.

A filly was born during my shift. It was very interesting because I had never seen it before. The foal is cute, and we are having fun with it. Apart from that, our 'usual pastime,' which I have told you more than enough about, carries on unchanging.

Did you feel like life here is much quieter and less hectic than life at your place? Except for the occasional minor depression, the general condition here is really good and peaceful. As far as daily life is concerned, we haven't noticed much of what's been happening to 'us' so far, except, of course, for those 'who know better.' Yet, on the whole, we are satisfied.

I imagine that the closure of the Working Village significantly reduces your chances of having a hakhshara with your parents. Are you still taking steps in that direction? Make every effort and do it quickly. Don't hesitate because we don't know what lies ahead.

I have to sign off now. Officially, I am already asleep – but I am lying on my knees while writing (I suppose my handwriting speaks for itself).

Many warm regards, also to your parents and your sister. I will return the photos to you – I understand from your letter that you want them back. I wasn't sure, and maybe I'm wrong.

Erco

The foal with its mother in front of the De Barchel farm of the family Oldenboom in Wilp

Wilp, April 17, 1941 (Letter no. 12 from Wilp)

Hello Ilse,

It took a while before I could reply to your letter. I spent the second day of Easter in Deventer. On the third day, one of the comrades celebrated his birthday, and we had to meet each other at a boring birthday party.
Last night, I worked until nine in the evening.
The color of the foal is the same as the color of a fox. You, lacking a professional eye, would say it is brown, but it is not brown. We are having a lot of fun with the foal. He gallops happily around the pasture. He was a little ill from having an inflamed navel, but that's all over now. If the pictures turn out well, I will send them to you; the roll of film is still inside the camera. The days are getting longer, and so are my working hours – recreational hours are getting shorter and shorter.
For the last two weeks, I haven't been able to do much. I had to go to Deventer all the time – half a night was lost because one of the cows had to calve. The calf came out along with the uterus. It was interesting because if you handle it correctly, everything will sort itself out. Don't be disgusted; I am determined to slowly turn you into a true farmer's wife.
In terms of work, we are somewhat limited now. The uncertainty about various questions does not instill confidence in the future. Jews in Gelderland now no longer receive housing permits. If an exception is not made for our movement, we will not be able to accommodate new members in our main Center. (There is a possibility that it will happen.) Even married couples have to separate.
You probably know about the situation in the pioneer Zionist movement. Because of all these circumstances, I cannot resign and cannot make programs at all, which is very annoying. You

are living in a kind of 'saying goodbye' state all the time.
That's all I have for now. Today, I received a letter from my mother via the Red Cross.
I don't know when I will be able to go to Amsterdam again.
Warm regards, also to your parents.

Erco

Elden

In May 1941, Erco moves to Elden in Gelderland. He lives in Huize Voorburg, a stately old two-story house on a dyke, located on the southern outskirts of Arnhem, which was set up as an agricultural school for pioneers aged 16 to 19. The residents work on the land attached to the house and on leased land nearby, where they grow potatoes and vegetables. The cultivation of fruit is their main activity; they have a large cherry orchard behind the house. The produce is mainly for their own use; the surplus is sold at auction. However, the harvest falls short sometimes, and the residents go hungry. 'The food was not good; often ensiled and partially frozen food. We ate porridge made of corn and received a piece of cheese once a week that was weighed by the headmistress, Lini de Bruin,' one of the girls who lived there later recounted.

Huize Voorburg in Elden was founded by the Jewish Center for Vocational Training, which had been established in 1940 as an umbrella body for all hakhshara institutions. The intention is to house mainly young people who have a certificate for emigration to Palestine but who could not go there because of the German occupation. The house is run by Werner Ahlfeld, 'a particularly pleasant and also very talented man,' according to Ernst and Lini de Bruin-Levie. She is a widow and brought her little daughter Hannetje with her. Initially, Ernst struggles to get along with her.

After the house and orchard are refurbished by quartermasters Shlomo Samson, Abi Meyer and Werner Ahlfeld, Erco moves in as one of the first residents, along with Marie Feingerscht, who takes charge of the housekeeping, and Miel Stranders, who teaches religion. Fokki Fuchs, a landscaper specializing in rock gardens, is one of the shift leaders. He is small in stature but exceptionally energetic.

Ernst immediately dislikes him immensely.

Ernst becomes madrich, a youth leader specializing in agriculture and horticulture, but does much more. He gives lectures on all kinds of subjects: culture, history and philosophy. In Elden, culture is important. There is a lot of reading and talking about literature, and they also pay a lot of attention to music. Jacques Presser, the later author of Ashes in the wind (The destruction of the Dutch Jews), and others regularly give lectures on all kinds of cultural subjects. In that book, Presser describes the intellectual discussions among the young pioneers. He remembers 'the wonderful atmosphere in which he [Presser] tried, with the aid of lantern slides, to give an impression of the work of great Dutch painters and the debate that arose concerning the Hebrew letters applied by Jan van Scorel to the hem of his Mary Magdalene's robe (Rijksmuseum), despite the fact that they (we) were already facing a dark threat.'

Huize Voorburg in Elden, 1940

Obtaining permission proves unexpectedly complicated. An extensive correspondence with the authorities is preserved in the archives of the Association for Vocational Training for Palestine Pioneers. It turns out that the establishment of the house in Elden violated the occupier's policy. The mayor of Elst, which included Elden, was ordered by the Germans 'for reasons of police security to prevent any settlement of members of the Jewish race in the province of Gelderland.'

The occupying forces wanted the Jews to totally disappear from Dutch society. Starting in 1942, they were concentrated in the Amsterdam Jewish quarter and in the many 'labor camps.' So, moving Jews to Elden was in conflict with that policy. It also appears that Jews were prohibited from leaving Amsterdam. For each future resident from Amsterdam, separate permission had to be obtained first.

When that fails, the Association for Professional Training Palestine Pioneers seeks permission further up the chain of command. On July 28, they have the chairpersons of the Jewish Council write a letter to Klaus Barbie of the SD in Amsterdam, assuring him that it concerns a limited group of carefully selected, healthy boys and girls. Apparently, the Germans then consider Elden a kind of Jewish labor camp because permission is granted.

When all permits had been arranged, 20 boys and 14 girls went and lived in Huize Voorburg. Their background is very diverse. Most of the young people arrived from Germany as refugees and previously lived in other hakhshara houses, but there are also several Dutch. There was a mix of Orthodox and traditional faiths and freethinkers. After some discussion, they decide to respect each other's beliefs as much as possible by observing kosher cuisine and respecting the Sabbath. Despite this, occasional disagreements still occur. Orthodox members want the boiler to be lit on the Sabbath by a non-Jew, the Shabbos goy. If one of the less strictly religious residents does so, they refuse to stay in the heated rooms and demonstratively take their food to the unheated bedrooms. Despite the major differences, the group develops into a very close-knit community. Ernst is very interested in Jewish culture and history and celebrates all Jewish holidays, but religion is not his forte. He also does not observe the dietary laws. He still enjoys the occasional piece of pork with the Oldenboom family.

Ilse visits Ernst even before all the young people arrive at Huize Voorburg. They spend their first romantic night together.

The residents of Huize Voorburg, summer 1941

Back row from left to right. Marcella de Vries, Ernst Cosmann, Bruno Slachet with Hannetje de Bruin on his shoulders, Hans Auerbach, Nathan Frey, Miel Stranders, Guta Lunsky, Arnold Koller, Hans Horowitz, Lini de Bruin-Levie, Ella Ahlfeld-Cahen, Hans Seemann, Leo van Esso, Esther (Eshu) Singer, Bernd Meyer, Fanny Zimet, Leo Goldschmidt, Gerhardt Sternlicht, Kela van der Walde, Manfred (Shlomo) Samson and Werner Ahlfeld.

Below: Ilse Birnbaum, Ferri Rosenberger, Betty Baars, Martha de Groot (above), Marie Feingersch, Hadassah Kalmar (above),

Greet de Winter, Siddi Schimmel, Rosa Kratzer, Dini Polak, Grete Lehmann (Rozijntje), Batja Rosenberger, Heinz Schlesinger and Mietje de Groot.
Ten of the people in the photo would not survive the war.

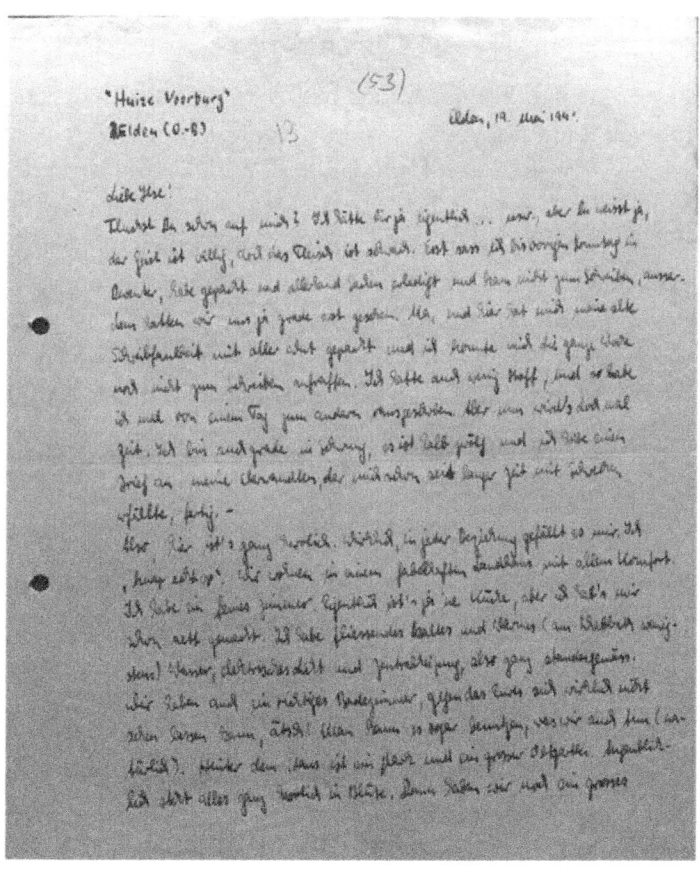

The first letter from Elden, May 19, 1941

Elden, May 19, 1941 (Letter no. 1 from Elden)'

Huize Voorburg'

Elden (O-B)

Dear Ilse,

Have you already condemned me? By now, I should be etc.... but you know, the 'spirit is willing, but the flesh is weak'. First, I was in Deventer until Sunday, had to pack and take care of some things, and just didn't get around to writing. Apart from that, we saw each other recently. Moreover, my old writing laziness infuriated me, an anger that hindered me from sitting down and writing quietly for a while! I also didn't have that much to tell you, so I kept postponing writing to you day after day. It certainly is high time now, and I am finally gaining 'momentum.'

It is now 11:30 p.m. I have written a letter to my relatives, which is something that caused me quite a bit of anxiety.

Well, it is really beautiful here in every way. I like it, and it feels like I am recovering and regaining my health. We live in a lovely villa with all the luxuries and refinements. I have a nice room, which is actually a kitchen, but I turned it into a nice room. On Saturdays, we have hot and cold water (the furnace burns uninterrupted; during the week, only a few hours a day as needed). Furthermore, we have electricity and central heating.

As the 'upper' class deserves, there is also a real bathroom, which absolutely cannot compete with the one you have at Stadionweg 117, Amsterdam. Don't laugh... we are allowed to use the bathroom, which we do, of course. There is a big park behind the house and an orchard with fruit trees, which are all in full bloom. In addition, we have a rather large piece of land. We are four chawerim and a chawera, who is surprisingly pleasant; we get along well, and there is a good atmosphere. We spend the evenings socializing with each other; we are like a family together. The chawera is very nice; she cooks delicious meals that are beyond our expectations, and she cleans the house. The work here is a real pleasure. The director of this farm is a particularly pleasant and talented man. All in all, I feel really good here.

But this life here will not last long. Today, we received a permit to have a hachshara kibbutz in Elden, and the chawerim will return here soon. There was an earlier attempt to populate the hachshara in Elden, but except for four members, none of us had housing permits, and we had to leave the house. What will I do then? Not sure yet. I think I will continue working here as an agricultural trainer, but that too is not certain. In any case, I will stay here for the next few weeks.

Actually, I wanted to invite you on Ascension Day, but unfortunately, we will have an important visitor here with a rather large entourage – a few leaders, etc. – in which case your visit here would be a waste of time. But maybe with Shavuot? Although, I don't know whether or not the students will be back by then. If so, we'll have to wait a while since no guests are allowed for the first few days. I hope you keep your promise and come visit me.

Packing my things was a horrible task. It frustrated me. You would have been a wonderful help. I ended up forcibly stuffing everything together; all my shirts had to be re-ironed… what does a person study for… You know what's the best thing here? I am far away from all the discussions, etc. It has been a while since I have seen any of the 'leaders,' so I feel really great. I got a report from Horst. According to him, the talks about merging are not moving in the direction I would have liked it

to. Isn't that just shameful? Now, I have been assigned an additional task; I have to go and teach Hebrew in Dieren every Wednesday evening. That is truly something I want to do...
At noon, we have a break of an hour and a half. We don't work on Saturday and Sunday. It's after midnight now, and I've been yawning for a good while. We have a lot of work to do tomorrow. After the long drought, it finally rained today, and now we can start sowing and grafting – all the things we could not do due to the drought.
Is everything going well on your end? Will your guest still be staying long?
Warm regards to your parents and to you, of course.
Loving regards,

Erco

Elden, June 3, 1941 (Letter no. 2 from Elden)

My dearest Ilse,

Although not even a day has passed since you left, I can't help myself, and I really feel like writing. I think you would be happy about it. Are you feeling the same way? I am very happy, and all I can think about all day is you. You know, I bask in the thought that we belong together now. I can't describe at all what I feel; happy and content don't even come close.
I've always had this idea that if you do not expect too much, a night like the one we had yesterday would be like the kitsch at the cinema, but it really wasn't.
It was my best and greatest experience so far, and I try over and over again to absorb and remember everything. I wish I

could describe it more concretely, but it is very difficult for me to do it in a letter. I'm sure you think and feel the same way, so you understand me completely.

The difference between your life in Amsterdam and here is reason enough to be sad. I can certainly imagine and understand your feelings on the subject.

Remember that we are connected and that nothing can prevent us from uniting and staying united. We will try to organize this time as best we can, even though it will not always be easy.

I am tired, and I'm going to bed early. Tomorrow morning, I have to be up as early as 4:45 a.m. (if the weather is nice) to harvest, and tomorrow night, I will drive to Dieren for a Hebrew lesson.

I have not gotten much sleep the past few nights. I think you, my darling, are also very tired. I am so happy about our last days; you being here was amazing. Don't be angry with me for writing such a strange letter. I am not used to such feelings, but I mean all of it completely truthfully.

Lots and lots of loving regards and kisses.

Write back soon,

Your Erco

Elden, June 8, 1941 (Letter no. 3 from Elden)

My dearest Ilse,

Thank you so much for your letter, which of course I am very happy about, which tells you that, like you, I am doing well. You are actually being foolish, my sweet. Everything between us has worked out, and I am so happy about it, but now you seem to be having doubts. Do I need to keep reassuring you that I really love you? Believe what I keep telling you: I am very honest and do not intend to see this relationship as an insignificant flirtation. These are my true feelings, my sincere thoughts. Could I possibly do more than this?

Does the fact that you are my first girlfriend (I only now know what it feels like) worry you? After all, I told you how much this relationship with you means to me. Have I appeased your mind? Or do I have to repeat it over and over again? I thought about you all week, of course. And when the chanichim[11] returned, I felt a little lonely. Today, another 16 or 18 boys and girls arrived, and I think there must be 30 of us now. Everything is, of course, very noisy and chaotic; I don't have much contact with these people yet, but they all know each other very well. Anyway, there is nothing better for me to do than to be with in thought and mind.

Shushu was just here, and he told me that there is going to be a small meeting in Amsterdam next Sunday. That means we will see each other. Would you like me to spend Friday night and Saturday with you? It is not absolutely certain yet, but for now, we can look forward to it. I will let you know.

Our headmistress, Lini de Bruin, arrived this week. So far, she is making a good impression. We may address her by her first

---

11 Pupils under 17

name.' It is too soon to tell whether we will get along. After all, we are still total strangers to each other.
Marcella is also here, and I get along well with her. Yesterday, we were together in Arnhem and in one of the stores, they addressed us as 'Mr. and Mrs.', which made us feel very proud ... afterward, we laughed about the double 'adultery.'

Marcella was a member of Hechalutz and also attended the individual training before arriving in Elden. Marcella is in a steady relationship.
Amnon Cohen was here on Friday; the merge will most likely not happen. It seems the eternal politicians won again.
I'm almost finished reading Claudius, which is a great book. Thanks again for lending it to me. Our 'culture...' assigned me another course on the subject of 'the history of Zionism.' I give it willingly; you know I am not willing to settle for just yard work. Although my attitude toward the 'community' remains unclear, it will certainly be difficult to build a close relationship with these people. For now, they see us as agricultural guides who have nothing to do with them. I decided not to be so snobbish so that I could establish a good relationship with them. Fokki is leaving us soon (if permit problems don't suddenly crop up).
Ferri and Batia, his wife, do not know for certain yet. They don't know what they want to do yet. They are hypersensitive and are easily influenced by others.
A few days ago, I had an argument with one of the boys who was totally against them staying, seeing that they had applied for immigration to Santo Domingo. I managed to convince the intern, but I still don't know what the others think.
What do you think of the photos? I really like them. The photo of the four of us – Hans with his serious face and me standing in such a strange position, has become a rather silly

photo, but the other ones are excellent. I keep looking at your picture.

Now I must conclude; I don't have any more to tell you. We will meet in six days – I hope. I think a week of not seeing each other is too long. I cannot imagine that less than eight days have passed since you were here; it seems a lot longer. Many loving wishes and regards,

Your Ernst

Ernst and Ilse, together with Ruth and Hans Stein, in the orchard

Elden, June 13, 1941 (Letter no. 4 from Elden)

My dearest Ilse,

At the moment, Marcella and I are planning to go to Deventer for the weekend. Since I know that you are waiting for a letter from me, I am writing a quick one before our departure.
I received the postcard and your letter, thank you very much. I can imagine that you are feeling all sorts of anxiety, but fortunately, everything has gone well so far.
The news has affected us in a depressing way, but although we cannot discuss the issue directly, we managed to calm down in some way. However, we are still far from a normal state of mind.
This is also why I would like to take advantage of this opportunity. I wanted to get away from here for a few days anyway to see friends in Deventer. David Levison will also be there; I hope it will be a fun few days.
Similarly, I hope we will see each other again soon; fourteen days is too long.
For now, there is a total ban on receiving guests. Well, we'll see. I hope you don't worry too much about me, everything will be fine. I have great faith in the future. Your letter was very beautiful. Think of me, as I think of you all the time.

Loving regards and best wishes,

Your Ernst

A raid on Palestine pioneers

The gravity of the situation under German occupation hit Ilse and Erco hard when the Nazis arrested about 300 young Jewish men during a second raid in Amsterdam on June 11, 1941. Many of them were Palestine pioneers. SD officer Klaus Barbie, later known as the 'Lyon Butcher,' had led the Jewish Council to believe that the German authorities would reopen the Working Village in Wieringermeer. The Jewish Council sent a message to all former Working Village residents living in Amsterdam that it was reopening and that the Germans would pick them up at their homes in the evening. They were pleased with the Germans' decision, as there wasn't much work in Amsterdam. However, they never returned to Wieringermeer. They were deported to Mauthausen via Camp Schoorl. The Germans arrested not only them but all Jewish young men they found in the neighborhood. One of them was Ilse's friend, Heini Pintus. In August, the news reached them that he had been murdered.

Soon after the arrests, the boys' obituaries arrived along with the offer to buy the cardboard box containing their ashes for a 'generous' 25 Dutch Guilders. Two of the comrades from the Working Village were able to evade the raid by hiding with the Birnbaum family, Else's parents.

No one had heard of Auschwitz yet. Mauthausen became the name that filled everyone with fear, just as the Germans had intended. The message was clear. No one came back from Mauthausen alive.

Elden, June 18, 1941 (Letter no. 5 from Elden)

My dearest Ilse,

Thank you very much for your letters and all the 'Schmonzes'[12] from Ruth; it was all (really) very tasty.
In the meantime, things have calmed down a bit on your end too, and so you got through your first frantic fear. I was glad Ruth drove to Amsterdam and could tell you about me; it must have calmed you down. I can only imagine the state you were in during those days of uncertainty. It was too close, and thankfully it's over now.
Let's hope that we are also spared the next time.
Don't worry, my dear, I promise to be careful. As you can imagine, I have been in a very unpleasant situation for the last few days. However, fortunately, the environment and work here help to calm me. The worst was on Saturday afternoon in Deventer. I was quite nervous there because of all the rumors, etc. I would give anything to have you by my side during these uncertain times. These are the kind of days when people need the person they love by their side. All in all, the weekend in Deventer was fun.
I stayed with Hans and Ruth. I got to know Ruth in Gouda, where she did staff training. I ate lunch and dinner at Beth Chaluz. The food was delectable, and I really enjoyed it. Compared to the food here, it was extraordinarily delicious. David was also there, so we spent a few fun hours together, although it was impossible to be in a good mood, of course.
I also visited my previous farmer. We were happy to see each other, just like before; they are good, kind people.
We cycled back home on Sunday evening. I am satisfied here;

---

12 Yiddish: all kinds of nice and tasty little treats.

the work is pleasant, although it has become very monotonous now.
I have a group of four friendly guys with whom one can have a very pleasant conversation. We talk about very 'important' issues regarding sex. We consider it from both a humorous and serious point of view. The agenda also included social issues as well as many other topics.

One very important topic: food! Even though the food here is very good, there is a lack of fat, legumes, rice, bread, flour, potatoes, etc., due to the point system and rationing. Vegetables and fruits are not enough; the boys complain a lot about their empty stomachs, but there is not much we can do about it. Of course, the administrators do what they can. For me personally, this problem is less of an issue. I do not eat much, I am used to working in the open air, and I am not growing anymore. Nevertheless, I also often go to work or bed feeling a little hungry. I buy food sometimes.
Fokki is still on the agenda. The organization promised that he would leave here, but since they don't have a job for him, he won't be leaving anytime soon. Now he (Fokki) is filing a complaint against me with Ru Cohen, the president of the Deventer Organization. I am making things difficult for him, I am trying to sabotage his status with the students, and so on. I really do not believe that I am to blame for all his troubles. Although, I must admit that the atmosphere between us has not always been cordial. Yesterday, a man from the organization came here for an explanation. He claimed that we were making Fokki's life miserable here. Then, a very angry letter addressed to Werner Ahlfeld arrived from Ru Cohen, holding Werner responsible for my behavior. That's typical Ru, ready to judge after one complaint! We don't have to defend ourselves at all – everything Fokki writes is the absolute truth

– despite his not-too-glorious name in the organization and despite him being overly sensitive and everyone knowing it!
We immediately wrote a reply rejecting all accusations and expressing our astonishment. The most interesting thing was that Fokki did not speak to us, but he turned to them behind our backs. I am quite upset by all this.
Fokki will most likely be replaced by a great guy from the 'Chuliot' group. We are happy about that because we are presently a group of five comrades. Of course, I hear all this news unofficially and am not allowed to talk about it either.
A week ago, the grandparents and both parents of a friend of ours were killed by a bombing in Gouda. It is such a tragedy; the boy was very attached to his parents. We are all very sad about it.

Our Hebrew teacher and his wife are expecting their second child to be born on Sunday. It is an absolute disaster; they already have a very difficult life. What will happen to these people?
Should they, God willing, emigrate? The first baby is just a year old.
I really hope that we will be able to see each other soon, but visiting me here is a big problem: we are not allowed to bring girlfriends here before July 15 (even the culture trainer's wife is not allowed to live here).
Hans Stein suggested that we meet in Deventer. You can then stay with Ruth and Hans. Secretly, I hope with my whole heart that this will happen. There, we are ... perfectly free and can do whatever we want. At home, you can maybe say that we are having a meeting there or something like that. However, I don't know when I will be able to get there; maybe not until three or four weeks from now, and that's a long time to wait to see you.

I just arrived back from a bike ride near Nijmegen with one of the chanichim; we brought back our third and fourth goats. Now, you can see that our herd is expanding. I have a chaniech to take care of the goats in their pen, and my job remains to keep an eye on things.

I must end this letter now. I have to go to Dieren to teach Hebrew.

I hope your mood has improved again; we do not want to give up, do we??? Think of me. I am sending you thousands of loving regards and sweet wishes.

Your Ernst

Your letters arrive here exactly one day after you have mailed them.

Ilse, squatting on the left. Elden, 1941

Jew or no Jew

In January 1941, it had become mandatory for Jews in the Netherlands to report to the population register and be registered there. Registration cost one guilder. Almost all Jews complied. A Jew was someone who had at least three Jewish grandparents. For those who adhered to the Jewish faith, two Jewish grandparents sufficed to officially qualify as Jewish. Since Ilse's mother was not registered as a Jew, Ilse therefore had two registrations. Her April 9, 1941 registration lists her church affiliation: Ni, or Dutch-Israelite. So Ilse was officially a Jewess. On October 8, 1942, she received a new certificate of registration. Now it states at church affiliation: none. So Ilse was now no longer considered Jewish, but officially as a 'bastard Jew.' That meant no J on her identity card. According to family stories, Ilse's father had paid a lot of money for this change.

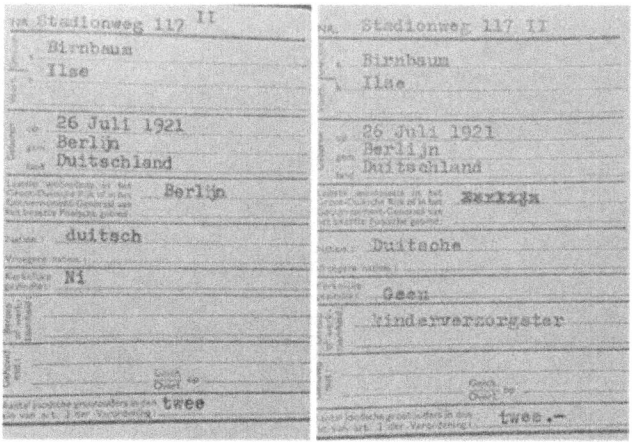

Ilses proof of registration dated April 9, 1941 (left) and the other dated October 1943 (right)

In the course of 1941, the personal identification card was introduced, and all Dutch citizens had to carry it with them from then on. In the case of Jews, a J was stamped onto it. Ilse, who still had German citizenship, used her German passport without the J. This allowed her to continue to move freely in the Netherlands and not suffer from all the restrictive measures imposed on Jews. For this reason, Ernst worried that, at some point, he and Ilse would no longer be able to see each other. Therefore, he urgently advised her several times to have a J stamped on her document. However, Ilse realized the seriousness of the situation and the consequences if she did what Ernst asked. As a Jew, like her lover, she probably would not have survived the war.

Ernst's registration as a Jew with the municipality of Voorst.[13]

---

13   Ernst's second name, Israel, on the certificate of registration was the result of a German regulation issued on August 17, 1938. Jewish men with names that did not sound Jewish were given the additional first name Israel.

Elden, June 23, 1941 (Letter No. 6 from Elden)

My dearest Ilse,

As always, receiving a letter from you made me very happy, and I want to reply straight away. You have no idea how I look forward to your letters. Every time one of your letters arrives, it feels like a celebration. The reason I don't write to you much anymore is because of your parents. I don't want to get you into any more unnecessary trouble.

Do you remember that some time ago, I advised you to have the letter 'J' added to your passport? I don't see any particular disadvantage in it for a girl, but with your passport, as it is now, without a 'J' that is, you should bear in mind that at some point, you would have to say goodbye to the two of us.

I can tell you this with a clear conscience, as I understand your decision and why you chose that side.

You write that you worry and fear for my safety. Look, I am not worry-free either. I have had quite a few scary and worrisome moments in recent weeks. Still, in general, I believe in the future, and when I think of you (which is quite often), it helps me overcome many things. My state of mind is usually quite good.

Actually, I had another fun day yesterday. It was the opening of the (official) hachshara.

It took place in the presence of a very small circle; only members of the management were invited. But of course, more people came, and before we realized it, ten members of 'Chuliot' had joined us. It was amazing. Hans, Ruth and David were there, and that's always the most important thing. You won't believe it, it is so pleasant to be with these people, as far as I am concerned they are second only to you... We talked about many pleasant but also sad things. Hans and David encouraged me to leave the Center. They feared that because of the ugly politics surrounding the main topic, my name could be badly damaged. I willingly heeded their words and listened to them carefully, although there are things that would make it difficult to resign these days. I might decide to resign anyway. After all, I have no influence over anything at the Center, and they don't share, ask or tell me anything.

In the long run, separating politics and personal opinion is impossible, or you must be fake and a hypocrite. Everything I have been doing lately has been to create peace for myself and avoid arguments.

I am tired of all the obligations/tasks of the 'Chalutz,' and I am glad I no longer have to waste my time on that. Much more fun wasting that on you or in Elden.

I would love to hear your opinion on this. I would be happy if you could write to me about it. Please don't try to convince me to go through with it. You already succeeded once (I assume you don't remember).

Sabbath in Utrecht sucked again; the clique was at their best again. I sat there as if we had just met five minutes ago.

This place remains beautiful and pleasant. There are now 31 of us, and the comrades are still behaving a bit awkwardly toward each other. It will take a while for everyone to get to know each other well, but the atmosphere is excellent. As long as my room is not needed as a 'sick room,' I can stay here.

We have a baking oven upstairs and showers too now, which is great, especially after work.

Tomorrow night, I will drive to Deventer for a meeting of the agricultural committee. There is nothing special on the agenda. Hans keeps asking about our visit. Hans and Ruth know how bad it feels when one can hardly see each other.

I have to go to Almelo on Sunday. In two weeks' time, on the Sunday, there will be a meeting with 'Chuliot.' (When could

you actually come? Will we be there from Friday for 8 days until the following Sunday?) I will cycle. That way, we can then share your travel expenses. So, I have already informed Hans, and now everything depends on you...
Many thanks for the ration points; we really needed it. Please tell your mother we were very happy.
I sometimes feel your letters are a little overly detailed, for example, what you wrote about Gideon Durlacher. It's not necessary, think about it.
I have to end this letter now; my girlfriend claims I go to sleep too late.
All my love and hope that we will see each other soon. I can hardly wait.

Loving regards and best wishes,

Your Ernst

Elden, July 2, 1941 (Letter No. 7 from Elden)

Dear Ilse,

Yesterday I received your letter (thank you very much). I wanted to answer you immediately, but due to the 'devouring of strawberries' in my room, nothing came of it. I have a lunch break now and, thus, an opportunity to write.
I hope your stomach problem has passed or, hopefully, almost. I still feel you should visit a doctor. Who knows, he might be able to help you. It's not wise to walk around ill during these times.
Listen, I hate to think of our date falling through. I'm looking forward to it so much. I'm always afraid your parents won't

let you go. But if you're not completely better yet, maybe we should postpone. Otherwise, neither of us will enjoy our time together. I will keep my fingers crossed and hope you get better soon. I'm not afraid that we will drift apart if we don't see each other for a while. When people think about each other as much as we do, it's just impossible. Don't you think so too? My mother always said, 'Absence makes the heart grow fonder.' I totally agree with her.

And you should not always be so pessimistic! I don't want to write too much because I hope we will see each other Friday night, and then we can tell each other much more.

Please write soon and let me know if and when you will arrive in Deventer. I assume that when you receive this letter, you will already have sent a reply to it.

You already received the letter from Hans and Ruth. I spoke with them on Sunday and stayed the night on Saturday. I always stay with Hans and Ruth when I am in Deventer.

Now, my love, I must sign off. I just wanted to let you know that I'm okay. Be careful with your stomach.

See you soon. Many loving regards (I will save the kisses for you),

Your Ernst

Should there be an unexpected change in plan, you can call me between 12:00-13:30 and after 19:00 at 251 Elden. On Friday, I will leave here at 18:30 in the evening. (I opened and closed this letter again)

Elden, July 11, 1941 (Letter No. 8 from Elden)

My dearest Ilse,

You must have been waiting all week for a letter from me. I thought we would see each other on Saturday, and talking to each other would have been so much better than writing a letter. I received your letter tonight (I received the first letter yesterday). I now understand that the two of you are not coming.[14] That is such a pity; I really looked forward to our reunion. Since last week, my longing for you has doubled. I know you much better now, which has increased my feelings for you. When I think of those two days, it makes me so happy. I am glad that we were together, that everything went well, and that we could spend so many hours together without interference from others. I hope that we will be able to see each other soon and often so we can be there for each other. Thoughts and letters can bridge the distance a bit, but what is it compared to being together!!!

Your letter again made both a nervous and an excited impression. My dearest, do me a favor: don't be so afraid. I don't know what messages you have heard again, but nobody here knows much about anything. Don't let all these things give you nightmares.

If you want to show me your love, then please try to overcome your pessimism. Know that I am also greatly concerned about the future, but I will not let these concerns control me. We must not lose faith that better times will come. I don't know how to convey my optimism to you, but I want to help you forget your concerns.

---

14 Ilse and her sister Margot would come. To facilitate her parents' permission to travel to Ernst, Margot had to go with them

It is very hot here, but not from the heat of a baking oven like in a city. We perspire quite profusely, but it doesn't affect me that much. I go to bed at 23.00 and leave all the windows open; the draft is cool and pleasant. I sleep in pajamas and a thin sheet over me.

Yesterday, I worked without a shirt for a few hours, but that was not a good idea, so I won't do that again. I normally wear underwear, a blouse and pants and that's fine. The heat is here to stay, so we will just have to get used to it; we have no choice..

I am so jealous that Lore's baby kisses you so much (who does it better?).

I don't have much news for you this week. Heavy work awaits me next week. We have to clean the drains. The mud splashes everywhere, so we wear rubber boots, but the water often seeps into the top of our boots and soaks our socks.

On Friday, I accompanied Frey to a horse show near here. It was very interesting. We saw beautiful horses (this region is known for good-quality horses). We treated ourselves to a 1.50 guilder ice cream.

I must finish this letter and mail it so you can receive it tomorrow. If I'm late mailing it, you will have to wait for it until Monday. So, my dearest, many loving regards and kisses.

Your Ernst

Your letter arrived at an incorrect address, namely in Voorburg; you wrote the address in a reverse order. (In Elden, the name of the house is 'Voorburg.') Here, you write the name of the street first, the house number and then the town's name.

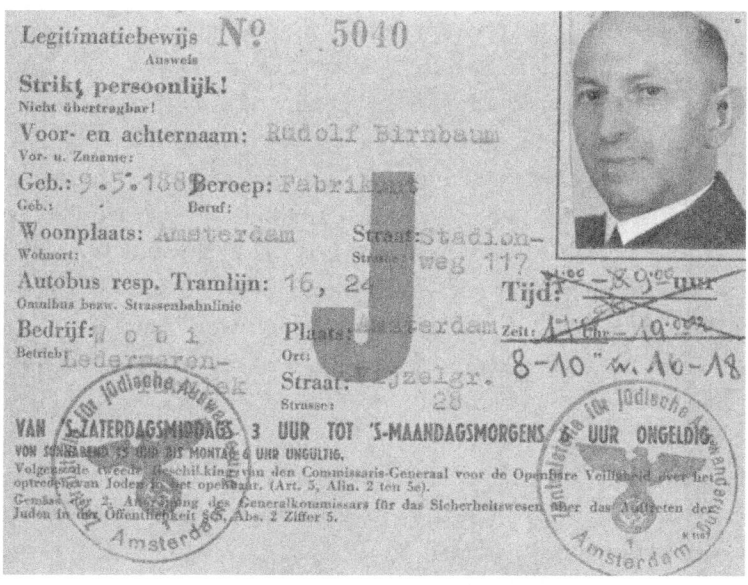

The personal identification document of Rudolf Birnbaum, Ilse's father.

Elden, July 16, 1941 (Letter No. 9 from Elden)

Dear Ilse,

Thank you so much for your sweet, precious letter. I was so happy to receive mail from you again.
The news about Chanan[15] really shocked me; I can't write about it. I'm sure you understand what I am feeling and thinking. My heart goes out to Lore. I can only imagine the situation she is in right now. Hopefully, we will get through all these dangers. When I read your letters, I always feel the mental pressure you suffer in your life and how anxious you are. Here, we

---

15 The Jewish name of Heini Pintus; Ernst probably used the name Chanan for security reasons.

experience the situation differently, and our nerves are stimulated a lot less. We feel less tension. If you are not in the thick of things but far away and only hear news about it, then things look different.

I am constantly wracking my brain on how to get you out of Amsterdam and bring you here to live with us. If we could be together more, we would get through all this much easier. It would be great if you could come here for a vacation in this neighborhood. Oh ... how happy that would make me! But Jews are forbidden in all hotels and tourist accommodations. I believe it might still be possible in Elst; it's very beautiful there. Would you like me to find out?

The only other option is for your family to live in Arnhem, but I suppose they wouldn't want to. Actually, what are the dates of your vacation?

I won't be able to get out again for the next few weeks. I must attend the 'Zionist History' course for the next 4-5 Sabbaths. In addition, it doesn't feel like I fit in that well with my comrades anymore; my friends are not local, which is not good. I was absent almost every weekend. Although mostly for the 'Beth Chaluz,' once for Chuliot... once with you in Deventer, and once with my circle of friends outside Elden.

The fact that Werner is absent every two weeks doesn't seem to be an issue because he travels to his girlfriend. Well, I don't owe anyone a report on how I spend my free time; otherwise, I would certainly have been able to explain my reasons. Werner told me with a grin that I should always say I am going to my girlfriend's.

Someone told Fokki that they see him as part of the community, and now he thinks he can upset us about it. It's an ugly game. He 'licks' the students' asses, and it seems he is turning them against us too. I hope he leaves here soon; we absolutely despise him now.

Sunday morning, we had a general talk about various social issues, such as 'accepting new members,' etc. In the afternoon, we went swimming, which was fantastic!!! As mentioned, it was the highlight of the day. It was the first time this year I was in the water. I wish you had been there; we could have enjoyed it together. We again had the same thoughts. It is the same with me, exactly the same. Something happy and nice happens, but then I only enjoy it half because you are not there with me.

I didn't stay over this time at Hans and Ruth's because we would've had to cross the bridge at 23:00, so we only went to sleep at 02:30.

I must sign off now. Many warm regards,

Your Ernst

I eagerly await your letter.

Erco with friends at the IJssel River. In the foreground, Hans and Ruth Stein

Elden, July 22, 1941 (Letter No. 10 from Elden)

My dearest Ilse,

After five days of disappointment (I have been waiting for your letter since Saturday morning), your letter finally arrived today – or rather the letter written in your spirit, some of which I was very happy about. To hear about your illness was less pleasant; I hope it is nothing serious and that you will soon be well again. Could it be 'vacation' excitement? It's wonderful that you are coming here without your parents. I am looking forward to it, and heaven forbid this should fail for some or other reason. That is strictly PROHIBITED!
Three weeks is really great. However, I fully realize that it will probably pass in the blink of an eye, but let's not be ungrateful. Tell Lore that I think it's very nice of her to come with you and that she shouldn't be afraid of the two souls residing in me. Sometimes, there is a 'third' sole, so for tactical reasons, it is good that we have a 'moral supervisor.'
After all, we must always have a 'protective' back.
Jews are forbidden from settling in Gelderland; they are only allowed to stay there for a limited period. In Arnhem, we are not allowed to enter cafes and hotels, but that doesn't bother us. I suspect you have found a room. There are no rooms available here. Have you booked with Gross? Or what's their name again...? Werner is frantically searching for a room for Ella Cahen, his fiancée. Her vacation is between August 1 and 15. I hope everything works out, and we will probably have written a few more letters by then.
As of this Saturday, I have already moved into my new room, and against all odds, it turned out nicer than I thought. On Sunday, I worked on the room and messed around in it all day. In the end, it turned out cozy and home-like. Everything

is very small, so I kept the decorating to a minimum – simple and well-organized, you'll see.

Last night, we celebrated the new rooms of the madrichim, which we had built for them in the attic. We celebrated with tea, small sandwiches and fruit. As it turns out, there was enough (seating) room for five people. I have many visitors; everyone wants to see the room.

Other than that, I don't have much to tell. I spend a lot of time preparing for my lectures on the history of Zionism. Yesterday, the Federation in Tiel invited me to give a lecture on the hakhshara in Elden next Sunday. I still don't know if I want to accept their invitation.

My dearest, do not be angry at me for writing so little today; I am exhausted and feel awful, but I really wanted to send you a letter. Please write back soon.

I wish you a full recovery. Much love,

Your Ernst

Elden, July 24, 1941 (Letter No. 11 from Elden)

My dearest Ilse,

Although you have just received a letter from me, I still have to congratulate you on your birthday 'as a courtesy,' so I decided to send you another. You already know what I wish you for this special day (actually, I should write 'us'); therefore, I don't need to list everything. We have already admitted that neither of us knows how to write birthday letters, although I believe that writing to you comes naturally to me. I must admit, everything sounds funny and banal now, so I had better give up. After all, I have often told you how I feel about you, my dear. Remember these things as if you are hearing them from me today. I hope we can celebrate our birthdays to come under different circumstances.

I actually wanted to send you a small package, but since you're coming here next week, I'll give it to you in person; that will be much nicer (then we can exchange it together...). I am sure you agree with me on that. Due to personal reasons, I could not accept your offer of not needing to give you a gift...

I hope you can spend your birthday with a bit of joy; I suppose it won't be much. Imagine I am there, telling 'rotten jokes,' ... alas. Instead, I promise to think of you the whole time.

There is not much to tell since my last letter, which was probably a bit strange (I was dead tired that evening). I also can't seem to concentrate, so I am struggling to come up with an idea. I am in Miel Stranders' room. We bought two kilos of gooseberries; there are just thirty left now. Miel is also busy writing letters to his friends; every few minutes, we stop and chat for a while. It is now 23:00, and so far, we have done very little (Miel has now finished his letter), but it is quite cozy here.

The weather is getting warmer again, and I have plans to go swimming, which is wonderful. Next week, we will swim together, and I am already looking forward to that! On Sunday, I will drive 36 kilometers to the Federation in Tiel to tell them about Elden and the hachshara.

Attorney Kish was here on Saturday and gave a very good lecture on 'social questions amongst people.'

Today I received your letter with great joy. In the meantime, I hope you stay in good health; try to be more careful from now on.

Well, my dear, best wishes and congratulations. Love and kisses,

Your Ernst

Elden, August 14, 1941 (Letter No. 12 from Elden)

My dearest Ilse,

I received your letter yesterday, and again I was very happy about it. I was longing for this letter. I am very grateful to you for keeping your promise to write soon. Now that you are no longer here, I can patiently wait for the evening to come. Everything is back to the way it was before you came. I think of those days with great wistfulness and joy that we were able to spend them together.
I believe that this week and a half has greatly strengthened our bond. I can feel my love for you growing stronger and stronger the more we see each other.

My love, I want to see you again as soon as possible.

As for the weather, you're not missing anything. It has not changed since you left – dark and cold (yesterday, I even had to wear a sweater) – and now it is stormy, and a lot of fruit has fallen from the trees.
Because you see, darling, you have been needlessly afraid again that I don't understand you or that I don't think well of you anymore. I completely understand your thoughts about Sunday night, and I understand your attitude very well. I believe we both made that mistake that night, if one could even call it a mistake. We were a little weak, and perhaps that was unnecessary. But in the light of day, everything looks different. When I think about it, I hardly ever have unpleasant feelings about something, like when someone says something out of anger or something you would rather have kept to yourself, but which is actually not that bad. I suggest you forget all about it; that is the best thing to do. Lastly, we have to expe-

rience some things first because we cannot know in advance what everything is and looks like. Next time, we will be wiser, but believe me, nothing has changed in my attitude toward you or my thoughts about you, my beloved. Can we consider this matter thus resolved and forgotten?

Life here continues as usual. On Monday night, Amnon and I chatted until after midnight; every time a Chuliot team member visits, I take the opportunity to catch up.
Yesterday we went to the concert I told you about. The musicians played the piano and violin, and they both played excellently. The program was also good: Schubert, Mozart, Beethoven ('Frühlingssonate'), Debussy, and Ravel.
Prior to each piece, we were given a brief introduction in which reference was made to the technique used. I can't remember if I ever told you that I don't know much about music; I enjoy it very much but don't understand what the composer actually wants to tell us.
The music is very conducive to my dreams and thoughts – you were on my mind all evening?
I have to stop writing; it's very late now. One of the boys visited me and stayed the whole evening. Marcella also came over for a while.
Will you write back soon?

Many loving regards and kisses,

Your Ernst

PS
I had to take something to the village this afternoon and passed one of the places we went on a walk together. I also passed by Paul Krugerstraat. And that always reminds me of

the many beautiful moments together with you and how I wish you were cycling next to me. 'And if not now...' Hopefully, it will happen in the near future.
I received pessimistic news again.
Don't be afraid, my love!
Everything will be fine!

Elden, August 19, 1941 (Letter No. 13 from Elden)

My dearest Ilse,

This will be a short letter because if I don't write it today, I won't have time to write until Friday, and I know you cannot wait that long.
I am very tired tonight and want to go to bed early. I have to go to the dentist tomorrow (and that is going to hurt). Tomorrow night, I will be in Dieren. On Thursday afternoon, I must prepare for my lesson on 'the knowledge of the country.' So you see, I am very busy. I received your letter today; thank you. Needless to say, it made me really happy. I think of you all the time, and it feels like forever since you've been here, but it was just a week ago.
What you wrote about Heini Pintus is incredibly sad; I was very upset about it. Let's hope everything goes well.
It's a shame that the relationship between you and Lore is not what it used to be and that it makes you feel more lonely. I understand it, though; in the end, the two of you are so different in many ways and how you live.
The other day, I was in Utrecht doing some shopping. Things there are going really well, and people can walk around more freely in a foreign city like that. I used to do that often in Bre-

men and really enjoyed it. Now I dream that the two of us can go window shopping in Tel Aviv together!
There is not much else to tell. My brother Heinz was here for the weekend and really liked it here. He has grown a lot and is already as tall as me.
We had many visitors on Saturday and Sunday; it was terrible – Federation members, chalutzim and various other old men and board members – it was swarming with people. My door opened continuously: 'Pardon me, just having a quick look at your rooms.'
Lini de Bruin has created a negative atmosphere. She has minimal contact with anyone, so she is considered a nuisance now. I agree with the de chanichim: she really does not fit here. Even when I try to understand her position and difficulties, it is impossible to recognize such a woman as madricha. It is a pity because, as a person, she is a wonderful woman. It is also unfortunate that it has a negative impact on social life and development here. I don't think she will leave here soon.
Hans, David and Rob want to visit this week or the week after. I am looking forward to that.
Sunday, Monday, and Tuesday, there is a seminar in Arnhem that I have already told you about. I will be there too, but I don't think anything special is going to happen.
What do you think of the photo? Nice, isn't it? It was taken during a meeting of 'Chuliot.'
I did what you asked and wrote to my mother about you, but only one sentence. I will tell her in small portions; otherwise, I fear she will find it difficult.
It's good that a raincoat can be repaired. If it's ready on Sunday, please give it to Werner. He will be in Amsterdam on Saturday and Sunday but don't worry if that's not possible.
I look forward to receiving it and am curious to see the pullover, but please do not spend too much money. Women in

love often exaggerate...
I wrote much more than I intended and didn't even have to chew on my pen (joke). I never do that anyway. Writing to you is so much easier than writing to other people. How is that possible? I hope my stories don't bore you.

Many loving regards, my love,

Your Ernst

Please give Lore my very best and tell her I wish her a speedy recovery. Will you write back soon? When will I get the promised photo?

Elden, August 20, 1941 (Letter No. 14 from Elden)

My darling,

I just received your letter, and now I am very sad. I have nothing to comfort you with except for what I have told you so many times: Don't give up! We must not give up hope regarding our future.
You know that I wholeheartedly believe that, in essence, people are good and that we will be happy. We have come this far and will make it through any future dangers.
My love, I am not simply writing words (to offer you momentary comfort); I am holding on to this with all my might. This is the faith that fuels my courage and strength. This is all I can tell you now.
I don't know what lies ahead of us, but together, we will endure. Together, we bear the uncertainty and worries because

we know we belong together, and our love will keep making us stronger. Stay strong, my love.
Tell Lore something on my behalf. I deeply sympathize but don't know what to say. Do you understand?

A thousand loving regards and kisses,

Your Ernst

Elden, August 26, 1941 (Letter No. 15 from Elden)

My dearest Ilse,

Several days have passed, and, at last, I can write to you again today and tell you all about my latest experiences. I received your letter on Sunday morning; thank you. Once again, you write with very little courage and utter despair.
I can't help you more than I've already tried, except tell you over and over that we must remain courageous and confident and that I firmly believe everything will work out fine.
Don't think I don't understand – you live under constant pressure and, therefore, in constant fear. If we could have been together, things would have been different. I think you would have been much calmer and everything much simpler.
I can hardly give you the same answer every time. In the long run, it won't sound credible anymore. Do you understand what I mean? Don't think I do not want to hear your concerns; you know how I feel about it, so don't be angry that I don't want to discuss it further.
The raincoat is great; I am very happy with it, so honestly, thank you. You are a very gifted woman! I was sorry it rained

yesterday and not today. I wore it anyway.
I attended the summer training of the Dutch Zionist Union from Sunday until today. It was quite interesting, although I didn't learn many new things. There were four lectures each day, lasting a few hours. The lecturers were Buechenbacher and the union secretary, who lectured on the trends in Zionism. Tini van der Heijden, secretary of V.K.L., lectured on issues regarding Palestine, especially about the Arab population. Dr. Spangenthal, who sits on the board of Elden, gave a lecture on the 'Chalutziut.' Werner Ahlfeld gave a lecture on the formation of the Israeli monarchy.
Josef Melkmann gave a lecture on the history of the people of Israel. Overall, it was interesting, and it inspired me, so I decided and hope to make a reading program for myself for next winter (the road to hell is paved with good intentions). I have compiled a comprehensive list that, in general, will be of value to me should I get around to it. Knowing me, I doubt I will succeed.
I also met a very interesting and nice man at the seminar; interesting because of his knowledge. I'm referring to Tini van der Heijden. We, the madrichim, had many in-depth conversations with him, lasting until after midnight. His lecture was about the religions of primitive people and was very interesting. Our last lecture this afternoon was by Dr. Spangenthal. Afterward, there was a nice discussion in which I also participated. I do not agree with the view that only 'real' Zionists can participate in a hakhshara; you are familiar with this Dutch view. However, according to this principle, you do get the best chalutzim. Our Dutch friends are all 100% volunteers and also very competent and good. But we, that is, the chalutzim movement, believe that because of this, the selection process is too strict, which leads to very few people joining. That is a pity because it's precisely the training that opens the eyes of

many... which ultimately, no matter how you spin it, is our vision. Let's absolutely not forget that.

It was already too late to talk about all the topics. It was impossible, and we were unable to convince each other. In any case, I could not persuade Dr. Spangenthal. He is no longer a child and has the right to have a different view from mine.

The farmers are disappointed with the people from the Working Village. As far as work is concerned, good people like Kurt Reilinger etc., perform no more than average.

Hans invited us to Deventer again. I immediately said no; you can't come anyway. I hope we can go there again soon. Then, we will do our best to be together as much as possible, even if it means enduring a few minor inconveniences. What use are we to each other if we only see each other once in a while? Last week, Heinz went sailing on a yacht with some friends on the Loosdrecht lake. Something went wrong, and the boat sank; they had to swim ashore. Heinz was sitting in the yacht's cabin while water rushed in through the door, and that's why he didn't notice anything. Somehow, he managed to get out (he had only recently learned how to swim) and made it to shore with the others. He was lucky. Fortunately, it ended well.

The 'organization of instructors' of all the youth houses was here today. They meet once a month. Maybe I should have been there, but I had a seminar, and we had an argument with Frey and Fokki. Apparently, 'their honor was violated' (especially Fokki, who is not welcome).

The attached photo is the one you wanted, right? (I assume.) Nice, isn't it? The weather is to blame for the photo not being very clear; it was very cloudy.

So, I think I've told you everything. You cannot call me a lazy writer. I hope I receive a really long letter from you soon. I am already waiting in anticipation.

Sorry, my sweet, but try to be a bit more cheerful. Do it for yourself and for others. In my thoughts, I am sending you many loving regards and a heap of kisses,

Your Ernst
Hans apologizes for not writing to you yet; he hasn't had time. Yesterday was his birthday.

Elden, September 2, 1941 (Letter No. 16 from Elden)

My dearest Ilse,

After all the hard work today, it's now your turn again. I long for
your letters and was very happy to receive a letter from you today, as always.
Yes, I understand that you are often nervous and anxious. I have made that clear to you in my letters, my silly girl!
What concerns me most in your letter are your professional plans. I couldn't figure it out and didn't get what you were trying to tell me. If I understand correctly, you want to quit sewing to become a maternity nurse. Or is it an evening course or something along those lines?
I assume that the new Nazi decree regarding studies for Jews has led you to these thoughts? If it is a so-called 'course,' then I can't really comment on it. Still, I don't understand why you want to learn something that (as far as I can tell) doesn't appeal to you at all?
But, if you are talking about a complete education, I have serious doubts as you have just finished your professional training

at Gerzon as a seamstress. Frankly, it doesn't seem like a good idea to me at all. I hope to read your answers soon so I can give you my 'actual' opinion on the matter.

There is not much to tell about my life here; there were no special events this past week.

On Thursday, we were all invited to Lini's place; she got her new furniture and decorated it very nicely. It was a kind of christening of the house.

We had chocolate milk and cakes as snacks, and there was beautiful music from records. It was cozy.

Lini has a rather good library, which I frequent fairly often (everyone does). I have taken on a heavy yet very interesting piece of literary work.

On Sabbath, we started reading the book *Krisis und Entscheidung im Judentum* by Jakob Klatzkin. The book is difficult to understand, so I prepared a summary of the passage with one of the students, which we can then read in an understandable way. This way, it is possible to understand the book.

We are now harvesting potatoes with a great group, which is really good farm work. We work hard, are industrious and return home exhausted.

On Friday night, I drive to Apeldoorn to Phillip and Betty (you only know their names).

On Saturday night, we have a Chuliot meeting.

When will we see each other again? Which should be soon, I hope.

In any event, I have to stay here for Rosh Hashanah; we have social obligations and are not allowed to leave. Can we then be together here in Deventer on Saturday and Sunday, the two public holiday days? Alternatively, there are still four consecutive days off during Sukkot, from Saturday through Tuesday. What will be most convenient for you? We should not miss this opportunity to be together for this length of time. Take

advantage of your parents' good humor.
I have been reading the book *Castellio gegen Calvin (Ein Gewissen gegen die Gewalt)* by Stefan Zweig. I also started reading the book *Junge Frau von* 1914 by Arnold Zweig today. Other than that, I am busy with Simon Dubnow.
This week, I received mail from my mother via the Red Cross and from my brother in Palestine; they are both doing well.
My dear, don't be angry with me for writing so messy and for my terrible handwriting today, which is even worse than usual. I am sitting on my bed and writing on a chair.
Marcella has no room and switches with Merry every month. She is sitting at the table now and sends many sincere, heartfelt regards.

Your Ernst

Write back soon and as much as you can.

Elden, September 9, 1941 (Letter No. 17 from Elden)

My dearest Ilse,

Sorry for writing to you with a typewriter; I forgot my fountain pen in Deventer, and I hope I haven't lost it. You understand, I hope. I received your letter on Friday just before my trip to Deventer; thank you very much. Why do you immediately worry when my letters come a little late? I don't always have time to write, and I also know you don't like me going to bed late. I also can't write when I'm very tired, and I don't like being hunched over a letter late at night.
I have been very tired the last few days. The work we are

currently doing is hard (digging up potatoes), and I also went to sleep really late. It was nice in Apeldoorn and in Devente – it was very home-like in Apeldoorn. I'm not as comfortable with Betty and Phillip as with Hans and Ruth. The food was nothing special either. In the afternoon, I ate at the Apeldoorn Bosch (Jewish psychiatric institution). In the evening, we had the Chuliot biweekly meeting in Deventer – we read portions of Martin Buber's Ich und Du (1923) and Worte an die Jugend
(1938), followed by a good debate. I stayed with Hans and Ruth Stein, and we had a wonderful breakfast on Sunday morning. It got quite late, so I drove straight to Oldenboom (the farmer in Wilp), where I enjoyed a delicious roast pig with all the tasty vegetables and potatoes to go with it for the first time since I had been here. I spent several good and enjoyable hours with them. They are wonderful people. They also invited me to join them on vacation. I haven't said 'yes' yet (who knows what will happen next). In the afternoon, I spent a little more time with the immigrant party. Marcella, Dudi and I ate supper at Hans and Ruth's (Marcella arrived unexpectedly, a nice surprise). Then we cycled back here with Hans. We had a flat tire on the way, but luckily, we found someone to repair the tire (it was after 22.00). We arrived back here in Elden five minutes before midnight.
You know, in the last few days, I realize more and more that I need a break now and then. I'm rather fed up with Elden, especially this last week, and frankly, for no good reason. Everything is as it always is, but I really needed to see our friends. I won't mention my desire to be with you because I can't achieve this on a bicycle. But now that I am back, my will to work is also back, and everything (almost everything) is once again at peace, 'and the sun is shining.' A new chaniech arrived today, and we immediately pranked him. We told him

that everything here is subject to strict rules; for example, we eat in a specific order, and there are strict punishments like fasting, etc. Apart from that, everything is shared with everyone. Money should not be kept in warehouse A. We are all acting, of course, but the poor boy hasn't caught on so far, and we keep bursting into laughter. He is clearly not very bright, but it is great entertainment for all of us.

What are we going to do on Rosh Hashanah? Perhaps it would be a better idea for us (should you be able to) to spend four days of Sukkot in Deventer. Hans and Ruth invited us. They said they do not mind us staying there for so long. If I may be honest, I think it would be better to be in Deventer for four days rather than two days here in Elden and two days there. We can be together much more in Deventer. After all, I have obligations here that I cannot easily get out of.

We will probably have a Chuliot meeting on Sunday, October 4, even before Sukkot. Is it possible to meet up afterward? Please try and do your utmost; I miss you so much.

If you want to read a very good book, you should try Junge Frau von 1914, written by Arnold Zweig. I read it in one go, wonderful. I discussed it with some of our friends, who also thought it was incredibly good. Next, I'm starting on Laudin und die Seinen by Jakob Wassermann. I usually read in bed at night. If I'm wide awake during the day, I focus on Simon Dubnow. As a matter of fact, I have absolutely no idea what you do in your spare time. Sometimes, you complain that I don't write enough about these things, but now it's the other way around. What do you actually read? Or don't you have time to read, or don't you feel like it? A good book at a time like this is a great distraction and provides us with a bit of artistic pleasure that we miss now that there are no more concerts, radio, etc. It offers a little counterbalance against all the worries and problems of the dark times we live in.

Write back soon.
I have to go to Deventer again on Saturday evening for a general meeting. I'm already getting sick of it. It's too bad this meeting is not in Amsterdam, my love. I must really finish writing this letter now.

Your Ernst

We have a very big cigarette shortage here. Perhaps you can find some? I heard that you can still get some in Amsterdam, preferably between 37.5 and 52.5 cents. In general, I smoke between 38.5 and 45 cents. Naturally, I will pay you back. Thanks for the blanket, Werner brought it. You really act fast.

Elden, September 14, 1941 (Letter No. 18 from Elden)

My dearest Ilse,

I have still not recovered my fountain pen, but since I don't want you to complain about my writing, I borrowed a fountain pen from one of my friends (there are more fools in the world).
I received your letter yesterday, and the package arrived today. I am honestly so happy and excited about it! The pullover is amazing and far exceeds all my expectations. Many thanks, my dear; I immediately put it on, of course, and it fits perfectly. Again, thank you very much. It's too bad that weeks have to pass before I can thank you in person, but until we see each other again, you will just have to imagine how handsome it looks on me. Try to picture it.
I'm sorry you are sick again; I hope you get better soon. I am very familiar with dysentery, so be careful not to worsen the situation. Try to eat as much as possible, because you are already quite thin.
You are right; my letters contain a little less content than usual. My dearest, I hardly remember what you look like anymore. We haven't seen each other for four weeks, so I can't wait for our next meet-up. Do you have any idea how desperate I am to see you on Rosh Hashanah? But it's better to postpone until Sukkot; that will give us more days to be together. We will spend four whole wonderful days in Deventer; happy days! (God knows... in this respect, we are spoiled).
Our Chuliot meeting (the center of Chuliot) will take place on the Sunday before Sukkot – October 5. After that, there are two Sukkot days, then four vacation days, and then the last (Sukkot) holidays on Saturday, Sunday and Monday. I know you don't want to come to the gathering (it's going to

be lots of fun because we're also celebrating Amnon's wedding there), but I, and also everyone else, would really like you to come.

Amnon told me that friends who cannot yet be included in Chuliot due to technical problems (such as the training period, the hachshara period, etc.) but who socially belong to the group can attend our conferences. I would love for you to get to know everyone. Hopefully, it will happen someday. Our meetings are truly different from other meetings I have attended so far in that there is an amazing social spirit – you know how enthusiastic I am about such meetings. Last week there was a big management meeting here. The three-month probationary period ended. Almost everyone was accepted, but a few must complete another three-month trial period. One boy and one girl were rejected permanently, but we have no idea what to do with them now.

The home of the Youth Alias is in Loosdrecht. If those two do not want to return, the only option will be the camp in Drenthe. The organization in Elden wants everybody to realize their full potential, but in my opinion, it is a crime against this boy; he will lose his way completely due to the bad influence of the youth in the Drenthe camp. A much wiser decision will be to accommodate this boy here in Elden.

The organization often tends to sacrifice individuals for the greater good. In this matter, however, it would be wiser to exercise a bit more caution. They are too principled in many things. We, the madrichim, were invited to a session where we had to spend hours hearing about our great responsibility in raising these chanichim. 'WE????' We all know the madrichim in Elden, don't we?! I was very angry about it and made that clear to them. They were talking about their 'experience' (of compassion). I responded that it is very easy to hand out instructions while sitting behind the 'green table,' but in reality, it's a very different story.

Of course, they were not willing to accept this criticism from us, and it was actually foolish of me to say something about it. Werner did not say a word even though he agreed with me. He just thinks, 'Let them talk'. Fokki, the 'righteous one,' justified management's actions (he licks their butts). Frey 'was impressed' by what he heard.

In the evening, Ru Cohen gave a speech about emphasizing the value of work more and more; culture has taken up too much space. From tomorrow, we will work an hour longer and study time will be reduced. They said that we will do more with culture during the winter months again. Everything was very important, of course, and against all expectations, everything went smoothly. This is good, of course, as we really do not need any crisis here. While sorting potatoes, a chaniecha and I humorously conceived the whole thing as a Bible chapter; we were in a crazy mood that day. On Saturday evening, we read our 'play' to everyone. It was a great success, especially because we spared neither the management nor the madrichim in our comedy.

This week, the work was very tedious. I had to sort potatoes with my group. We made lots of noise: we sang, laughed and yelled a lot, and threw potatoes. We finally concluded that despite the difficult work, we had a lot of fun.

Have I written to you yet to say that I am receiving dental care? I have several cavities that need fillings; it's so annoying. I visit her (the dentist) once weekly, and she fills a cavity. Fortunately, I went to the dentist on time. Luckily, my teeth have not been neglected, so the treatment does not hurt.

Thank you for the cigarettes that arrived just in time. I was almost becoming desperate because I can't buy them here; there just aren't any. Can you take care of that from now on, too? Naturally, I'll pay you back for everything.

My dear darling, I hope I have told you (written) enough for today. Please write back as soon as possible, and especially write that you are healthy again.

And again, thank you very much. I wish you a speedy recovery.

Many loving regards and kisses.

Your Ernst

Elden, September 21, 1941 (Letter No. 19 from Elden)

My dearest Ilse,

Today is Erev Rosh Hashanah. I want to write a quick letter so you will receive it tomorrow. Usually, I'm not so much into 'wishing each other.' I don't usually send New Year's wishes, but I think we both couldn't wish ourselves enough this year. The past year has cost us a lot. We are terribly exhausted and don't know what lies ahead. How long must we still wait before we can think about the future calmly again?
Despite all the misery, we have also experienced beautiful moments this past year. I believe and wish that all the beautiful times we have had will continue and never stop.
Whatever happens, I hope we will never lose our courage and that everything will work out.
The two of us will also celebrate our private Rosh Hashanah tomorrow, the beginning of the third year of our relationship. My love, we know we belong together, and nothing could ever change that. Tomorrow, we are going to think about each other all day long, even though we are apart from each other, geographically speaking.

Because of Rosh Hashanah and our private anniversary, I plan to send you a package with a gift tomorrow.
I must sign off now. We have a session in Loosdrecht this evening.

Many warm regards and a kiss (1)

Your Ernst

Give my regards to your parents as well.

Elden, September 29, 1941 (Letter No. 20 from Elden)

My dearest Ilse,

This morning I received your postcard. I'm terribly sorry that problems keep cropping up and that our plans must change again. Apparently, all we have is bad luck this time, which is hard to accept. These changes are painful and hard to swallow. I fully understand that you want to be with Lore now, but after two weeks, surely you can take a break after she has gotten over the initial shock? That should be possible; it must be possible.
Yes, the first few days are terrible and impervious, but I hope time will help Lore calm down a bit.
I have no desire to come to Amsterdam. You know that in Amsterdam we can hardly be together and enjoy ourselves. Two days in Deventer is better than three days in Amsterdam. My dearest, you must understand and remember that you have an obligation both to yourself and to me.
Not seeing each other for so long is just ridiculous, and more-

over, it's sad. I don't want others to take you away from me every time. We only have a few occasions to see each other, so we have to utilize every opportunity.
Well, be sensible, I beg you! We must hurry, as we may not be able to travel at all in the near future. Who knows...
Try to come this week. If not, then next week, but to DEVENTER!
I will write you again in a few days. Until then, loving regards and kisses

Your Ernst

Write back soon.

Elden, October. 8, 1941 (Letter No. 21 from Elden)

My dearest Ilse,

Thank you so much for your letter; it made me very happy. I totally agree with you.
I arrived here safely. It was very nice at Ruth and Hans' place. I was at the Oldenbooms on Monday evening until 9:45 p.m. As always, it was lots of fun.
On Tuesday, I cycled back to Deventer around 3.30 p.m. Everything is fine here.

We are now eating in the Soeka, which is really nice. The 'pious' eat in the dining hall where it is less cold.
We had quite a lot of excitement here today, so I decided to go for a bike ride. It was a good decision, as it calmed me down. Don't be angry that I write so little this time. I am very tired,

and it is already late. I had many visitors, and they had just left.
Many warm regards and kisses,

Your Ernst

The first big raid in Gelderland

On October 8, the Netherlands suffered its fourth raid. This time, close to where Ernst was, in the Achterhoek, Apeldoorn, Zwolle and Arnhem. This was probably at the request of the highest SS officer in the Netherlands, Hanns Albin Rauter, in order to further frighten the Jews and break the resistance. According to Lou de Jong, Rauter had shortly before asked his boss Heinrich Himmler for permission to take some three to four thousand communists and Jews between the ages of 18 and 35 to Mauthausen.

Seventy random Jewish men were deported, and almost all of them were killed immediately.

Ilse's parents insisted that Ernst seek refuge at their home in Amsterdam, as they worried that Ernst would also be nabbed on the street one day.

Elden, October 11, 1941 (Letter no. 22 from Elden)

My dearest Ilse,

Finally, there will be no more visitors, which means it's your turn now!
Today, I had a busy day. At eight in the morning, while still in my pajamas and on my way to the bathroom, Hans, who has to be here early for various things, met me on the stairs. Ruth was now home alone. I even had to teach a lesson before dinner. Miel Stranders went away for a few days, so I had to be his substitute. In the afternoon, I teach a Bible class, also as Miel's substitute. This afternoon, I teach another Bible class. Then I have to do something for Hans again, which, of course, I do with the greatest pleasure. By now, Hans is back home again.
I received your letters; I understand that you are extremely anxious; the situation here has not changed, but fortunately, nothing was wrong anyway.
You can stay calm; I am as careful as a person can be. About the offer to come to you, I hope it never comes to the point where I have to take advantage of that. But if it does become necessary, I certainly will, so don't worry unnecessarily. I didn't want to call you and definitely didn't want to be the first to contact you because I knew you would be shocked, and I certainly didn't want that. If you want to know more, go see Werner. He will be in Amsterdam during the holidays.
I was so happy that we were together again, and I can hardly describe to you with words how much strength this gives me every time and the feelings I take home with me. I know how strong our love is, and that gives me full confidence and a lot of strength. On days like this, when you have someone to think about and whom you are close to, you are stronger. You never leave my thoughts, especially during critical hours, and

that helps me overcome my fears.

Now, after the holidays, life is back to normal here. The weather here is bad; it was impossible to work outside yesterday. In the early morning hours, I typed many letters on behalf of the house. In the afternoon, I went with one of the boys to get vegetables for the holidays, and I got completely soaked as it rained non-stop.

Your offer to lend me money is very generous, thank you very much, my dear, but I really don't need it.

I don't know what else to write. I want to tell you and say so much, but I'll just have to put it off until we see each other again. Do you think you can get permission to come for Ruth's birthday? If not, I am considering coming to Amsterdam, to you, before then. I fear they will impose a travel ban soon, maybe even within the next two weeks.

A thousand kisses,

Your Ernst

PS: I did not catch a cold.

Some of the residents of Huize Voorburg, including Werner Ahlfeld (with pipe) and Ernst. Dudi Rosenbaum and Eshu Singer are standing on the right, October 1941

Elden, October 20, 1941 (Letter no. 23 from Elden)

My dearest Ilse,

This evening, I was free to write you a letter, but everything changed as all the madrichim suddenly had to attend a meeting with Lini. It ruined my whole evening plan. Now it is already quite late, and I am very tired, so please forgive me if this letter is not perfect.

I received your letter, and frankly, I was very surprised, and that's putting it mildly. How someone like you can harbor such infantile desires is beyond my comprehension. Worry and despair, knowing you, I certainly understand, but losing control of the situation and common sense altogether is something I cannot understand. I was totally shocked when I read your thoughts on the 'Labor Service,' etc. I don't wish to argue 'for' or 'against' at all, but these thoughts are completely absurd. Apart from that, you should always take some time to consider what you can or cannot write in a letter; I have spoken to you about that many times.

I beg you to stop saying such nonsense; I cannot express in words how disgusting it is.

Things here have not changed much; the atmosphere is good, and there is a lot of work. I fill my free time with reading and other stuff, like culture, etc. We had a concert on Sunday. Ella Cahen (Werner's wife) played the piano, and another woman played the violin, which we actually thought was not very well played.

Other than that, nothing new. David was here on Sunday, and Fokki was once again unbearable. He makes us want to be physically sick; we are constantly getting angry with him. What will happen on November 1? The best thing would be if you could come to Deventer... see what you can do.

I will write to Hans.
My dear, don't be angry that I don't write much today; I am exhausted. You will get another letter soon. I'm also waiting for a letter from you.
Many loving regards and kisses,

Your Ernst.

Elden, October 26, 1941 (Letter no. 24 from Elden.)

My dearest Ilse,

Finally, after a week of hard work, I have time to write to you again. I wanted to reply immediately after I received your letter, but I was busy every evening, and in my free time on my lunch break, I couldn't get around to it either.
Because of last week's storm, we had over 900 pounds of apples flying off the trees. Since we couldn't do anything with them, we had to peel and dry everything. We do this work in the evenings because during the day there is a lot of other agricultural work to do and we need all abled bodies. So, we have been vigorously peeling and drying the last two evenings. It was fun and cheerful, but it was a pity that we had to waste so much free time doing it. Nevertheless, we diligently carry on (also this week).
On Thursday, I have to prepare a 'meeting' with Marcel, and it cannot be postponed either.
Yesterday, I read all day. The mail doesn't get to Amsterdam until tomorrow evening anyway, so today, Sunday evening, it's still early enough.
I was very happy with your letter. This time, it was more

confident and attentive than your previous letters. The tone in my last letter was a little sharp. Please forgive me. I was in a terrible mood that evening. I was irritated and also really shocked by your letter, believe me.

Your pictures are nice, but why are you letting yourself be photographed with this dummy? He ruins the whole picture. It is already quite cold here. Yesterday, I put up a sign here in the attic with the words: 'To the exercise area for Arctic studies' (no need for an explanation, of course) as it was freezing cold in the countryside this week. We had to harvest vegetables until 10 a.m., and everything was soaking wet. Now, the motto is: do all the work as fast and hard as possible, such as digging, sowing, and harvesting vegetables: red beets, carrots, lettuce, cabbage, etc. Everything must be done before the heavy rain and frost. 10-15 men are incessantly digging in the earth with shovels; it is manual plowing, actually. Werner is picking apples with a group of guys, and I am digging up potatoes with another group. Everything is full of mud, which also sticks to everything. Our farm manager is leaving this week, which is very unfortunate. He got a new job, probably better and certainly safer. He was rock solid in every way.

In the meantime, we are running everything ourselves until there is a new manager.

Frey, undoubtedly the most abled of us all, is actually now the one running things around here. This is how things have been working for a few days, and it's going quite well; we can handle it!

The spanner in the wheel is Fokki. He opposes anything and everything and incites trouble (we are not afraid because no one really takes him seriously). People are looking for another workplace for him, but the big question is whether he will leave. The current situation is not clear. It is getting harder and harder to deal with him, which is very disturbing because,

in general, everyone is dependent on everyone and affectionate to everyone. Frey, Werner and I run the business here and always find a peaceful solution to everything.
Yesterday and today, I read a good book, The Living Thoughts of Spinoza, by Arnold Zweig (in Dutch). It was not easy. Furthermore, I have read Die Geschichten Jaakobs by Thomas Mann, the first part, and found it very interesting, although the style is rather complicated. Next, I want to try to read an English book, Eastwind Westwind, by Pearl S. Buck. Let's see if I succeed. We have established an English reading club here. I do not participate, but the others are managing nicely. They read three pages per hour, but I get bored that way, you understand?
Moreover, I know the level of the participants.
Every Sabbath evening, there is a poetry class – Miel Stranders gives poetry lessons. So far, we have learned to sing a lot of songs as well, something I think is very important for the youth here in Elden and, of course, just as important outside of Elden. Miel is doing a great job, and we are all enjoying it. Now, my little one, what is going to happen to us this week? I asked Hans to write to you, which I assume he has done. I really hope you get permission to come. Please answer me as soon as possible so I can take time off. Actually, I'm going to Deventer anyway, or do you think I should come to Amsterdam? I leave it up to you to decide. There is still hope regarding the 'travel ban,' although only a little. See if anything can be done about this. Sweet of you to buy the present (one less worry for me). 3 guilders in these times is really good and enough. Will you send it in case you can't come? At least write that it's from me too! Otherwise, it will be embarrassing for me. I keep the faith that we will be able to meet this week; my fingers are crossed for us.

Loving regards and kisses,

Your Ernst

Marcella has just come back from Deventer; everyone is sending you warm regards. Everything is fine in Deventer. I would prefer to travel to Deventer on Sunday to pick up my winter clothes; my summer coat is no longer adequate for this cold weather.

Elden, November 5, 1941 (Letter no. 25 from Elden)

My dearest Ilse,

Actually, I don't have much to write about, but since I know that you pine for my letters, I will try to fill a page anyway. I returned home very satisfied after being with you, and every time I think back, it fills me with a special feeling that is hard to describe. I believe it could perhaps be called 'happiness.' This is how I know that the things I told you about our bond have been reaffirmed and strengthened. I hope we can see each other again soon. How was your trip back home? It must have been horrible to travel back home alone? What did you tell them back home? Everything here is fine, but winter being early limits us as far as work is concerned. Our carrots are still stuck in the ground. Carrots are an important part of our nutrition. I hope we can get them out before it freezes.
My plan was actually to write you a letter last night, but then we suddenly received a notification, after which I couldn't even think of writing (but it made me think of you even more). Our people here remained relatively calm, although

the situation was obviously very serious. We received better news today, and life has returned to normal. You were probably very worried again, and I can certainly understand that. I'm sure I'll get a trepidatious letter from you tomorrow; I don't know what people are telling you.
My dear, you can stay calm.
I am signing off now; I simply have nothing else to tell you.
I will write to you again at the end of the week. Until then, many loving regards with the necessary accessories.

Your Ernst

Wow, how wonderful! My bed has arrived. It is already quite cold upstairs, so we no longer use our bedrooms.

Elden, November 8, 1941 (Letter no. 26 from Elden)

Dear Ilse,

I have the pleasure of starting this letter, then Ernst has less to write, at least, that's what he tells himself! However, I just want to thank you for the book I received.
Other than that, just my kindest regards. I heard from Ernst that you are doing well, so I don't need to inquire about that anymore.
I hope you continue doing well!

Kind regards,

Marcella

My dearest Ilse,
Waiting for a letter is very difficult for you, so I will do my best to write another letter soon. I was very happy when I got back from the trip, as I always am when I've been with you. Although we did not have complete freedom in Deventer this time, it was wonderful to see you. Hopefully, we will see each other again soon, but then without the 'supervision'... we need to spend some time alone.

On Monday, I arrived safely in Loosdrecht and even caught the bus. It was very pleasant. I talked with my brother for hours (his voice is breaking now). The next day, early in the morning, all 7 of us left Loosdrecht. Luckily, everything here in Elden is going well. Everyone said it was much cozier and more homely without us (but we also stated that it was much more fun for us without them...).

In the afternoon, we went back to work and soon forgot about our trip to Loosdrecht. Well, that was the case for me. When I went to bed in the evening, Amsterdam seemed far away. If it wasn't for my thoughts of you, the trip would already have been a distant memory.

Last night, we all sat mending socks together. Imagine me (yes, I participated as well). I have never mended a sock before. Until now, that is. Everyone thought I was an excellent student and mastered the task well. Actually, I wasn't going to tell you about it; I don't want you to get any ideas in the future... but as you know... out of the abundance of the heart, the mouth speaks... etc.

The winter cultural program started today.

I had the whole morning free, and so I learned Hebrew, something that, since I have been in Holland, has not happened yet. I enjoyed it very much, and now I have decided to continue with it.

I was supposed to drive to Dieren tonight, but I don't feel

like it. For me, it would be a lost evening as I have much to do here. Maybe Kurt Reilinger can take over this task (I'm going to try anyway).
I think I have written enough for today, or at least I have told you all the interesting things about the last few days.
What I forgot to tell you is that it was not easy for me to leave Amsterdam, certainly less easily than you might think.
I will write to you again at the end of the week. Until then, I hope to hear from you in the meantime.
Give my regards to your parents. Thank them for me and tell them that I had a pleasant time with them, etc., etc.

And to you, my loving thoughts and kisses,

Your Ernst

Elden, November 24, 1941 (Letter No. 27 from Elden).

My dearest Ilse,

It is high time I wrote you a letter and therefore I want to use these free morning hours for that. Many thanks, I received your letter with great joy.
You say we should not be so attached to each other because we have almost no opportunity to get to know each other better. Listen, my dearest, love is primarily based on emotion. And just as one does not know and love so much even before one professes mutual love, this is the time before there is communication so that one can love even after that. There are weaknesses and advantages to 'her and him' that one does not know beforehand and which only become apparent in daily

life. It is simple: either you love each other, or you do not love each other. In my opinion, that is just the way it is, and that is why I am not afraid of anything. Except, of course, for the fact that I want to be with you much more, certainly much more than we are together now (and not just to get to know you!).

From my side, there is not much more to tell (these days, we say 'thank goodness'). Our cultural program is beginning to run nicely; everyone is learning diligently. If only they were as diligent when working in the field!

Currently, Werner and I are free in the mornings. In the afternoons, we work outside until 5 p.m., then spend 2 hours with Batya in the kitchen.

The others: Frey and Fokki are out until noon and then in the kitchen until 5 p.m. From 5 to 7 p.m., they are free. It is much more pleasant to get the morning hours. First, while the dining room is being cleaned, we chat with Lini or go to the 'teaching room.' The great thing for us is the wonderful silence when only a few people are home. Yes, people have work hours and study hours, but it is still very noisy when they are all here. Evening work in the kitchen is less fun; I have already had to wash cups, plates and pans alone a few times.

Besides Hebrew, I am also volunteering to learn literature, which fills my time completely. I am in a reading club with Marcella, and the subject now is the philosopher Jakob Klatzkin, which also takes up a few evenings.

We also have professional first aid and economics classes four hours a week, which I also participate in. Just maybe I'll take another course in Hebrew. So you see, my dear, I really have to make an effort to find time to write letters. Lucky for me, I love writing to you, but to others...????

Yesterday, we had a 'Hebrew day' for the first time; it was a little strange to speak only Hebrew, but it went quite well. Fokki, Frey and Merry do not speak a word of Hebrew; they

had to speak German or Dutch. Lists of words associated with a room were posted in all the rooms, for example, kitchen: the names of utensils, vegetables, etc. In the teaching room, the names of writing utensils, smoking utensils, etc. Even in the toilets (in the boys' toilets, at least), lists of appropriate words were not forgotten, and there (at least in the boys' toilets), the appropriate lists with appropriate words were posted prominently. In the afternoon, Pnina Carmi taught Hebrew; everyone had to say something in Hebrew.
Then we had a discussion about the Arab matter.
Marcella just returned from Deventer in a cheerful mood and sends many warm regards and also 'news' (she wants to tell us the 'news' later). I think it might be about her marriage. Friday, Marcella and I will probably drive to Deventer.
On Saturday evening, there is a bi-weekly meeting of Chuliot. We will then celebrate the inauguration of Rivka and Amnon's house. Marcella says it is nice, and they enjoy living there.
Jaap and David have the flu; Jaap has very severe flu with a fever of 39 degrees.
A newsletter recently arrived stating that it will be possible in the future to move from Amsterdam to the provinces to change professions. It is actually unclear how this will be done. In any case, it's not bad news at all (I hope it will make something possible for you soon, really important), don't talk to anyone about it for now.
I have to end this letter now.

Your Ernst

What did the fortune teller predict for you?
She's probably a very rich woman...

New anti-Jewish measures

In the fall of 1941, new anti-Jewish measures rapidly follow one after the other. Already in August, Jews had been forced to transfer their bank balances in excess of one thousand guilders to the Lippmann-Rosenthal Bank, a former Jewish bank taken over by the Germans. From September 1, Jewish children must attend separate schools. From September 15, Jews are no longer allowed to visit parks, zoos, cafes, restaurants, hotels, theaters, cinemas, sports facilities, public libraries and museums. Signs reading 'Forbidden for Jews' are hung at entrances. In October, the Jewish Council is obliged to register all Jews in the Netherlands and create an extensive cartography.

Jews could practice certain professions only with a permit. In addition, it becomes much easier to fire Jews. On November 7, the dreaded ban that Ernst and Ilse feared the most goes into effect: Jews need a permit to travel or move.

Elden, December 1, 1941 (Letter No. 28 from Elden)

My darling Ilse,

Actually, I wanted to write to you from Deventer, but I was very busy all day and simply didn't get around to it (In Deventer, the day also starts very late).
I received your two letters, one of which Werner brought this afternoon.
My dearest, I really don't know what to answer anymore. Due to all your great worries, it seems you really don't know how you should and can move about. When I read the article in the newspaper, I immediately thought of you.
We can only take comfort from the fact that others have experienced a similar fate and endured it as well. What difficulties and obstacles these new laws will cause us is still unclear. Now, we just have to wait and see what it all actually means. Should you be able to come to Sabbath, I will jump with joy. Moreover, we can then talk at length and in peace with each other about all these things. Should you get permission, you could also stay here longer, and if you like, we can also drive to Deventer. Just let me know in time.
Don't worry, and don't be afraid; I won't drive without a 'travel permit.' I had fun again in Deventer, although it was much less fun without you. It just so happens that when you spend time with someone somewhere and then suddenly find yourself in that same place again but then 'alone,' something is missing. In my case, you are the one I was missing.
Marcella and I started the day already at 05.45 in the morning because we couldn't miss the 07.30 bus; it's really no fun sitting on a bus in the cold so early in the morning – we thus had a really long day. The work here in Deventer starts at 09.30 in the morning (remember this! This is also how we will do it later!).

Hans invites us again, and (he says) we should never be ashamed.

We spent Sabbath evening with Amnon and Rivka for the inauguration of their house. None of us felt like going there, but in the end, it was very pleasant, homelike and cozy; everyone was 'disappointed' for the better. Besides Stein and Spits, there were a few other friends with whom we gossiped a lot. We also studied a chapter in the Mishnah, which, as you know, is a custom associated with the inauguration of a house. We had delicious food and drank two glasses of delicious wine.

We also discussed various issues, including future work.

During the day on Saturday, I made my regular visit to the sweet, cozy Oldenboom family (the farmer) and then did some shopping in town.

That night, we slept like 'bohemians.' I slept in a room together with Ruth and Hans.

Sunday afternoon, I was invited to the Oldenbooms' house for lunch. It was so pleasant and homelike, so I stayed for dinner, and we ate delicious bacon sandwiches. I also helped with the milking, which was wonderful.

Since being here in Elden, I have not yet had the opportunity to milk a cow.

In the evening, the Chuliot committee had a meeting. Iss (Isaak) and I were upstairs with Ruth. At midnight, we had doughnut balls (it wasn't even New Year's Eve). I am now very rich again; I received 15 Guilders from Cologne. Besides that, Heinz and I got 30 Guilders from what was left after the sale of the house in Bielefeld. It is not much, and I don't know what the overheads were; there were also duties and liens on these houses. In any case, I consider this money to be money I have earned because I never thought I would ever get that money.

I have already spent some of it, among other things, on a good long pair of warm underpants. (It proves that I am responsible…).

I forgot to write that I also became a teacher. I have to teach at a children's institute in Arnhem every second Saturday. Last week, I was there for the first time, and it was quite nice. Four girls and a boy. Your friend Thea Lindberg is also there (she knows you from Amsterdam). Therefore, you have to tell me in time when you are coming, because, if you come, I have to postpone my lesson in time, which is easy; I just have to announce it, and that's it.

It's great that you can get pipe tobacco for us; I'm very happy about that. However, please remember one thing, and because I know you, I will say this in advance: do not add anything extra, and you can forget about 'sharing' the cost! A 100 grams lasts me a very long time, so I don't need extra. Besides, it's way too expensive.

Marcella and David are getting married soon but don't yet know what they are going to do for the wedding. Do me a favor and don't talk to anyone about it, not even David, who is coming to visit you next week.

We are currently preparing for Hanukkah. Fokki is preparing a 'show,' they say it is going to be very lame. A few guys are playing a piece in Yiddish. I think everyone is going to do something. Werner and Miel are also preparing something. I hope it will all be fun.

We want to do everything in two parts:

Days of Yesteryear!

Days of the Present!

In the first part, the days of yesteryear, we speak and read about the times of the 'Maccabim.' In the second part, we want to draw parallels with our times and thus talk about pioneering. Do you have some or know of any literature on pioneering?

Or equivalent material? Like descriptions... But please, not: *Israel, People and Country, Working Women's Tales,* or *The Song of the Valley* by Sjolem Asch. Try to think of something; sometimes, women also have good ideas....
I must end this letter now. I hope you can come to visit soon; I miss you very much.

Many warm regards and a big pile of kisses,

Your Ernst

Elden, December 7, 1941 (Letter No. 29 from Elden)

My darling Ilse,

I now have my first free hours on Sunday afternoon, and I am using these to write to you.
Thank you for the letter you sent along with Marcella, and of course for the excellent tobacco, which I am so happy about. I immediately dried it and put it in a tightly sealed glass bottle (jam jar). I intend to keep it as my 'emergency' stash. I expect tobacco will soon not be available anymore. One thing you should not have done, which I absolutely 'forbade' you to do, is buy me a double portion, not more than I ordered from you. However, it is sweet of you, and I thank you for it.
It would be great if you could get a job in Arnhem. As soon as I see Amnon again, I will talk to him about it.
Actually, I don't know what it's about at all. In fact, when you spoke to Amnon about it, it seemed like such a pipedream to me that I didn't pay attention at all.
Do you really believe that you can teach? You must know all

the subjects much better than the others. Anyway, we are going to do our best and the sooner, the better.

Great joy this week: on Wednesday, I received a Red Cross letter from my mother. It was dated September 10. She is doing well but was not allowed or able to write more.

There is not much news about here. Everyone is busy with Hanukkah, and it demands a lot of preparations.

We have canceled all classes in the evening because we have so many preparations. Our heads are spinning like crazy from all the songs we are writing. I have also promised friends to help them with their songwriting (friends who have trouble writing songs). You know, the songs that people give each other along with the gifts.

Mill and I wrote a song about Fokki, and we did quite well. He is going to turn green with envy, though, because we did not mince our words, to put it mildly. The music for it is *Eine Seefahrt, die ist lustig* (it was once at the top of the hits list in Germany).

Fokki is going crazy. He is also organizing a show, but his co-workers think it's no good (I heard that two days ago).

Other than that, it's going to be fun at Werner's place. One evening, there will be a singer accompanied by a pianist, and another evening, there will be a lecture on 'Hanukkah topics.' There will also be classical musicians on one of the evenings and on another evening, we will have fun singing, dancing and giving gifts to each other.

I'm sure these evenings will be fun.

What do you think? Would you be able to come? See what you can do. Your suggestion to come to Deventer for Christmas is not such a bad idea. I don't yet know what our working arrangements will be during Christmas, but I think it's probably possible. We will have four workdays in a row off again because we don't work on Christian holidays. We have to respect our Christian neighbors, and that's why we don't work these days.

Werner was in Deventer yesterday. Hans had a bad temper because the dentist hurt him, and thus, he could not eat, which was a big deal for Hans. Marcella is there today; she was actually supposed to come back yesterday. I think she wants to stay in Deventer for a while. She called today to say she will be coming later. They are having a good time this week; Werner has three days off. They are getting married on Wednesday or Thursday, with only a few guests. The ceremony (*chuppah*) will be held in the synagogue.

On Friday, I plan to drive to Deventer, where we are having a Hanukkah gathering.

We drew names to see who would give who a gift. I have to give a gift to one of the boys that you do not know. I'm sure it will be lots of fun.

On Sunday, we will drive back to Elden early, as we also have to celebrate Hanukkah here in Elden.

Now it's your turn to tell me everything.

Many warm regards,

Your Ernst

Elden, December 13, 1941 (Letter No. 30 from Elden)

My darling Ilse,

This letter is definitely not going to be a long one; the package must be taken to the post immediately, and, of course, I want to include more Hanukkah greetings. I hope you like the gift (I chose it myself); you have always been so enthusiastic about it, which is why I thought (and believe) you would be happy with it.

Thank you so much for your letter; it made me happy as always.

You must be wondering why I am writing from Elden and not Deventer today. Thursday, for no reason at all, I suddenly didn't feel like going to Deventer at all. Deventer without you has much less appeal than it used to for me, as I've told you before. The news of the past few days also dampened my desire to go there.

Apart from that, or because of all this, I also feel that I have been traveling quite a bit lately. I hope to be able to go to Deventer again in two weeks.

So, my 'main reason' is that peacefully staying here in Elden for four weeks in a row is not such a disaster.

In the end, I was also very tired from all the preparations for Hanukkah; after all, all the hustle and bustle in Deventer severely affected my nerves. So, to everyone's surprise, I abruptly changed my mind and let my travel permit lapse.

What David told you about the 'cold' here is absolutely not true. During the same Sabbath that he was here, the furnace suddenly went out, and the religionists did not let it burn again because of the Sabbath. It is always pleasantly warm here, and we never suffer from the cold. On the contrary, we have it a lot better than you do. Our living rooms, bathrooms and the kitchen are all heated. It's even cozy in my little room; there's no heating, but the room is surrounded by heated rooms, which, of course, is also nice. I sleep with a woolen blanket and another blanket, and even though I have more blankets, these two are more than enough.

Do not be wary, my little one.

I have nothing more to tell you except that I must hurry to the

post office, which closes in half an hour.
We have paid the main preparations for Hanukkah; we will distribute the gifts tomorrow night. For Merry, I bought a bag with writing paper.

Many loving regards and well wishes,

Your Ernst

Elden, December 18, 1941 (Letter No. 31 from Elden)

My dearest Ilse,

Finally, after all the fuss and fatigue of Hanukkah, I have time to write you a letter to thank you for all the beautiful gifts that made me so happy. Your pictures are so much nicer than the copies I had before. Naturally, I look at them all the time(!). The book is wonderful; you probably want to teach me a correct view of women. Other than all the praise to women, it (thankfully) also contains many truths.
First of all, the most important thing is that I totally agree with you about going to Deventer at Christmas. We don't work during Christmas, so I have vacation days. It only depends on you or your parents whether we will be seeing each other there. Please do your best to make it happen; we haven't seen each other for so long.
The Chanukah celebrations have been successful so far. It started on Sunday evening with lighting candles, etc. After the meal, we distributed the gifts.
All the songs were read out loud, and most of them were written with a lot of humor. Miel and I read everything aloud.

And everyone was happy with their gifts.
The carpentry people put a lot of effort into making all kinds of folders, sewing boxes, etc. I received a notebook and a pack of cigarettes. The atmosphere was great and very positive for everyone.
On Monday evening, it was our pleasure to act as host, which was not particularly successful. We lacked equipment, and there were some other minor glitches.
Tuesday, the 'Nelson Revue' singer was here, accompanied by a pianist. They sang some songs, although he was banging the piano keys too hard. He also made some jokes. Some of the excerpts were quite nice, but overall, the evening was nothing special.
Yesterday, our production shows were presented, all of which were followed by thunderous applause.
Fokki's show was more fun than expected, but still nothing special. There were a few very charming pieces, and we really enjoyed them. Everyone was enthusiastic about the evening.
Yesterday, we played board games and laughed a lot, especially with the game with the flute. You know which game I mean. We laughed like we used to before the war started, so you can understand that, for the time being, we are very content with just our circle.
I got an interesting assignment today. I have to measure our areas and then create a map. This is going to keep me busy until Christmas.
I heard from relatives of mine in Germany that one of my father's cousins is being deported to Riga. I don't know whether they are already there.
I have nothing else to tell you, and it doesn't matter because we will see each other next week.
I am strongly convinced that everything will work out, so your pessimism, at least in this respect, is not justified.

To avoid misunderstandings, I am free until Sunday and even until Monday morning if I want.

Many loving regards,

Your Ernst

Elden, December 31, 1941 (Letter No. 32 from Elden)

My dearest Ilse,

Just as I was starting this letter, I received your letter, and as always, I was overjoyed. Especially since I have been thinking about you incessantly these past few days. It is the same for me as for you; every time we are together, my feelings for you grow increasingly stronger.

I hope we will see each other again soon. I especially hope we can see each other more often. The days and weeks that we don't see each other are becoming more and more difficult and unbearable.

I wish you could come somewhere near here; I can hardly wait anymore. If there's any way I can help with that, I will, of course.

The trip up here on the bus on Sunday was quite tedious, and I nodded off every now and then. I arrived here just in time for dinner but wasn't hungry yet. That night, I could not sleep, nor was I tired at all, and just lay thinking about all kinds of things, which was certainly no reason to feel miserable, on the contrary.

These days, I sleep in the 'Boys' Dormitory.' It's much too cold upstairs now. Fokki continues playing the hero and still sleeps upstairs, but I am not that crazy. True, my room at the farmer was even much colder, but I am not a 'masochist' who 'enjoys' the cold up there.

Yesterday, I talked to Marcella about David's (Marcella's friend) proposal to you. They would love for you to come, but David's parents are a big problem. They understand your reasons for not wanting to work there. Marcella asked if you would like to work at her mother's house in The Hague. I immediately laughed at them. Why...? Increase the distance between us even further?

I don't have much to say about my work. On Monday, I did some repair work on the electricity, and today, I am mapping the fields (which I already told you about).

I will finish the maps before the weather turns bad. I have been working on them since the summer.

We had a very interesting visitor yesterday – I want to tell you about that in person – remind me when we see each other.

I can wear the corduroy suit again; everything that needed to be repaired has been repaired. The suit is really beautiful, and everyone is jealous. Werner and Marcella say that the jacket cost at least 15 guilders. If this is true, I made a good buy after all that 'haggling.'

I will buy you a pair of wool socks; they are very good and cheap here.

My love, the morning is over, and I must end this letter now. I hope to hear from you soon.

Many best wishes and a thousand kisses,

Your Ernst

Could you get me some tobacco? It's almost impossible to get cigarettes of normal quality here.

Elden, January 4, 1942 (Letter No. 33 from Elden)

My dearest Ilse,

Until now, I have been working on our accounts, sacrificing almost all my Sunday free time. I am setting it aside now to write to you. After all, I know how you pine for a letter from me.

It was with great joy that I received your truly precious letter yesterday. If only you knew the emotions that course through me when I open your letters and read the sentences from which your love gently caresses me.

You complain that I give you very little opportunity to enter 'my' emotional world. My dear beloved, I am not the kind of person who likes to talk about their feelings (that is, it is okay to talk about them without liking doing so). You will have to be patient until you know me completely. I have told you so many times how much I love you, so never fear that. Exactly a week ago, at this time, we said goodbye to each other; it seems like half a century ago. I hope we will see each other again as soon as possible.

I spoke with David again yesterday about his proposal, which he keeps repeating. They (i.e., David and Marcella) understand why you refuse the offer and agree with you.

I explained why you can't leave Amsterdam. They didn't quite believe it at first, but then they understood. I also regret that you can't go there. David's parents must be very nice people. Had it been in another city, I would say 'take the offer.'

We have a new game. On Fokki's recommendation, we (the group leaders) bought a 'Monopoly' game. Do you know the game? It's really fun and exciting.

It will probably become a lifelong habit for Fokki; he nags us every night to play the game with him. Who has time to play every night? I don't have that much free time. I desperately need my free time for various things.

In general, Fokki makes me want to puke (sorry). It's getting worse by the day. I already discussed it with Marcella. The worst is when I return from Deventer, where I get to spend time with nice people. When I come back here, I feel the difference even stronger. Last Sunday, I honestly could not exchange even one word with him.

I have read an excellent book by Johan Huizinga, *In the Shadow of Tomorrow*. He calls his book 'A Diagnosis of the Modern Distemper', and in it, he paints a clear picture of the decline of our culture. He talks about the trends in politics, art, social attitudes, etc., during these times. His predictions are unfortunately very bleak, as he believes that the youth of today is the only chance for a revival of culture and civilization. I am very skeptical about it.

I would recommend you read the book (if you can find it); it is well-written and fluent.

I went to the photographer yesterday and can collect the photos on Wednesday. I suspect that they are not good; I kept making stupid faces. We'll see.

In our literature circle, we are currently reading *Götz von Berlichingen* by Goethe in divided roles. It went fine the first time, but there are a few people who cannot read well. It is difficult because we also have Dutch girls in this literature circle; I prefer they don't read.

I am in the process of finding a suitable place to hold a seminar in Hebrew. An Arnhem boy took the burden upon himself and has already found something. I will probably not participate; it is difficult for me to get away from here. I drive there every now and then, either in the afternoon or in the evenings.

The afternoon has come and gone, and I must end this letter

now. I hope to hear from you soon.

Many best wishes and kisses,

Your Ernst

Elden, January 10, 1942 (Letter No. 34 from Elden)

Thank you so much for your precious letter, my dear. I understand how it feels to be alone all the time; I feel the same way. I miss you very much and always. With less and less patience, I await the next time we will meet, but when????? I hope we will see each other again soon.
This week has gone by smoothly and without any 'getting on my nerves.' It is quite cold here, although, so far, it does not affect me. It is quite warm in our dormitory this year. At night, I can lie in bed reading without my hands freezing, but it's terrible in my little room upstairs. I was there a moment ago cleaning up a few things, and now my fingers are so frozen that I can barely write. Fokki, the terror, is still upstairs and will probably stay there.
The farm manager was here on Thursday. We drew up a sowing plan together for next year. This is not a simple task, but still very interesting work. Of course, we have to take essential nutritional needs into account, but if the crop is more or less in order, and if we don't have to hand over more than last year (instructions on this can change), we could manage until the end of the year.
I spent the Sabbath quietly with a book and a stroll (regretfully, without you) in nice weather.
I continue to keep myself busy with culture a lot, and since I

cannot study according to my own expectations, I decided to attend history classes with Werner. He is doing a great job. He is still studying history very diligently and with great pleasure. He is always reading all kinds of commentaries on the Bible and other books. There are only four of us, which makes it easy for us to study well.

I bought a grammar book for my Hebrew lessons and ordered another textbook with all kinds of reading sections. And I am also getting a new Bible. We got a very cheap offer from the Christian Bible Society for a Bible that comes in three or four parts. More people were interested, and so we decided to organize a raffle. For the first time in my life, I won a raffle, and then for a Bible ... something to think about! Well, it really doesn't cost much, but I have to pay for it...

One of Fokki's sisters is here today. She works as a cleaner in Amsterdam, and she is also a singer. We don't know which of these two things she is better at. She is giving a concert this afternoon. Whether she is going to sing the way she looks... well, we'll see...

I did not like the book *Jahrgang* 1902 by Ernst Glaeser. The man delves into one-sided descriptions more than you can imagine. I don't believe this represented the face of the generation.

This week, my brother Heinz sent me two letters from my mother and my brothers through the Red Cross. I replied immediately.

How do you like the photos? Some of them I really quite like, especially the one I'm smiling in and the one with my arm; the others are terrible. As a matter of fact, I was told yesterday that when I read it, I had exactly the same expression as in the awful photo. My answer: so I've been told. Just find one or more photos you like, mark them on the back and send them back with the next letter.

Thanks for the good advice regarding the documents. I have two photos for my birth certificate. Why a person needs a passport photo, I really don't know. It isn't good for anything, and it adds no value.

I think we will get a 'residence permit' like friends who are 'stateless.' I heard something like that here.

At present, there are tensions again between the Orthodox and those of us who are not Orthodox. They are accusing us, and they are partly right, but we are also partly right. Do you understand our point? On Sabbath, we all sit around the heater. A gentleman comes and stocks the heater with wood and coal, and WE pay him. The Orthodox are in no way willing to contribute.

On Monday, we are holding a board meeting to discuss this matter. And, among other things, it will be decided which newcomers will be hired, for whom the probationary period should be extended, and who no longer needs probation. We are expected to voice our opinions about various members or prospective members. Most of the time, we are all in agreement.

I don't have more 'material' to write about. Besides, this letter must be posted right now, or it can't be posted until tomorrow.

Many loving regards and best wishes,

Your Ernst

Zentralstelle für Jüdische Auswanderung

Foreign Jews in the Netherlands, like Ernst and many of his comrades, were subject to separate rules. At this point, they were already being registered for 'voluntary emigration.' On December 5, 1941, it was announced that all non-Dutch Jews must report to the Zentralstelle für jüdische Auswanderung (Central Office for Jewish Emigration) in Amsterdam. Ernst also received a call but wasn't very concerned about it. Before he had to report, he had to fill out a very detailed form consisting of 30 pages, with all personal details – including real estate, movable property, bank accounts, entitlements, apartments, businesses, valuables, and even clothing and trifles such as a lighter, cigarettes, pipe, reading glasses, number of socks and handkerchiefs and toys.

The Zentralstelle organized the persecution of Jews. This organization was anything but focused on the voluntary emigration of Jews, but instead had to provide the *Endlösung der Judenfrage* (Final Solution to the Jewish Question) and organize deportations to camps in Germany and Poland. This service was paid for by the Lippmann, Rosenthal & Co. bank with money stolen from Jews. This office registered all movable property that Jews had to leave behind: if they were deported, they also had to hand over their house keys at that office.

The organization organized the forced removal of Jews from all over the country to Amsterdam in anticipation of their deportation. From October 1941, the Zentralstelle had a card system of all Jews, compiled by the Jewish Council on the basis of data from the population register.

The Zentralstelle also had its own police force consisting of *Ordnungspolizei* (order police), auxiliary police and its own personnel, among other things. They also assisted with the deportations and carried out evacuation operations such as that of the Jewish psychiatric institution Het Apeldoornsche Bosch and, from the end of September, also carried out raids.

Elden, January 18, 1942 (Letter No. 35 from Elden)

My dearest Ilse,

Thank you so much for your letter. I have been waiting for so long and impatiently (even though you didn't write later than usual).
A bit silly of you to cut the film (do you read my letters with so little attention?). Fortunately, it is not that bad. I believe they can copy it, nevertheless.
I really don't know when it will be possible for me to be in Amsterdam again. It is impossible to cross the bridge due to the amount of ice on the river. This is why a ferry trip takes so long, and there is about a one-hour waiting time.
Saturday, I have to go to the children's institution for my bi-weekly reading. I have already postponed it once due to the bad weather.
As I have said many times, don't worry about my clothes. I have four warm sweaters with long sleeves, three with short sleeves, and a sleeveless leather jacket (very warm) to wear under my winter coat. Furthermore, I also have some coats, corduroy pants, a leather hat with earmuffs, many shoes that I wear and more shoes that I don't wear, etc. etc. etc. All your worries are absolutely unnecessary. Nor do I suffer from starvation, as I have assured you several times. Before I eat, I am always starving, but after, the hunger is gone, so there is no question of 'starvation.' I also have enough tobacco for now (one of the few here who smoke). I am also sure that Marcella

can get tobacco for me.

I don't know when I have to go to the Ministry of Emigration in Amsterdam. I think we, 'the pioneers,' will be among the last.

When will I see you here in Deventer? Christmas is four weeks away; for God's sake, do your best. Do everything you can to get out of the house again.

Right now, we are all on the ice. Our lake is frozen, and we can tie the skates behind the house. We do not have enough skates, so we have to share what we have among ourselves, but we are doing quite well. Can you imagine that I, too, (unexpectedly) got a taste for this sport? I like it and succeed better than the others, who fall quite a lot, but we are all learning and are turning into fine skaters. Yesterday, we had a skating competition. Today, it was 'figure skating.' All of us are also our own spectators, of course ... which is also possible to do from the window. Even the working hours change because of this. We have been given 'ice-free' hours on several occasions now. So, you see, we are quite sporty, and the cold really doesn't bother us. Working in the hayloft is nice; it is warm there, and there is almost nothing to do outside. A few times, the boy who was helping me and I froze considerably. We had to knock the dust out of the capuchins, which we did with the help of the wind. We stand on the dike, where the wind is very strong; our ears were literally flying off our heads. Despite the leather jacket and all kinds of covers, we froze and had to quit, and now we are waiting for better weather. For example, I am now doing some surveying again, which is also not very pleasant, as I also have to work outside for that. Every time it gets too cold outside, we are given the opportunity to continue sketching inside so we can defrost and get a little warmer again. The whole house, including the hallways, is pleasant and warm. After much effort, the heater is finally working properly. For-

tunately, the parts that were broken were discovered in time, when it was less cold. We have coal, and if it gets too cold somewhere in the house, we can turn on another stove. On Monday, we processed the legumes by hand. It was an enjoyable job that I had never done before. The pace was good, and it was really fun.
Last night, we had another gramophone record concert – Beethoven's violin concerto played by Fritz Kreisler, accompanied by the orchestra of the State Opera in Berlin.
Fokki's sister sang really beautifully on Sunday evening. She sang *Hallelujah* by Mozart and *Shema Israel* from Mendelssohn's Elijah oratorio, some Schubert songs, some Yiddish songs and some opera. The accompaniment was not very good, but she was, and we enjoyed it.
Yesterday, David was here again. We gossiped a lot; it was quite emotional,etc.
Over and over, it is confirmed to me what a great guy he is.
My dearest, I must finish if I want this letter to reach the mail today. Last Sunday, two boys forgot the letter at the reception desk, and that's why you didn't receive it until Tuesday.
Many sweet regards and kisses,
Your Ernst
PS I couldn't even reread this letter before sending it off; that's how quickly I had to send it to be mailed.
Elden, January 28, 1942 (Letter No. 36 from Elden)
My dearest Ilse,
It probably surprised you to not hear anything from me for so long, but you are going to laugh when I tell you why – I was in bed with the flu. Admittedly, it was not that bad. I went to bed (temperature 39 degrees) on Monday and got up today at 10 o'clock. Now, I am sitting in a warm room, warmly dressed, with nice weather outside, and I can't even go out for a while; it's such a pity. I'm still a little weak in my legs, but it wasn't

annoying today; I had lots of visitors. I can tell you that just about everyone was with me. I also had plenty of books, so it wasn't all that bad. I was in the sick bay and was treated well. The days before that, I was incredibly busy and, therefore, had no time to write.

On Sunday, we had a 'Hebrew day,' which was fun. Many friends translated songs from German into Hebrew, told stories in Hebrew, and played games in Hebrew; it was a wonderful day. During the morning hours, I translated two songs by Wilhelm Busch, and I got a nine for it. That doesn't say much because almost everyone else got an eight or a nine.

Saturday afternoon, about ten of us went to Arnhem to attend a lecture by Prof. Kantorowicz. The topic was 'The Nature of Religion.' It is the same Prof. Kantorowicz who lectured at the seminar last year (you were not there), and it was interesting then as well.

It's cold, but at home it's fine. Outside, the wind blows right through your clothes. Sabbath wasn't very pleasant; the Shabbos goy couldn't get the stove going. I went to Frey and Batya; it was nice and warm there.

Sunday afternoon, a water pipe suddenly burst, and we had flooding on all three floors. Fortunately, nothing was damaged. My bed just survived.

There is great excitement today: Miel Stranders got married. The date that you suggested for us to see each other again is not encouraging. Do you not see any opportunity at all for us to meet up sooner? I totally support you enrolling in a hachshara. I have always said so, but if you think it can't be done before July 1942, why do you want to write to Emmy about it now? On the other hand, it might be good to enroll yourself early.

Another thing: it's better to also add the word Gelderland after O.B (Overbetuwe) on the envelope of the letters you send

to me. I have had a few letters arrive via Germany. Perhaps there is also an Elden in Oberbayern...
As for tobacco, I have enough for now. David managed to buy some.
I have to end this letter now, my dear. I am still a little weak, and thus find it hard to concentrate.
I'll write to you again soon.
Many regards, and if you are still coughing, please get well.

Your Ernst

Elden, February 1, 1942 (Letter No. 37 from Elden)

Ilse, my love,
I was very happy to receive another letter from you. Especially because, after such a long time, it sounds a bit like the 'old' you again. It arrived together with the postcard, now I really feel obliged to answer you as soon as possible. Thanks so much for the nice pictures. I don't understand much about pirouettes, but I can definitely see that the movement is not easy; I certainly won't imitate you. 'Flying' on the ice rink is more than enough for me. My pride is to leg over, and this winter, I also learned to skate backward. I love horseback riding (just like the guy in the show); I've done that a lot (generally with girls... ha, ha). Well, skating is over now, although it's ridiculously cold again today.
I really hope your cough is over by now; I am also still coughing quite a lot and still have a runny nose that I treat with the help of a pack of Tempo tissues.
It is nice that you have some more distractions now and you are not so alone all the time, which is clear from your letter.

It seems you have had fewer dark and heavy thoughts in the last few days; hopefully, you have been able to let go of these thoughts a bit.
I will not come to the meeting next week, despite all your reasons; I have not been invited!
The meeting is meant by Shushu for comrades who work at the farmers and for whom twenty places are needed, while at the same time, they will get more contact, inspiration, etc. That's really true, and I'm not sad if I'm not there. You know how much it interests me. For the two of us, being together is very important. For us, it gets further and further away. Although I can still come to Amsterdam sometimes; you know how much I 'love' that... Can you come to Deventer in the foreseeable future? Or at least to here? I don't believe it's impossible. So far, it has always proven the opposite of your pessimism. Do your best, I finally want to see your sweet face, not only in pictures.
I can only send you the pictures during February. Because of the bad weather, I only brought the roll to Arnhem eight days ago. The connection to Arnhem is very bad. There were only a few days on which we could cross the ice (and it was not exciting at all), but now it can only be done by ferry, which usually takes an hour and a half. If everything goes according to plan, then I plan to be there the following Saturday. I am going to try to find 'Kaloderma cream,' although I think the chances of that succeeding are slim. Maybe I could still find it in Elst; there are still several things available there.
Meanwhile, I received the Bible – I had written to you about that – four volumes in synthetic leather, beautiful printing with interpretations in Latin. It's too bad that I don't know enough Latin to understand it – 1720 edition – but I am very happy with it. I also bought tables of world history, that is, the history of the nations that were or are important.

Everything is arranged by political, economic and cultural events; it's great. I got the latest edition.

Today, Miel and his young bride are coming here. A great excitement. The carpentry made a set of 2 armchairs and a table as a gift from all the friends, which is really very nice. The guys, together with Fokki, did an excellent and tasteful job. Saturday until midnight, I was wallpapering the walls of their room, which is not that easy. It looks good despite some air bubbles; it was a nice job.

Friday, I played electrician. I pulled a new line for the bell, and contrary to all expectations, it worked the first time. My physics classes at school gave me useful lessons for life.

Our literature class is fun for all participants, and many new people are joining. I am not that enthusiastic about it because people read very poorly, but that is what the 'people' want.

Now we are reading King Lear, and maybe we will also start with Richard the Third. I read many plays by Shakespeare at intervals. I knew only a few of them, and now I want to fill this gap in my development. I recently also started a book by an English author (in Dutch translation) on modern physics. Even though I do not understand everything, I do understand quite a lot.

The cold has done a lot of damage to some of the potatoes; they are frozen. These potatoes taste disgusting, and now all we can do is hope the freeze continues because if it thaws, everything will rot within a few days. The rationed portion of bread (grace) has now been reduced. Up to now, we have received an extra portion for 'hard workers,' but it is freezing outside, and we are not working that hard at the moment (which is true). We gave the corn to a miller, and now we get a hearty PORRIDGE MADE from cornflower instead of the bread, which is very filling.

I don't know if I have already written to you that I now go to a children's institute in Arnhem twice a week and speak to children there (only the Zionists among them). I began by talking a lot about Klatzkin's book, which we have been working on nicely and intensively. I know it well, and the children cooperate very wonderfully.

Yesterday, I heard that all the Jews have to leave Arnhem. Don't worry, it certainly won't affect us. Except that, in the fall, we saw that not everything that happens there happens here right away.

Now, my dear, I must quickly finish this letter, the boy who takes the mail is leaving immediately.

Forgive me for not having time to read this letter again carefully before sending it. Please write back soon.

A thousand kisses and good wishes,

Your Ernst

Winter in Elden. Ernst, front row on the left

Elden, February 7, 1942 (Letter No. 38 from Elden)

My sweet little one,

I waited for your letter for a day and a half, but yesterday, as always, I received it with great joy.
I can understand how excited you must have been these past few days and what the mood of you two was (and maybe even is now). I hope everything works out, as it is unthinkable that anything could go wrong. Hans and Ruth are both bright and experienced enough to take care of anything well, which is why I am actually less apprehensive. I am glad you were able to help them so well. It always means a lot to help a friend. As the English say, 'a friend in need is a friend indeed.'
You know, by now, you are really easing into our circle. Six months ago, you were a stranger to everyone. Now, you have already helped solve difficult, important, and most personal problems. I am very happy about that.
When will we see each other again? If you only knew how I miss you. We haven't seen each other for almost two months, which is really too long. I wish you could come from time to time, but for just one day, it makes no sense. The road to Arnhem is long and difficult and, above all, takes a long time, but if there is no other possibility... In fact, I can also come to Amsterdam. It may be the last thing I want, and it makes me feel stuffy, but what won't a man do to spend a little time with his darling? I suppose I'll be in Amsterdam next month for Marcella and David's wedding.
Try as much as you can and use all means of pressure and lies so that we can be together again soon. Here, everyone asks me why, contrary to my habit, I have been traveling so little to Amsterdam lately.
How many times do I have to reassure you about my feeding

here? Your concerns are sweet but completely unnecessary. I really do get enough to eat. Everything is calculated so that we get enough nutrients. The situation here is incomparable to the situation in the city. For example, we have now abolished the extra portion of bread for several weeks. Currently, because of the frost, we are not considered 'hard workers' (because we do not work outside), so instead, we now get an excellent, hearty porridge made from our cornmeal every day, which is a good replacement for bread. This applies to other things as well.

We have reasonable amounts of potatoes and vegetables, and I am really full every day. Our slices of bread are thick and spread (thick) with nice cream butter. No one here has lost weight, even I haven't lost a gram since last summer. I lost weight when I stopped eating fatty peasant food, but that is natural anyway. So: please stop worrying. Marcella explained that David is spreading these rumors around; he (David) has the same fears about her.

I stopped writing for a few hours, walking with Marcella in Arnhem. We wanted to go pick up the photos and take care of a few more things. The photos won't be ready until after the frost. The photographer's water pipe is frozen; he can't work. So you have to wait patiently for it. The walk was stone cold but nice. We were well dressed. It was the last time I walked with Marcella; she leaves us on Sunday.

It is very unfortunate that she is leaving (although I wish her well). She belongs to our circle; she is the only one here with whom I have a little personal contact. I get along very well with Batya and Frey, but that's all. I will now have much less contact with Miel than what I have had so far. His girlfriend is here; I believe she is quite nice, but very cold and I am afraid she is also very annoying.

It doesn't seem to me that she is a force like Marcella; I think the golden days of the warehouse and the rest of the housekeeping services are probably over, which is very unfortunate. But it remains to be seen, who knows....

Sunday, they came here, and there was huge excitement (don't know why). They were met with great joy, and people welcomed them with a hora dance. In the evening, there was a feast, also because of Toe Biesjwat. There were many pastries (do you know poppy seed strudel?) and many more delicious dishes. Two boys wrote and quoted a nice song. Miel spoke about the marriage tradition of Sheva Berachot. Werner told a story about an Arab (Muslim) wedding; it was really fun to hear. It seems that once, while in Palestine, he was invited to such a wedding.

I have taken an important step in my cultural work lately. I have been taking Hebrew classes with Werner in a group at the second to highest level. This way, the study is systematic, which is very important and binding for me. I manage pretty well, and I follow it well, but I have to work hard on the grammar, and I repeat a lot. I study really hard. We have a lot of homework, and I'm constantly fighting for time. When I finish this letter, I have to sit down and learn words. Tomorrow morning, there is a Bible class (the first hour), which I won't participate in for now; it's just too much. First, I have to finish repeating the grammar.

My literature class (which I teach) continues to attract participants, probably people interested in general education. Today, we started with Julius Caesar.

I am now reading an interesting book about the modern scientific world, especially about new theories in physics, written by an Englishman, Sir James Jones, translated into Dutch. It is very difficult. I understand only half of it because I never had enough physics and mathematics, but there are things I still understand reasonably well, including the theory of relativity.

Could you do me a favor? I am sitting here with nothing much in terms of good novels. Could you send me one of your books? Werner will be in Amsterdam next week. As long as the drive to Arnhem remains difficult, he doesn't want Ella to travel here. Could you send me something? Your book *German Antiquity in Renaissance Myth* is still with me. I haven't read it yet; it has 500 pages. My God, this is not a novel after all.

Today, I suddenly remembered our visit to a cabaret performance. Marcella was wearing another pair of thick stockings that didn't fasten properly over her thin stockings, so they kept sliding down. I had to keep walking slightly in front of her (to avoid being seen), and thus, she tried to win the 'fight' with the stockings.

So, I have reached the end of my wisdom again, almost 5 pages ... absolutely enough.

You already know what the weather is like; we are always inside. Maybe we will get a vacation soon. There is no work here. At least people are discussing it.

The mail comes very irregularly and never on time.

Lots of sweet wishes and kisses,

Your Ernst

Elden, February 12, 1942 (Letter No. 39 from Elden)

Ilse, my dearest Ilse,

Yesterday I received your letter, and the day before yesterday I also received a letter.
Since I know what kind of days you are going through now, I am writing back very soon, so you won't have to wait long for a letter from me.
That such a terrible thing would happen to Ruth, I could never have imagined in my worst dreams. I read your letter, and it touched me deeply. I hope she doesn't have to suffer too much. Once again, we see what often happens to women and that these things don't just happen in books.
I really feel what you are going through, my dear, that you are having such an incredibly hard time with your parents, and I am very sad about it. I wish I could help, but I have no idea what to do or what I could do.
We have to wait five more months, until July, then you will be 21 years old. Hopefully, your status will then change. By law, you will be an adult and be able to make your own decisions. In any case, despite all the misunderstanding and lack of love on the part of your parents, you know that there is a person who is completely yours and wants to give you all the love you otherwise don't have.
I don't know what mood you are in at the moment, so I want to throw this letter in the mail without additional stories about the past few days. In general, there isn't much to report either. I need to make it clear to you that my thoughts are always with you.

Many sweet regards and kisses,
Your Ernst

Werner won't be going to Amsterdam this week.

Elden, February 17, 1942 (Letter No. 40 from Elden)

My dearest Ilse,

I received your letter yesterday with great joy. It looks like you have gotten through these difficult days, and I so hope you will soon calm down from this nasty excitement. I hope you never have to go through it again. From what I hear, things on your end are turbulent again; I hope it is not serious.
Let me start with the most important thing first. In eight days, on Saturday, Marcella and David are getting married. It will be a civil wedding ceremony in the town hall. I have been invited, and David plans to invite you, too. Maybe he has visited you already.
They are not throwing a big party but are keeping it very modest. For us, it's an opportunity to see each other. Try to come. I hope your parents will give you permission.
Since I didn't know exactly whether you would want to come to this wedding, I asked David to speak with you personally. In a few weeks, they will hold their chuppah in Amsterdam. I will come for that, of course, and I hope to see you then. Please do not disappoint me – we must get together again. I am already looking forward to it!
These next few days I have to fill out an emigration questionnaire – it is a terrible job – I am already nauseated when I think of the 'clothing list' I have to make… it is a pity you are not here; you could have helped me a great deal with that.
As for the photos, you still have to wait. I was at the photographer's in Arnhem again on Saturday and was told that

I would have to wait another eight days. At least, I hope they will be developed and ready after waiting all this time.

On Saturday, David came to pick up Marcella – the goodbye was not too dramatic. We read her a nice song we wrote for her, and then there was some good food. Afterwards, Marcella, David and I talked (chatted) until 0:30.

Last week I read *Caspar Hauser* by Jakob Wassermann. What a story...I found it very interesting. Now I am reading *De Lente*; I forgot the author's name. I'll have to run upstairs to check. It's a good English novel about the lives of English soldiers who were prisoners of war in Holland during World War I. Other than that, I'm currently reading *Egmond* to exercise my brain a bit...

The last eight days passed by without much news. On Saturday, we enjoyed another evening of music, a Beethoven quartet. We have one of those habits – on a Saturday evening, once every two weeks, we listen to a gramophone concert, and the following week, we sing and learn songs.

My Hebrew is improving well; it's going better than I thought. One learns a lot with Miel. Most importantly, I am again delving into the secrets of grammar that I forgot long ago. I exceed others at translating, which has always been my strong suit in all languages (it is also the easiest). For the translation exercises from Dutch to Hebrew, I have surprisingly gotten a good grade; I am very proud of this. I really enjoy learning Hebrew much more than before.

Every Sunday evening, we have a 'Hebrew club,' and we speak only Hebrew with each other. For every meeting, someone has to prepare something, tell a story, or start a discussion – then a fierce debate ensues, and certainly not without mistakes, but pleasant. It is spirited, and this is how one learns well. We often continue chatting in Hebrew even after the official lesson; that's how much fun we have.

You don't have to send *Ariane*. I read it a long time ago, and I didn't really like it.
The work remains monotonous, sorting potatoes and legumes and cutting trees. Soon, we will not have enough work for everyone. We hoped it would start thawing, but there is no end in sight.
Herewith, I end my ramblings; it is also very late.

A thousand kisses and many sweet thoughts,
Your Ernst

Werner won't be going to Amsterdam this week either.

Elden, February 23, 1942 (Letter No. 41 from Elden)

My dearest Ilse,

I received your unfavorable answer about the weekend with great disappointment and with great sadness. It is actually very childish; we should not have spent the night with Hans and Ruth at all.
That the chuppah of David and Marcella will take place a fortnight after that is not a problem, because the 'party' this week is for the closest friends only. Only family members are invited to the chuppah; none of us will be there.
I will come to Amsterdam for the ceremony — for you, too, of course. Obviously, if your parents are automatically negative about every trip or object to every trip, nothing can be done, but in my opinion, this (the chuppah) could certainly have appeased your parents — which, after all, is the truth.
The train connections are back to normal, and this, too, can-

not be used as an excuse – but if you don't want to or can't, then don't. If only you knew how I look forward to the time when you are no longer at home with your parents; the situation as it is now is unbearable. I am just jealous of all those who can always or almost always be together undisturbed and without any objections. I trust your common sense, and five months is not an eternity – although it often feels that way.

It's great that you are already preparing for your hakhshara and buying everything you need for it. If I can help you, I will do so with pleasure.

Washcloths are definitely still available (we have good relations...) Shampoo? Don't know, I'll have to ask. Kaloderma cream is no longer available anywhere, not even in Elst – where we could still get quite a few things. Anyway, I plan to take an empty tube with me to Deventer. Sweet of you to buy 'Biomalz' for me; I refuse (sorry) to drink it even though you claim it has so much nutritional value (who wears the pants at home???). I don't have weak bones, my knees are strong, and nothing is falling off my body. How many times do I have to make it clear to you and promise you that the food here is absolutely good enough?

As for the list of my clothes, don't worry about that. I only have to write down things I am NOT taking with me and valuables I don't have.

I'm a little hesitant and worry about the property we had in Germany on 01/09/1939, and now I have to add it to the list. Germany has long seized it by now, anyway. I must ask my uncle about it; he helped us with everything related to these matters after my father's death. There is also a good reason why I have been writing less these last few days – which I have already written about to you – and I have even told you that I am not very good at expressing my thoughts on paper. Moreover, I don't like doing so either. I think letters, at least from people you like, are cold, and they cannot replace a personal connection. That's why I almost never feel like writing. I'd rather not write than just write for the sake of writing. Most of the time, I don't even know what to write.

I'm sure you were expecting this letter two days sooner – for various reasons, I didn't get around to writing Saturday or Sunday. I was in Arnhem with my youth group on Saturday, which takes many hours. The journey there and back already takes two hours. On Sunday, I was busy filling out the form. In the afternoon, I took a nice bath. Those who want to take a bath have to heat up the big boiler where the vegetables are cooked and then transfer the boiling water to the bath; this takes quite a long time.

Then I taught some girls chemistry. They made a chemistry assignment today. We need to work hard to cultivate an understanding of natural sciences among the girls – the tests are tough, and it's a lot of work.

Thus, Sunday went by without any free time for myself.

A while back, we received two letters from the Red Cross from my mother and from my brother; they came via London, and it took only three weeks to arrive. My mother is doing well; she has a new job that she is content with. My brother Werner is in a Medium Training Group.

The work here has become even more relaxed; only the loggers are still working. We give the boys time off every afternoon because we have no work for them anyway.

My relatives in Cologne, who I thought had already left there, have been informed that they can stay (in Cologne), but they have to move to a nursing home for the elderly, which is not the worst thing.

The morning hours are over, my dear. I have written you everything I can think of.

I hope to receive a letter from you soon.

When will we finally see each other?

Many sweet regards and a whole pile of kisses,

Your Ernst

Elden, March 3, 1942 (Letter No. 42 from Elden)

My dearest Ilse,

Now, after my trip and after Purim, I finally have time to write to you again. As always, I had lots of fun in Deventer, and I missed you sorely. Without you there, it was only half the fun. The civil ceremonies of Jacob and Ziona's and David and Marcella's weddings were really great fun. The mayor himself conducted the ceremonies and gave a speech in honor of the two couples; he spoke beautifully. Afterward, we enjoyed delicious cake at Jaap's, and from there, we were invited to Amnon and Rivka's for lunch.
I have yet to tell you about the 'witnesses.'
At Jacob's wedding, the witness was Hans Oldenboom.
At David's wedding, the witnesses were Hans and Jaap.
In the afternoon, I briefly visited Oldenboom and Beth Chaluz, where the Hengelo branch had a meeting. There, I met many comrades whom I had not seen for a long time. Among others, Gunter van der Haal, Hannemann and Horst were also there.
Hans Eisner, I assume you know him, is lying in a hospital in Deventer with open pulmonary tuberculosis. Once his health improves a bit, he will have to go to a sanatorium. He is very optimistic and hopes to be completely recovered within a year

and a half. Whether he will ever be completely healthy again is a big question – he will have to change his occupation in any case. I was with him again on Saturday evening until very late, and we had an elaborate dinner at 0:30 (there were three of us).

On Sunday, I was invited by the Oldenbooms for lunch. I was at Amnon's in the evening, where I had supper and also stayed the night because Hans was in Zutphen that same day. You probably know that Ruth is currently in Zutphen to recover a bit. She is much better, and hopefully, she will return home by the end of the week. Hans says the mental reaction to the whole thing came later, and it was very difficult for her. When talking about you, Hans couldn't say enough. He praised you highly. He and Ruth endlessly thanked you for your help. Hans 'congratulated me on my excellent, successful hunt' ... (he meant you, of course), as if he were telling me something I didn't already know... On Monday, I drove back to Elden. In the evening, we read the Megilla (the book of Esther) as we should with Purim. On Tuesday, we shortened the work hours in honor of Purim, and after a good meal, we watched some pretty good movies. Ru Cohen was here with his wife and daughters; he also gave a speech.

I obediently take the 'Biomalz.' Hans also highly recommended it, and it tastes
all right. Washcloths were nowhere to be found – neither here nor in Deventer, but I did find some good woolen socks for you. I must finish now. There is a Hebrew lesson in a little while, after which I can continue writing in the evening – which means this letter can be sent early tomorrow morning.

Anyway, I will go to David's chuppah, which is about a fortnight from now – could you buy a present for me (for the couple)? You know, for about 3 guilders.

Many regards,

Your Ernst

Elden, March 7, 1942 (Letter No. 43 from Elden)

My darling girl, my dearest,

I have just now received your letter, which I have been waiting for for a long time.
Let me begin with the most important thing first – when will we see each other?
Did you perhaps see David's advertisement in the newspaper? The announcement of the chuppah that is going to take place in Rapenburg Street? This way, we can't go on with our little deception. Besides, I wanted to come anyway. David and Marcella have made it more than clear to me that it is their wish that I be present at their chuppah. Now what? What do you think would be better? Shall I come to you all weekend until Monday morning? Or is it better that I come to Amsterdam Sunday morning until Sunday evening after the chuppah? The wedding party is on the weekend after that in Deventer, so you can come too. I assume you will get your parents' permission for that.
The week after that is Passover, then we have four days off. Anyway, I have to spend the first two seider nights here, but what do you think about coming here? Both festive days are going to be very beautiful. I can definitely get away from here for a while during the last two feast days, and then we have four days off together and with each other.
I suppose you're not allowed to travel twice in one month, so we can really only consider one of these two options – I'll

leave the decision of how to arrange all that to you – it just depends on your parents. For me, it would be better to come to Amsterdam only on Sunday, because I would like to hold the kidush here on Friday night. (To my regret, I have to postpone the conversation with the children in Arnhem again, for the second time now, and I will only be able to see these children again in two weeks, which is really not good.) If we can see each other soon after that, it won't be so bad. After all, you know how much I 'like' staying at your place; you yourself wrote about the bad situation at your home.

This week is going to be very long; I will be waiting the entire time for Sunday to arrive so I can finally see you again. My dearest, if you only knew how much I miss you! I keep thinking of you and of our upcoming visit.

Hans and Ruth aren't planning to come to Amsterdam.

Nice that you like the pictures; I am really happy about that. I still owe you one, and of course you will get that one too. It hasn't been developed yet, although I should have gotten it a long time ago. I paid for it two weeks ago.

I think what you are writing about relates to this; this is exactly the case (leaving the house, etc.), but let's talk about it in person on Sunday; that's better than writing about it.

It pains me to read that the atmosphere at your home is so bad now. It is very sad, but I know exactly what you are talking about.

How long this harsh winter will last is anyone's guess. Someone told me he heard from the Meteorological Station De Bilt that the frost is expected to last into early April. Great predictions... This kind of weather is catastrophic for agriculture! Spring cultivation should have already begun. The farmers are complaining a lot; presumably, much of the grain has been destroyed by the prolonged frost and will have to be re-sown. Therefore, this year's harvest will also be much less than usual.

We will have a lot of work and are talking about maybe asking volunteers (from the pioneer group) for help. However, we are also a bit against this proposal. I think that with (a very big) effort, we can handle it ourselves.

Today, we began preparations for Passover. We elected a committee of six members who will plan the second Seder evening. This means that they must change the entire haggadah[16] into a current haggadah. We will keep the first Seder evening traditional – after all, we have to consider our Orthodox friends. It is sure to be a lot of fun, and perhaps Prof. Levkowich will also come.

Friday night at dinner, I read The Story of Little Muck by Hauff. For me, it was important to show my comrades how beautiful legends can be. It was a very successful evening.

You may have heard that they are now dismantling the Beverwijk kibbutz, which is really bad news. Until now, I had always hoped they would make an exception as far as learning farms are concerned; we are still here.

Hopefully, Werner will bring a book from you tomorrow. I'm looking forward to reading some literature.

Although you can always find something to do here, I always like to fill my free time with good literature. Yesterday, I borrowed the book Florian Geyer, written by Hauptmann, from the library, and another book, Reis naar India, written by Bousels. This book is about the worldview of various philosophers. In addition, I am reading a novel by author Kellerman.

I must finish this letter now. Miel is waiting for me; we must begin Passover preparations.

I hope to receive a letter from you before next Sunday describing how you plan to 'construct' our weekend...

---

16 The Haggadah is the story of the exodus from Egypt, which religious Jews read on Seder evening, at the beginning of the Feast of Passover.

Goodbye my dearest
Many loving regards,

Your Ernst

*Notification of the marriage of David and Marcella,
Het Joodsche Weekblad, March 6, 1942*

Elden, March 19, 1942 (Letter No. 44 from Elden)

My dearest Ilse,

The house is already asleep. Admittedly, it is already very late, but on Monday morning at 9:20, you will be waiting for my letter, and I don't want you to run to the door in vain.
Needless to say, we arrived here healthy and cheerful. We had good standing places with a beautiful view from the train.
The two days with you were fantastic. I'm glad I came, although I didn't feel like it at first because of Amsterdam, etc. – it has only one drawback – now I long for you even more than before and can hardly wait to be with you again. I hope our planned meeting will go ahead.
Now, please pay attention: Yesterday, two officials from the Jewish Council checked our immigration papers. They said that I would probably have to go to Amsterdam to meet with the Jewish Council and the Gestapo within a week or two weeks from now. It takes two days, so how about we meet in eight days on Friday in Deventer, or will we still see each other the last two days of Passover? The Sunday and the Monday after that is Easter. Whether we will work on that Monday then is still unclear. We need permission from the mayor of Elden to work on a public holiday. But because of the terrible weather that we've had here in recent weeks, we hope to obtain this work permit for 'vital jobs in agriculture.'
In any case, it means we have at least three days to ourselves, which is also worth a lot, but if we meet soon in Amsterdam, then yes, these two things are incomparable. I'll leave the decision to you – you arrange it as you like, as it suits you best. Hans called today and very cordially invited us to come to Deventer for a few days. In any case, they will stay in Deventer for the next few weeks. My questionnaire (immigration form)

was fine; I only need clarification from Germany about my 'property' on 01/09/1939. I wrote to my uncle about this. On the question about what I am taking with me, I listed only hand luggage; I can't take anything else, anyway.

Spring at last. We have switched off our central heating; it is warm enough at home without it. On Monday, I 'moved' back into my little room, which is much cozier than the 'boys' dormitory.' Working outside is really enjoyable; people liven up and really start living again. I'm sure you are also feeling better; are you working already????

Other than that, I have nothing to tell you except that I hung eight dead mice in the girls' room today, and the girls threw a fit ... the screams could be heard throughout the neighborhood...

The book Cimarron is very good; I have already read more than half.

Your sweets were very tasty. I am very stingy and frugal with them, which is why I still have some left over. We also got cigarettes this week.

Many sweet wishes and kisses (finally, we know again what a KISS is)

Your Ernst

Elden, March 23, 1942 (Letter No. 45 from Elden)

My dearest Ilse,

To avoid mistakes, I want to write quickly about our meeting – at Hans and Ruth's. I was wrong when I thought Easter would be after Passover. In the meantime, I found out that Easter comes after the first two feast days of Passover.
So, if you are not coming for the weekend, it would be best to meet from Saturday, April 4, until the second day of Easter. Hans will be there with you these next few days, so it would be best to arrange the date with him. Should that also be impossible, we are left with the date eight days after Easter, but rather not the last feast days of Passover.
I received both the express letter and the second letter. It is best if we speak about it in person.
For me, our conversation had a different effect – well, until Friday night. I am already looking forward to it.

Warm regards,

Your Ernst

Elden, March 24, 1942 (Letter No. 46 From Elden)

My dearest Ilse,

Just a quick note: Today, I received word that I have to report to the Jewish Council on Monday, March 30, at 2 p.m. and on Tuesday, I have to meet with the Germans.
Could I possibly stay with you from Monday morning until Tuesday afternoon?

Is it then possible for us to travel back to Deventer together? Would something like that be possible? Think about it for a bit...
Other than that, there is no news. There is plenty of work now; spring is beautiful.

Many fond regards.

Your Ernst

PS
What I wrote in yesterday's letter remains unchanged, and if you want, we can also go to Deventer on another day.

Elden, April 9, 1942 (Letter No. 47 from Elden)

My darling girl,

I just received your letter, and I want to reply to it at once because I know you are probably already looking forward to receiving a letter from me.
My dear, you write about the situation at home with your parents and how desperate you are about it.
I am wracking my brain about it, but I don't know how to help you. I understand what you are talking about and all your difficulties. All I can tell you is that we have to endure it for a few more months. And above all, trusting that we love each other and belong together should help us overcome this situation. We see each other so little, so for God's sake, let's try and get through this time together. I have been fantasizing for some time about when we will be together for always, or at least a

lot more.

After you left, everything here felt empty. My room feels lonely and alone. I stare out into space, see you with needle and thread in your hands, dream of our future, and imagine us being wonderfully together alone. For now, we must be content with what we have, with the few hours we get from time to time, which have become precious memories of many shared experiences that belong only to us.

My dear, we have to bite the bullet; we have to go through these difficult times together.

As for personal concerns, we have some control over that. At least we have the ability to defend ourselves, to make sure we do not drown in our worries.

The external worries are increasing, and we have to leave the uncertainty about our health and our lives in the hands of fate. My little one – chin up; the past few days have been wonderful.

Professor Levkowich was very good. Werner is more or less healthy. He is walking around again but complaining of frontal headaches. He will be seeing an ENT doctor tomorrow.

Rolf Schloss was here several times and told us a lot about Gouda[17] – more bad than good things. I decided to go there myself to see it with my own eyes.

The festive days are over. I am sitting with Werner and the

---

17 The Catharinahoeve in Gouda was a youth farm, initially for Dutch youth, where they prepared for their future in Palestine. In April 1943, deportation loomed, and the residents went into hiding. Ultimately, of the 27 members, 18 survived the war.

whole time, people are clattering past with the chametz[18] tableware they are taking back downstairs again.

The chocolate is excellent; I am truly enjoying it. I doubt it will last four weeks here; it is far too good, and I have already devoured most of it.

Werner asked you to get the books he requested from the University Library for him when you get there. You can get the first book at the National Library in The Hague.

My dearest Ilse,

A thousand loving thoughts and kisses,

Your Ernst

Elden, April 15, 1942 (Letter No. 48 from Elden)

Although I am dead tired, I want to write a few words so that you won't have to wait too long for mail from me. I received your two letters; thank you very much.

I was very happy that you spent beautiful days with Hans – a positive change in your monotonous life.

I hope the second thing you wrote succeeds, but do me a favor, be careful with your letters! Don't write everything; it's really very unsafe.

Too bad you didn't come to Arnhem on Sunday. At least we could have seen each other for a while. When will we see each

---

18 Passover has ended. Chametz are foods with leaven, which is forbidden on that Jewish feast day. For eight days and eight hours, Jews are not allowed to eat or possess chametz. They also use special tableware that has never been in contact with leaven.

other again? Another century has passed since we saw each other. Our days are again dominated by work. My day starts at 7 a.m. until 6:30 p.m. with a one-hour break in the afternoon. I am outside all day; the weather is lovely, and we all enjoy it immensely. We are all very tanned after these few days outside.

Yesterday, I opened 'shower season,' and now I shower every night if possible. It is wonderful. A beautiful time is now beginning here. We can feel that it is spring – the fruit bushes are already starting to bloom.

Yesterday, Werner told me about the first blossoms on the pear tree, and he immediately made fun of 'the blooming Birnbaum.'[19]

I'm very much looking forward to Hans and Ruth coming this weekend; it is definitely going to be fun.

I have nothing more to write; I am about to go to bed (9 p.m.). The first few days of being outside and working make you tired as a dog; you really need to get used to it.

A thousand loving regards and kisses,

Your Ernst

---

19   Birnbaum, Ilse's last name, means pear tree.

Elden, April 21, 1942 (Letter No. 49 from Elden)

My dearest Ilse,

Now, after a long, difficult and strenuous day, I finally find time to write a few words to you.
The reason I did not write earlier was because I was kind of hoping to see you here on Sunday; I was waiting for you.
Sunday and yesterday we had visitors from comrades of Chuliot. Hans, Jaap and Ruth, Amnon and Iss were also here on Sunday, so I was obviously constantly busy.
Ruth and I went to the train station on Sunday afternoon to (possibly) meet you. There was only one train, and we thought you might be on that train, but you didn't come.
It was fun with Hans and Ruth, but I missed you. I hardly spoke with Hans; he was constantly engaged in conversations. I spent the whole time with Ruth, and all in all, they were here for about five hours.
I was very pleased with the 'little things,' and although they are handmade (which is not usually the case), they are very useful. I like using them; they come in handy.
I was very happy with your letter; I am always happy when you are in a happy and confident mood – which unfortunately is rarely the case. What will happen to us if we don't learn to enjoy life as much as possible, especially in times like these?
Spring is great; we are all already tanned – and enjoying the weather. On Sabbath, I sat outside in the sun all afternoon reading. Work after all these long winter months is doubly enjoyable; we manage to get a lot of work done. And everyone works with great satisfaction.
We completed the work plan for the month of April in less than a week. It was really amazing how much we got done; we amazed ourselves.

I don't know if you've heard, but chances are Ruth might have a job for you. The odds are in your favor! It will be with the Levison family in Zutphen. The Steins (Hans and Ruth) always talk about this family. I believe it is not a bad idea, although I hardly know this family. Ruth and Hans say they are very nice people; they have two small children and a third one on the way. They are very wealthy people.

For the two of us, this will be very beneficial: vacation days, easy train connection, bus, bicycle, etc. Well, nothing is certain for now, but July, and thus your birthday, is already in sight! Would it be possible for us to see each other before Pentecost? Since knowing you, I don't find the expression 'thirsty for someone' at all funny anymore.

Much love, my little one, many sweet thoughts and many kisses,

Your Ernst

Eshu and Dudi feeding the baby goats

Elden, April 28, 1942 (Letter No. 50 from Elden)

My dearest Ilse,

Although I do not have much news to tell you, I believe it is most important for you to hear from me anyway.
I realize more and more and also clearly see again and again that your mood probably depends primarily on the weather. The latest letters sound completely different from the previous ones.
I hope that the job with the Levison family is still happening – that would be great, but if it doesn't work out, we will certainly find something else. That's not the main thing – the main thing is to get away from there first.
If what your mother said to Mrs. Pintus is true, it would be a very positive thing – but who knows... perhaps your mother just wanted to 'brag'.
Around here, everything is happy and cheerful! Our goats are about to give birth! I spent the night from Friday to Saturday half awake, half asleep with my friend who works in the goat barn. At 8:30 in the morning, two goats were born; a boy and a girl. What a huge joy that was for everyone; we were all so excited about it. Today, it was another goats' turn – the previous night, we were half asleep in Lini's room (office) and spent the whole day sitting in the pen, and even though it seemed like it was going to happen, several times, it didn't... Presumably, I won't be making my bed again tomorrow morning... Now, everyone wants to witness the birth, and when it happens at night, they ask to be woken. I, for one, am already a little tired of it all.
On Sunday, I was near Wageningen with my new teacher, who is a very nice man and is very knowledgeable; he is an expert in soil theory and fertilization – two subjects I desperately need,

which I never learned and don't know. They live very nicely in a lovely little villa at the foot of a little hill on the edge of a forest. From now on, I am going to bike there every week on Tuesdays, which means I have to stop my work here an hour early.

At the moment, there is still more than enough work for all of us, but because of the drought, we can't do much, and most things have been done.

Today was quite a rotten day, with a cold wind. It was particularly terrible in the morning.

I have to finish this letter now – I am tired and still have to go to the goat pen.

Many loving regards and kisses,

Your Ernst

Elden, May 6, 1942 (Letter No. 51 from Elden)

My dearest Ilse,

I am writing to you mainly so that you get mail from me and not because I have much to tell you – in fact, I have nothing to tell you at all.

I still 'relive' that brief hour we were together and could spend with each other on Sabbath. Even though it was almost nothing, at least we could talk to each other. Now, the weeks until Shavuot will pass twice as fast.

If all goes well, the Chuliot meeting will continue. It will then be the second day of Pentecost. If you want to, you can come, but I don't believe you will enjoy it. We will discuss it.

Again, thank you very much for the book; I don't think I've thanked you enough for it. In any case, you are entitled to many more kisses (always, of course). I have already read a large chunk, and as I progress, I like the book more and more. It's an excellent book.

It is getting more beautiful here by the day; trees are in full bloom, which is absolutely beautiful. I wish you could see it sometime!

On Sunday, the Board had a meeting. They praised us a lot for the work we have done so far and also praised our management. They also expressed their satisfaction in another way, by increasing our salary. I now earn 7.50 guilders, which is really quite good.

The goats are cute, and they are all doing well – because of this beautiful weather, they spend all day outside and incessantly jump through the field with great joy.

What was it like when you got home on Saturday? Did your parents suspect anything, or did your 'bluffing talent' – which is admirable – work as always? I am expecting a letter from you soon; I am eagerly waiting for one. 14 weeks from tomorrow, you will turn 21.

Many fond regards and kisses,

Your Ernst

There are some surplus ration points for meat now that are being exchanged for a lot of other items. Maybe you guys are interested and have a surplus of certain ration points?

The Star of David

As of January, Jews already had a 'J' stamped onto their personal identification cards. On May 3, it became mandatory to also wear a visible identifying mark: the six-pointed yellow Star of David with the word 'Jew' in the middle. This made people recognizable as Jews anywhere and anytime. This way, the Germans wanted to further separate Jews from the non-Jewish Dutch. Not wearing the star visibly resulted in severe punishment. The Jewish Council was ordered to distribute the stars to the Jewish Dutch within three days. Jews had to purchase four stars per person at four cents each. All Jews over the age of six must wear it.

Ilse had 'mixed' status and was not required to wear the star. Worried that this would make it even harder for them to interact in public, Ernst asked Ilse to wear the star anyway.

In July, Ilse went to work for the Levison family in Zutphen, which was near Ernst, meaning there were more opportunities for them to see each other.

Elden, May 14, 1942 (Letter No. 52 from Elden)

My sweet angel,

After a long meeting regarding the issue of a professional hakhshara, I finally have time to write to you again – I was very happy with the two letters I received from you, especially since the journey to your hakhshara is now in sight. How glad we will be if everything goes according to plan! In any case, we can then go to Zutphen next week.
Tell me, what is the situation? Do you already have permission from your parents regarding Shavuot? Shavuot is in eight days, and I hope these eight days fly by... I can hardly wait... Are you looking forward to it too? Do you think you can come for all four days? The Chuliot meeting is most likely going to take place in Deventer rather than here in Elden, which has one advantage and one disadvantage. The meeting is going to last two days, and you can definitely attend. By now, you are no longer a stranger here, and in six months, you will be accepted anyway.
So, what are you going to do with the stars? Will you take them with you? I believe it has advantages even if you don't wear them permanently... travel permit, etc.
Jaap and David were here for a few hours on Sunday to talk about the meeting, and so we had our own 'little meeting.' The weather is beautiful; I sit in the garden all afternoon, doing my homework.
The agriculture classes are going fine. I am driving there again this afternoon in about an hour.
The flowering of the fruit trees is almost over; it was beautiful. Several varieties did not live up to our expectations.
I took some sweet pictures of the goats; I'll send you a few copies.

As for the meat, don't worry about it. For now, we have no problems; we will get it. But what's so bad about not having meat? I can live without meat if I have to. You probably think like your mother when it comes to food.
Did you also have one of those beautiful thunderstorms with lots of lightning at your place on Monday? I was standing at the window upstairs and had a beautiful show; it was amazing. I tried to take pictures of it, but I don't know if I succeeded.
Well, if I forgot anything, I will tell you in person next week.

Many loving regards,

Your Ernst

Elden, May 18, 1942 (Letter No. 53 from Elden)

My love,

Before we see each other again, I just want to quickly send you my loving regards. I am already excited and can hardly wait for the next three days to pass. Hans was here today, and he told me that you won't arrive until late in the evening. I am arriving late as well, as we will be working until 6 p.m. I don't know yet whether I will come by bus, train or bicycle.
I have nothing else to write about. I will tell you more when I see you.
I could have just as easily sent you a postcard, but that's just not possible because of your parents.

See you soon, my love.

A thousand loving thoughts, and the rest will keep for later.

Your Ernst

Elden, May 27, 1942 (Letter No. 54 from Elden)

My dear angel,

I have just received your letter, and it made me so happy. I think you got my letter at the same time.
Last night, Troostwijk came to visit me (the boy with the nasal voice), so I did not get around to writing.
When I think of our four days together, my feelings, the emotions I am experiencing now, cannot be described with words. On the one hand, I am insanely happy: we were together, we shared so many good things together, and we love each other so much. On the other hand, I am sad: time flew by so quickly, and now I will have to be without you for so long again. I think a lot about all these things, but you know how hard it is for me to put it in writing. In any case, my thoughts are full of love for you, my dear.
After we said goodbye to each other, although God alone knows how hard it was for me, the ride home wasn't too bad in the end. I cycled back fast, in about two and a half hours, with heavy headwinds and without any stops; not bad at all. I think I never really appreciated my own strength and perseverance. The cycling was not tedious at all because I finally knew what to think about...and I did! It was raining, but not much, but when I got to the dike close to home, it started pouring. My raincoat, although not impregnated, was still pretty water-repelling.
By 11:30 in the evening, I was still cheerful and amazingly

still not tired.
Everything here was running its course, and everyone wanted to know everything; all the news, Jaap's jokes (the ones I could still remember), etc.
Sad news: Our non-Jewish neighbor hanged himself on the second day of Pentecost; he had stomach cancer. So you see, not only Jews have problems; other people have big problems, too.
I unpacked the gifts from my suitcase with joy, especially the beautiful photograph that I immediately hung on the wall during my lunch break. It looks beautiful, especially when the sun shines into my room (which doesn't often happen, and when it does, it only lasts for a brief moment). I always look at it as if I have another window in my room. I now have three reproductions of Van Gogh hanging next to each other on the wall in my room.
I have to go downstairs, more for the sake of discretion (don't laugh!) than necessity. Strangely enough, I am still not tired.

Many loving wishes,

Your Ernst
Who loves you very much!

Elden, May 31, 1942 (Letter No. 55 from Elden)

My dearest Ilse,

Even though we have congratulated each other on our first anniversary, I would like to put something on paper in honor of this important occasion.
During this first year, we had many difficulties and obstacles

to overcome; we saw each other very little, and we had many worries. And yet I feel that, despite all this, our love constantly grew and strengthened, and we have forged an inseparable bond. If we recall all the days we spent together and had an unforgettable experience because of it, this year of our lives has been the most beautiful.
And if we continue loving each other as we have until now, no force will be able to match us. We will weather everything together, and should they rip us apart, we will reunite. I believe this with all my heart, so do not be afraid of the future. Together, we will overcome everything. Today, I will be with you even more in my thoughts (if this is at all possible), and we will be together, if not in person, at least in our souls.
Heinz was here yesterday. I asked him for these two pictures. I am sure you will like them.

Many loving regards straight from my heart,

Your Ernst

Elden, June 3, 1942 (Letter No. 56 from Elden)

My dearest Ilse,

I was overjoyed to receive your two letters; thank you so much. The postcard also arrived yesterday; you can't imagine how happy it made me.
It seems I have proved my optimism 'right' again. You really must hurry now. The sooner you come, the better. You leave Amsterdam on Friday, stay here for the weekend, and drive to Zutphen on Sunday. Agreed?

We no longer get travel permits, and that's very bad. We must be glad this doesn't apply to you as it does to others.
We don't know what will happen to Werner and Ella now. Anyway, their chances look bleak. On Sunday, Ella left Elden with a heavy heart. My professional agriculture classes will have to stop if we can't solve the problem with the travel permit.
Fortunately, Heinz was here on Friday and Saturday, which was his last chance. It was great spending time together. Unfortunately, it was too short. Actually, it was only for one day because he had to be back in Loosdrecht by Saturday evening. The Arnhem floating bridge caused him to miss the last train, and so I gave him my bike so he could cycle to Utrecht.
The work here is really wonderful at the moment – we are tanning browner and browner, and we work up a good sweat. At lunchtime, we stay in the field. Merry brings us food by bicycle. We built a trailer, which is fantastic because it frees us from walking half an hour back and forth, which wastes time and strength. In short, it is really great here now. Please come soon. I hope that by the time you come, the weather will be the same as it is now.
Did I write that on June 20, we will celebrate the first anniversary of the hachshara of Elden? We are very busy with the preparations. I am writing the history of the year in rhymes, including cartoons and slides. I hope it will be fun. My friend, the 'poet,' is sitting behind me and insists that I stop writing to you. Besides, the mail has to be sent. So, in all haste – THE END.

Many sweet thoughts,
Your Ernst

Elden, June 10, 1942 (Letter No. 57 from Elden)

My dearest Ilse,

I am collapsing with fatigue, yet I don't want you to wait too long to receive a letter from me.
I got up at 03:45 this morning, and together with Frey, we spent the whole day harvesting hay with a scythe. It was very hard. My bones are aching, but it was very satisfying.
Thank you very much for your letter. I have already heard the news about Horst! You have been a bit careless again in your letter; you MUST be careful about what you write.
How are the preparations coming along? When can I finally expect you here? I'm already so excited; please make haste.
I don't have much to tell you; life goes on as usual.
I'm still working on our 'Elden, annual anniversary.' I'm sure it will be a hit.
My love, don't be angry that I don't write a longer letter. I really can't, and I'll probably be just as tired tomorrow, and even after that, you'll have to wait a while. I hope you write to me soon.

Many loving regards and kisses,

Your Ernst

The anniversary

On June 22, 1942, the first annual anniversary of the hakhshara home in Elden is celebrated with events such as sports that could be watched from a grandstand built in the former carriage house. Canvasses with pictures of the past year are hanging on the walls in the barn. Since it is not possible to project an actual movie, they reenact one. Ernst, Fokki Fuchs, Shlomo Samson and Hans Seemann put together the program. It begins with advertisements from Arnhem businesses and then a preview of the 'movie,' *The Women's Regiment*, to be filmed the following week. The leading role, Countess Caroline, is very reminiscent of the director of Huize Voorburg, Lini de Bruin. After the weekly review, mostly about that afternoon's sports games, the 'main movie' is 'screened,' comprising reenactments of moments of life at Huize Voorburg over the past year. Then, the girls perform a piece portraying what it would be like in the hakhshara home if there were no girls. A couple of boys reenact a board meeting. They play Lini de Bruin and the directors of the Deventer Association, Ru Cohen and Mau Reichenberger. The evening ends around 11:30 p.m. with the traditional folk dance, the hora.

Elden, June 17, 1942 (Letter No. 58 from Elden)

My love,
Thank you for your letter. Let me start with the most important thing first! Will you come? When are you coming?
It is obvious to me and of the utmost importance that you come here a few days before you have to leave for Zutphen. After all, we haven't seen each other in four weeks, and you know that it will be difficult to ask for vacation days in the first few weeks after Jetty Levison has given birth. You should be able to leave Amsterdam a few days early; it must be possible!
It will be idiotic if, now that you will no longer live at home, we will meet as little as before. We don't have to ration our love of our own free will. If you don't want to wait until the weekend, during the week could also turn out to be convenient. Every week, six people are on vacation at the same time; we can do what we want because it is forbidden to work!
I can take my vacation the following week from Monday to Sunday, and should the week after that suit you better, that's fine by me too. You can come whenever you want as I have unlimited time for you! Just write to me as soon as possible about your plans and options so I can tell the people here when I want to take my vacation. Agreed? Don't cause a fuss, mind you!
For the last few days, I have been busy preparing for the anniversary celebration here in Elden non-stop.
Everyone is training enthusiastically. We want to organize a 100-800 meter run (shorter for women), high jump, shot put, weightlifting, tug-of-war, horse-mounted battles, a relay, etc. etc. We also planned evening shows.
 A couple of guys, along with Fokki and I, are doing a kind of cinema 'movie reenactment,' consisting of 'commercials,' the

'news,' coming soon,' followed by the 'main movie.' We have more than a hundred pictures and cartoons that we have drawn on canvas using a diascope. The drawings were made on transparent parchment and attached to a thin cardboard frame exactly the size of the slides. Thus, we have slides in color. I composed the main film using all kinds of scenes from the past year and rhymes. Fokki designed, created and then added cheerful drawings. It is a complicated process. The script comprises 6 full pages written on the typewriter.

The images must be drawn first, then we must go over the drawing with a color pen suitable for a screen. In some instances, we only need to paint the outlines, but sometimes, we need to paint whole patches. We then have to cut small frames out of cardboard and glue the paintings on them.

We have already completed most of the work, and we are enjoying it immensely. Every night, we work until the early morning hours.

I haven't read a book since Saturday evening, and that's saying a lot!!! I don't even read before falling asleep; imagine that...

The weather is bad, really rotten. I hope it improves in time for vacations. Sometimes, it is so cold that we have to wear coats, which is very unfortunate.

My dear, my afternoon break is over, and this letter must be mailed to you immediately so that you can reply immediately.

A thousand sweet thoughts and kisses,

Your Ernst

Elden, June 26, 1942 (Letter No. 59 from Elden)

Ilse, my dearest,

The weather is too nice to sit inside writing, but this letter is way overdue for you.
This week, I will finally have my vacation. I couldn't wait any longer for you to come. Besides, I don't expect you to be able to come here during the week.
In the end, it worked out well. We are lazying outside and on Mondays, even with music by Bach and Mozart.
Yesterday, we went on a bicycle trip through the Betuwe and also cycled to Nijmegen. It was wonderful. We got home all brown-tanned and totally exhausted. For the first time in my life, I experienced a flat tire – and a proper one – six holes – one after the other in the same inner tube.
Such a shame you couldn't be here. It would have been really good for you to be out in the sun all day.
The first annual anniversary was a hit; everyone was happy. In the afternoon, we played several games, followed by lemonade, sandwiches and cakes; what a treat that was. The buffet was in the hayloft. The whole hayloft was decorated with photos, paintings and songs from the past year. The performances were in the evening.
We titled our performance 'Cinema on the Spot.' It was a great success, and many people shook our hands and thanked us. We really created a lot of fun, even if I say so myself.
The other performances were also very good. The girls pranked the boys: 'Elden without women.' Before I even realized it, I was on the stage; they (the women) dragged us onto the stage by our clothes.
A few boys performed a hilarious board meeting, including a Lini de Bruin character wearing her clothes and even her typ-

ical hairstyle, a knot at the back, which, of course, could not be left out. We had a great time and laughed ourselves to death all evening. We ended the evening with a long hora dance.

We have to surrender our bikes in an hour, which is very depressing. We are still clinging on to a tiny bit of hope. Until a final decision has been made, I remain optimistic, be it with my last strength.

I have nothing more to write, and the orchard is calling me.

Many regards and loving thoughts,

Your Ernst

Recently, I received letters from my mother, dating from March and April.

She is doing well and has a job with many responsibilities, which gives her great satisfaction. She is (noticeably) very worried about us.

The Extermination of the Jews gets underway

In late June 1942, the realization dawns on the always optimistic Ernst that the German occupier's plans for the Jews do not bode well. No one at the time knew of the plan that was concocted in a villa on Lake Wannsee near Berlin in January to exterminate all the Jews of Europe, but their lives were made unimaginably difficult that year.

After the numerous anti-Jewish measures that were implemented in the first two years of the war by which Jews were totally removed from society, the actual physical removal of Jews from public life was now underway. Jews were no longer allowed to study, were fired from every job, were robbed of their bank balances and valuables, were no longer allowed to travel or move, and had to wear a Jewish star. They even had to surrender their bicycles, as Ernst wrote. Signs saying 'forbidden for Jews' or 'Jews not welcome' appeared everywhere.

On June 26, 1942, it was announced that Jews were going to be deported to Germany for 'work creation' or 'employment.' On July 14, 1942, the first train carrying 800 Jews departed from Amsterdam to the Westerbork camp. Many were taken straight to the concentration and extermination camps in the east. A total of 107,000 Jews were deported from the Netherlands, of whom 102,000 did not survive.

Elden, July 1, 1942 (Letter No. 60 from Elden)

My dearest Ilse,

It is late, and I have to leave my room soon. I have offered my room to one of the girls for her week off, but I wanted to write a few quick words to you first. I hope this letter reaches you in Zutphen. I also hope you recover from your illness soon. I received both letters; the second one shocked me terribly[20]. It is probably not as bad as you heard, but it is bad enough. Werner received a letter from Ella; she knows the precise details. You are right, we must remain courageous, and I still hope that everything will work out. It is a race against time or with time... In any case, I am already over my initial shock. I think our senses are becoming less and less sensitive. Besides, the news is not that surprising ... now we'll just have to wait and see how things play out. What I fear most is that they will separate us for a long time. The new measures bring us new difficulties, but either way, I think we can keep doing what we are doing for now. Please allow me to congratulate you on starting your hachshara.[21] My love, I wish you lots of success. My thoughts regarding all this and my opinion about it and that I waited for this moment in anticipation is old news to you, so I don't have to explain it to you again. As a result of this change, we are now literally

---

20 Ernst may be referring to news about Camp Westerbork. On the day this letter was written, the camp was handed over to the Nazis. The camp now became a transit camp to the camps in the east. It is possible that news of the upcoming deportations was already known during these days.

21 Ilse begins doing her hachshara as domestic help with the Levison family in Zutphen.

approaching each other with a big step in the right direction, and our lifestyles are beginning to become more and more similar. You will have to overcome several difficulties, but I am sure you will prove yourself. I'm not one bit worried about it because I know what you are capable of; you are a champion!!! I want to tell you more, lots more even, but since I hope and am absolutely sure to see you here on Sunday, I prefer to tell you everything in person. Try to come, even if only for a short time.

As for how to get here...I honestly have no clue, but I'm sure you will easily manage to find a way.

Your Ernst

Elden, July 9, 1942 (Letter No. 61 from Elden)

My dearest Ilse,

I have received your express letter. I would like to repeat what I told you on the phone yesterday!
Do NOT do anything without talking to me about it in advance, especially not bring anything here – I cannot use anything, neither a bicycle nor other things – you need all these things much more than I do.
For now, there is no reason to panic. The biggest mistake is to lose your cool and to do something for the sake of 'doing something.' I don't want you to go crazy or drive me and others crazy. Sometimes, it is best to just do nothing for a while. You would be amazed at how calm all of us are here.
I hope you will come here on Saturday or Sunday, then we will

talk about everything calmly. As I said: don't bring anything!

Many warm regards and all my love,

Your Ernst

I am trying to get Heinz here – I think that would be best.

Elden nears its inevitable end

On July 6, Jews are banned from visiting non-Jews. They are also forbidden from having bicycles or making telephone calls. Ernst and Ilse's future becomes increasingly uncertain, and it becomes more difficult to keep in touch because Ilse is officially a non-Jew. She increasingly urges Ernst to go into hiding, and she tries to arrange a place where he can hide out.

In Elden, deportation to Camp Westerbork in the near future seems inevitable. Everyone prepares a backpack with bare essentials in case they suddenly have to leave. The Jewish Council even gives instructions on what they should pack. But it is difficult to find suitable backpacks. The JCB officially appoints women as 'backpack seamstresses' so that there would always be enough backpacks in stock. Mau Reichenberger is responsible for the production of backpacks in Arnhem. These backpacks come in very handy later.

Elden, July 16, 1942 (Letter no. 62 from Elden)

My darling Ilse,

Thank you so much for your letter, which I just received. I understand that you are completely exhausted; working late every night is no joke. Speaking from experience, let me assure you, YOU WILL GET USED TO IT. The beginning is always hard, difficult, and depressing, but after a while, everything becomes automatic, and there is nothing you can do about it... You will just have to bite the bullet.

I don't understand what request your father made to the Gestapo? It would be a great shame if you had to leave there. Amsterdam is hell on earth now, and the atmosphere is completely unlivable. It's hard for us to fathom here.

Ella (Werner's wife) updated us again yesterday – actually, there is nothing new. Ella has lost a lot of weight and looks terrible. The mother of one of the girls here is suffering from a nervous breakdown – she's certainly not the only one... I'm sure you'll soon be angry again; after all, you know what awaits you back home in Amsterdam.

We are constantly busy with preparations, such as repairing shoes and clothes, etc. We will receive train times soon. We will probably all get backpacks; if not, I will have my backpack repaired so I can put more in it.

Can you bring me some things from Oldenboom? Things I didn't think were important before. I need my cutlery and my side backpack; I think those are still there. Also the shoes, but I already asked you for those. Maybe some leather straps to tie rolled-up blankets, etc. If I remember correctly, there is also some shoe polish and such, and if the polish is finished, at least bring me the brushes.

I hope it is not too heavy (weight) for you, I am so sorry to burden you with all that, but I see no other way to get it. Perhaps, if Hans were to come here, he could bring some of it – has he managed to get a travel permit in the meantime?

One more thing about our last conversation on Saturday night. Do you really believe you were right? I think you need to understand me, my status and my surroundings a bit better. Do you think that I, someone who lives in a society like this, can just disappear completely and then only show up for dinner? Or, that it is possible for me not to exchange a word with anyone? If you think about it with a little common sense, you will certainly see that I can't have neglected you, not even a little bit...

Another thing, let's not be so obstinate! Never admit a mistake?

I got that impression from you on Sunday – I often behave that way, too – but it really doesn't make any sense. We then get angry unnecessarily and deeply regret these unfortunate conversations afterward.

It is cold and unpleasant here at the moment. We stay inside almost all day and keep ourselves busy doing boring tasks.

It is getting late, and I also still want to write to the Oldenbooms.

Stay healthy, my love, and don't work so hard.

Many loving regards,

Your Ernst

Some friends here send you their regards.

Elden, July 26, 1942 (Letter no. 63 from Elden)

Highly esteemed birthday girl!

One thousand ninety-two weeks ago,
You leaped with joy, your face aglow,
Into the world, to come to me
Still very young, as all can see

At birth, you weighed a little less,
Two kilos, if I had to guess,
You grew up quickly, without a doubt,
Growing, yes, you figured it out.

Your childhood days were full of cheer,
(Children lack virtues, it's often clear)
But you were soon sent far away,
To England, where you had to stay.

In British classrooms, you excelled,
In wonder, all were surely held,
They took you in, gave you a start,
To raise you as a lady, smart.

But once you had it figured out,
Back to Holland, without a doubt,
You joined Gerzon to learn a trade,
They took you in, and there you stayed.

But the end of that fine course came fast.
So now you have success at last,
As a seamstress, loyal and quick,
You cut up many yards of fabric.

Now you stand on your own two feet,
Now your training feels quite complete,
You handle all tasks in the home, it's clear,
You even teach children to use the potty here.

Maccabi Hatzair brought you great joy,
Learning values you employ.
There, we all liked Calvary's nonsense,
Although it never made any sense

The Movement has been good for us too,
Without it, I'd have never found you,
Irony aside, let's make it plain,
That meeting you, was my ultimate gain.

Congratulations, I will spare,
You know how much I truly care,
My wish is simple, small, and sweet:
To live a life together, that's pure and complete.

Although this poem may have no worth,
I felt compelled to give it birth,
Since you once said I write with flair,
This little rhyme I had to share.

(219)

I.

Elsten, 26. Juli 1942.

Hochgeehrter Geburtstagskind!
Vor tausendneunundneunzig Jahren
kamst Du in die Welt gefahren.
Zu kurz war die Entwicklungszeit —
manchmal merkt man das noch heut'...

Da du nur wenige Pfund wogest,
hat man dich mühsam großgezogen.
Doch du entwickeltest sehr schön dich,
bald war dein Umfang ganz ansehnlich!

Nach sehr wechselvoller Jugend
(Kindern fehlt ja manche Tugend),
ward'st in das Ausland du geschickt,
ganz England war darob entzückt!

The first page of the birthday poem

Elden, August 2, 1942 (Letter no. 64 from Elden)

My dearest Ilse,

Today I am free in the afternoon (and these hours are when I miss you the most). I wanted to write a few words to you, just a short letter. I received your letter – thank you. Actually, I don't know what to write – everything is 'supposedly' taking its course.

Ella has given us some hope again; the educational farm in Gouda has not yet been dismantled – we will just have to wait and see what happens to us. We can discuss the contents of your letter in person on Sunday.

The week has been very boring; we only got to do some useful work here these past few days. As far as work is concerned, things are picking up again.

This week, I received another letter from my mother on a Red Cross form. She is doing well.

I am ending the letter now:

First, I don't have the necessary peace and quiet to write.

Second, I still have things I need to do.

Third to sixth... I have another headache.

For the last two weeks, I have been suffering from constant headaches. If it continues like this, I will have to go see a doctor.

We are getting the second vaccination[22] this week; none of us had any side effects or pain.

Don't be angry that I write so little and superficial. You will be here next Sunday, won't you?

---

22 Against smallpox. The Dutch vaccination program continued as usual during the occupation. In Germany, the Nazis abolished compulsory vaccination because infectious diseases would help kill 'inferior people.'

Many loving regards,

Your Ernst

Elden, August 23, 1942 (Letter No. 65 from Elden)

My dear, sweet girl,

I was very shocked yesterday when I received your letter, for I really had not seriously considered this possibility. I was firmly convinced that everything had gone well. Now, I am severely blaming myself for the fact that, because of me and my carelessness, you have ended up in such a situation. I am so terribly sorry, and I really don't know how to make amends. I only hope it won't get too bad and that you, my dearest one, won't have to go through such suffering. But I can hardly imagine that it could be too late after only a few days, can it? However, I am glad that you are so brave and determined.
After all, I know how it is. You carry all the burdens and suffering, and all I have to do is sit here and write you a letter, but what else can I do?
Please know that I think of you incessantly and that your worries are mine, too.
Farewell, my love, and be strong in all that we have to go through now. For I love you so much!

I embrace you and kiss you deeply,

Your Ernst

Elden, September 2, 1942 (Letter No. 66 from Elden)

My love,

Although I hope to see you on Sunday, I still want to write a few words to you.
I was very pleased with your letter. There is not much to report from my side.
The latest announcement, which came this week, stated that (for now) we will not be leaving for the camps until November 1; at least, that is something!
Work is fun now. We are harvesting wheat and hay (all with a scythe). This is our favorite work, and everyone is very enthusiastic.
Mrs. Pool was here this weekend and sang songs from the Dreigroschenoper and Flemish Legends – and recited various things. The Dreigroschenoper was pretty shabby (I mean the way she expressed it). I expected something a bit better. Needless to say, we hear the Moritat von Mackie Messer and especially Mutter Courage und ihre Kinder around every corner here. Tonight, we played the records twice (that's why it got so late). I still haven't sent my stuff – now that it's not as urgent, I want to change some things, and we also need to talk about the address. Lini told me today that she got a letter from you – she wants to wait and see. You can talk about it on Sunday. If you MUST talk to her, I think it would be better to write to her – she often leaves on Sunday afternoon – and I don't know exactly when you will be here. I must end this letter now (and so on...you know...!). Will I get another postcard from you about this?

Many loving regards,
Your Ernst

The Westerweel group

In August 1942, it became known that all 49 young Palestine pioneers from the Pavilion in Loosdrecht had gone into hiding. On August 18, the last youths and their leaders were taken to hiding addresses throughout the Netherlands. One of these children was Erco's brother, Heinz. He ended up at a hiding address in Rotterdam and survived the war.

The youth leader in Loosdrecht was Joachim 'Shushu' Simon (1919-1943). This man had been in a German concentration camp. He therefore had no illusions about the Nazis' intentions with the Jews. He said the children he was responsible for 'should not have to go through what he had gone through.' Not only did Shushu organize the hiding of the Loosdrecht children, but he also created an extensive network to accommodate other people in hiding and provided escape routes to safe countries like Switzerland and Spain. He did this together with the Rotterdam teacher, Joop Westerweel (1899-1944) and his wife, Willy. This led to the formation of a special resistance group consisting of Jews, especially Palestine pioneers, and leftist, pacifist non-Jews. Members of the Deventer Association participated fully, and Ilse was also involved in this group. Thanks to the Westerweel group, hundreds of people were saved. The leaders of the group paid a heavy price: Joop Westerweel died in front of a firing squad in 1944, and Shushu Simon committed suicide after being arrested because he was afraid of betraying his supporters under torture.

Although going into hiding was considered the only way out by many, the Deventer Association remained hesitant. From the beginning of 1942, when they heard that a number of Palestine pioneers from the former Working Village of Wieringermeer had successfully gone into hiding, they talked a lot about doing so. All the raids that took place also confirmed the urgency of going into hiding. However, the Deventer Association remained of the opinion that those engaged in agriculture had nothing to worry about because they were indispensable. They could always go into hiding later.

Ru Cohen, founder of the Deventer Association, was also strongly opposed to people from Elden going into hiding. Erica Blüth, as secretary of the youth aliyah committee involved in the hiding of the Loosdrecht children, recalled: 'when Shushu suggested to him that the house in Elden should also go into hiding, he abruptly declined.' Hans Seemann remembers that the leadership in Elden discouraged the hiding of students. They feared reprisals from the Germans. Moreover, they believed in the alleged agreement made with the German authorities that the residents of Huize Voorburg did not have to go to the camps.

From 1942 onwards, it became easier for Ernst and Ilse to see each other. Ilse had been working as a housekeeper for the Levison family in Zutphen since June. As she did not wear a Jewish star, she could move around freely, and she visited Ernst every week in Elden. On July 26, she turned 21 and was thus of legal age. In September, Ernst and Ilse decided to get engaged, even though it was forbidden for Jews to marry non-Jews. Together, they wrote a letter to Ilse's parents.

Elden, September 8, 1942 (Letter No. 67 from Elden)

My beloved Ilse,

I want to quickly take advantage of the lunch break to write to you. I haven't had a moment off since Sunday, and the highlight is that tonight, we have to prepare the beans to dry (we all do it together).
It was the first Sunday of the month again, which is when I have to do the bookkeeping. This time, it took a lot longer to get done.
It was such a shame that you could not come on Sunday. I was really looking forward to it, so I was greatly disappointed. I am sure you will come this week???? If you could be here on the two Rosh Hashanah days, it would be amazing – or do you think it won't be possible? We probably won't do anything special here. Professor Levkowich canceled his arrival, so there will be a lot of free time. Do your utmost. I hope it works out. I will be so happy.
I understand all too well that you are fed up with working yourself to death while everyone else is just slacking off. It was the same with me when I worked for the farmer, but in the end, I/you are the laborers, aren't we? I could never get used to it, and it made me angry over and over again.
But you have to persevere because, ultimately, it is also a life lesson.
During the next week, although it is forbidden, I am going to prepare a package for your parents. There is not much to choose from, a few pears and some onions. I will ask the neighbor for onions because ours are not big enough yet.
Herald Simon is getting married (civil) today – his girlfriend is 19 years old. I wrote a short congratulatory letter to them.
I received a letter on Saturday from a distant aunt who I met

15 years ago. She got my address from an uncle in Wiesbaden, Germany. She lives with her family in Dinxperlo, a small town southeast of Arnhem, not far from the Dutch-German border. She writes really nicely; I will definitely reply to her.
I suppose you also have heard about the terrible situation currently in Amsterdam. Be glad you are no longer there.
I very much hope to see you this weekend, here with me.

Until then, many loving regards and kisses

Your Ernst

Enclosed are two pictures – did the others fail?
I opened this letter again – should I write a letter to the Levison family for Rosh Hashanah? Or is that not necessary?

1942, Deventer, the last meeting. Ernst, second row, third on the left

Elden, September 21, 1942 (Letter No. 68, the last from Elden)

My dear, sweet girl,

I waited for you last night and also this morning. I kept thinking you might come after all, although my hope gradually faded. Now, I am very disappointed that you could not come. First of all, because I was sure you would. I was looking forward to your visit. I suppose it was impossible for you to come. I don't think they could have easily kept you there otherwise.

It's quite boring here today. I stayed in bed with a book until 11 o'clock this morning. Every time someone walked up the stairs, I hoped it was you. In the afternoon, I slept for a few hours, something I never do during the day, but I am really very tired.

For the last few days, I have gone to sleep very late (or early...), not before 3 a.m. We are hard at work preparing for an 'agricultural exhibition' that we want to hold during Sukkot. It racked my brain about it; I wanted to do something different for a change. I believe the exhibition will be fun. Seven of us comrades are working on it very energetically. We make models of farms, we paint posters, etc. I don't want to reveal too much about it, because you will see everything for yourself on Sunday.

The letter from your parents was very pleasing. It's great that they didn't 'make a fuss.' I thought they would write to me as well; it's 'supposed' to be that way anyway... but so far I haven't received anything. I received a package from them at the beginning of the week (before they got our letter).

I find Oldenboom's offer exceptionally sweet. I haven't written anything to them yet because I knew Herman and his friend were coming by here. But when they came, I did not manage to speak with Herman alone, and I could not bring that up in front of his friend – but I will write to them. Their visit was really nice, even if it was a little uncomfortable because it prevented me from working. I actually invited them to come on Sunday because I knew you wouldn't be here then.

This very minute, as I am still writing to you, I received a letter from your parents that says the same as the letter they sent you. I will write back to them immediately. I have to thank them for the package I received from them, anyway. I'm not sure now how to sign the letter: with my full name, Ernst Cosmann? Or just Ernst? Or Erco? Or E.C.?

I have spoken to Lini. She suggests you inquire about the doctor's rates so you can tell her on Sunday. For now, she will stick with her regular doctor and treat her eczema with ointment only.

I don't have any more news.

Ella still does not have a travel permit. She will stay here for now, also because she has been ill all week. She now has to go back with a one-time-only travel permit.

This week, we – my group and I – are going to work outside again. We are harvesting potatoes at the neighbor's house.

Did you know that Jacob Lebel and his family were deported? I believe this is one of the most tragic cases of all. He is so terribly ill, and the baby is still so small. Batya's sister is also there; she only had a brief moment to speak with her.

I immediately wondered what the reason for your trip to Amsterdam might be – I read in the newspapers about the mobilization call. Of course, I was also a little afraid that it might be something worse. Heaven forbid we have to deal with one more worry.

My dearest, write back to me soon, and even better, please come here as soon as possible! I long for you so much. I can barely wait until the weekend. It's going to be a long, slow week here until I see you again.

Many loving regards,

Your Ernst

The letter to your parents was remarkably easy for me to write, covering almost two pages. I wrote that they should not worry about your future; we can be just as happy as other people.
I divided the speech into three parts:
Work
Leisure
Business Opportunities.
What do your parents think about us? Did they say anything?

Kisses,

Ernst

Go into hiding or not?

At this time, many of Ernst's comrades began thinking about going into hiding or fleeing abroad. Others thought it was still too soon. Werner Ahlfeld, the leader in Elden, later recalled why he did not allow the residents to go into hiding: 'I was always of the opinion that the Germans would lose the war. I had no illusions about the fate of the Jews, even though I had no idea about the Germans' plans. Isolation from foreign countries made it feel as if we could do nothing. I wanted to avoid panic, and above all, I wanted the hachsharah organization to continue operating, which the Germans allowed us to do during the first two years of the war.' According to Ahlfeld, in the spring of 1942, Elden's leadership did arrange hiding addresses in the area for the children on their own initiative. Ahlfeld also provided himself with a false identity card in case of emergency.

The residents in Elden still felt safe because, as agricultural workers, they were exempt from the Arbeitseinsatz. However, some chawerim from Elden did not wait for what was to come and managed to flee to Switzerland.

Ilse also did her best to find hiding addresses. Erco, however, turned everything down. He also declined an offer from the Oldenboom family. Ilse also found a hiding address for Lini de Bruin and her little daughter, but Ernst wrote to her, in a secret language, that they were staying put: 'For the time being, she remains with her regular doctor, treating her eczema with ointment only.'

'The elder chawerim consulted with Werner and me about the measures to be taken in case of an incursion on the house by the Germans. There was a search for hiding addresses in the area, but not systematically. Mau Reichenberger (of the Deventer Association) would warn us through his relations if a raid was imminent,' Lini de Bruin, the headmistress in Elden, later recalled. That warning, however, came too late. In the early morning of October 3, 1942, Huize Voorburg was surrounded by the Germans. All thirty-eight Palestine pioneers living there are detained and taken to the Westerbork camp.

As for Ilse, she now knew what she had to do. Because she was still free, she had to help and support Ernst and his friends as much as possible.

When she heard that the residents of Huize Voorburg had been taken away to Westerbork, Ilse wrote a short letter to Ernst, expressing her despair. She never sent the letter and always kept it:

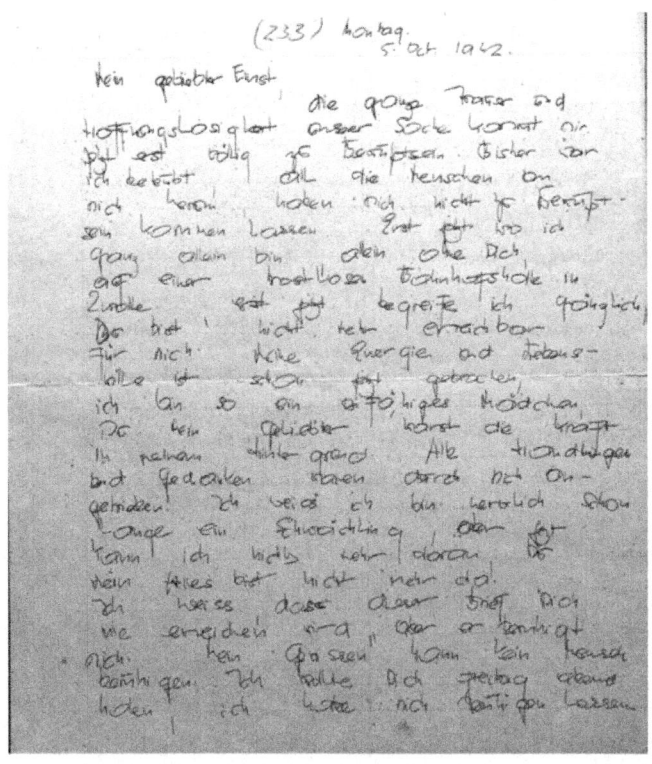

Ilse's letter to Ernst. Monday, October 5, 1942

Monday, October 5, 1942

My dearest Ernst,

All our tragedy and hopelessness have only now dawned upon me. Until now, it seems I have been in a coma. All my friends around me failed to wake me up to reality.
Now that I am sitting here alone, without you, in the dreary hall of the train station in Zwolle, it's clear to me: you are no longer within my reach. My strength and zest for life is gone. I am but a simple girl – and you, my love, are my pillar of strength. Everything I did and thought was based on you.
I know I have always been weak at heart, but without you, I cannot do anything because you, my everything, are no longer here!
I know this letter will never reach you, but writing it calms me. No one can calm my conscience. I wanted to come and get you on Friday evening but did not have the necessary strength. I was too lazy – my love, I can never undo it.
What do you think, my Blondie, if I were to be with you now? Why choose a life partner if you are not with him during his most difficult hours?
Oh, my beloved – I don't know what else to say – I'm as empty as a desert. My light is gone, you...

Ilse

In 2019, a memorial stone was placed at Huize Voorburg in Elden.

Erco in Westerbork

In the early morning of October 3, 1942, Huize Voorburg is surrounded by police and SS. Everyone is still in bed because it is a Jewish holiday, the eighth day of the Feast of Tabernacles. The Palestine pioneers are ordered to leave the house within twenty minutes. They must walk to the train station in Arnhem.[23] They do not know what is going to happen, but they are prepared: everyone has a to-go backpack for if they should suddenly have to leave. In Arnhem, hundreds of Jews are standing on the platform, desperately wondering where they are going. The SS men present herd the people into a waiting train and are unwilling to provide information. It turns out that they are being taken to the Westerbork camp.

Camp Westerbork

'The Westerbork camp, surrounded by heath and dark brown moorland, lies in the desolate and barren Dutch province of Drenthe. As far as the eye can see, there is nothing but poor, desolate earth, with only a few scattered small farms. The camp is lonely out here, ten kilometers from the nearest village called Hooghalen,' Zwi Durlacher, one of the chawerim, described his first impression. Once inside the camp, this impression becomes 'very positive.' 'Here, you see straight streets surrounded by modern brick buildings. If you were not aware that you were in the infamous deportation camp, you could just as easily have thought that you were in a very modern suburb of Amsterdam.'

---

23 According to Shlomo Samson, they were taken to the station on the back of open trucks.

When the Germans invaded the Netherlands in May 1940, Camp Westerbork already existed. After the Kristallnacht of November 9, 1938, life had become truly impossible for Jews in Germany, and there was a large flow of refugees toward the Dutch border. Many of them were sent back or stopped at the border by hundreds of additionally deployed border guards. Those who did enter the country were mostly accommodated by private individuals or, like the Palestine pioneers, ended up in labor camps and training centers where they prepared for transit to Palestine.

Approximately 10,000 Jewish refugees were eventually admitted, and the government decided to build a central camp for them. A site as far away from the inhabited world as possible was chosen, on the heath near the village of Westerbork in Drenthe. The Jewish community had to pay for the construction

of the camp themselves. The first 22 refugees arrived at the camp on October 9, 1939. After the capitulation in May 1940, 749 refugees lived there.

They came to the camp voluntarily because they thought they would get a good education and that there would be various recreational opportunities. In reality, they had to work hard to build up the camp. One of the first residents was Werner Bloch. He recalled, 'The further away we got, the lonelier it became. At one point, you only saw heathlands. Occasional groves. And where eventually the refugee camp would be, there was a vast plain where there was only heath and sand, and it was very desolate.'

After the capitulation, the Dutch authorities decided to house all Jewish refugees in Westerbork and military police were assigned to guard the camp. The camp was only taken over by the Nazis in July 1942 and then transformed into Polizeiliches Durchgangslager Westerbork. It was now no longer a refugee camp but a place where

Jews, Sinti and Roma from all over the Netherlands were gathered in order to be sent on to camps in the east. Most of them died in Auschwitz-Birkenau and Sobibór. A total of 101,525 people were imprisoned at Westerbork, most of them only briefly.

When the Germans took over the camp, they found a tight, military-based organization set up by Dutch commander Jacques Schol. The residents of the camp were assigned all sorts of functions within the camp administration. Schol, who was not a Nazi, thus hoped to keep the Germans out of the camp. These, however, felt that the Jews were 'treated far too humanely and that, because of the attitude of the camp commander, the Jews felt very comfortable here.'

The first two German directors were soon dismissed because of their cruel behavior. Keeping so many people in check succeeded only with a very different approach. The new commandant, Albert Konrad Gemmeker, transformed Westerbork into a camp where conditions were relatively good compared to other camps. People were not mistreated, families could stay together, and there was enough food, thanks to what the camp residents themselves managed to organize. All kinds of amenities were available: a store, playground, schools, an excellent hospital, theater performances and concerts. Gemmeker maintained order through a cunning system in which victims were used to victimize their fellow men. Jews guarded Jews and even largely determined who was on the train to the east. All Gemmeker cared about was that the train was filled every week.

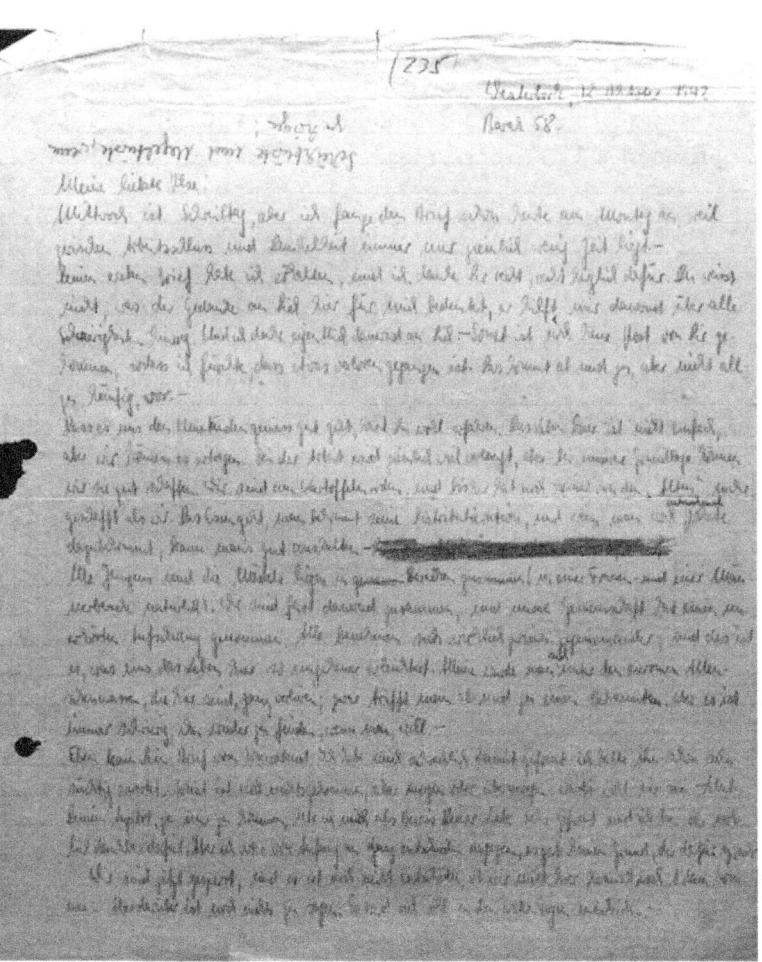

Ernst's first letter to Ilse from Westerbork

Westerbork, barak 58, October 12, 1942 (Letter no. 1 from Westerbork)

My dearest Ilse,

Wednesdays will be 'letter days,' meaning the day when the camp is willing to send letters. Today is Monday, and I want to start writing now because there is very little time between when work ends and when it gets dark.
I received your first letter, for which I am very grateful. You don't know what it means to me to think of you; it helps me overcome all difficulties. In fact, I think of you all the time.
Except for the first letter, I have not received any other mail from you yet. I fear that a letter may have gotten lost – it happens from time to time, but fortunately, not that often.
You may have heard that we are doing quite well under the circumstances.
Life here is not easy, but it is still bearable; we can handle it. The work requires a lot of effort from us, but our group can do it. We harvest potatoes, and so far, we are much, much better than those who arrived here before us.
The food is tolerable. You receive rations, and if you get the occasional parcel, then it is manageable. All the men and women are put in barracks (men's barracks and women's barracks, of course).
Our group is very close, and we try to be together a lot. We are very considerate of each other, and that makes our lives bearable here. On your own, you could truly get lost here among this 'mass of people.' Now and then, you run into an acquaintance, but it is impossible to find him again.
I just received your letter from Saturday. I am so happy about it; I have been waiting in anticipation.
Apart from this letter, I haven't received anything else yet.

Hopefully, I will receive something tomorrow or the day after. Your offer to come here made me very happy and proves your love – and I thank you from the bottom of my heart. But I have been absolutely against it from the beginning, so there is no reason to even talk about it.

At the moment, we are locked up here, so there is no choice on whether we can come to Amsterdam from here. Therefore, for the time being, the issue is not open for discussion.

It will probably be decided within a few days.

I will first list all the things I need here: my pair of high shoes, the leather gaiters (they should still be in the box), shoe polish, a pair of pants (if they are still there...), 2 pairs of long underpants, toilet paper, a notepad, drinking glass, ski cap, some cans, some jam jars, detergent (also for Asher Gerlich), a candle, and leather shoelaces. And a decent large backpack, if you can get one. The one I have here is a little too small. The backpack should be bigger than the typical backpack for outings – if you can't get it, then never mind.

Can you send newspapers and magazines or weeklies? We have very little reading material.

Send only inexpensive stuff; don't spend money on books that are even a little expensive.

I see now that it is a long list, but you can imagine that we really need all these things. Fortunately, I have my warm clothes here, which is the most important thing, so at least I am well equipped with that.

You just have to write the name plus the address:

Barracks number 58
Quarter number 323 Hooghalen
Westerbork East.

We are always allowed to receive mail, and I would appreciate it if you write to me often. I don't have to tell you how desperate I am to receive mail from you. Please also ask others to write from time to time; we are happy with each bit of information from outside.

I can write once every two weeks, and only one page.

I think of you a lot and remember all the wonderful things we went through together.

You cannot imagine how I look forward to the moment when we will see each other again. Hopefully, it will be soon. We must not lose our courage; we must conquer all difficulties. I am not afraid – my dearest, please don't be afraid either.

I must finish this letter now. Fortunately, my neighbor has a small piece of candle. Otherwise, I would have been sitting in total darkness. Borrowing or giving are unfamiliar concepts here!

Now, I still have to wash, which is very important here; we all do our best to keep ourselves as clean as possible. Occasionally, we may shower with hot water in the camp bathhouse. So far, I don't have eczema, etc. In this respect, our barracks are outstanding because all the people are very clean and take great care to keep it that way.

I forgot to thank you for the 'wash bag.' I have a whole pharmacy now, but this 'wash bag' is an important asset. The nasal ointment is excellent and helps me cure my colds despite my always having wet feet.

Now, my dearest, all my love and a thousand kisses.

Your Ernst.

Can you get me some cigarettes? Only one weekly dose at a time.

And spare flashlights.
Should you find another jacket or battledress among my things, please send it.
If there are any, also a hand and shoe brush.
Don't forget to send warm greetings to all our friends and acquaintances.

Westerbork, October 17, 1942 (Letter no. 2 from Westerbork)

My dearest Ilse,

I don't know if you received my first letter sent last Wednesday. I have the opportunity to send a letter now, and I want to take advantage of it.
Thank you very much for your two letters and, of course, for the two fantastic packages that helped us tremendously. Without these food parcels, the situation here is extremely bad. Please ask other people to send something from time to time, and please ask Oldenboom, too.
I also received the dyno torch; thank you very much, my love. I was worried that it might be lost as I was convinced that you had sent it to me earlier. Fortunately, it arrived yesterday. I hope I can give it back to you soon.
On the 'particular' Saturday, October 3, I lent my own dyno torch to someone during the evacuation of Elden. That 'someone' 'forgot' to give it back to me. Those dyno torches are very handy because now we don't need batteries.
I wrote you a long list of things I would like you to send, and I now ask you to do it as soon as possible. Although I'm doing fine with the things I have now, I will greatly appreciate the

additional items. For example, I believe I still have a green or gray jacket, of which I really would have loved one, and a few more of my pants.

You've already sent a few things, and that's wonderful. You chose the correct items; well done.

Can you send hairpins? The girls/women are in desperate need of them.

Not much to tell from here. The work is not too pleasant and very hard. We are often soaking wet, and many people suffer from severe colds.

Thanks to my generally good health, I have had no problems so far, not even stomach problems. I do have a slight cold, but that is a normal autumn cold that I would have gotten anywhere else.

Yes, I am very careful, as life is quite difficult here. The day lasts until 19:00 in the evening, and it is dark by then. Every little thing, like food etc., takes an eternity here because you have to queue for everything. I have gotten used to that, along with all the other difficulties.

I put up with the situation as much as I can, and about everything, I say, 'Alright... it is what it is...' That doesn't mean that I simply accept everything, but I try to avoid becoming irritated as much as possible. I have to control my nerves; I can't get angry about every little thing. Here, you are always on edge anyway, like you could lose your balance at any moment. You curse and grumble about everything minor and major. Up to now, I have remained calm, and I don't want to complain about rickety nerves; there are many here who seek and especially need attention and comfort.

Our group is doing great – most are behaving nicely, sharing everything with each other and helping each other as much as possible.

Fokki, on the other hand, is an exception, and Merry (the

woman who was the cook in Elden) is not the nicest person in the world either. We are relatively lucky with our group of people in our barracks. The men are excellent, neat, clean and quiet. The women have a harder time because of the screaming children. They don't have enough tables, and sleeping is almost impossible.

We have relationships here that make our lives a little easier. We get our laundry from the camp laundromat, which is managed by some older camp residents – Abi Meyers' father from Elden works in the laundromat.

Every evening, we get a little extra food (the taste is good, the content is less) in a good way and on time. If you work very hard, you also get a bit more food.

The evenings are pointless – visitors, acquaintances, like our friends' parents, like our parents, walk to and fro aimlessly. At 21:45, we go to sleep, and we fall asleep immediately because we are exhausted from work and also from the long journey to and from work.

The fact that you cannot come to Westerbork is very good! I absolutely do not want you to experience the things that are happening here. As far as I'm concerned, it's manageable, but it is far worse for women – and good for any woman who doesn't have to go through this.

I am not afraid that we will become 'strangers' if we don't see each other for a long time. We will feel comfortable with each other in no time. There is still a chance that we will get out of here – let's hope... Please write to Oldenboom that I got the package with fruit and the cake. It is so sweet of them, and I thank them with all my heart.

I think of you a lot – write to me soon.
Lots of loving regards and lots of kisses,
Your Ernst

Westerbork, October 24, 1942 (Letter no. 3 from Westerbork)

My dearest Ilse,

I am trying to write quickly because I have to go somewhere and the letter has to be sent soon.
All your letters have arrived nicely on time; I am always happy when I receive mail from you. Write as much as you can. I tense up every time they announce that mail has arrived.
I already wrote in my last letter all the things I need. Try to send it as soon as possible because I need all these things here more than I can explain to you. It is best not to send food items in the same package because then the package will arrive faster.
We currently have a food problem – all packages containing food were confiscated today, and we do not know whether they will be released. Please postpone sending food – I will let you know when it is possible again. All your other packages have arrived with most likely everything in them. Only the last package, which you wrote about and finally did not send (and then did send), has still not arrived, but it seems to me that it is still too soon.
Lenie thanks you for the medicine you sent for Channa'le. She is very happy with it and uses it a lot. The second package for Channa'le has not arrived yet.
Other than that, there's not much news. The roads here are literally a swamp, and the moisture manages to penetrate every shoe, even boots.
Potato harvesting is coming to an end – we don't yet know what will happen next. (I mean, what kind of work we will do next.) The 'SPERRUNG' has been postponed, which is very good.

I have to stop now. I will continue as soon as I can.
Please do not send cigarettes in the package. Send them with someone instead.
Many loving regards, also to your parents – I will write to them.

Your Ernst

Please put a note in each package: Who the sender is.
Please tell Oldenboom that we need bread and butter more than we do cakes.

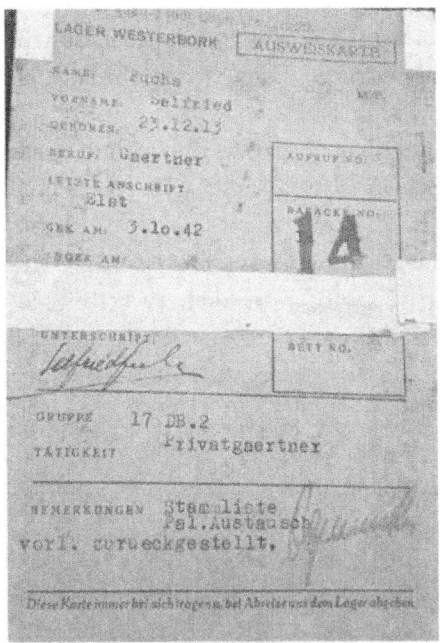

Ausweiskarte of Selfried (Fokki) Fuchs from Westerbork. It shows that he was Commandant Gemmeker's private gardener and that he was temporarily blocked from deportation (zurueckgestellt) because he was on the list of Jews to be exchanged with ethnic Germans in Palestine.

Westerbork, October 26-29, 1942 (Letter no. 4 from Westerbork)

My dearest Ilse,

Although I don't yet know when this letter can be sent to you, I am writing it in advance so that I can send it at the right time. (Writing a letter undisturbed is not an easy task here, and thus, it takes a lot of time to write a letter).
I assume you have received my previous letter (number 3) by now. You already confirmed receiving the second letter, and you probably haven't received the first one yet. They probably hold the mail for quite a long time. In any case, I was very happy with your letters and hope to receive another letter soon. You can imagine, in this isolation, the joy one feels here when mail arrives, especially when it comes from a person who is always in your thoughts. It is not possible for you to visit; all visits are strictly forbidden!!!
As much as I would like to see you, it is better this way.
We have been here for more than three weeks, and it feels like an eternity. Elden belongs to the 'distant past' but remains a wonderful memory.
When life stops abruptly, and you suddenly find yourself in a completely different place, especially the way it happened, it is very different from when you move to another place and have had the time to prepare beforehand. And yet, one gets used to it. People compromise in this new way of life; you come to terms with the altered situation.
Of course, we are all aware of where we started and where we are now, and the situation here is not good (I cannot say that the situation here is good, etc., etc., even though we know that our situation is better than other people's in other places).
Life here is very unusual, and it is difficult to describe it on

paper. The impressions are still too fresh to put into words.

I sometimes try to observe these things from a distance. I can afford it for now because, so far, fear has not been an issue for me (I hope the devil doesn't hear me...). Still, all the conditions of normal life and the interests of the people here are totally different.

When they finished working (i.e., collecting papers among the camp paths, sweeping barracks, all kinds of digging work, etc.), the intellectuals sat around all day 'and did nothing.' Rich merchants are not interested in anything except food.

At the same time, all the old antagonisms of the different 'classes' remain. In daily life, there is no sense of a society that (must) share the same fate.

There are people here whom I have never met before, the lowest possible proletariat, a crowd not even described in books. I cannot identify with these people, yet I try hard not to be condescending and know exactly what a bitter fate they have had in the past and what fate they have today.

Some people try to evoke pity and beg for a slice of bread, which they then sell at the high price of half a guilder per slice ... and the language you hear here ... until now, I thought I could speak and understand a rough peasant language, but what you hear here is almost unintelligible.

Here (almost) everyone is very selfish; only good acquaintances help each other, which is understandable since every object and piece of food is invaluable here.

We also behave this way, even if it is difficult for us to refuse something, such as a cigarette, etc. We quickly realized this at the beginning and decided that we had no choice; we had to think only of ourselves!

Within our group, everything is different, of course – we share and help each other.

Every Sunday, there is machsan.[24] We knit socks, and the girls/women do the more complicated repairs. As a result, our clothes are in reasonable condition.

For your information: You now have a 'sister-in-law': Rozijntje. Rozijntje is now my sister. When we left Elden, I suggested that every man should take responsibility for a woman. That means helping with everything, especially looking out for her and never letting her out of his sight. Each man, one woman! I chose Rozijntje, the weakest and most dependent of all the women. I was really very worried about her – she couldn't carry her luggage, she always lost her possessions, and she didn't know how to pack. I arranged everything for her and helped her carry the packages. She was very happy – our love as brother and sister was evidenced one night when we slept side by side on our backpacks. We behave accordingly, like brother and sister, and the others treat us the same way. What will happen to Rozijntje in the future if, God forbid, she should have to leave alone without proper help. I honestly don't know. Without help from others, she is completely lost. There are a few others in the same situation,

including your friend Clarie (the dark, skinny girl). She has a real problem (she has a screw loose) and does not understand at all what is going on here. We have received a temporary 'SPERRUNG' for all the pioneers who are here, which is indeed the best that can be achieved in this bizarre situation – we are obviously very happy about it.

I received your letter yesterday; you really don't have to worry, all your letters and packages arrived. In fact, four parcels from you and a parcel from Oldenboom arrived yesterday – it was like a birthday. Our biggest luck was that they had not been

---

24   Literally: storage place.

looted. Many food items have been confiscated lately; some packages have arrived empty. Nevertheless, the packages must continue because, without them, we struggle very much. The best thing is to make up small packages – you can send butter as a letter package and so on.

The packages you send are really great, and you always manage to send exactly what we urgently need. All my friends and I thank you, and everyone loves you very much. The girls were very happy with the shampoo and the hairpins. Can you get more hairpins? And also shoelaces, sewing utensils, thimbles, handkerchiefs, and don't forget my work shoes that are still at your place.

The pants and jacket were perfect, thank you very much for them, and I found the 'notes'...

I cannot express with words how happy I am with the parcels and how grateful I am to you for them – you are really too sweet. I am glad that I have you and that you help me with all these problems directly and indirectly.

Listen: If you need money to buy the more expensive things, you can sell all my things, anything you wish. I am not attached to anything anymore. When you are here, you look at everything differently – nothing except life has any value.

Don't hesitate for a moment; I agree in advance with everything you do and decide.

Now, my love, this letter must be sent, and I also need to go to sleep, although there will be another deportation tonight, so we won't be doing much sleeping.

As for me, please don't worry...I am fine. I am feeling well and trying to influence others to stay in a good mood.

I think of you constantly.
Many loving regards and a thousand kisses,

Your Ernst

Please send a ration certificate for sewing supplies – packages should be sent to Mr. Samson, Barracks 18.
It is not possible to come visit.
Please include a small writing pad and a few envelopes.

Give your parents my regards. I believe I received a package from your parents, but it arrived without the sender's name, so I am not quite sure. I will write to them soon.
The same goes for Oldenboom.
I will write to my mother using my previous address.
Greetings to Levison, Aunt R and Uncle H.

October 31, 1942

This letter has still not been sent – today I received your letter 'D,' thank you very much. I don't need to answer it because I have already written about most of it.
I received a letter from Heinz; he is doing well.
I haven't heard from my mother in two months, which is strange. Others get regular mail from Palestine via the Red Cross.
I did not understand your comment about 'a BLESSING in DISGUISE.'
Can you send me the shoes as soon as possible so that I can use them instead? The shoes I have now are 'half' a shoe.
Could you please also include some razor blades? The best ones are the ones with the elongated hole, but should you not be able to get those, then anything will do; don't make too much of an effort.

Definitely the end.
Many loving regards and kisses

Your Ernst

By the way: the small packages are arriving in good order now. O's tin of cookies arrived in order as well.

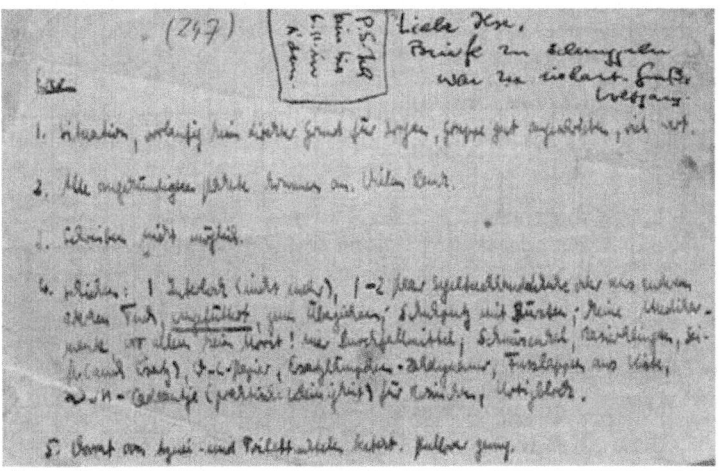

On a small piece of paper, apparently smuggled out of the camp by someone at a time when no letters were allowed to be sent, the following is written:

Hello Ilse,
Smuggling letters was too big a risk. Regards, Wolfgang
P.S. I will be in Amsterdam on November 6

In Erco's handwriting:
1 Situation for now: no immediate cause for concern. The group has developed a good reputation, and that is worth a lot.
2 All announced packages have arrived.

3 Writing: currently impossible.
4 Send: A pair of gloves made of tarpaulin or other strong fabric, without lining, to be worn over ordinary gloves. Shoe polish with shoe brush and laces. Razors, soap or soap substitute. Toilet paper, foot rags (are in the box).
Bulbs for flashlight, pocket dynamo.
Hanukkah gift (something small and useful) for Rozijntje, a small notepad.
5 Our supply of medicine is good and is more than enough at the moment. Have plenty of pullovers.

Palestine pioneers in Westerbork

The first group of Palestine pioneers, who arrived in Westerbork in July 1942, were immediately sent on to Auschwitz. The 36 people from Elden who arrived on October 3, including Ernst, escaped this fate due to fortunate circumstances. The evacuation of Huize Voorburg was part of a large nationwide raid. On the night of October 2 and 3, 1942, all the Jewish men who were housed in the dozens of labor camps that existed were taken to Westerbork under the pretext of family reunification. At the same time, their wives and children were taken from their homes. Between 25,000 and 30,000 Jews arrived in Westerbork that day. The chance of being put directly on the train to the east was thus small.

Shlomo Samson, one of the comrades from Elden, also played an important role. In his memoirs, he describes how tremendously relieved he was when the train, in which the people from Elden had been herded in by the SS at Arnhem station, headed north and not east. His family had arrived in the Netherlands in 1938, and since 1939, the family had lived in Westerbork. So Shlomo knew Westerbork well. When the Germans took over the camp in 1942, they had left part of its organization untouched to the 'Alte Kampinsassen,' the German refugees who were already living there. As one of the oldest residents of Westerbork, Father Samson had an important position there. Among other things, he determined who was allowed to work outside the camp. Because of his intervention, the Elden group was not immediately sent on, and they were allowed to stay together on the grounds that they were hard workers. Shlomo Samson was their contact with the camp leadership and, therefore, crucial to the group. He provided them with the 'vitamin C' (connections), as it was called in the camp, that was necessary for survival.

Philip Mechanicus, the journalist who, during his stay of nearly a year in Westerbork, made merciless observations of the society there, described in his diary the impression Ernst's group made on him: 'Imbued with a strong spiritual consciousness, physically burly and strong, courageous, they are the predecessors of the new generation, which has also gathered here in Westerbork as members of the Hashera, favored by the commander: young farmers preparing to leave for Palestine, often educated young men from secondary schools.' He expected that they would also do well in Poland. 'The young generation, insofar as they come from a hard school, is maintaining itself beautifully here, [...] If they are given reasonable opportunities in Poland, the same image will manifest itself there too!!'

A German soldier poses while behind him new prisoners arrive at Westerbork, October 3, 1942, Ernst was one of them that day (Coll. Karl Schneider, Bremen Staatsarchiv)

Paul Siegel, a pioneer who arrived in Westerbork a little later, also wrote that Commander Gemmeker valued the group. This gave them a false sense of security. He opined: 'We owed our security to the fact that the camp commander needed us. We did all kinds of functional work for the camp that also benefited the residents.' Erco and his group drew hope from their good relationship with the camp's German leadership, and that was one of the reasons they did not want to try to escape for the time being. Commander Gemmeker, however, did not care who exactly was on the weekly train to Auschwitz as long as they met the number dictated by Berlin.

A close-knit group

'Our group, about 70-80 chawerim, lived together in a barrack; when chawerim or young Zionists arrived, they joined us if at all possible. We had a good social and cultural life; we also learned Ivrit,' survivor Lotte Wald, who arrived at the camp in January 1942, later recalled. Paul Siegel, who had also ended up in the hakhshara barracks, described how 'the Elden group formed a close-knit unit,' so much so that they were initially unwilling to share food parcels with the others in their barracks. Later, the group of mostly German Palestine pioneers became increasingly unified, a group that felt privileged and relatively safe.

Erco felt it was very important to keep the group together and to take care of each other as best he could. He took care of Grete Lehmann, nicknamed 'Rozijntje' (Raisin) because she was so small. Unlike Erco, she did survive the war[25] because she belonged to the group of 222 people who were exchanged for German Protestants

---

25   Rozijntje settled in the Alloniem Kibbutz, where she started her family. Clarie, whom Ernst mentions in the same letter, also survived Bergen-Belsen and settled in Jokne'Am in Israel.

in Palestine – the 'Templars' – via Camp Bergen-Belsen

Westerbork, November 3, 1942 (Letter no. 5 from Westerbork)

My dearest Ilse,

I can send this letter tomorrow, so now I have to hurry with writing, and I don't have much time because we have to appear before Commander Gemmeker to try to arrange our Sperrung.
I received your letter (marked 'D') on Sunday and was so delighted with it. And today, I received the package with the many useful things we so badly need; everyone cheered with great enthusiasm.
I conclude from the handwriting and the warm greetings that it is a package from Mrs. Levison; give Jetty my most heartfelt thanks. They are truly all things that we sorely lack here.
I hope you can send the rest soon, especially the shoes. It is terribly wet here, so we often need to change shoes.
Send it to Wolfgang, then it will arrive here in good condition and quickly.
I confirmed all the packages from last week, so no need to worry. They are here; nothing is missing!
Wolfgang received a registered parcel; I assume it's yours – I'm going to pick it up right away, thank you very much.
Today, I also received a parcel from Oldenboom containing butter and bread, and just in time. The packages are arriving. Bread and butter are the most important things. I thank you so much for it; we all thank you for it.
Try to advertise: 'Who can send packages?' We need bread

and butter more than anything else. Without bread, we won't make it. It is not enough to send a one-time package; it must be done regularly.
Spread the message in Deventer as well – we don't see or hear anything from the people there.
The package your parents sent on October 22 arrived, I am very grateful for it. The package with the work clothes arrived today – I don't know if there are things for me in it.
Yesterday, we had the 'first big experience,' but since it is already over, there is nothing to worry about. You don't have to worry about anything. It was announced that all the madrichim except Lini de Bruin (Lini de Bruin has a different kind of 'Sperrung' – no hachshara) and Fokki (who is currently in the hospital) were on the deportation list. We were sure we would be on that transport; the first hours of the night were hopeless, with no chance of being rescued. And when we started walking, there was no hope of going back inside. On the way to the train, they called us back, saying we were released and not to be deported.
Later, a telegram arrived from Dr. E. Sluzker of the Jewish Council, stating that it had been decided that Frey, Werner and I were exempted, something very special, unique! This 'release stamp' from Westerbork almost cost us our necks. We kept very calm, and everything went well. The hardest part was saying goodbye to our comrades. That was very difficult for all of us – but there was great joy on Monday when we returned unexpectedly, a celebration for all of us.
I can't put everything into words, but I hope someday someone will come to you and tell you about it. Anyway, we are safer now than before, you don't have to worry.
Should Wolfgang and Tzippi come to Amsterdam, you can talk to them about this. It's late, the letter has to go, so I need to end it now. I can write more often now, and naturally, I am

going to take advantage of this opportunity.
Could you send me one of those little bags, one that can be tied around the waist, for my documents? Maybe one that is made of oilcloth or something.
At this very moment, my gray coat is being taken out of the package, fantastic! This will allow me to keep my winter coat. Will you keep my picture? I would have loved to see it. I'll let you know when it's possible to send it here.

Lots of sweet wishes and kisses,

YourErnst

Warm greetings to the Levisons, to the Oldenbooms and to your parents.
Yesterday, another one of your letters arrived. I put it somewhere, but I have no time to look for it now.
Reply as soon as possible.

Westerbork, December 11, 1942 (Letter no. 6 from Westerbork)

My dearest Ilse,

Finally, I have another opportunity to write to you, albeit briefly.
I received your letters and was so happy with them. You cannot imagine what it means to me here in Westerbork to receive a letter from you, to receive something personal, to touch something dear to you.
Your packages have also arrived. There are no words to describe how grateful all of us here are to you. If you only knew how much you are helping us with all the little things you pack... you solve many of our worries. None of our other friends help us as quickly and efficiently as you do.
My dear, everyone here speaks highly of you.
The Chanuka days were quite fun – every night, there was something. We organized two evenings – just imagine, one evening, even the commander of Westerbork, Gemmeker, came to visit us. On the last evening, all the chalutzim and all the youth movements were here, well over a hundred people. So you see, we organize our life quite well here. All our friends are together, and they are doing well.
A few of our comrades are distancing themselves, including Merry, who miraculously found an 'idiot.' Frey and Batya are also keeping to themselves, which is very disappointing.
Today, again, many people from your neighborhood arrived. Of course, I do not yet know who they are.
I am going to visit Mr. H. tomorrow; I suppose he will be here again tomorrow.
Apart from that, I don't have much to tell you – in general, I am doing well. I had the 'camp sickness' (dysentery), fortu-

nately not badly and also only for a few days.
All of us have become a little more nervous, but that, too, is bearable.
As far as the future is concerned, we are currently at ease here and quite calm. Our status is currently positive.
Things are probably looking good with Otto Sluizer as well, even though it seemed bad at first. I think of you a lot and also long for you very much. Visiting me here is almost impossible, and for various reasons, I wouldn't want you to do so, but I hope we can see each other soon.
The clogs are no longer urgent – I have new ones. It might be nice if you could keep a pair of clogs for me as a spare. I'll write to you when I need them, that would be really good. The foot patches are fine. Could you send me my leather jacket? It may come in handy here, but please don't send it by mail – for now, I have enough and actually insufficient space for it all.
If you have a small to medium case (not as big as your blue one), that would be good, but it must be an old case.
I just received your package of Benelac milk powder. Thank you very much. We desperately need it here. The day before yesterday, the four packages with the coat hangers, etc., arrived. In fact, we are getting all the packages at the moment.
This evening, I was told that my uncle from Wiesbaden, who did a lot for us in the past and whom we loved very much, had died suddenly.[26]

---

26 This uncle, Erich Cosmann, the brother of Ernst's father, was a notary until he was no longer allowed to practice that profession in 1933. He was arrested during Kristallnacht and taken to Buchenwald concentration camp, where he was severely abused. After he was released, he had to support himself and his family by working as a road worker and in a cardboard factory. When he had to report to the Gestapo in November 1942, he said, 'They will not get me a second time.' He drank poison and died

My dearest, I wish you the very best, lots of love and kisses,
Your Ernst

Dear Ilse,

Finally, I have a chance to thank you for all the things you have sent us.
You have no idea how much we need it, thank you very much. What is the situation like here? You know. The packages we get from you contribute a lot to our well-being (although it sounds a little 'dramatic'), but it really is. Thank you very much on behalf of everyone, especially from us women.

Stay healthy,
Hadassah (group from Elden)

Please forgive me; my letter is a little weird – I cannot tell you how often I am disturbed while writing. It is impossible to write undisturbed for a period, not even for a moment..
Westerbork, December 13, 1942 (Letter no. 7 from Westerbork)

My dearest Ilse,

This letter has still not been sent, so I can add to it, although there is not much time.
From 11 a.m. to 3 p.m., we made sandwiches. Hadassah and I are with the Samson family, and we handed out cakes and fruit. This is my job; I am responsible for the comrades' inventory, and we share everything! As for me, this work is not easy, and especially not the responsibility. Almost every evening between 8 p.m. and 9:30 p.m., we work under heavy pressure. I am already very skilled in cutting and buttering bread – I can even cut a sausage

by eye in equal sizes for the required number of sandwiches. Although it is a lot of work, it is also enjoyable, so I feel like I am doing my bit for society this way. What is also wonderful is that I am spending the evening in a heated room. In the main camp, where the elderly live, there is a central heating system connected to the steam system. That alone is worth a lot.

A lawyer, Aaron, visited me today – I couldn't remember him. He gave me your greetings and told me about your requests. I considered everything, but I want to wait a while longer. I also spoke to Mr. Samson about us, but he cannot help us.

Your letter of December 11 arrived – I am delighted with it – also my many thanks for the packages. Sometimes, it makes me very uncomfortable to constantly send you requests and give you so much work, but you must understand that in our situation, it is very difficult to be independent and to make do with what we DO have.

We have more or less gotten used to life here; we have regular living habits, especially in terms of food, and the relationship between us is excellent. We try to make everything as homely as possible. On Sabbath and Sundays (not meaning a day off – but because we don't work Sunday afternoons, unlike Sabbath), there is a tablecloth on our table. We sit, we read (rarely), and we are also tailors.

The women share the other half of our barracks. We, the men, are also often on the women's side.

By the way, speaking of 'house,' there must be a game among my papers, 'Mikado,' thin wooden sticks. It says: *Eins, zwei, drei, wenn's wackelt ists vorbei*. We want to play this game here. Could you send it with someone?

Cigarettes, send those just for Ella. Mr. H. will only take one pack.

We got clogs. We needed them badly, and finally have no more wet feet and no more dripping shoes. Sometimes, it rains here

for weeks at a time, and everything turns into a big swamp. My new shoes are fantastic.
Now I have to end this letter. I have to hand out bread, and then we will have ourselves disinfected against lice. Everyone must go there, even if our group is not affected.
Many loving regards,

Your Ernst

Many warm regards and kind wishes – Werner Ahlfeld
Kind regards from me too – Gitta Lonsky – Elden
Also from me, kind regards and thanks for everything, dear Ilse – Eshu – Elden
Also from me – Asher Gerlich – Elden.

Dear Ilse,

Erco finally remembered that I wanted to write something to you too. First of all, thank you so much for the handkerchiefs. I was so happy with them and used them right away. This shows you just how much I needed them. It was such a great surprise. I already thanked Erco, and I can also thank you directly.
I must tell you, you raised that boy (Erco) very well. He takes good care of all his things and mends his socks himself. The sewing equipment you sent helps us a lot. On behalf of all the women and girls, we thank you for the packages you send all the time; we are always very pleased with them, and we really need everything.
Lots of warm regards,

Rozijntje

Chanuka

On December 11, 1942, Ernst wrote: 'The Chanuka days were quite fun – each evening, there was something. We organized two evenings – just imagine, one evening, even the commander of Westerbork, Gemmeker, came to visit us.' Prisoner Paul Siegel was also present that evening. He later recalled more details: 'Another experience that contributed to strengthening the camaraderie was the successful Hanukkah party celebrated in our barracks and attended by all the members and almost all the barracks' residents. Ernest ('Erco') Cosmann, one of the leaders in Elden, gave a lecture in which he told how the Jews suffered under the yoke of the Greek occupiers and about the heroic deeds of the Maccabees who led the Jewish people and managed to liberate the country. It just so happened that at that moment, camp commander Gemmeker and his entourage entered the barracks for a routine check. We all jumped into position, as was required whenever the commander or anyone else in German uniform entered the barracks. Gemmeker ordered us to proceed. We sat back down, and Ernst resumed his lecture. Gemmeker remained in the barracks for some time. Later, we learned that after leaving the barracks, he asked the Jews accompanying him to explain the meaning of the Hanukkah festival and wanted to know more about our group. It turned out that he was impressed by the atmosphere that prevailed among us. Since then, the group has held an exceptional position.'

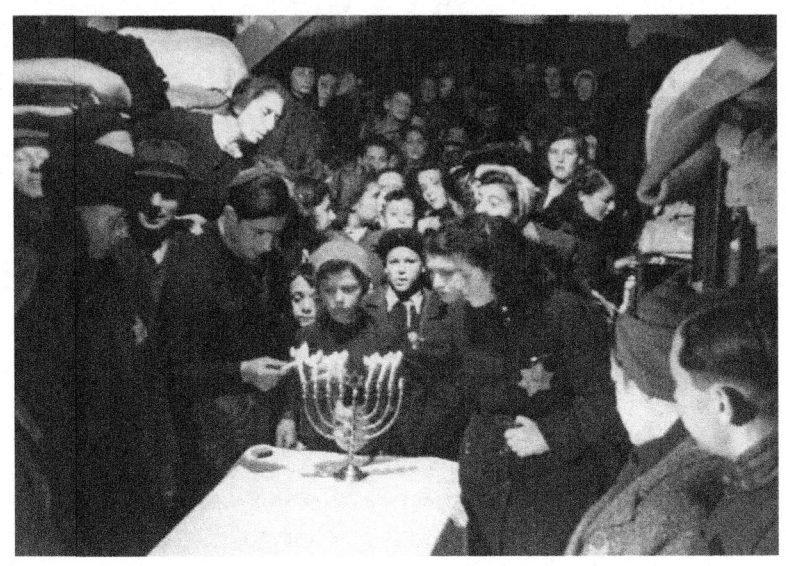

The Chanukah celebration in barrack 64 in Westerbork (photo: Rudolf Breslauer, National Archives)

Westerbork, December 23, 1942 (Letter no. 8 from Westerbork)

My dearest Ilse,

Even though I don't have much to report, I'm going to quickly fill a page. At least you'll receive a sign of life from me.
I couldn't write to you on the official writing day because I had to express my condolences to my aunt about my uncle's death, which I did on a twelve-line postcard.
Also, there is no fixed writing day every two weeks; the writing days are not regular and are often at long intervals. It is impossible to rely on or know when these days will be.
I received the packages and the letters, and again, I was so very happy with them.
I found your last couple of letters a little happier; it gave a more relaxed impression, which made me happy. You see, my dear Ilse, we have to accept the given situation as it is; there is no point in complaining. After all, it could have been worse. I have genuinely come to terms with this reality.
I was glad to hear that you spent such a nice Sunday at Oldenboom. I am really jealous of you. The Oldenbooms are wonderful people.
The 'Mikado' game arrived today and was received with great joy.
Mau Reichenberger, a Deventer hakhshara activist who, so far, has been exempted as an official of the Jewish Council, is coming tonight. He was given permission to visit Westerbork in that capacity. He was 'our man' in Arnhem and thus also 'our man' in Elden. He was also a member of the board in Elden.
In any case, the 'Mikado' game will have to wait until another evening. We will have fun with it at Christmas.
From Thursday afternoon until Monday morning, we are

free. However, we might have to work on Saturday. In any case, enough time to get a good rest.

What silly questions you ask: 'Do I think about you sometimes?' Of course, rest assured, my thoughts are always with you, yet I'm glad we are NOT together here – even though it's not that bad here. In the evening, we sit with the women, where it is more sociable and also more cheerful, which is good for the general mood. The group has changed slightly; some new people have joined us.

Kela and Eshu's friends are disappointing; Martha, Dini, Frey, Batya and Merry. Martha and Dini are behaving ... dismally! Claartje, too. They flirt with all sorts; the community does not interest them, as if it does not exist here. They are only part of the group when there's food.

Are you coming to Amsterdam soon? If at all possible, you should visit Ella. She is ill, and Werner would like to hear from someone else how she is doing, maybe write about it.

After everything I have written, I really don't know what else to add. Writing is difficult here, with all the interruptions, and forgive me if the sound of my letters is not as cordial as you might expect.

When I am alone, I remember all that I wanted to tell you, but when I am in here with all the hustle and bustle going on and all the noise and a thousand distractions, it is just impossible to concentrate for even a minute, and then the thread of my story instantly disappears.

My dearest, you know my intentions, what I mean and how much I love you, even if I can't always express it.

Now I must end this letter.

Many loving regards and many kisses,

Your Ernst

Mau Reichenberger just arrived – can you send cigarette paper? Maybe it is in my leather jacket?
Happy New Year – hope it will be a better one than the last year.
Hanna'tje, the daughter of Lini de Bruin, was very happy with the package, and so was Mrs. Samson.

Westerbork, January 7, 1943 (Letter no. 9 from Westerbork)

My dearest Ilse,

Today, I can write to you again, and I will, of course, use this opportunity to do so.
First of all, my thanks and everyone's thanks for all the packages. Everything arrived fine, and as always, it is all very useful. We have not lacked any food lately, and we have not gone hungry for a long time. The opposite is true; I think I have gained weight. My 'knickerbocker' can no longer close. Every evening, there are some leftovers from lunch and sandwiches from the comrades. I am now lucky enough to work for a farmer near the camp – we sort potatoes for the camp kitchen.
Eshu also works here and cooks a pot full of stew every day. It helps a lot, and we can put food aside.
Perhaps you will be interested to know that I have now been appointed as the responsible 'group leader' of two groups leaving camp to work for farmers in the area.
This is not important because of the 'honor,' but still very important to me. It shows that I have a good name with the

director for all 'outside' work, which is an important thing here. The advantage of it is that I get to go to the farmer much more than others – you know how much I like doing farm work – without many people around me, without crowds. I assume I will be doing this work for at least a few weeks.

You probably overimagine how cold it is here – it really isn't! Sure it's cold at work, but with the clogs and with the leather jacket (thank you very much, I really need this jacket) I can definitely bear the cold – I don't wear gloves, I wear half gloves without fingertips.

Inside is fine; it's really not that cold – I sleep in pajamas + a pullover and without an undershirt. I have two blankets, and I'm nice and warm.

Please, no unwarranted worry! No need.

Greetings from Dr. Aarons – he is doing well. I tried my hardest for them; I hope it helped a bit, but I'm not sure.

Our laundry gets washed for us here in the laundromat. Maybe we can send our laundry to the laundromat in Apeldoorn again; it was extremely good.

Hadassah washes the socks for me; maybe you can send laundry detergents again? I mend my socks myself (only here... beware, I won't do it in the future...).

Rozijntje takes care of the rest of my laundry. She usually sorts everything out as soon as the laundry comes back from the laundromat. I get everything back neatly folded. She takes really good care of me; I often have to stop her from attempting to mend my socks.

I was glad to hear that your days in Amsterdam were more or less good, although I always hear here that the situation in Amsterdam is terrible.

I am also glad that the relationship with your parents is good now.

Mau Reichenberger tells me that you look good and are doing

well, which makes me very happy.
Apart from everything I have written, there really isn't anything new to tell you. All our comrades are also doing well, except that we are all a little nervous, which is no surprise in this sea of people.
My dearest, I must end this letter, I have a lot to take care of today.

All the best, many warm regards and kisses,

Your Ernst

Greetings to Oldenboom, thanks for their letter. The Mikado game has gained many fans here. Of the packages you mentioned, two arrived today with the sewing utensils. Hadassah was overjoyed with them and thanks you on behalf of all of them. She says Rozijntje is very happy with the soap box. Don't send carrots; we have plenty of them here!

Westerbork, January 13, 1943 (Letter no. 10 from Westerbork)

My dearest Ilse,

As always, my heartfelt thanks for all the packages and letters; I was overcome with joy.
What can I say to convince you? I am not hungry, nor am I cold. I am not freezing! I am positive that I even gained weight, and I was never cold (not even once). We did have two really cold days, but I was well dressed.
It was also nice and warm inside; we wore no more than usual.

The hygiene warning is really unnecessary. Of course I am very careful... what do you think of me...? We also warned the others about it, and I 'lectured' one of the boys about it today. I got the gloves; did I not tell you? I thought I did. They are excellent and wonderfully warm. I use them under ski gloves. The pullover is also lovely, but it hasn't been cold enough to wear it yet. I would have sweated terribly if I had worn it. Please thank the Oldenboom family on my behalf.
You can't visit the Samson family: A. It's impossible. B. It's no fun for me at all because you can talk to them by yourself, so such a visit is totally useless.
Maybe someone can explain it to you sometime, but I don't need money here. My only expense is for stamps, and we have a common fund for that.
The packages I hadn't confirmed arrived a day later. As always, everyone was very grateful for them. Everything was very useful. The women were especially pleased to have their personal requests fulfilled.
I am glad that you are acquiring the personality of a hakhshara woman more and more, which is how I predicted it to you a long time ago. Whether that this will make me love you less ... surely you don't believe that.
Apart from all this, there really isn't much news around here. Life here is boring, more or less the same day in and day out. Sunday night, there was an information evening about the youth care that is now being held here.
We heard an excellent violin concerto; it was very special also because it was the first time I heard good music here. I also recited a piece.
People want me to take up a training position for the youth group. I don't know if I'm going to do it; it's too difficult to commit to obligations here. I have almost no free time anyway, and what little I have, I need to relax.

Besides, you can imagine that I also have other things on my mind besides talking to people. But if no one else can do it, then I will have to anyway. Working with the youth here is more important than anywhere else.

I cannot understand, cannot justify, your complaints about your work. In my eyes, your life is a life of luxury. Had I been allowed to be 'out there' like you, I would give anything to be able to do whatever. If you have to work a little longer on Sunday, just remember that we usually have to work on all Sundays; even the Sabbath is a regular working day. The work you do is most certainly not comparable to our work here and certainly less demanding. You really shouldn't complain; we know that our situation is still pretty good. It all could have been much, much worse.

Now I have to finish.
Many loving regards and kisses

From Ernst, who loves you so very much.

Meeting up with Ilse

During his stay in Westerbork, Ernst and Ilse manage to meet up twice. The first time is when he was sent to Apeldoorn. That is where the Jewish psychiatric hospital Het Apeldoornsche Bosch is located, which Ernst has visited many times before when he still lived in Elden. On January 20, 1943, it is evacuated with the help of the Ordedienst of the Westerbork camp. Nearly 1,200 patients and 50 staff members are taken directly to Auschwitz in a freight train, where they are murdered immediately upon arrival. A week later, Ernst arrives with a group from Westerbork to clean up the building and pack up all the valuables left behind for shipment to Germany. The hospital is to be turned into an Erholungsheim for the Waffen-SS. Despite the horrific events in Apeldoorn, his stay there feels like a welcome break from his life in Westerbork. He wrote, 'Although the work there is terrible, it feels just like being on vacation.'

Ilse arranges to be smuggled in by a Dutch military police officer and finally sees Ernst again for the first time in four months.

The final time that Ilse and Ernst see each other will be in early August when Ilse visits Ernst at the farm where he works outside the camp.

My dearest Ilse,

Many dear regards from a pleasant 4-day trip to Apeldoorn. All of us here on the train are in great spirits now. We do not yet know what work we are going to be doing. Other than that, everything is fine. You can send letters to Heinz Schlesinger and Arnold Koller (Barracks 64). Many regards,

Your Ernst

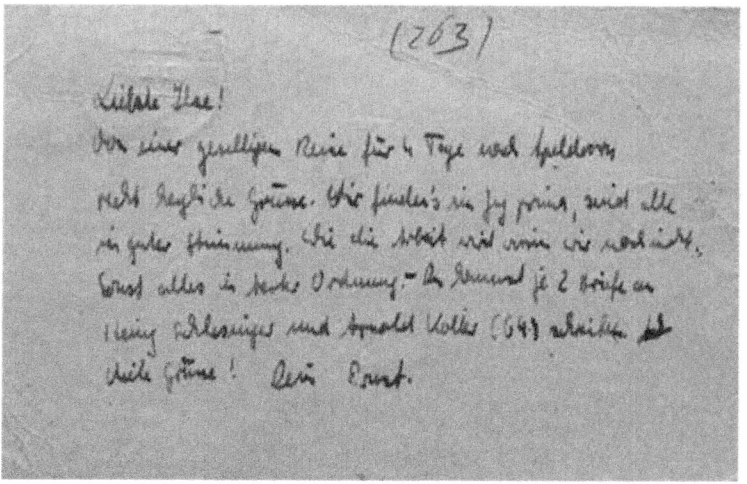

A postcard, sent from Zwolle station, en route from Westerbork to Apeldoorn, January 27, 1943.

Apeldoorn, January 31, 1943 (Letter no. 1 from Apeldoorn)

My dearest Ilse,

Once again, for as long as I still have the opportunity, I would like to write a few quick words to you.
First of all, I want to tell you how happy I was to see you again and to be with you, my dearest. Those were the most beautiful hours I have had in a long time. You can be sure that I will remember and enjoy these hours for a very long time.
It is wonderful, despite everything we are going through, to suddenly be able to see the person I love so much, to be next to her, to be with her.
I hope the trip home went safely and without incident. I am quite worried and look forward to hearing that you arrived home safely.
The seemingly beautiful days here end tomorrow afternoon (Monday). We will return to Westerbork again, to an environment that is now going to look much uglier for us after we were allowed to enjoy some freedom and comfort for a short time (also seemingly... very ironic, lugubrious, macabre). It was 'granted' to us, so to speak.
But we will get used to it again, and after a while, everything will remain a pleasant memory.
I thoroughly enjoyed these days – first and foremost, of course, because I got to see you.
Although the work there was terrible, it felt like I was on vacation. Nevertheless, I feel like we have regained more new strength, a bit of freshness and courage.
The very best, my darling. Perhaps, now that you have seen me, it will be easier for me to convince you that I am doing quite well.

Many loving thoughts and a thousand kisses,
Your Ernst

Warm regards to all our acquaintances – and very special regards to the Levison and Oldenboom families

Westerbork, February 8, 1943 (Letter no. 11 from Westerbork)

My dearest Ilse,

Today, we have a writing day. I immediately took advantage of it to fill my page. I received your letter; thank you very much. Heinz thanks you too and was pleased to receive your regards. On Monday at 3 a.m., we returned from Apeldoorn, and everyone welcomed us with great joy. It was as if we were returning from a lengthy, weeks-long journey.
The morning after that, we immediately resumed our regular work. There is not much to tell other than the same old, same old: We work as usual and get soaking wet every now and then... All the parcels arrived, thank you very much!
The rags for mending clothes are very good. We will use them a lot; they come in handy.
Three parcels from your parents arrived. Please write to your parents that the women and I use it – really great. The girls and women are very embarrassed. I hear they lack everything; could you do something about it?
Eshu also has a private request: Her boyfriend's birthday is January 15. Could you get her some handkerchiefs? He needs them bitterly. I don't know when this letter will reach you, but it won't be a disaster if the handkerchiefs arrive after his birthday.

Have you heard that Mrs. Samson's baby died last Saturday? The baby had jaundice and something else. The first few days were very sad, but they are bravely trying to get over it. We made sure that a parcel of baby clothes meant for the little baby goes to Heinz Wertheim's wife – they are expecting a baby in a few months. If Mrs. Samson had received the parcel, it might have made her sad again. The Levison family took another parcel to the hospital. Don't write to her about it; that will reopen the wound that needs to heal.

Could you make a copy (about 6 or 7) of the photo of us with the friends of the hachshara in the Elden orchard? Some friends no longer have a copy.

I really have nothing more to tell you.

Loving regards,

Your Ernst

Yesterday, I started taking vitamins. Let's see if I become big and strong now.

Could you get a strong pocket knife that is not too small for Honki? I think it's impossible, but I'll write to you about it.

Dear Ilse,

It's been quite a long time since I received the blouse from you, but I actually didn't know it came from you, so I couldn't thank you. It looks good on me, and it's lovely. Kind regards,

Rozijntje
Kind regards and all the best, Honki
Kind regards from Eshu

Kind regards, Arnold Koller
Kind regards and all the best, Hadassah
Dear Ilse, Ella wrote to me that you had called her and had a lot to tell her.
Warm regards, Werner.

Westerbork, February 14, 1943 (Letter no. 12 from Westerbork)

My darling Ilse,

I want to write you a couple of lines quickly and, first of all, tell you that I have received all the letters and parcels. As always, I was very happy with them.
The rubber boots are great; you can't imagine how handy they come in here.
I am very grateful to the comrades who sent them.
A while ago, you wrote about shoes for 'Rozijntje.' Have you sent them yet? In any case, they have not arrived! Is it possible to send them soon?
I think that you have probably received my last letter from last Monday by now.
Werner at least got a reply from Amsterdam. It sometimes takes a long time for letters to make it through censorship here.
There is not much new I can tell you. Of course, we have the occasional excitement, but our life here is a mundane routine. Last night at Shlomo Samson's, we listened to great records. Can you imagine hearing a real concert again after four months? I was 'starved' for good music. Especially since everything around us here is so ugly, and then you suddenly get to enjoy something beautiful. I have been re-invited to Beethoven's violin concerto this afternoon.
Recently, I received mail from old friends in Bielefeld. I also received a letter from my brother Heinz; he is doing well. I have not heard anything from my mother for a long time.
That is all I have to tell you.
Another big thank you for the hair growth product that I actually use regularly and secretly.

Many kind regards and kisses,

Your Ernst

The women desperately need sanitary pads – can you get them? Are these still available?

At the bottom of the letter, added later by Tzippi Fränkel, who traveled back and forth between Westerbork and the Jewish Council as a courier and had apparently smuggled this letter with him, the following is written:

Dear Ilse,

Erco asked me to tell you that for everyone who tries to escape, 10 people are deported as punishment.

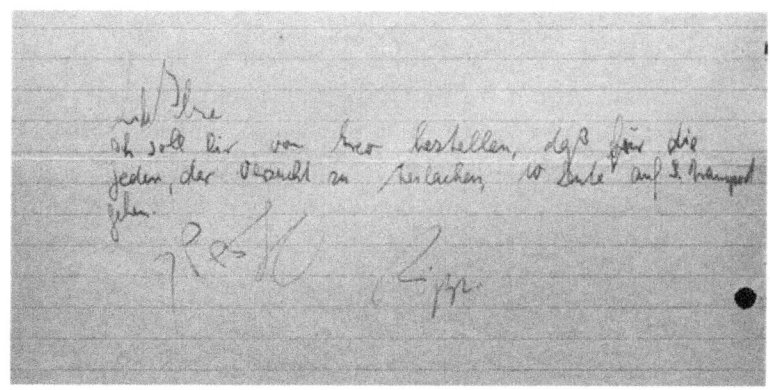

Westerbork, February 21, 1943 (Letter no. 13 from Westerbork)

My darling Ilse,

I am already in bed, the light is still on, and I am not that tired on Sunday evenings, so I want to write to you.
The letters and parcels have arrived and, as always, are received by everyone with great appreciation. People are so happy with your parcels. The women were especially grateful this time, and thank you sincerely.
You complain that I hardly write a full page, but keep in mind that you are not the only one reading the letter. Despite everything, it is very hard to tell you things. I cannot write anything that will cause us tension or agitation here.
You may hear some alarming news from here, but don't worry about us; we can still be optimistic about the future, as far as that is possible here.
While it is true that we had some major concerns over the past few days – the situation was not looking good – we are all looking forward to the future calmly and peacefully. We resolve to believe that even the very worst will not be that bad. However, it has not come to that yet, and no one knows what is going to happen. In any case, people are slaving away greatly for us...
We are working on the moors; the weather is a bit better, and we are also enjoying the work. Yesterday was great; it was a proper spring day.
The weather here is usually worse than in other parts of the Netherlands.
I am now reading Madame Curie, a great book. Do you know it? My bed is right under a light bulb, so I can read every night

– I sorely missed reading.
It is now 11.15 p.m., and everyone is asleep; one only hears snoring. Our friends are doing pretty well, although some women have less 'spirit.' A new couple, Hadassah and Ludwig Hoffmann, has been here for a few days now. Due to a lack of time, Hadassah no longer helps me supply our friends. Hans Auerbach helps out now.
Fokki is wearing an engagement ring now that his bride (16 years old) is no longer here. She has gone to Barneveld with her family. Apart from that, I have no more gossip to share.
Bella Shenkar arrived yesterday and is now in our barracks; I don't know what will happen to her. Kela is in hospital with angina, and Dini is in hospital with jaundice. Betty has been discharged from the hospital after having recovered from an illness of which I have forgotten the name, and she also had a gum infection. Tamar is in hospital with jaundice.
Fokki has been discharged from the hospital with an illness that neither he nor we know what it was. Eshu and Rozel Kerzer are in bed with chicken pox but are already recovering. It all sounds dangerous, but it's really not; you go in and out of the hospital much faster here than usual.
In recent weeks, many have been ill, presumably related to the bad weather. I am perfectly healthy and feel fine, as you know! Were you in Amsterdam? Ella wrote that it was your intention. Werner and I constantly exchange news from the letters you send us.
Hadassah asks for a 'fine' comb, but not made of wood – she has one of those. I think it is impossible to get the one she wants. The women here need it. They are afraid of having their heads shaved in case lice are discovered. For now, that hasn't happened to anyone here.
I don't have any requests for a change.
Please pass on my warm regards to Oldenboom, and many

thanks for the parcels.
Warm regards also to the Levison family. We all thank them for everything they send us.

Lots of love and kisses

Your Ernst

This week, I received a letter from my mother; she is doing well.

Westerbork, February 23, 1943 (Letter no. 14 from Westerbork)

My darling Ilse,

There is not much news; I just want to reply to your postcard from Amsterdam.
Don't worry about us unnecessarily. At present, our position here is reassuring and without much change. We have good reasons to believe that our near future is not in imminent danger. I don't know if Tzippi talked to you about it, but in any case, you will hear it from me again now.
Today, I received your letter dated February 17.
Your fear of becoming strangers to each other is unfounded; why do you even think that?
I feel exactly the opposite. Stay calm, my little one.
To everyone's delight, all the parcels from Amsterdam arrived today. It sure was a huge job to gather all these things. Why were you in Amsterdam, anyway? If you are in Amsterdam again soon, please try to get me a windbreaker from Ella, one

produced by J.C.B., but there is really no hurry, so don't go to too much trouble.
I cannot confirm the parcels yet; we usually get them on Wednesdays. Other than that, I am doing well.

Your Ernst – who thinks of you all the time

Almost forgot:
I sent you a parcel today with two pairs of pants that I could not mend here. Is it bad of me to ask you to mend them for me? They started mending the brown pair here, and that's why they frayed. The woman who wanted to mend these pants for me was transferred to another job, and it will take ages before I get them back from the 'sewing workshop' here. It's not urgent; I have enough pants. Can you sew a pocket on the back of the brown pants for me – I simply don't have room for my wallet with the necessary certificates.

February 24, continued.

Today, I finally received your letter, which I have been looking forward to so much, and Werner too; we didn't know if you and Ella had calmed down by now. We are glad you were not feeling anxious for too long. Although, it was long enough.
H. talks too much, although there is some truth in it, but we are in a special situation.
I would like to know how Jaap is doing; I'm glad he is recovering. Should you see him, give him best wishes from all of us.
Eight parcels arrived here today, and everyone was overjoyed, especially the women. The shoes for Rozijntje are fine; she is very happy with them.
The copies of the photo of the friends from Elden are great;

you should have seen how happy everyone was – please make 5 more copies.
The remainder of this letter has become longer than I thought – everyone sends you their warmest regards.
Otto Sluizer and Heini Fraenkel just shouted across the bunkbeds, 'Enough for today.'

Many sweet thoughts and kisses,

Your Ernst

I will write to Hans soon.

Divide-and-rule politics and false hope

The 'Jewish town of Westerbork, the Jewish capital of the Netherlands,' according to Jacques Presser, had a highly variable population. The vast majority of residents stayed there for only a few days or weeks, and others for many months or even years. Pioneer Paul Siegel wrote: 'Westerbork was literally a big human warehouse. People came in and went out as if they were goods. On some days, when more came than went, the crowdedness was unbearable. Thousands squeezed into the more than overcrowded camp, and in some barracks, three people had to share a double bed. We had become the most stable group in the camp and were therefore envied by many.'

A train usually left from Westerbork every Monday and Friday, from the beginning of 1943, every Tuesday. In total, between July 1942 and September 1944, 65 trains went to Auschwitz and 19 to Sobibór, always with about 1,000 people on board. In addition, 11 more deportations left for Bergen-Belsen and 17 for Theresienstadt. The inhabitants of the camp did not know what awaited them in the East, but it was clear that it was worse than where they were. So they did everything they could to stay in Westerbork as long as possible. The number of German SS guarding the entire camp was no more than 20 to 30 men. The way in which a small number of Germans managed to keep a large number of people who had little to lose under their thumb was through a clever policy of divide-and-conquer, bestowing false hopes and suddenly taking them away again. The residents of Westerbork were constantly working to obtain the proper stamps on their camp passes or to acquire a place on one list or another in order to be safeguarded from deportation to the East that way.

The camp leadership took advantage of the dislike that the German and Dutch Jews had for each other. The Germans blamed the Dutch for the fact that when they came to the Netherlands as refugees before the occupation, they had not been properly received but had been placed in Westerbork. The Dutch envied the Germans with their privileged position in the camp. The German Jews were the first to arrive, so they held the most important positions in the camp.

They had the 'Ordedienst' (OD – body of order service) that functioned as the camp's police. This consisted of German Jews, and the Dutch called them the 'Jewish SS.' The day-to-day management of the camp consisted of a staff of German Jews (the alte Lagerinsassen) headed by German-Jewish refugee Kurt Schlesinger.

No one knew exactly what Auschwitz was. The Germans called it a labor camp. It was clear, however, that things were a lot worse there than in the relatively 'free' Westerbork. The permanent fear of being deported loomed over the residents of the camp like a dark cloud. The train full of people to an unknown destination that first departed twice a week and later only on Tuesdays was a constant reminder of this. The weekly rhythm of the train determined life in the camp.

An important part of the diabolical divide-and-conquer system introduced by Commander Gemmeker was the list of people who were not directly deported. For many different reasons, people could be on a list of barred people, and the prisoners did everything they could to get on such a list. They spend all their free time and money on it. For example, there was the Calmeyer list of people who had objected to their registration as 'full Jews' because they claimed to have 'Aryan' ancestry, there was a list of baptized Jews, of World War I veterans, of people of foreign nationality and so on. One of the most important lists was the 'List of 2000,' the list of indispensable prisoners: doctors, nurses, members of the Order Service, artisans, cooks and farmers. The 'alte Kampinsassen' were on it, as well as Erco's hakhshara group. Ernst's group believed they were indispensable because of the work they did inside and outside the camp. Their function gave an exemption from deportation, but such a Sperrung was always 'bis auf weiteres.' Philip Mechanicus cynically wrote, 'A list is a collection of Jews who are going to be deported at a certain time. Such a list could suddenly be declared invalid – platzen (implode), as it was called in camp jargon. Every Monday night, it was possible that even people who felt safe would be sent to Auschwitz the next day.'

Shlomo Samson described the strange ambiguity in the camp: 'Everybody hated Westerbork and everything it represented, and everybody was willing to make any sacrifice to stay in Westerbork and not be deported. People clung to every possibility, even doubtful ones, and paid to get on new lists that would then 'platzen' sooner or later on a deportation night. They tried everything, and every day could be conclusive.'

The List of 2000 was also suddenly cut in half. A thousand people, including many Palestine pioneers, who had felt safe, were earmarked for deportation. Ernst, however, could keep up his hope of being spared because he had a certificate for emigration to Palestine. The Jewish Council, the organization that represented the Jewish population to the Germans and had to organize anti-Jewish measures, issued them, among others, to people whose parents lived there.

Ernst's mother and his brother lived in Palestine, so he was eligible. The Jewish Council checked and, through the Amsterdam branch of the Dutch Red Cross, sent telegrams to the Jewish Agency in Palestine, which represented Jews in the British Mandate Territory of Palestine. The Jewish Agency, in turn, notified the Jewish Council through the Red Cross. The applicant received a confirmation signed by Gertrude van Tijn of the Committee for Jewish Refugees or her secretary, Dr. Kurt Albersheim. Ernst's card from the Jewish Council's cartography reads 'possesses Albersheim Decl.': a medical certificate indicating that he was physically fit for pioneer work. Only the letters RK (Red Cross) appear on the back of the card, probably indicating that a message had been received from the Red Cross.

The Germans were willing to let a limited group go to Palestine to trade them with the British authorities there for a group of ethnic Germans, the 'Templars,' who had been living in Palestine since the nineteenth century. Since the British only allowed people with certificates, the Germans had to therefore choose people from this group.

A drawing, made by Erco, of the interior of a barracks. The three-story bunk beds on which everyone also had to keep their personal belongings can be seen clearly. (coll. Ghetto Fighters House Museum, Israel) Ernst's card from the Jewish Council's cartography shows, among other things, that he was 'gesperrt' (blocked) because of his position in the camp.

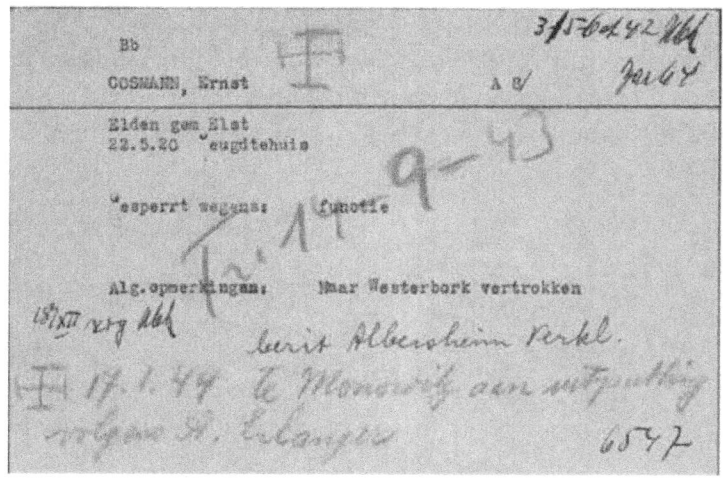

Ernst wrote on March 9, 1943, that they had received certificates, which meant they would be spared from being deported for the time being. However, in July 1943, the Albersheim declaration was already declared invalid again, so many, including Ernst, were still eligible to be sent to Auschwitz. Of the 1,500 people who had been spared in order to be sent to Palestine, 350 remained. Yet, by the end of the year, nearly 1,300 Palestine certificates were issued again, many in the names of people who had already been deported to Auschwitz in the meantime, like Ernst and his group. Jacques Presser wrote: 'Now and then, when the deportation at Westerbork was short of a couple of hundred people, hundreds of people for whom the Palestine certificate numbers had arrived too late, also disappeared; the mindset of certain official bodies, which had already been flagged several times, cost the lives of a group of Palestine pioneers.' Ernst was one of them.

From January 1944, however, people left Westerbork via Bergen-Belsen for Palestine, who were exchanged for the ethnic Germans living there. Of the 1297 certificate holders, 222 eventually arrived in Palestine. Among them were Lini de Bruin and Grete

Lehmann, who they called Rozijntje. For a small group, those certificates brought salvation, but for most, only false hope. Those who were exchanged were women, children, and some elderly men. By order of the Germans, no boys and men between the ages of 16 and 45 were included.

Westerbork, March 9, 1943 (Letter no. 15 from Westerbork)

My darling Ilse,

At last, I have the opportunity to write to you again. I really want to write as much and extensively as possible.
First, thank you again for the many parcels and letters. Everyone was so pleased again. Everything is very practical. We can use all of it except for the strange bags; we don't quite know what to do with those. We had quite some difficulty getting rid of the strange material (shirts for the dead – or whatever it was). Everything else was excellent; people literally grabbed things from our hands.
Were the boots meant for a particular person? I gave them to Honki, who has the biggest feet around here.
A special thanks for the parcel for my 'anniversary' of 7 years of hachshara. Very nice of you to remember. You really made me very happy. I like the book, and I read it in one go. I would hardly want to remember this day. I said it was my 7 fat years so far – I hope the 7 lean years don't come.
By the way, the parcel arrived on March 1. The pants fit really well, just the way I wanted them to, and I enjoy wearing them. Regarding the question of whether it is advisable to go to the farmer or to stay with Levison, I think you should stay with

the Levison family. First of all, I don't think you can just leave them considering they have helped both of us so much, with money and a lot of other things. They are very cordial and generous with everything we need. I think it would be ungrateful to leave them.

But on the other hand, if you feel that from a safety point of view, you will be better protected at the farm, then you unfortunately have to leave the Levisons. The important thing is to avoid danger. It's hard to judge from where I am. In any case, I don't think it matters much whether you are on hachshara a little more or a little less. Now is not the time to start a regular hachshara; you should put that on hold for now.

Werner has requested a vacation, and I hope he gets it – I'll let you know in advance so you can meet him and talk with him.

Work is quite pleasant now because the spring weather is lovely. I spent another few days with our group at the farm, and it was great. Each day, we bring bouquets of flowers, which now adorn our tables. Hopefully, we will be there again next week. Tomorrow night, certificates will be distributed, which will allow us to leave our barracks briefly in the evening between 7 p.m. and 8 p.m. We waited a long time for this, about two weeks. It was really very inconvenient that we had to finish sandwiches by 7 p.m. in the evening; we had to do everything at a crazy pace. Our situation remains comfortable, so there is no reason for immediate concern.

Our working hours are a little longer now, from 7:15 a.m. to 6 p.m., with a one-hour lunch break. Starting tomorrow, we will stay outside all day, and the packed lunch will be delivered to us outside in the field.

I speak to the Aharons from time to time. They always send you and the Levisons their regards.

Give my warmest regards to Oldenboom, and thank them for

all the parcels that arrived. I don't write to them because I think it is better if I don't; it's safer for them.
The women thank you for the sanitary towels. For now, they have enough in stock, so don't send any more. You shouldn't have such high financial burdens either. I am also grateful to your parents for constantly sending wonderful parcels.

This week, all the parcels arrived opened. Nothing was missing at all; we got exactly what was written in the letters.
Work is a real pleasure now: springtime sunshine, we eat our lunch outside, we lie down from time to time for a nice rest, and sometimes we dash through the fields like madmen.
We do wrestling exercises – we need to get rid of excess energy. Soccer matches are held every Sunday. Elden defeated the 'individual hachshara' with 5-0.
We will celebrate Poerim with a performance by Max Ehrlich. I am on the preparation committee, and if everything goes according to plan, it will be great.
We have received certificates confirming our 'provisional' Sperrung – this is really good news; we currently have some 'assurance' (at least according to the rules here).
I have to end this letter now. Why don't you write more often? You can send more letters.
Could you arrange a pair of sunglasses for me? If possible, no green lenses, and with a metal holster if possible. I left my sunglasses in Elden. They gave us safety glasses here.
Mijn darling, all my love, sweet thoughts and kisses,

Your Ernst

We greatly enjoy being able to go outside in the evening; it is difficult to sit in the stifling air of the barracks all evening. You can also arrange many things.

Today, during a visit to the hospital, I met Mrs. Dorenberg from Apeldoorn. She normally serves on the board of the hospital, but she is ill now. Bella Shenkar is also in the hospital and will be discharged tomorrow. She has shingles and also some problems after having a molar extracted.

Entertainment in Westerbork

To make life seem as normal as possible, Commander Gemmeker encouraged all kinds of entertainment in the camp. There were variety evenings featuring cabaret, singing and dancing, and theater performances. There was plenty of talent among the prisoners. They included the jazz duo Johnny & Jones, very popular in the Netherlands, and the famous German entertainer Max Ehrlich became the leader of the Gruppe Bühne Lager Westerbork, a theater company consisting of well-known cabaret artists. There was also a symphony orchestra composed of musicians from, among others, the Concertgebouw Orchestra. There were also sports competitions: soccer, athletics and boxing.

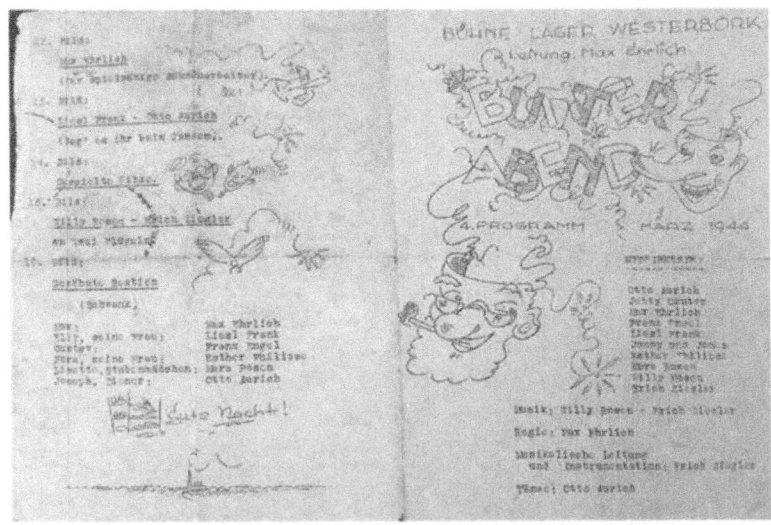

Variety evening in Westerbork

Westerbork, March 21, 1943 (Letter no. 16 from Westerbork)

My dearest Ilse,

Today, I have the opportunity to write to you again. As usual, first of all, thank you very much for the letters and parcels, which all arrived intact. The 'Poerim' parcels also arrived on time; we added them all to the festive meal, which even included a nice cake. We couldn't do much on Poerim.
We are all doing well, and we all look like we have just gotten back from a vacation. The great weather of the past few weeks is the reason we are so nicely tanned.
Work is a real pleasure at the moment.
We start the work day at 7:30 a.m., we remain outside the camp during lunch, and we return to the camp at 6:30 p.m. Lunch is brought to us, then we lie in the sun, and we read or sometimes sleep a little.
The work shirts were a huge success. Everybody wanted one, so we finally decided to hold a lottery among the comrades.
I am sitting on my bed thinking about what to write to you. There is simply nothing much to say – there aren't any topics even. The past few weeks have been relatively quiet. Perhaps we will move to another barracks in the next few days, but even that is not clear yet.
A few days ago, people from Bielefeld who have been here in Westerbork for a long time invited me over. We talked a lot, or rather SHE talked a lot. Many people and events were mentioned that I haven't thought about in a long time – it was all quite nice.
Anyway, my need for things from the past has been satisfied for now. Despite an explicit (really cordial) invitation, I doubt whether I will be visiting them in the coming weeks.

It's not clear how and when Werner will have his vacation. I hope that will be decided in the coming week. Thank you very much for the windbreaker; how did you get your hands on one so quickly? It is great, and I enjoy wearing it.
Give my warmest regards to Levison, Oldenboom, and your parents. They are all so kind to us.

Many loving regards,

Your Ernst

All our acquaintances send you their warmest regards. Rozijntje is in the hospital with jaundice and is trying hard to get out of the hospital immediately. Being ill offends her honor. As small as she is, she is stronger than all the women here. Just imagine, it is the first time in eight years that she is ill.

Dear Ilse,
I also want to write a few words to you. How are you and your family doing?
Could you send me a tube of 'Lacson' and a toothbrush?
Erco wouldn't ask for it on my behalf. He says I should ask for it myself. So, now you see, I asked for it myself.
Erco wants to continue writing, so I have to stop now.

Sincere regards,

Fannie

Westerbork, April 18, 1943 (Letter no. 17 from Westerbork)

My darling Ilse,

You haven't heard from me in a long time. To my regret, my last letter came back with a note: 'Moved to the Vught camp.'[27] I hope you have recovered a bit after the excitement of the past week. Well, at least what is meant by 'recovered' these days.
I received your postcard. It seems to me that you have been through quite a lot...
Why don't you want to go to the farmer? Or why aren't you allowed to? I hope to hear everything in detail soon; you know how anxious I am to hear all about your upcoming plans.
Everyone here is interested in you, and everyone wants to know what you are doing and how you are doing.
How are your parents doing? They are certainly very nervous, more nervous than before. I can only imagine the situation in Amsterdam. They (your parents) are probably happy to have you with them for a few days.
The parcels from Zutphen and Amsterdam arrived well.
The clothes were for immediate use, which came in handy because some things show wear and tear after a while. People are also somewhat vain and don't like to wear the same thing all the time.
At the moment, we are all properly outfitted, so we will look

---

[27] The Levison family, with whom Ilse worked and lived, was arrested much later because David Levison was a member of the Jewish Council in Gelderland. They ended up in Vught, one of the three concentration camps in the Netherlands, along with Amersfoort and Westerbork. Camp Vught was under the control of the SS; the regime there was particularly cruel compared to Westerbork. After a short time, the Levisons were taken to Westerbork.

party-worthy on Saturday and Sunday.
The food supply has decreased a bit, but we have no reason to complain; we have enough. I have just opened a few parcels now — everything is in order.
We are saving the apples for Seder Night, and we are always grateful for the cigarettes and tobacco.
I hope Passover will be wonderful. On the first evening, we will be invited into different groups with different people — I am with Shlomo Samson. On the second evening, we will participate in a big 'Seider' in the barracks. I believe that despite all the difficulties, the holidays will still be pleasant. After all, the exodus from Egypt deeply appeals to us here in Westerbork.
Except for these two days, life here continues as usual.
For the past week and a half, I have been doing digging work in the camp with a group of 30 people. From tomorrow, Frey and I will each work with a group of 20 people doing peat extraction and land clearing. Don't be jealous of anyone serving as team leader; I would have preferred not to have accepted this position, but for various reasons, I could not refuse.
On Sundays, we enthusiastically engage in sports — playing soccer and volleyball. For a whole week, I could hardly do anything but crawl — that's how bad my muscles were aching. Hans Auerbach and Honki are surprised that they have not heard from you — you wanted to write to them, didn't you?
Right now, they are talking about 'moving' again. We don't yet know the number of the barracks.
Did you hear that Lini de Bruin and little Hanna have been

transferred to Barneveld?[28] For many of us, it was difficult to say goodbye to them, and for Lini and little Hanna too, of course. I am sad that we had to part; we were all together on their last evening.

To my regret, I can't write to everyone. Thank your parents and Oldenboom for me and very much on behalf of all of us. All in all, our life here is pretty good at the moment. The frequent stirrings have now subsided, and day-to-day life continues calmly. Of course, there are always things that keep us in suspense, even if they don't concern us personally, but the news often passes through here anyway; oh well, and then...
If only you knew how much I miss you! I think of you more and more and have almost no patience left to wait until you are with me again. I don't want to write too much on this subject because it will surely make everything even more difficult for you.

I recently received a letter from my mother. Naturally, she is very worried.

Dini Polak now works as a nurse in a hospital. Two weeks ago, I accidentally found two old aunts of mine, my grandfather's cousins – I thought they had long since died in Germany. They recognized me immediately (after 15 years). They are both in excellent mental condition. I expect they will

---

28 A group of prominent Jews, exempted from Arbeitseinsatz and deportation by the Germans, were housed in Castle 'de Schaffelaar' and Huize De Biezen in Barneveld. On September 29, 1943, the Barneveld group was nevertheless taken to Westerbork, but they held special status there. Most members of the group were eventually deported to Theresienstadt. The majority of them survived the war.

be deported next Tuesday.[29]
My love, two full pages should be enough for today.

Many loving regards and kisses,

Your Ernst

Sincere regards, Rozijntje

Thank you so much for the tobacco. You literally saved us, Efi Kohler.

Westerbork, April 24, 1943 (Letter no. 18 from Westerbork)

My dearest Ilse,

Although I don't have much to say, it is 'writing day,' and so I must write to you.
All the letters and parcels arrived; thank you so much for everything! The others were also extremely happy with them, of course.
Your parents have also sent us a lot; it is really tremendously kind and sweet of them, especially now that it is so hard to get everything. I appreciate it enormously, and thank you very much for it. Unfortunately, I cannot write to them. We talk about your parents here a lot among ourselves – they

---

29 Those two elderly aunts were Sara Cäcilia and Ida Cosmann. The two sisters had fled to the Netherlands in 1939 and lived in Dinxperlo. On April 10, 1943, they arrived in Westerbork. 10 days later, they were deported to Sobibór. They were murdered there immediately upon arrival, aged 81 and 79.

gradually became a part of us.

Passover is not very noticeable; work and food continue as usual. The Orthodox are struggling greatly, abstaining from eating bread, of course.

The first seider evening at Shlomo Samson's was cozy and home-like. Mrs. Samson and Eshu, despite the difficulties, went to great lengths to make everything as beautiful as possible. Traditional melodies, cultural contributions, and, most importantly, delicious food helped us to forget a lot of misery for a few hours. Because the curfew was delayed by an hour (until 11 p.m.), we had enough time to enjoy the evening. This evening was a pure pleasure.

The second Seder Night was disappointing. We were in our barracks. The night before, there was a great cantor whom everyone was enthusiastic about, but due to various technical failures, things did not go as planned. Besides, the second evening of Seder is never as nice as the first, especially if it is held exactly the same way. Of course, we can't do a lot of things anymore. Perhaps Miel Stranders will read the Song of Songs to us.

We recently received letters from Ru Cohen and Mau Reichenberger mentioning your help and work with great praise. I am so proud of that!

The women ask if it might be possible for you to send some sanitary towels? Talk to Ella about it.

I'm starting other work this week – land reclamation – along with 20 other people. Pretty fun work. Could you possibly get me a pair of dust goggles? It really is needed here. I have such goggles at the moment, but they will most likely break before long. It's not very urgent, so there is no rush! Maybe you happen to meet a former biker who has a pair and doesn't need them anymore.

Do you already know what kind of work you are going to do

in the near future? Needless to say, I would really like to know. Please write to me as much as you can and in as much detail as possible.

You can capitalize on all my 'reading time.' You are the only one around here who sends me any mail.

Fokki is asking for some books from Ella – they are 3 books about flower gardens. Ask Ella for them. As if that's something we really need here... typical Fokki.

That concludes the topics for today.

Until we meet again, my love, many sweet thoughts and kisses,

Your Blondie

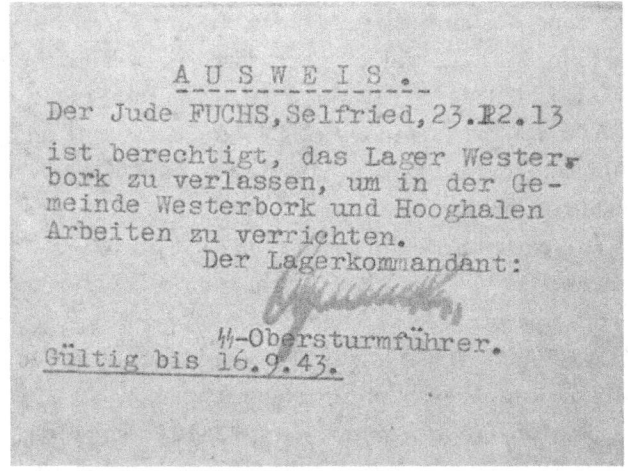

A permit (for Fokki Fuchs) to leave Camp Westerbork
Westerbork, May 2, 1943 (Letter no. 19 from Westerbork)

My dearest Ilse,

I know for sure that you long for my letters; I, too, am always happy when I can write to you again. I know what a 'sign of life' can mean to someone in these times, even if it can never fill the gap of someone's absence.

I can answer all your questions in the letters, but this way (through a letter) is so incredibly difficult for me, especially when you write about the relationship between you and me. I don't understand why we should distance ourselves from each other and why your relationship with others would weaken our relationship. After all, it is the same for me. I am very attached to other people, and I know that my attitude towards you, my love, will not suffer because of it.

Why are two people who love each other supposed to be alienated from each other just because they have different experiences against their will for a certain time in their lives? Some men spend years in a war with no change in attitude toward their wives.

I don't know your thoughts on the matter or what you feel, so I can only write how I think and feel about it.

In any case, there is no doubt about my feelings toward you.

I kindly ask you to write things clearly; reading veiled hints is stressful and makes it impossible to piece together the whole picture. Which makes me afraid of possibly misunderstanding what you mean.

There isn't much to tell you from my side. I continue to work with my group outside the camp. My task as team leader causes me a lot of irritation, very little joy and a lot of anxiety. I don't know how to get rid of it. Can you imagine how impossible it is to lead such a heterogeneous group? To manage a group of elderly, more elderly and young people all mixed

together with each other?
You are constantly struggling with all kinds of difficulties, you have to take responsibility for everything, and you reap very little reward.
This past week, we had a talk to determine who actually sees themselves as belonging to the community, to the comrades? Some immediately announced that they were leaving the group; they did not see themselves as being part of this group. After all that, we decided to put a bit more effort into our social life, more meetings, gatherings, etc. For now, it seems to be working pretty well. We elected a committee: Fannie, Werner and me.
Dr. A visited me today; he is doing well. He receives the parcels regularly. The parcels from you also arrive here well, and as always, thank you very much. We know only too well how difficult it is to always scrape things together to fill a parcel. We are doubly grateful for it. The women would like to especially thank your parents as well.
On Tuesday, we will send you a parcel with packing materials and glass jars.
Presumably, the parcel will reach you even before this letter arrives.
That concludes the topics for today – oh, I almost forgot to congratulate you on the new job. I hope you will succeed.
Please describe your work to me in detail so that I can imagine accurately what your job is like.
Regards to the Oldenbooms. I thank them for their letter and parcels. No doubt they will understand why I cannot write to them.

Well, my love, many sweet thoughts and kisses,

Your Ernst

Dear Ilse,

Thank you so much; the blouse is beautiful, and I am thrilled with it. It was a real surprise, and it fits me perfectly. I shortened the sleeves a bit. You have surprised me so often, and to my regret, I can only thank you by letter.
There is not much news from here.
Thanks again with all my heart.
Kind regards,

Rozijntje

Westerbork, May 17, 1943 (Letter no. 20 from Westerbork)

My dearest Ilse,

Werner asked me, 'What are you writing to Ilse?' He finds it difficult to write Ella a full letter. Unfortunately, I could not give him an answer because there really isn't much to tell; at least, nothing worth writing about.
I received your letters. I was so pleased and happy with them, especially with the last one.
Although your answer did not surprise me, and, of course, deep down, I had no doubts about it either, your answer did me a lot of good. I read it over and over with love, again and again.
I can picture quite well what your life is like there, and I think it is, in a way, similar to ours, at least in terms of inner feelings and reactions. On the outside, our lives are very different, although, to some extent, I think you are not free like a bird ei-

ther. In short, you do not control time nor what you do. Here, we organize time for leisure, entertainment and recreation, albeit all in a very primitive way.

I have just returned from a wonderful evening of music featuring a string quartet. We often hear music, even in our barracks. I try to read a lot. During work breaks, we have a lot of time — after a good meal, we lie in the sun and rest up.

Sometimes, we go to the classrooms in the school, where we can read quietly, which is very convenient for us.

My evenings are almost always devoted to the community, especially the early evening hours, where we discuss all kinds of things.

At present, there are many people in the hospital again. Some have severe angina with a high fever, and others have scarlet fever. In this place, people go to the hospital very quickly, even with diseases that could very well be treated at home, but patients cannot be treated in the barracks.

For now, everything is more or less fine; there really is no need to worry unnecessarily.

The situation with the working group is improving day by day. Most of the problems have been solved.

I believe people are very satisfied with my team.

I have written a little about our life. I know it is not enough for you, but you must understand that I cannot write more. I think of you all the time and try to imagine what you look like, and I miss you terribly. How much longer do we have to wait?

I assume you have arrived at your new workplace by now, and I hope everything is to your liking. Tell me as much as you can about everything. I am very interested.

The parcels arrived, and everything was great, as always. Everyone is very grateful to you and your parents.

We are now only allowed to receive parcels from Jews in

Amsterdam. From May 20, parcels from NON-Jews will no longer be delivered.
Many loving regards and many kisses,

Your Ernst

Dear Ilse,

Once again, my heartfelt thanks for the blouse. I am saying it again because I wore the blouse again this week, and everyone loved it. As do I, of course.

Many kind regards,
Rozijntje

Dear Ilse,

It's been a while since you've heard from me.
I am glad Erco left some space for me so I can write a few words to you.
Thank you so much for everything you send to us women. Every night, we hold a fashion show and every time another parcel arrives, the party starts all over again. It goes from woman/girl to woman/girl until together they decide who looks the best in it…then that person gets to keep it!

Goodbye, dear Ilse,
Gustel

Westerbork, June 2, 1943 (Letter no. 21 from Westerbork)

My dearest Ilse,

Today we have a writing day, and now I can finally answer all your letters, which I received with joy.

First of all, I am glad that you are satisfied with your new workplace, although the short working hours are not desirable but it might be enough to start with. I understand that you are tired in the evening.

I was very happy with the presents I received from you and your parents for my birthday, and I thank you for them.

The friends made sure I had a nice day. In addition, I got a few little things: the girls baked a cake for me and wrote a few songs in rhymes that I got next to my bed early in the morning, which instantly put me in a good mood. Lots of sweet wishes, lots of handshakes, until my hand started aching – I had reason to be happy that day.

That day, Marie Feingersch got married. She married Gerrit Kleinkramer. (Remember her? She was our cook in Elden.) The following day, we held a 'chuppah' for them. In the evening, we all celebrated together in a cozy atmosphere.

It is beautiful that, despite all the limitations and obstacles we struggle with here on a daily basis, we find ways and means to enliven gray days to make our lives as pleasant as possible and spend our time as well as possible.

On that day, another couple got married. The room was decorated with flowers and a sickle (the sickle, which is used for many agricultural activities, is the well-known symbol of our group).

The rabbis also spoke in Hebrew. After the 'chuppah' of these two young couples, we danced the hora around them. Such an event provides strength and courage for months to come. Even the older guests who were there were very impressed by the spiritedness they saw with us.

Occasionally, we gather in the evening for a gramophone record concert.

There is a 'kiddush'[30] every Friday evening. Roosje Pool (who is also here now)
organized the last meeting. We also meet for other events, such as a lecture given by Mau Reichenberger.

The Levison family is doing a little better – as of yesterday, they are staying in our barracks. They suffered tremendously, especially the baby who almost died, but luckily, he is much better now. We help them a lot, of course. I try really hard to at least reward them for the help they have always given us. She, Jetty Levison, is a wonderful woman, but she does not know the meaning of the word 'order.' What a mess she makes, but she is a thoroughly pleasant, funny woman.

After a period of not going outside the camp, I am back doing groundwork with my group. I am writing this letter while sitting on a carriage at the farm after a delicious lunch. A few comrades here and there on the hay around me are sound asleep.

I suppose you know who among our friends has come here recently. Of those closest to us, actually, is Hans Moser (Hamo), a Deventer pioneer. I meet up with him from time to time.

We try to help everyone as much as we can, which goes without saying.

My relatives who wrote to me but whom I don't actually know

---

30 The blessing that is pronounced at the beginning of Sabbath and Feast Days.

suddenly showed up here. They are very boring, and I try to visit them as little as possible. They talk all the time about the 'family' being able to arrange 'Austausch' papers. I personally don't believe in it and have little hope in it. I have written everything worth writing about today.

Many loving regards,

Your Ernst

Westerbork, June 16, 1943 (Letter no. 22 from Westerbork)

My dearest Ilse,

We are on a lunch break now. We are at the farmer's, and this is the best time to write to you. This place has enough distractions, too. Heated discussions are happening all around me, and yet it is more pleasant here than in the barracks, where one is constantly disturbed and called upon. In the evenings, I am always very busy with the needs of the community, both material and spiritual; it takes up much of my time. I get back from work at about 7 p.m., change clothes and eat. Then it's almost 8 p.m., and I only have two hours left. There is always so much to do, so much running back and forth. Reading in quiet is not possible. Lunchtime is really the best time for peaceful, pleasant reading.

Our food is delivered to the field, which saves time. You don't have to wait, etc. The work is really pleasant and enjoyable. We have a mandatory quota, and we are making a great effort to deliver it. We are a good team. Everyone does their best and works hard so we achieve what is demanded of us. Because of this dedication, we have built a great reputation here, and I see time after time that they are very satisfied with us.

On Saturday night, we had an evening we won't easily forget, even if you haven't experienced something like this in a long time. We had a real concert performed by a philharmonic orchestra. The camp has an excellent orchestra, which could basically perform anywhere.

The program was very impressive:

```
         KONZERT-     UND     LIEDERABEND
          des Symphonieorchesters - Lager Westerbork
                   Dirigent: Heinz Neuberg

         Solisten: Erna Weiss, Sopran - Mendel Rokach, Bariton

1. Ouverture zur Oper "Oberon"              Carl Maria v. Weber
2. Lieder                                       Franz Schubert
      a. Geheimnis
      b. Die Forelle
      c. Frühlingsglaube
      d. Heidenröslein          (Klavier: Mark Velt)
3. H-Moll Symphonie ("Unvollendete")            Franz Schubert
                         P a u s e .
4. Valse Triste                                  Jean Sibelius
5. Prolog "Bajazzo"                              Leoncavallo
6. Ungarische Rhapsodie II                       Franz Liszt

            Saaleinrichtung: Eugen Frankenstein
            Beleuchtung:    Technischer Dienst
                Beginn des Konzertes: 20 Uhr.
         Die Programme sind nach Ablauf am Ausgang abzuliefern.
```

You can't imagine how excited we all were.

It was two hours of FREEDOM. Everyone is trying to go to the concert one more time. Let's hope we succeed.

The Levison family is doing well. They are cheerful, and everyone loves them very much. Jetty (Levison) told me that she wrote you a long letter, so I won't have anything new to say to you about the Levison family.

When you receive this letter, everything at Edith's will already be over; you have written to me about that already. Tell them

I am thinking of them and wish them all the best, etc. I hope everything goes well – we are all anxious.

I cannot write to Oldenboom; I am only allowed to write a letter once every two weeks and I write to you, of course, and I suppose that, in all modesty, you wouldn't want to change this. Please give the Oldenboom family regards from all of us, and many thanks for everything they send us. Also, our sincere thanks to you and thanks to your parents for the parcels, which, as far as I can tell, also came in part from the Jewish Council in Deventer.

We are happy with everything and use everything. Especially the women and girls, thank you for everything you send. You are pretty much their only resource.
Unfortunately, I cannot send back packing materials because it is no longer possible to send parcels from here. It is very inconvenient for us, and we know that parcel deliveries to you will be even more difficult. We are all sorry, but there is nothing we can do about it.
It's great that you can get clogs – we need four pairs.
Sizes 20 and 21 for Levison's children, size 24 for Rozijntje, and size 28 for me.
Thank you very much for all your best wishes.
Shlomo is okay; I don't see him much. He rarely comes to see us. I see Dr. Ahlfeld often; he always sends you his warmest regards: 'regards to Mrs. Ilse,' he then says.

My love,

Against all odds, I managed to write a full letter. I really didn't know what to write at first. You already know how much I think of you and how much I miss you, so I don't need to write about that.

My darling Ilse, never doubt my love for you.
I wish you all the best. Many kisses,
Your Ernst

Westerbork, June 30, 1943 (Letter no. 23 from Westerbork)

My dearest Ilse,

I am lying outside under the sun's rays – currently taking a lunch break.
Today, the sun is shining again after not having done so for a long time, and everything instantly looks different.
All your letters have arrived. What a joy – at least for the most part.
Parcels have also arrived from your parents and from the Jewish Council. We are very happy with everything, they are all things that we really need here.
Nowadays, we hardly receive parcels from other places. That said, I can tell you that there are still no problems with delivery to our group. We really thank you all for all the expenses and hassles.

I could say many things in response to your last letter, but such a letter is difficult to answer and write. I am not accusing you of anything, and I believe I understand you very well. Nevertheless, I must tell you that the things you wrote hit me hard, and I still feel it. All these years, and especially the last three quarters of this year, I have never doubted you or our relationship. The thoughts of you and our shared future are the only certainty I have in all the uncertainty we are constantly floating in. You must understand how it makes me feel. If my conviction disappears, then the whole situation will change for me; it will become unbearable. You must also imagine how much the words in your letter torment me.

I don't seek pity for myself, and I don't want to influence your decision; everyone has the right to make their own decisions. I just want to warn you not to react impulsively, to decide things in a moment of lightheartedness that you may regret afterward, and then not be able to resolve (because you have to think of me too). Everything is so difficult and complicated.

You live your life, which is definitely not an easy life, and I live my life here, which is definitely not any easier. Each of us lives in a different environment and has different experiences that affect our daily lives.

Do you believe, my dear, that love and all that was between us is not enough to bridge these times?

Do you believe that true friendship – and we felt such a thing existed between us – is bound by time and place?

We have to really grit our teeth, but I think we will be fine.

I have learned a lot these past few months, my beloved. Imagine if we were together now, with each other, were all alone, and I told you all these things – what would you say to me?

Look, I give you complete freedom and do not want you to do anything for me that is contrary to your thinking and to your feelings. My letters may sound dry and impersonal, but believe me, it is because of the external situation. My thoughts are like before, full of love and longing for you.

Do me a favor, my love, and answer me quickly because uncertainty is the worst thing there is.

That's all on this subject.

Recounting my usual day is very difficult, as always.

I assume you have heard who of our comrades arrived here.

I am in regular contact with Jaap S. He does not change; he remains as he always was. He is with us a lot and might also come and live in our barracks. Ella has recovered quite well and works with the women outside, which she really enjoys. Werner and Ella both don't seem to mind too much that she came here to Westerbork because it is easier together anyway. Ella sends you her warmest greetings.

When you have the opportunity, give all our friends my best wishes and warm regards.

I will write to everyone personally at the first chance I get.

Regards also to Oldenboom. If possible, I will write to them.

The clogs have arrived; they are great. I kept one pair for myself and gave the other pair to a very good friend, my bed neighbor, and my partner for long night talks. He is Eshu's friend, Dudi Rosenbaum. That is enough of an introduction. He also wants to add a few words to this letter.

Rozijntje is happy with her clogs and thanks you for them. Her birthday is on July 9, maybe you could write a few words to her?

Could you get another pair of clogs for Fritz Ziesel? He doesn't know what to do; he can't handle the clogs provided here in the camp. His has size 28.

Aarons' family sends you their warm regards – I speak to them often; they are wonderful people.

A. arrived here with her husband. I didn't even recognize her, even though I had a terrible fight with her about 10 years ago.

My dear, the page is full, and my handwriting is terrible. My attitude and the quality of the paper are to blame.

All the friends send their warmest regards, but the most loving wishes and kisses come from me.

Your Ernst

Dear Ilse,

It will definitely surprise you to get a letter from me, especially since you have never seen me, let alone gotten to know me. I have wanted to write to you for a long time.

You probably know that I have been Ernst's 'bed neighbor' for the past six months.

The downside is that I am a very light sleeper, and I wake up every time Ernst talks in his sleep. The name Ilse plays a prominent role in his dreams – but I do not object to that, of course.

What may interest you is that I was in Loosdrecht and that your friend Eshu is also my friend.

For today, many kind regards,

Dudi Rosenbaum

Westerbork, July 14, 1942 (Letter no. 24 from Westerbork)

My darling Ilse,

First of all, although much too early, as I am only allowed to write once in two weeks, sincere wishes for your birthday.
Your birthday has never been celebrated in such difficult times as this last year. I know, for example, that you have never had to look back on a year with such sad memories as you had this past year. Therefore, we hope more than ever that the beginning period will be the beginning of your happy period – OURS, too, of course.
My dearest, you know how much I would like to be with you on this particular day to personally offer you all my blessings. We are not together right now, so you probably cannot be truly happy – it was exactly the same for me on my birthday. Rest assured that we will soon be united again and live our lives as we wish. I wish you a day as happy as possible. Imagine that I am beside you to give you birthday kisses.
I received your letters with great joy. These letters prove that nothing has changed. Everything between us remains the same. You just don't understand how happy and delighted I am with this news. You see, we are meant for each other even though we are not together.
I think it is silly that you want to drive to her house with Winnie. I would first check whether her relatives are there at all – otherwise, you will only see her, and that won't accomplish anything.
Maybe you obtained a bit more information in the meantime. As usual, there's not much to tell from here. I am working with my land-clearing team and enjoying it. It will come to an end soon because we are going to help the farmers in the area

harvest the wheat. This is really great, and not only are we 'seasoned farmers' happy about it, but so are the others.
I don't know yet when exactly it will happen.
Many wonderful parcels from the Jewish Council and from your parents arrived again, and once again, we were very happy. All the things could be used immediately, and we thank you for them.
We started a cultural program on Sundays, during which we had maximum participation every time. We hope it will continue this way. The community is experiencing great difficulties; I think I have already written about all of it. We all seriously believe that things cannot continue like this. A decision was made to improve the situation. I hope so. It will be very unfortunate if things fall apart.
We are trying to arrange other accommodation for the whole group – whether we will succeed... I don't know, but we are trying!
Werner sends Merry his regards; he will write to her soon.
My dear, I must stop – due to a local disturbance, I must finish this letter very quickly. I have far less time to write than I thought. The moment I can, I will write much more extensively.
My darling,
Many sweet thoughts and kisses,

Your Ernst

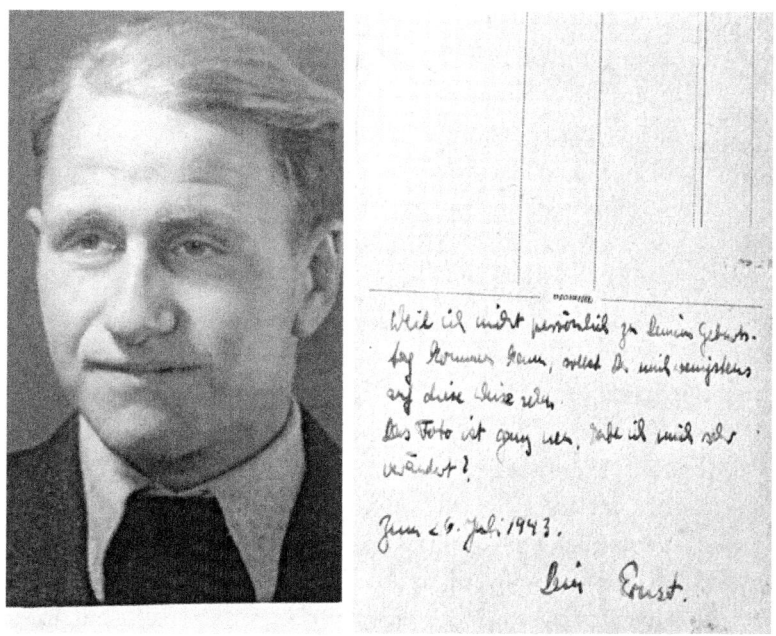

Erco sends Ilse a birthday card from Westerbork, including a photo of him, July 26, 1943

Westerbork, July 27, 1943 (Letter no. 25 from Westerbork)

My dearest Ilse,

Although I am very tired from having worked all day in the sun, I just can't let a writing day pass without writing to you. I received several letters with lots of loving regards that made me very happy. We are all overjoyed about the photos. I am really happy that you are having such a good time there. Do you already know how to milk a cow? I mean when it sounds like a steady stream, and a thick layer of foam is formed in the bucket. Have you already experienced hostility when milking a cow?

I read your postcard in which you wrote with particular concern. You need not worry at all – you should know and understand our status by now. Please don't worry; there is nothing to worry about. At the moment, we are not worried at all either. I hope someone has the opportunity to explain that to you sometime. We have good work now. We are working well and harvesting at the farmers' all day. We are working hard but having fun. That is Dudi Rosenbaum, Rachel Livschitz, another friend and me. It is quite far away from the camp; walking there and back every day is strenuous. We are exhausted at night.

You should see what a hassle it is in the morning when we all go to work. About 200 people head out of the camp in small groups. At noon, we pass through one of the villages and meet dozens of acquaintances.

Ella is not doing well. She is ill and very depressed. Her mother was deported not long ago. It's so sad; we all sympathize with her.

How was your birthday? I thought about you all day, and according to Dutch tradition, everyone congratulated me on your birthday. I hope you had a good time and didn't worry too much.

Just so you don't get upset again that I don't write everything... I was a bit ill last week. I had diarrhea and a slight fever. I was in bed for a few days, but in the meantime, I am healthy and in one piece, and everything is over. Don't worry about what is in the past.

All the parcels from the Jewish Council arrived.

The apples are delicious. Everyone was so happy with them. My love, for today, I must end this letter.

Many loving regards,

Your Ernst

The Levison family is doing well. Habakkuk, their little one, is growing nicely. We are good friends. We have fun and 'talk' with each other, etc.
All the other friends are also doing well.

Don't forget to give the Oldenboom family my regards.

Dear Ilse,

I was pleased with the letter that I received yesterday. I can answer it right now. What a tasteful gift you spoiled me with; a wonderful choice. You have truly lavished me.
Unfortunately, I was sick on my birthday; I had diarrhea all week – and on top of that, the excitement about my mother. I hope to fulfill your request regarding Ernst. Whether he likes it remains to be seen – I will try. We are all grateful to you. Next time, I will write more.

Your Ella

Did you have a nice birthday? We were remembering this same day, but then a year ago.

Kind regards,
Hadassah

Dear Ilse,
I am standing next to Erco's window. The notepad is lying on the blackout curtain, an interesting form of writing.
We worked at the farmer's all day – we harvested rye.

Kind regards,
Rozijntje

A page from Ilse's photoalbum: Ilse on Hachsjara in Wilp at the Oldenboom farm, 1943.

A page from Ilse's photo album: Our last encounter.

Westerbork, no date, somewhere around the beginning of August

(Letter no. 26 from Westerbork)

My dearest Ilse,

Just a quick note on how to get here. You can choose any day of the week. You can spend at least one night here, but I think you could possibly stay longer. Perhaps you could come on Friday? Some of the women want to see you on Saturday; they can't do another day because of work. I leave this decision up to you; you come when you want and when it suits you best.
Write to me when you will come (write it via Tzippi, not by post, for God's sake). There is very strict censorship. Besides, we have not received any mail for a week, but we get letters and postcards.
The people's name is Jonkers. They live in a village called Zwiggelte. You drive up to Beilen, and from there, you will see signposts for Zwiggelte. Chances are you will be picked up.
The farm is on Zwiggelte's main street – it's a big house with a big front garden and a red letterbox.
Let me know in your letter whether you will bring your bike. If you like, you can bring my camera with you, if you can still get a film for it somewhere. Anyway, to buy a roll of film you have to take the camera with you, as not every film automatically fits.
Well, that's enough for today! I hope everything is sorted now. I am already very happy.

Many sweet wishes,
Your Ernst

Meeting for the last time

In early August, Ilse and Erco met one last time. This time in Zwiggelte, a town near Westerbork, where Erco worked for a farmer. They could not arrange anything by mail because everything was subject to censoring, so it had to be arranged through Tzippi again. But Erco did provide directions in a letter. Ilse took Erco's camera and took pictures during their last meeting. These photos have been preserved.

Dudi Rosenbaum, Rozijntje, Eshu Singer, Ilse and Ernst in Zwiggelte

Censoring

At the beginning of August, Erco wrote: 'Write to me and let me know when you are coming (send it via Tzippi, not via mail, heaven forbid). There is heavy censoring. Besides, there hasn't been any mail for a week now, but we do get letters and postcards.'

The censorship was indeed very strict, and that is why Erco could not say everything he wanted via mail. 'You must remember that you are not the only one reading the letter,' he wrote to Ilse. Anyway, there were all kinds of channels to pass on information – information that we unfortunately cannot derive from Erco's letters. The most important things they needed to tell each other were conveyed orally by camp visitors. One of these visitors was Alfred 'Tzippi' Fränkel, courier and liaison between the Jewish Council and the camp institutions of Westerbork and active in the underground resistance that arose from the Zionist youth movement. Because he could travel freely back and forth between Amsterdam and Westerbork, he was the main source of information for Erco's group. Sometimes, Ilse hid messages in the packages she sent. 'The pants and coat were fine, thank you very much for them, I found the 'notes'...,' Ernst wrote on October 29. Ilse and Erco also shared what they could not write in the two face-to-face meetings they had.

Westerbork, August 17, 1943 (Letter no. 27 from Westerbork)

My love,

Today, you are receiving only a few short, sweet words and wishes from me.
I don't have much to tell you yet, another dreary day, but with memories of us being together.
I decided it was better not to come on Sunday as it's too dangerous. I hope this is all right. I am very worried; I hope I make it.
Oh, I forgot, the Levison family asked for fruit.
Will you have the watch repaired?
I got the camera. It was lying neatly in the basket; the search was not particularly thorough.
The train schedule should be in your bag, and the photo for Shushu is in your wallet.[31] I took it out of the passport.

Loving wishes and kisses,

Your Ernst

---

31   Apparently, the escape plans had not yet been abandoned. The passport photo was probably used for a false identity card. Shushu Simons was able to take care of that.

Stay or flee?

The relatively great freedom in Westerbork meant that escaping would not be difficult, especially for Ernst and his group, who worked outside the camp every day. The difficulty was deciding where to go. But the chawerim had a solution. They had contacts, such as the group of Joop Westerweel and Shushu Simons, in which Ilse was also involved, who could provide transportation and hiding locations. Yet, the prisoners stayed where they were for various reasons. Werner Ahlfeld wrote: 'The strong bond within the group meant that especially the older chawerim did not take the opportunity to flee for fear of reprisals and in order not to undermine the cohesion of the group.' The Germans made it clear that for everyone who tried to escape, ten relatives or friends would be put on the next train. If an escape attempt succeeded, and it occasionally did, relatives of the escapee were immediately taken to the prison barracks and then transferred. Escaping or an attempt to escape came at the expense of others. Moreover, Ernst was optimistic. He relied on the good reputation he had built up with the camp leaders to keep him from being sent away, and he thought the war would end soon. In the spring of 1943, reports of German troops losing battles in North Africa and Russia reached the residents of Westerbork. News of the uprising in the ghetto of Warsaw also came through. Jews were fighting, enjoying initial success against

photo of Ernst made in Westerbork

the Germans, which made a big impression.

Ilse did not succeed in convincing Ernst. She went to Drenthe one last time on the Sunday after their final meeting, where she met a girl from the pioneer group outside the camp. Ilse had brought a bicycle and clothes for Ernst, but in vain. Ernst did not show up. In the end, however, he did seem convinced of the need to escape. He wrote, 'I am very worried; I hope I make it.'

A day before he was taken to Auschwitz, Ernst wrote to Ilse: 'Don't worry too much, even in the worst case, all is not lost – it is only a matter of a short time, and we will triumph!'

Erco was one of the five leaders of the groups who worked at nearby farmers every day outside the camp. Each morning, they left the camp accompanied by Dutch policemen, usually to plant or dig potatoes by hand or to cut peat. It was not difficult for these young farm workers to flee. But they almost never did. They all knew that escaping meant that those left behind would be severely punished, and the group's bond was so strong that it therefore did not happen. Moreover, escape was not possible without outside help. Westerbork was very isolated and far from civilization; it was impossible to reach a safe place without means of transport. The members of the hakhshara group regarded the farmwork in Drenthe as a step closer to Palestine, as a continuation of their pioneer training. 'As group leaders, we conveyed this to the others with great success. More and more young people wanted to join the hakhshara group and tried to move to our accommodations,' Paul Siegel wrote.

Nevertheless, plans were forged. Via Ilse, Ernst and Werner Ahlfeld received a stack of forged camp passes, identity cards and stamps with the signature of camp commander Gemmeker, which had been made by the forger Frans Gerritsen. According to Ahlfeld, this saved at least one person already at the beginning of 1942: Max Windmüller, a member of Joop Westerweel's resistance group, escaped from the camp a day after his arrival. Paul Siegel described how the preparations for the escape of all the hachshara went: A passport photo was taken of everyone, supposedly for a sports certificate for the camp. The photos went to Amsterdam, where false personal identification cards were made. Tzippi ID Fränkel smuggled them back into the camp and Werner Ahlfeld hid them.

The pioneers wanted to escape only if they could do so without endangering the lives of those left behind. In early 1944, when Ernst was already gone, they finally found a way to escape without the Germans noticing. Those who wanted to escape volunteered to be transferred. They joined the crowd that was leaving on the train, put on a band of the Jewish Order Service, the camp police, got off the train again as ODs and hid in the camp. The next day, they joined the work crews leaving the camp. Thanks to their false Ausweis, they succeeded. Once outside, they were met by members of the Westerweel group, often Frans Gerritsen, Lore Durlacher or Mirjam Waterman, who took them to the station in Beilen or Assen on the back of their bicycles.

The train to Auschwitz

The Germans spread information that things were not as bad in Poland. Prisoners would be performing labor over there. People in the camp did not always believe this, as alarming reports filtered in from the outside world. On July 27, 1942, writer Thomas Mann, in one of his much-lauded radio messages on the BBC, already spoke of the mass murder of Jews in Eastern Europe. He also said: 'There is a detailed and authentic report that states that 11,000 Polish Jews were killed in gas chambers.' On October 9, 1942, Anne Frank wrote in her diary: 'The English radio mentions gassing...' The Palestine pioneers had also heard this. Since they never received messages from Auschwitz, they devised a plan. They were tasked with cleaning the train that ran back and forth between Westerbork and Auschwitz. To find out more, they asked the deportees to hide notes on the train. This did not yield much because the notes only ever described the journey. One saved note reads: 'We passed Auschwitz. A group of about 15 men took the train... We see a lit building in the distance. Bye, boys, it seems we will return soon.'

One of the German pioneers, Fritz Lustig, who had been deported to AuschwitzMonowitz, where Erco later ended up, managed to smuggle a note out of the camp in early 1943. He gave a Dutch worker, who volunteered to work there and was going home on leave, a letter for Ru Cohen of the Deventer Association. He asked Cohen to make sure that 'under no circumstances must anyone come here.' When Ernst's group arrived at the camp in October, they met Lustig, who 'completely astonished' asked them: 'What are you doing here? I specifically wrote and told Ru that no one should come here!' Hans Mogendorff confirmed this. In his diary that was later published, he wrote how, in April 1943, he 'received a dreadful message about what was happening in Auschwitz.'

Ilse wanted to convince Ernst to run away, to disappear, but then 10 others would instantly pay the price, Ernst had told her. As far as he was concerned, trying to escape was therefore not an option. In reality, almost everyone boarded the train to the East sooner or later.

In the second week of September, it slowly became clear that Ernst's group was in danger. All kinds of plans were forged, but in vain.

Westerbork, September 7, 1943 (Letter no. 28 from Westerbork)

My love,

Thank you so much for your sweet wishes. We'll have to wait and see what happens. I don't have much to tell you; you already know my thoughts. I hope everything will work out. We are experiencing anxious times. I don't know if you can imagine our mood. We go from hope to.. well, never mind, it will be all right.

I won't be returning my wooden clogs – we are allowed to take them with us.

My love, stay strong. I am also trying my best to stay strong.

Kisses,

Your Ernst

Ilse did not receive this letter until after Ernst had already been sent away. The date of departure is written on the back.

Westerbork, September 13, 1943
(Letter no. 29 from Westerbork, the day before he was taken to Auschwitz. The last letter.)

My love,
Just a quick few words; I currently do not have the necessary peace to write a long, detailed letter. People are probably telling what is going on here.
As for our meeting, I promise to do my utmost to make it.
You know my one condition that I cannot ignore. Do not worry too much; even in the worst case, all is not lost – it is only a matter of a short time, and we will triumph!
I want to make one very important thing clear to you and assure you that I will not let negative thoughts influence me. During the past few days, Werner and I have succeeded in dissuading a number of comrades from volunteering for transfer. You will hear from me as soon as possible, either verbally or by letter.
My love, stay strong. Believe in our love and in our common future.
A thousand kisses,

Your Ernst
Ella's address: Jonker, Nieuwe Markt 1 (?)

Goodbye

Completely unexpectedly, the thing everyone feared the most happened. There were persistent rumors that lists with names, including those of the Palestine pioneers, had been 'cracked' again. But this time, it turned out to be true. Paul Siegel recalled: 'We didn't believe it. We owed our safety to the fact that the camp commander needed us. We did all kinds of functional work for the camp that also benefited the residents. Despite this, doubt gnawed at us. Another night of horror awaited us. Like every Tuesday, at exactly midnight, the head of the barracks arrived, accompanied by officers, and they read out a list of names. They had hardly begun when I heard the name of someone from our group and understood that the time had come. [...] The list contained the names of most of the leaders of the house of the Aliyat ha-Noar from Elden: Erco, Ferry and Batya, Emil Stranders and many, many comrades who, like me, had worked as pioneers with farmers in the Zutphen area and with whom I had a shared past.' Siegel himself was still spared: he was not yet twenty – only the older chawerim were being transferred this time.

On September 14, Philip Mechanicus also witnessed the departure of Ernst's train, the train on which he should have been. He was removed from it at the last minute. 'Furthermore, a number of members of the Hashera who were over twenty-one years of age and who were working here in the field were taken as well. The Obersturmführer gave them a letter in which he asked the commander of the other camp to assign them the same kind of work they did in Westerbork – fieldwork – and to not split up the group.' The commander is a bit sentimental,' he wrote sarcastically.

Thirty-seven young pioneers under the age of twenty-one, who had Palestine certificates, were taken off the train at the last minute.

Their place was taken by other prisoners who had volunteered to accompany their relatives to Poland.

When the train carrying 40 pioneers (12 women and 28 men, including Ernst) was about to depart, the people staying behind, who were ordered to remain in their barracks, snuck out to the platform. 'The train doors closed, saying goodbye weighed heavily on us. We all sang Hatikwa (Hope) and Techezakna (Keep courage). My voice broke, and many of us cried,' Paul Siegel recalled. 'The whistle of the locomotive signaled that the train was about to leave. A group of very special people was being taken away.'

Zwi Durlacher, one of the people who remained at the camp, described the departure: 'Most of the chawerim quickly packed their belongings. We walked from one person to the next. We couldn't believe it. It slowly became time for the chawerim to leave the barracks. Everyone was standing around talking to their friends. Many chawerim who were staying behind were crying, but only for a moment. Everyone realized that they should not make it even harder for those who were leaving. Then, it was time for them to exit the barracks and board the train. We carried their luggage, as we did with all other transfers. It was almost time for the train to depart. The moment was getting closer and closer. The commander walked along the train; we stared at it. Did he know what was going on inside us? In any case, we had to step away from the train. A quick, light handshake, then we waved from a distance. Soldiers walked past the train and locked the carriages. The locomotive then blew its whistle, and the train slowly started to move. The chawerim sang the Techezakna and Hatikwa. We tried to sing along, one last shalom, and then the train disappeared out of sight.'

Ernst's good friend and 'bed-neighbor,' Dudi Rosenbaum, wrote a letter to Ilse the day after the train departed. He, too, described the comrades' touching farewell. Moreover, he wrote that they had tried everything to save Ernst, even 'Onkel Teilach,' camp jargon for an escape, but they had to refrain from doing so due to 'compelling reasons.'

Shortly after Ernst and the 39 other members of the group were taken to Auschwitz, the fear of reprisal was abandoned, and the plan to help the remaining members of the group escape gained momentum. It had now become clear that the chawerim were more vulnerable than they thought and that the documents, stamps and certificates that were supposed to protect them from being transferred had little value. They also had fewer and fewer illusions about the situation in the East.

Werner Ahlfeld had been sent to Amsterdam to clean up the building of the Jewish Council, which had recently been dissolved by the Germans. He stayed with Ilse and her parents on Stadionweg and, via her, made contact with the 'illegal Hechaloets' who were going to organize a mass escape. A Dutch military police officer was bribed to help the pioneers get through the cut barbed wire and into stolen Wehrmacht trucks, which would take them to a hiding place, from where they would then be taken to safe houses. A coded message arrived by telephone the day before the planned escape: 'No suitcases will be sent'; the action had been called off.

Westerbork, September 15, 1943 (A letter to Ilse Birnbaum from Dudi Rosenbaum)

Dear Ilse,

I will try as much as possible to somehow write a normal letter. I am not sure if I will succeed or whether I can handle it. Due to technical reasons, I cannot describe the exact details of Erco's departure. Tzippi will definitely tell you everything in person. We tried everything (even 'Onkel Teilach,' but had to abandon that for compelling reasons), but all in vain.
Everything happened so unexpectedly – because otherwise, we would have been much more careful.
Enough about 'if', etc. I am unable to write the details of the departure; my hand is shaking. As I write these words, everything seems false and hypocritical to me; it's not possible to put it into words.
No words can describe the great atmosphere our friends left in. Practically speaking – they had a decent carriage all to themselves, all the friends together. Erco was appointed 'carriage manager.' Thirty-eight comrades left Westerbork together in this carriage. We had previously arranged the carriage in a special way.
As for the food supply, we feared that some would not make it due to overeating – that's how much food we put in the carriage.
Despite being ordered to stay in the barracks, we stood alongside the train. As the train slowly departed, we all sang the *Hatikwa* and *Techezakna*. This is how we said goodbye.
It may all sound kitschy, but such moments cannot be described.
Personally, I'm completely devastated. I held up pretty well all day, but at night, when it became clear to me that Erco

was not lying next to me, I couldn't help myself — I can tell you this because I don't have to feel ashamed with you — I cried like a baby, something that hasn't happened to me in four years.

It affects us both so deeply, although I understand that I should not and cannot compare myself to you.

A great void has now been created here that cannot be filled. Now, when I enter the barracks, no one comes up to me. There's no commotion, no discussions, no arguments.

The silence is terrible. I'll stop writing about it now; otherwise, I'll go crazy.

All these things brought us together, namely the community of 'Elden' and the few left of the 'Deventer Organization.' You must forgive me a thousand times for writing so pessimistically — and as for myself, so unmanly — it's because of our state of mind here.

We are mostly optimistic, and we hope to see them again. We owe this optimism to the only example we have, to our friends who are now gone.

As for you, I feel confident as you have known Erco for a long time and know him well, you know what kind of person Erco is. As far as we are concerned, we have to remember that we only have a short time left.

I am working in Meppel now. I will write the address of my workshop, and perhaps you can come visit us sometime. Then, I will tell you everything in person. I will also tell Tzippi or Fokki everything accurately. Please write to me only through Tzippi or Fokki and not in the usual way. I must end this letter now.

Stay strong,

Dudi

I almost forgot the most important thing: they received a letter of recommendation from the commander of Westerbork camp, Albert Konrad Gemmeker, specifically recommending them as an excellent group of workers. This is very important and will certainly serve to their advantage.

In Auschwitz

The train's destination turned out to be more gruesome than they could have imagined at Westerbork. Lotte Wald, one of the people on the train, later recounted: 'On September 16, [she was mistaken about the date] the elderly chawerim were to be transferred to Poland, but they were taken to Auschwitz instead. Although certificates had been requested for us, they came too late, as I heard later. There were 40 chawerim, including about 12 girls, traveling in a cattle carriage. At the time of departure, we and those who stayed behind sang the *Hatikwa*. Of this group, only 10 girls and 2 boys returned. In Auschwitz, all the girls entered the experiment block; I was sent to Birkenau in the summer of 1944 because I refused to submit to the experiments. [...] Our chawerim were sent to Buna, where conditions were so horrible that almost all of them died after only a few weeks.'

The women ended up in the barracks in Auschwitz, where medical experiments were conducted. Of them, ten survived. The men were put to work, as Commander Gemmeker had requested, in Auschwitz-Monowitz. This camp, also called Auschwitz III or Buna, had been established by the companies IG Farben and Krupp. It was indeed a labor camp where Jewish prisoners had to perform slave labor under inhumane conditions. The prisoners were hired by the companies from the SS for three or four Reichsmarks per day. Writers Elie Wiesel (*Night*) and Primo Levi (*If this is a man*) recorded what it was like in the camp.

When Ernst arrived, there were about 6,000 prisoners. At IG Farben's Buna factory, they made synthetic rubber from coal. Those who worked in the factory survived an average of three to four months, and the miners lasted no more than six weeks. The prisoners lived in inhumane conditions. They were forced to work as hard as possible while being subjected to constant beatings. The food, consisting of the notoriously watery Buna-Suppe – which was called that because it tasted like the synthetic rubber produced there – and bread with occasionally a bit of butter, cheese or sausage, was insufficient to sustain them. People were slowly turning into what was called a 'Muselmann' in the camp: someone who is scrawny and unable to work, who, due to exhaustion, hopelessness and hunger, has become nothing more than a shadow of a human being. According to Primo Levi: 'An emaciated man with a drooping head and crooked shoulders, with an expressionless face and eyes.'

The management of the companies located in Monowitz felt that the barracks did not serve to house the sick and weak. There was a hospital, but only for people with relatively minor ailments, who were expected to heal quickly. Really sick or seriously weakened prisoners were sent back to Birkenau to be gassed, or they were murdered in the hospital. It was in this hospital that Ernst, who had arrived at the camp on September 16 as a healthy, strong young man who was used to hard work, died of hunger and exhaustion on January 17, 1944.

Arnold Erlanger was the only one of Erco's group to survive the camp. He was there when Erco died. After the war, he wrote a letter to Ilse describing Erco's last days.

Enschede, July 9, 1945

My dear friend,

You have no doubt heard the details about Erco from Martha de Groot.
Nevertheless, I would like to answer your letter personally. I was very sorry that I could not talk to you when I was in Amsterdam and that Martha could not reach you by telephone.
I might be in Amsterdam again soon, and if you write me your address (I am sending this letter via Martha), I will be glad to visit you and tell you about Erco if you like. Today, I will do so again in writing.
As you know, we (about 50 friends) were sent to Auschwitz by train on September 14, 1943. We were all courageous, which changed somewhat after our arrival, although we still did our best to remain brave.
Some of our friends, including Erco, were 'lucky' to get a job in the barracks: night watch, cleaning, etc. As a result, they got a double portion of food and sometimes even more than that. This work did not exempt them from regular work. These comrades had enough food to give to other friends as well, friends who did not have double work. As a result, we held out reasonably well for the first three months despite the heavy digging we had to do. After this period, the barracks were switched up, and most of the friends lost their positions. The situation of our comrades deteriorated very quickly; one by one, they became a 'Muselmann' who was then 'transferred' to Auschwitz. We could deduce from previous transfers what that meant. It meant being gassed.
I had an accident in December. I broke my arm and was taken to the hospital. After lying there for about two weeks, Erco was suddenly brought in. Because each bed was for two patients and I was still alone in a bed at that time, I asked them

to put Erco in my bed because we were such good friends. I was happy to share my bed with such a pleasant man.

Erco came to the hospital because of a boil on the back of his neck, really nothing serious, but after three or four days, he developed diarrhea – which was one of the worst diseases in the camp. Despite my pleas and the doctor's advice, he wouldn't eat anything, claiming that he knew himself better and that if he didn't eat for two days, the situation would automatically improve quickly. It was a terrible mistake because, after two days, he was so weakened that he no longer had the minimum necessary strength to eat, and he literally fell into a state of total starvation. These were terrible days for me; seeing my good friend in this state was horrible. When death appeared upon his face, it took five days before he was relieved from his agony.

I sacrificed nights to accompany him when he had to get out of bed so often and helped him as much as I could with little things that were still somewhat possible, but there was no chance of saving him anymore. In the last few days, he also did not have the necessary strength anymore. Since none of us believed in the possibility of ever getting out of this hell alive, he no longer cared what would happen to him.

Erco was fully conscious and reacted normally. The last few days, he could no longer talk, but I could see that he was happy to be freed.

It was awful seeing a human being starving like this.

Erco passed away on January 17, 1944.

Of our group that was transferred, I am the only one to survive until today, and I don't understand why I was chosen to survive.

Arnold Erlanger

| Nazwisko | COSMANN | | Nr | 150630 |
| Imiona | Ernst | Oznaczenie | J. | |

ur. _____ w _____
Narodowość _____ Przyn. państw. _____
Zawód _____ Uwagi: † 15. 1. 1944 r.

Książka zgonów KL Auschwitz III

Źródła i materiały

Syg. D-AuIII-5/4 nr inw. 156998 str. 31

KRAK 4, Sarego 7 — 154/67 — 278 000

Death certificate from Auschwitz

Ilse's war

After Erco and his comrades were deported to Camp Westerbork, life seemed bleak, a future without hope. Ilse, however, managed to regain her footing quickly and began devoting her life to helping Ernst and his comrades as best she could. She became the indispensable link between the pioneers in the camp and the outside world. Ilse sent whatever was needed to Erco. In his letters, he writes a lot about things they needed. Ilse apparently took care of not only Erco's needs but also those of the whole group. Everything was in short supply: clothing, food, shoes, women's sanitary products, tobacco, cigarette paper and so on. In a letter to Tzippi Fränkel, the Jewish Council's courier, Werner Ahlfeld expressed his concern that Ilse was not sufficiently supported in this by the Jewish Central Vocational Training Center, the umbrella organization of hakhsharah schools: 'Ilse also sends us very much. I believe she and Erco, respectively, pay for that themselves. Talk to her sometime. I think the J.C.B. should pay it back to her.' Ilse used all the contacts she had to scrape things together. Her parents helped her, as did the Levison family in Zutphen, with whom Ilse lived in the house for a while until they, too, were rounded up. Farmer Oldenboom in Wilp, where Ernst had worked, also provided a lot of fresh produce from the farm. In addition to caring for Erco's group in Westerbork, Ilse was involved in illegal activities, according to stories from others. After the war, Ilse did not reveal much about her activities during the war after Erco was arrested. She discussed it at greater length with Israeli historians twice, once in 1957 and again in 1987.

Ilse talking with Gideon Drach, March 1957

'Because of my relations with Hechaloets and as I often visited Beth Chaluz on Tolstraat, I knew all the chawerim in Amsterdam. Since I did not have to wear a Jewish star, it was easy for me to help with the illegal work. I had a German passport and could thus give Lore Durlacher my identity card. She could use it to move around freely.

I took care of several people in hiding, visited them, arranged money and food, etc.

In mid-1942, I went on hachshara as a domestic helper for the Levison family in Zutphen. I could move around freely, so I traveled around the country a lot.

For example, I visited the house of the Youth Aliyah in Elden every week. My friend was a youth leader there. I consulted with him about his going into hiding.

I believe there was no general plan for the children in Elden. On October 20 or 23, all the Elden children were arrested and sent to Westerbork.

At that point, I began to help more intensively. First, I helped the chawerim in Westerbork by sending food and clothing. The Levison family and a Dutch farmer, Mr. Oldenboom in Wilp (Deventer), supported me. The farmer donated a lot of food for the chawerim for over a year.

In March 1943, the Levison family was also rounded up and sent to Vught.

I looked for a job with a vegetable grower in Twello and again sent parcels through the Jewish Council in Deventer to Westerbork on a daily basis. Those food items came from Dutch friends.

Meanwhile, I was regularly visited by Kurt Reilinger, who gave me various assignments. I also took care of Fanny and Manfred Reinhold in Terwolde, Hans and Ruth Stein in Terwolde, Werner and Lenie Rose in Wilp and Fieke de Winter and Hans Mogendorf in Terwolde.

Lenie and Werner, for example, lived in the most appalling conditions and had no contact with the chawerim until mid-1943. They had no coupons for food. No money, no clothes, and on top of that, Lenie was pregnant. Their host was terribly poor; he was a day laborer at a large farm, who incidentally paid Werner and Lenie with foodstuffs.

Ruth Stein also had a child (July 1943) in a Catholic hospital in Deventer. This child was hidden with Dutch people, devout Catholics. The child survived the war.

Ruth Stein and her infant son Michael, born in 1943 in Deventer. Ruth and Michael survived the war.

The Germans allowed me to handle Mr. Levison's affairs while he was imprisoned in Vught. (He was a rag merchant with many relations and supplies in the country.)

I always met him in Arnhem, and he gave me most of his money for our illegal activities. I delivered many thousands of guilders to Lore Durlacher.

Through my relations with several farmers, I was able to find some hiding places. It was very difficult to find them. I often felt that the Dutch could have provided more assistance, but they were usually uninterested. Conversely, many people, especially in religious circles, provided selfless help. For example, I knew a family with 9 children who also kept 5 Jewish children in hiding.

In September 1943, after my friends were deported out of Westerbork, I returned to my parents in Amsterdam. Before that, I had visited Westerbork once and found a chawera at a farmer's house outside the camp. I had brought a bicycle and clothes to help my friend flee.

However, the longer the chawerim were in the camp, the less courage they had to flee; they feared being put on punitive transport if they were caught again or of reprisals against others.

From September on, I had more contact with the chawerim and helped with the work by taking care of matters assigned to me. As my parents officially lived in Amsterdam, I was somewhat limited in my work.

When the news of the arrest of the chawerim of the Paris leadership reached us, it was not only a great blow to us, but it paralyzed all our work. We could no longer send chawerim across the border, and they had to remain where they were hiding.

In Amsterdam, on Prinsengracht, a nurse named Tieke housed 9 Jews, including chawerim. In the fall of 1944, all the people in hiding contracted typhoid fever, and Tieke nursed them until she became ill and died. The people in hiding all survived the war.

In the fall of 1944, the biggest problem was getting food. We rode bicycles across half the country to find food.

Once in Amersfoort, my companion Ruth Stein and I could not continue as we had no strength left. I went to the Ortskommandatur (local German headquarters) with my German pass to ask if we could travel on with army vehicles. (I subsequently used that pass more often; Frans made the passes).

I later heard that Ruth had weapons in her suitcase for an illegal Dutch organization.'

Ilse working on a farm in Wilp, 1943

An interview with Ilse Mandelbaum (Birnbaum) by Yigal Benjamin on February 17, 1987

What do you know about the preparations made in Elden for going into hiding?

I really only know what Erco and I discussed. I did not wear a star and could go there every week. I went there every week, and we always wrote to each other between visits. I kept suggesting he should leave, but he kept saying he could not leave the Chevra (community). I believe Loosdrecht had already gone into hiding by then, and I had the impression that nothing at all was being done for Elden.

Did Erco, who had a leading role in Elden between July and October 1942, tell you anything about preparations to go into hiding?

I was not informed about that, and neither was Erco. I kept telling him: 'Pack up and come!' I took his things, such as his camera and typewriter, and I had even found a place for him in a small town near Zutphen where he could hide, but I don't remember exactly where. I could not convince him; he felt he could not leave the Chevra alone. Furthermore, I know that I found a (hiding) place for Lini de Bruin (the person responsible for Elden) and her daughter. How and where, I don't remember. Then Erco wrote to me in one of his letters: 'Lini will remain with the same doctor for the time being, and he will continue to treat her with ointment.' That meant that she would stay there in hiding.

Did he ever mention any talks with Shushu about an organized hiding operation?

I think that if he had known anything, there would have been a duty of silence, and he would have kept quiet about it. I was with him a week before Elden was raided (October 3, 1942). If I had been there then, I would have been taken too. I thought about going to Westerbork voluntarily – a foolish idea – as I was obviously worth much more to the Chevrah outside the camp. Two days before he was taken, I wanted to go fetch him. I called him at the time, which was not common practice, and I blamed myself greatly for not persevering and not actually doing it. His friends Hans and Ruth Stein did go into hiding. Ruth later had a child (June 1943), and I was there. (He calls them friends in his letters, just like his former employee, farmer Oldenboom, with an 'O'.) After all, he knew about the opportunity to go into hiding, yet in all his letters, he wrote to me that I was too careless. He had much less courage than me and was far more anxious and anxious for me. Later, we bumped into each other a few times, for example, when people from Westerbork were sent to Apeldoorn in February for 'clearance work' after the deportation of the residents of the Apeldoornsche Bosch in January. A trooper smuggled me into the complex, where we met up. I told him, 'Erco, come with me now; we are leaving.' He said: 'No, I can't do that.' He couldn't abandon the children as he felt responsible for them. We had a fierce discussion about it. Two weeks before they were deported, they held a big agricultural show in Elden, for which they had worked very hard. Kurt Reilinger and I developed a close friendship; he always gave me coupons and had many other contacts. I can't remember all the details, but I know that I suffered terribly. You simply cannot tie someone up and then try to pull them out forcefully.

This mindset was actually expressed much more strongly in Westerbork, wasn't it?

Much stronger. You can read that in all of Erco's letters. We are in the Chevrah, we are organized, we eat together, we cook together, we work, we have a good name. Even now, after 45 years, you still want to jump out of your skin, but no one can imagine something like that. Every letter contained, 'We are young, we are strong, we persevere.' That was the preconception about most of them, but of course, in Westerbork, every individual attempting to escape risked reprisals against the group. For example, Dudi (one of the chawerim) ran away twice, and they brought him back twice. He had a lot of initiative. I don't remember when he was transferred, but apparently, it was only at the end.

Did Erco ever speak to you about existing plans in Elden to go into hiding when he was already in Westerbork?

No, never. In fact, if such plans had existed, he would naturally have said something in passing, such as: 'Too bad it didn't work out at the time.' Or: 'Too bad we didn't follow through then.' Because by then, any secrecy would, of course, have become moot.

What did you do in the period after October 1942?

First, I was still on hachshara at Levison in Zutphen as a maid. That was a household that is hard to imagine now. I then found a place through Kurt R. in Twello under my own name with a vegetable grower – impoverished farmers and wonderful people. Two British pilots were stashed at their place, and I didn't even notice; it was unbelievable that I didn't notice a thing. But I was busy, of course. I was allowed to live there with the understanding that I would work in the vegetable garden when I had nothing else to do. Then I did something stupid and stole the daughter's identity card, and naturally, they immediately suspected it was me. Then Kurt got me to a contact address in Deventer with an elderly lady who was always very nervous but who helped us a great deal. I stayed there for about six months. Then it got too risky; after all, I looked like a stranger. After that, I stayed in Teuge in Apeldoorn, and during the Hunger Winter of 1944/1945 (when there were no more raids), I went back to my parents in Amsterdam because my mother was very ill and got an ulcer due to malnutrition. My mother was supposedly 'Aryan,' which wasn't actually the case, and she kept telling me that I was endangering the whole family. In any case, I did not live in the house with my parents but in someone else's attic.

Did you begin your illegal work with Kurt after Shushu's death?

I gave my ID to Lore (Durlacher) when she became illegal. Kurt then said that two people with the same name could not live at the same address. I had a German pass, which was renewed once via the proper channels. The second time, I was too afraid to have it renewed at the Gestapo, and then Frans Gerritsen 'renewed' it for me. That all sounds improbable now, but in my idiotic innocence, I walked around with it. I don't know where I got the courage. Once, when the Germans nabbed me, I gave them such a big mouth that they immediately let me go. Ruth Stein was Jewish, and after her child was born, the baby was moved from one place to the next. Kurt said the two of us shouldn't go out into the streets because we looked like 'the entire Jewish community,' but I always kept in touch with Ruth. I was strongly influenced by her; she had a strong personality. Then a time came when it became very dangerous, and the others (chawerim) decided that Lore could no longer remain Ilse Birnbaum. She then became Els v.d. Bergh. I remained Ilse Birnbaum on my German pass, which was safer. We simply figured that a German pass would not be overly scrutinized.

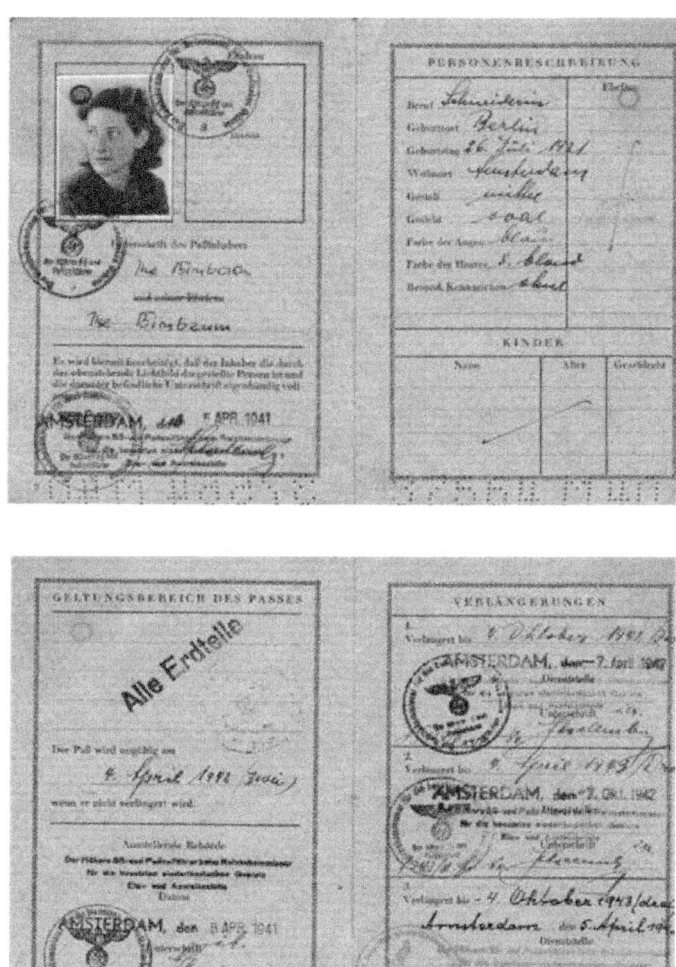

Ilse's passport, 'extended' by Frans Gerritsen.

Ilse and the Westerweel group

In Amsterdam, Ilse often visited the Beth Chaluz house on Tolstraat until April 1943, when the Germans found out about it. This house served as the headquarters of the Palestine Pioneers resistance. Several chawerim who worked for the underground movement lived there. They warned comrades of danger, provided hiding places, arranged falsified papers and voucher cards and delivered them to comrades throughout the country. Since early 1942, Jews had been prohibited from traveling, so someone like Ilse, who could move freely, was of great importance to the organization. They also tried to get in touch with other Dutch resistance groups that could be of interest to their organization. This resulted in the forming of a resistance group consisting of Jews and non-Jews, which was later named after Joop Westerweel. The Jewish part of the group came from the Hechalutz – the Zionist youth movement that prepared Jewish youth in the Netherlands for a life as farmers in Palestine. They were led by Joachim 'Shushu' Simon and Menachem Pinkhof and his friend Miriam Waterman. They asked a teacher, Joop Westerweel, for help when they needed hiding places for the pioneers from Loosdrecht who had to go into hiding in the summer of 1942. They succeeded. When the Germans came to take them to Westerbork, the Pavilion in Loosdrecht was empty.

The graphic designer Frans Gerritsen was an important member of the group. He knew how to masterfully forge identity cards and other documents, making him an indispensable member.

The raids made hiding increasingly dangerous and safe houses difficult to find. So the group tried to find a way to take hiders to Switzerland or Spain. Shushu Simon found a route to Spain, but he was arrested at the Belgian border in early 1943 and committed suicide to avoid betraying his comrades under torture. Another pioneer, Kurt Reilinger, who was good friends with Ilse, later managed to find an escape route to Spain. He arranged for pioneers to work as laborers for the Germans on the Atlantic Wall, and from there, with the help of the French resistance, they escaped to Spain. Many of these refugees escaped from Westerbork with the group's help. About 70 people fled to Spain, and 80 others hid in France. About 100 survived the war as hiders in the Netherlands.

Although Ilse did not talk much about those days, it is clear from statements by others that she was an active member of the resistance group around Joop Westerweel. The Dutch Jew Herman Italiaander, for example, only came into

contact with the Palestine pioneers while in hiding. Later, while in Westerbork, he lived in their barracks. He wrote that he was in contact with Ilse Birnbaum when – even before Ernst was sent to Auschwitz – they were organizing a mass escape for the entire hachshara group. The operation was canceled at the last minute. After October 1943, when Erco was already no longer in Westerbork, contacts with Ilse, Lore Durlacher and Frans Gerritsen intensified. Italiaander escaped with their help and was smuggled to Spain via France and reached Haifa in November 1944. Manfred and Fanny Reinhold, who hid in the chimney of a tile factory during the war, also said Ilse was one of the members of the resistance group that helped them. Fanny gave birth to a son in August 1942. Because it was too dangerous to leave the baby with them and because they did not want it to live in the unhealthy chimney room, Ilse's group found a woman who could take care of the child. Occasionally, Ilse or Lore Durlacher would bring the child to its mother for a while. All survived the war.

Paul Siegel, a Palestine pioneer who escaped from Westerbork with the help of the Westerweel group, also mentions her several times in his book *Locomotieven Trekken de Wagons*. In it, he describes, among other things, his life in Westerbork, where, aided by the strong group spirit of his comrades, he maintained himself for more than a year. He describes how, partly due to Ilse's good care, the group lacked very little. After he escaped from Westerbork, he encountered her again as she was a 'courier for the organization.' At his request, she will then try to inform his parents, who are in hiding, of his escape. However, the people with whom they are hiding do not want to speak to her for fear of traitors. With Joop Westerweel's and his organization's help, Siegel managed to reach Spain via France and across the Pyrenees. He arrives in Palestine at the end of 1944. When he is safely in Spain, Ilse delivers a letter to his parents.

1945, after the liberation, in Ilse's handwriting

After the liberation

After the Germans surrendered and Holland was free again, a confusing time filled with mixed feelings began. Slowly, friends and acquaintances who had survived the camps returned, and the obituaries of others arrived. At the end of May, Ilse received word that Erco was not returning. A letter from Ilse to Ruth Durlacher paints a clear picture of this period. After staying in the factory chimney in Terwolde, Ruth and her husband Zwi had been smuggled to Palestine via Spain by the Westerweel group.

Amsterdam, June 11, 1945

I was delighted to have received your letter of May 16 today. Yes, finally, we are free, but we still feel utterly shackled. You are healthy and on your way home. What a notion that is, returning home, it is almost impossible to understand. I do not yet have the concentration to write you a good, sensible letter. The constant intense emotions and different messages, then good and then bad, make it difficult to focus on anything. Personally, I have been very lucky, although the raids were often too close for comfort.
In retrospect, it seems like a miracle.
Because of my special position as a half-Jewish woman, I was fortunately often able to make myself useful. Unfortunately, I was not able to help my closest and dearest friends.
Two weeks ago, I received the news that my friend Ernst Cosmann, you may remember him, was killed in Auschwitz as recently as March. If I dwell on that thought, I might fall into despair, but I do not have time to think.

You ask about friends; it is difficult to give you an answer. Every day, I hear the names of others who have been saved. I will hereby include a short and very incomplete list of people who have been liberated from the camps or who have resurfaced here. These are the names off the top of my head. We receive new names every day. They include the most wonderful cases of happiness and the most terrible tragedies.

I sign off and hope to hear from you again soon. Please see if there is any possibility that we, too, can come soon. I still don't have a certificate.

Give my regards to Zwi as well.

Heartfelt greetings from me,
Ilse

Lotte Löwenstein surf.
Paula Kauffman lib.
Eva Fränkel lib.
Hans Moser lib.
Werner Ahlfeld en vrouw lib.
Lore Durlacher surf.
Heinz Frankl lib.
Alfred Fränkel (gen. Zippi) lib.
Paul Wolf lib.
Susi Herrmann lib.
Lola Eckard lib.
Heinz Cosmann surf.
Meta Walde lib.
Rokel en Ruth Karlsberg surf.
Wolfgang Zielenzieger surf.
Lore Pintus lib. And parents Ludwig Hoffmann lib.
Abbi Pinkus lib.

Chaja Rotstein surf.
Esther Singer lib.
Hess Cohen lib.
Hermann Cohen lib.
Ruth Stein met kind surf.

After the liberation, Ilse was with the Oldenboom family in Wilp, with soldiers from the Jewish Brigade, a part of the British army made up of Jewish volunteers from Palestine. After the liberation, they were stationed in the Netherlands and Belgium, among other places, where, against the wishes of the British, they helped Jewish survivors emigrate to Palestine. Ilse, with the dog, is standing next to her friend Lore Pintus, who would marry the soldier on the far left, Gaby Herman, that year. Lore remained in Westerbork for about three months after the liberation because she had nowhere else to go.

Ilse in Castricum, where, in the summer of 1945, the Zionist youth movement Hechaloets organized a large gathering. Holocaust survivors gathered here with, among others, the Jewish Brigade.

PART 2

The second generation

We are the generation that had no choice, the generation that carries the burden on its shoulders.
We are the generation that has seen the numbers on the arms.
We are the generation that heard the screams in the still of the night.
We are the generation that should not have asked about **IT**.
We are the generation that wanted to know about **IT** but had no one to tell them about **IT**.
We are the generation that was greeted with sorrow every day.
We are the generation who had to walk on eggshells.
We are the generation whose parents refused to board a train.
We are the generation who grew up in a house full of secrets.
We are the generation for whom silence played a starring role, who were not told the horrors, but even without hearing about **IT**, still understood **IT**.
We are the generation without grandparents, uncles or aunts.
We are the generation where bread was never thrown away.
We are the generation that always had sugar, flour, salt, rice and oil in the house.
We are the generation that was not allowed to disappoint.
We are the generation that was not allowed to be teenagers.
We are the generation that was not allowed to complain.
We are the generation that understands it is impossible to

prepare for Satan's kingdom.
Our generation is a living monument.
Our generation perpetuates memory and records.
There is no diploma for the second generation; its burden is to be the world's memory.
Often, our shoulders cannot bear the burden. Yet, it is our sacred duty in honor of our grandparents, uncles, and aunts to carry this torch with pride and tell future generations the story of what took place in Europe during the previous century.

Something that should never ever be forgotten.
There is no diploma for the second generation.

Ilse and David

Summertime, August 1945, the sun is shining, and the weather is nice. It is nice weather to say goodbye to the beautiful city of Amsterdam. A small suitcase with two dresses, two pairs of pants, two blouses, some underwear, a photo album and Erco's 105 letters. With these possessions, Ilse leaves her second homeland. She is assisted by The Joint (American Jewish Joint Distribution Committee), and together with a few friends, she sets off to the port city of Marseille in sunny southern France.

Ilse in La Ciotat

The small medieval town of La Ciotat, not far from Marseille, has an abandoned castle that has been converted into a temporary shelter camp for all the refugees who want to leave Europe after all they have been through there.

The long wait in La Ciotat is enjoyable and wholesome for the refugees. The weather is beautiful, as are the surroundings; it seems like a long vacation. The young Jewish men and women there experience a long, unexpected period of recovery. They are the remnants of their families, the scarce survivors, with memories of the many who are no longer there. It is better to not think about it, at least for a while ...but that is impossible.

Waiting for a ship to Palestine

In December 1945, Ilse became very ill with scarlet fever, followed by Bell's palsy. Her face twitches, one corner of her mouth droops down, and the eye on that side can no longer close properly. She is treated with old-fashioned electrical equipment at a hospital in Marseilles; she receives painful electric shocks. The treatment helps, however, and Ilse gradually recovers. In this unlikely situation – a beautiful young woman with a distorted face – a beautiful boy comes to the hospital every day to encourage her. This helps her to get better, and she falls in love, a feeling that was unimaginable after Erco's death.

Ilse and David

Cupido shoots his arrow; he knows what he is doing. He brings feeling back into the world where emotion has lost its way in dark, musty basements. There is nothing stronger than life itself! The impossible suddenly becomes possible again: a gentle caress, a warm hug, a lingering kiss, nerves awakening, not out of agony, but out of passionate love.

    David Mandelbaum and Ilse Birnbaum are together, and they are in love, no matter how their different backgrounds. David comes from a very religious, Polish-Jewish home, while Ilse comes from an assimilated German-Jewish home. David's family was warm and loving, with a Yiddish mother. Anything was allowed as long as the children had fun. Ilse's home was cold and strict – Prussian upbringing applied: children should be seen but not heard ... but the family was also loving and caring.

David survived eleven concentration camps; Ilse was fortunate never to have been in any of them. David lost both his parents. Ilse still has her parents.

David and Ilse come from families who lacked nothing financially before the war. They make a strikingly beautiful couple; they both have beautiful curls and blue eyes. Together, they have one goal: to leave the blood-soaked European continent as soon as possible.

Ilse and David in Marseille

Palestine

On March 17, 1946, the time has come for a large group to leave La Ciotat. They are bound for the port of Marseilles, where the ship Tel Chai will anchor. The ship could carry about 400 passengers, but almost twice as many board. It is impossible to refuse even one person a place on board. However, the organizers do ask that no luggage be brought on board; there is no more room for that. After all, they had to take a lot of extra food on board.

David, a true survivor, smuggles a suitcase with down blankets on board. Of course, the source of these down blankets is a mystery – in such chaotic times, one can only guess... Likewise, about the source of a gold Omega ladies' watch and a Doxa men's watch....

Ilse, a true Jekkette, as German Jews are called in the Hebrew dialect, obediently does what is demanded. She brings nothing with her except for the bare necessities. And so she boards the ship with a dress, a pair of shoes and a handbag ...a handbag containing a photo album and the 105 letters from Erco.

The ship departs with 736 illegal immigrants on board. The journey becomes a ten-day hell. The people lie on wooden bunk beds, and there is no room to stand or sit down. The only luxury consists of climbing on deck

Immigrants hoist the Zionist flag.

every now and then to catch one's breath or to vomit in the sea. They twice encounter stormy weather, which causes unwelcome delays and even more discomfort, impatience and seasickness.

On March 26, the lights of the port of Haifa become visible in the distance; a few hours later, the Tel Chai anchors off the coast of the Promise Land. The sparse remnant of the great European Jewish community can finally taste freedom again.

All 736 stateless refugee survivors stand on deck and sing the Hatikwa. The dock workers standing on the dock wave with tears in their eyes. The crowd on the dock shouts loud, clear and heartfelt: WELCOME! The survivors are finally on safe ground.

*The Tel Chay anchors. English soldiers stand guard.
No one is allowed to leave the ship.*

Ilse loses her left shoe in the scramble and takes her first steps with her right shoe. Does it predict happiness? No one knows; the next few days will tell. Her first steps in Palestine, with one shoe, a dress, and a purse filled with Erco's letters.

Free, but no freedom.

Palestine is governed by the British Mandate, and the illegal, stateless, surviving immigrants are sent to a detention camp in Atlit, where they are prisoners once again.
They are released after a short period of time.

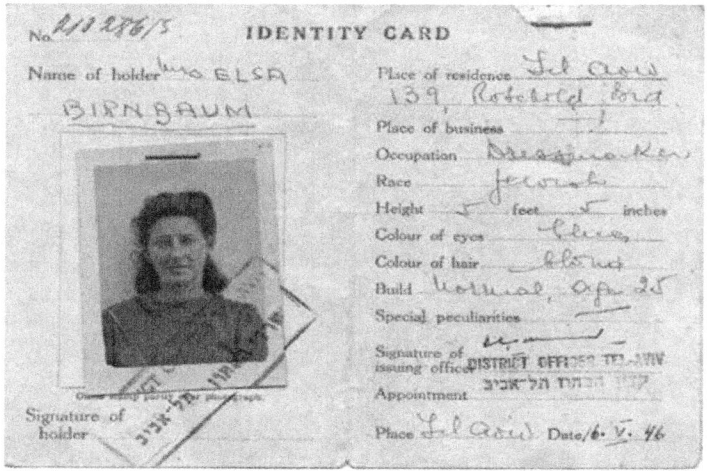

Identity card, British Mandate in Palestine voor Elsa Birnbaum

Ilse has a married niece, Steffi Hirsch, who lives with her husband Akiwah and their four-year-old son in the kibbutz Ramat Ha'Kowesh. Steffi is a niece; a niece means 'family,' and one goes where one has a family. Ilse and David settle in the kibbutz Ramat Ha'Kowesh.

Steffi immigrated to Palestine with the Youth Aliah from Berlin back in 1936. She met Akiwah Hirsch there. They married very young and settled in the kibbutz.

David Mandelbaum and Ilse Birnbaum begin their new life. Free at last. Ilse writes enthusiastically to her parents in Amsterdam. She finds it strange; what should she tell her parents now that she is changing from a Birnbaum to a Mandelbaum? She writes, 'his name is David Mendelssohn,' which she thinks is fancier. But how long can David remain a Mendelssohn?

May 10, 1946, on the promenade in Tel Aviv

On August 11, 1946, David and Ilse get married in the kibbutz. There is no money for a ring; it is borrowed from someone before the ceremony. Ilse does not have a white dress with a veil, and David does not have a tuxedo. The kibbutz organizes two boxes of grapes and a box of broken cookies from the kibbutz's cookie factory. For the toast, they have cold water. There are about 10 guests, including Eshu, who also came with the Tel Chai, and my uncle Joseph, my father's brother, also an Auschwitz graduate who, against all odds, survived hell. Joseph was liberated by the U.S. Army at Dachau on April 29, 1945. As an older brother, he felt a responsibility toward his little brother and initially had objections about the bride. After all, the bride is not of Polish descent...

Oh well... so much for not being of Polish descent. Soon, all is forgotten. Ilse gets a great Polish brother-in-law and Joseph, a lovely, smart German sister-in-law.

David and Ilse's wedding photo, August 11, 1946

Life in the kibbutz is not easy. The kibbutz is poverty-stricken, Arab neighbors infiltrate every night, and there is a lot of vandalism and even murder and manslaughter. Night after night, men lie in wait in the trenches around the kibbutz, guarding the residents but also the kibbutz itself.

Women with children are evacuated. Women without children and pregnant women remain in the kibbutz for essential work, like caring for the livestock, chickens and horses. The cookie business must also continue as the factory is one of the few sources of income they have at these times. People never complain. On the contrary, the wheat fields surrounding the kibbutz, the warm, caressing sun, and the sweet-smelling orchards with orange, grapefruit, lemon and tangerine trees make up for everything. At night, all the intoxicating scents are released, and the smell of nature's perfume hangs in the air under a cloudless sky full of twinkling stars. Ilse and David breathe freedom deep into their lungs ... Ilse's tummy grows. Ilse is carrying life in her belly.

Haya

February 18, 1947, almost on the day two years after David's liberation, Ilse and David embrace a daughter; they embrace me. Haya is my name. My grandmother, who did not survive, was named Haya. Haya means 'life.'

The kibbutz was at the forefront of the Zionist attempt to establish a state, a project that soon succeeded. Life in the kibbutz is conducted according to socialist doctrine and socialist values. Everyone is equal, men and women, and everyone works together. Everything is for everyone, and everyone is there for the community in the kibbutz. Babies stay with their father and mother until they are six weeks old, and then they move to the children's home, where there are nurses who take care of the babies. The mothers return to the work they were doing until shortly before their babies were born.

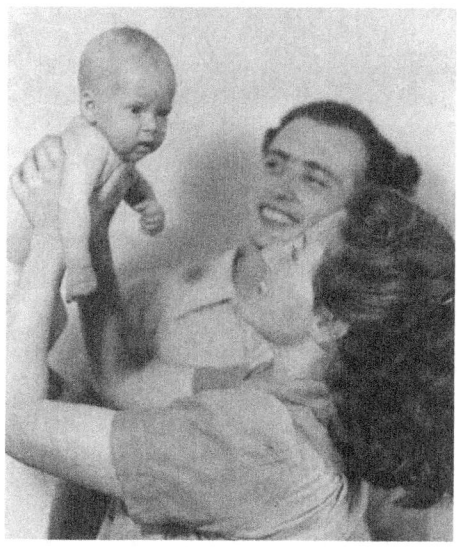

At four in the afternoon, the parents return from work, and little ones and parents are together until seven in the evening. Then the little ones return to the children's home where they are washed, given their evening meal, read to and put in their beds. The nurses sleep with the babies. A crying baby is tended to by a nurse and not a mother or father.

Babies with a childminder in the kibbutz

Physically, Ilse and David, my parents, survived the Holocaust. Mentally, they hadn't yet. Immediately after my birth, my mother falls into a severe depression. She cries incessantly. In her imagination, she sees trains with small children going east. My birth turns out to be a traumatic event. In the kibbutz, struggling with too many problems of her own, chawera Ilse's situation receives little understanding. She is left without help and without support. Ilse's mental state does not fit into this community of tough people who have to face major existential problems every day.

Because of the 'precarious' situation (according to the 'scholars' of the kibbutz), I am moved to the children's home as quickly as possible. The intention is good, but the consequences will manifest themselves for years. However, my mother does come to feed me. Not at night, as that's not allowed according to Bolshevik rules. That's what nurses are for, equal rights and duties for everyone. Very quickly, Ilse completely breaks down.

A kibbutz fighting for survival is unable to solve the problem of chawera Aliza, as Ilse has now been named. Slowly, Aliza/Ilse regains her strength without professional help, simply because the reality of life demands it. Then, a new problem surfaces in the family.

At just twelve weeks old, I become ill. I cannot digest food, have diarrhea and vomit constantly. I am admitted to Tel Aviv's Assuta Hospital. The diagnosis is dystrophy, the painful degeneration of tissue due to malnutrition. There is no pediatric ward at that time, so I lay among all kinds of sick people with various diseases and connected to IV tubes from head to toe. To this day, I bear the scars on my body.

My mother gets to be with me for an hour every day, and she is here for that hour without fail every day. She drives three hours there and three hours back. The kibbutz gives her the money for the bus, which is very special. She does everything she can in that one hour: washing me, taking me for a walk in the sun, and especially turning me over regularly. My weakness and lack of supervision have caused bedsores. The situation worsens by the day and seems hopeless. Professor Meyer, head of the department, invites my parents and says, 'The child is dying. You are young and healthy; make a new child. Forget this child.'

My childhood in Israel

Times were hard and difficult. Many were wounded by the War of Independence going on at the time, and there were so many sick and traumatized Holocaust survivors. And everyone needed treatment. Blinding the senses was probably an existential need, a necessary self-defense in these times.

No bad intentions, but stark reality. There, a newborn baby lies ... Is there a God in heaven? Perhaps there is.

That same day, my parents, Ilse and David, returned to the kibbutz, sad and crying. A member of the kibbutz, a tractor driver, waits for them outside their front door and tells them, 'I arrived back today from the Ha'Emek hospital in Afula, where sick children are being successfully treated.' The following day, they return to Assuta

Hospital in Tel Aviv to fetch me and, take me to the hospital in Afula, about a hundred kilometers from Tel Aviv.

My condition continues to deteriorate overnight; I am actually dying. The hospital warns my parents that they are taking a dying child out of the hospital, and they have to sign a form that they understand. They do.

There is a war going on between the Arabs and the Jews; the road to the north of the country is extremely dangerous. The kibbutz provides an armored vehicle, and thus, I am transferred to the hospital in the north. The road is long and difficult, death lurking under the blanket, but they succeed in this impossible task. The hospital is in sight, and when they arrive, they receive a warm welcome and encouraging words: 'Yes, we have good experience with these cases; everything will be fine. We are optimistic!' Hearing these words made the dangerous journey worth it.

David and Ilse are not allowed to stay in this hospital either, and so they drive back to the kibbutz in the armored vehicle. From that moment on, my parents have no contact with the hospital. It is impossible to make the drive to the north of the country again. It is too dangerous as there are snipers along the roads, and many roads are blocked.

They can't make phone calls either. The only phone the kibbutz has is an 'emergency phone' to be used only in an emergency, not for a deathly ill child. Times are hard, and so are the people; their survivor mentality leaves no room for compassion. The strong stand a chance; the weak do not.

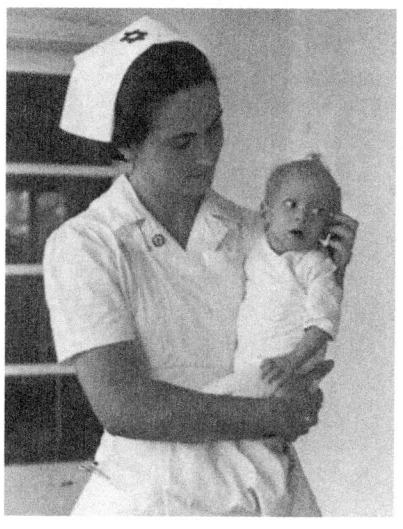

Chaja, 8 months old, Ha'Emek Hospital in Afula 1947

I was never told what my parents' mental state was during these times. About nine months go by. Then the same tractor driver of the kibbutz, located in the north of the country, decides to go and see what happened to the kibbutz's little chawera. He meets a vivacious little girl with a mouth full of teeth and a head full of blond curls running happily down the hospital corridors toward him. 'This is the hospital's little doll,' the nurse tells him. 'The whole medical staff here is her father and mother, her family. We absolutely adore this baby.'

*January 1948, at the Ramat Ha'Kowesh kibbutz
in Palestine during winter*

I don't know when my parents finally got to hug me again, but I was about a year old when they brought me home. The whole kibbutz – men, women and children – greeted us with tears of happiness and with great excitement.

The war of independence is in full swing. Women with children are being evacuated to another kibbutz, a kibbutz a little further inland that is not directly on the border like Ramat Ha'Kowesh is. The men stay behind. After being evacuated overnight, Ilse, my mother, comes back to the kibbutz alone, without me. She left me in the care of another woman...

Why? I don't know. Perhaps she was afraid of losing another man in her life? Again, I am left on my own for a while and again under the supervision of others.

The war of independence continues. Akiwah Hirsch, the husband of Steffi, Ilse's niece, is killed. Exactly two weeks after the birth of his second son. Ilse is determined to leave the kibbutz.

My parents fetch me again, and we depart. The kibbutz is furious with David and Ilse, and they are prohibited from taking anything with them. And so they leave the kibbutz with me, wearing only a shirt. Nothing more is allowed: no shorts, no blouse, no blanket or sheet, and no diaper; everything is the property of the kibbutz. For a whole year – possibly even longer – after they have left, David goes to the kibbutz every night for surveillance and patrols. He considers that his personal duty. The women with children no longer living there meant that there were a lot of unused cribs. David asks if he can borrow one of those cribs for me, but the kibbutz refuses; it is the property of the kibbutz.

Still, David keeps doing his duty every night. These are hard times, hard people, and that harsh reality is impossible to judge now.

The family moves to Sde Warburg, a beautiful pastoral village. They rent a small room. Ilse works as a seamstress and cleaner, and David works in the military industry. After a while, David enlists in the army and becomes a soldier.

Has the time come to say goodbye to Erco's letters? Ilse feels obliged to give the letters to Thekla Cosmann, Erco's mother. Those letters are the only thing left of Erco, her son. She takes me with her to the Dovrat kibbutz and parts ways with the letters. Many years later, she told me that it felt like an amputation but that it had to happen sometime. Mrs. Cosmann reads all the letters, and after a few months, she invites Ilse back and says:

'These letters are yours,' and that is how the letters end up back in Ilse's possession.

January 1949 in Petach Tiqwah, Israel

About a year later, the Mandelbaums move again. This time, they go to Petach Tikwa, a small town where they rent a two-room house. The toilet is in the garden, and there is no bathroom; they bathe in a tin tub in the kitchen, like in the Wild West. Water is heated on a primus stove in a large washtub. David constructs a nice couch from old orange crates, and Ilse sews the upholstery. To this day, I remember the nice sofa set my parents made. It became cozy; it was a home. Peak Street No. 23 in Petach Tikwa becomes our palace.

Food is still a big problem, as it is for many. It is difficult to get food, and after standing in line for hours, with fresh memories of the Hunger Winter in Amsterdam in 1944, my mother does not and cannot accept the fact that I do not want to eat. She knows what hunger is and what hunger means, and she forces me to eat.

I often vomit, and then I have to eat my own vomit.

When I vomit in kindergarten, my nanny assures me that she will not tell my mother. 'This is our secret,' she says. Many times, at ten o'clock in the morning, she would remove the accumulated food from my cheeks as I refused to swallow the food. I was not the only one; there were lots of children who reacted the same way. Our parents had suffered hunger, and so we were forced to eat. It was traumatic, and it still is.

Purim 1954, dressed as a girl from Volendam on Rothschild Boulevard in Tel Aviv

Regardless of how small I still was, the motto then was, 'Your father has suffered enough; you must not add to it. You have to eat!!!!!' (I was about 4 years old at the time.)

Ilse continues to work as a seamstress and cleaner, and David is now a professional soldier. Many packages arrive from Amsterdam containing everything they need. Between the years 1949 and 1959, everything is rationed, including food. There is no hunger, but there is only a small selection of food items on the shelves in the stores, and thus not much to buy. Agriculture doesn't yield much yet. The trees are still young (except the citrus trees). Apples, pears, peaches, bananas, avocados, everything still has togrow. Tomatoes are given to the industry, but one can buy 'secondhand' tomatoes at the greengrocer ... measly leftovers. The same applies to cucumbers and other vegetables. During these years, more and more immigrants arrived from all over the place. There just wasn't enough, and yet it was enough; there was absolutely no hunger! Some of the best cookbooks were written during these times. A zucchini can be used to make:

A) An appetizer: chopped zucchini with onions, tastes like chopped liver. Delicious with a slice of black bread (there is no other bread).

B) Second course, zucchini soup (with a slice of black bread).

C) Main course, zucchini patties with lots of fried onions and potatoes (with a slice of black bread).

D) Dessert, zucchini compote with cinnamon and lemon, tastes exactly like apple compote.

Who is still hungry after that much bread?

Every now and then, when the Americans are pleased with us, as in 1956 when Israel, at America's request, withdrew from all of conquered Sinai, we get American treats. All of a sudden, we could buy salted butter, as much as we wanted, which is subsequently used for and in everything.

In 1952, my grandmother comes to visit, and I am given my first doll. Ilse also receives a present: a wedding ring, something she still didn't have at that time. David solemnly blessed her again with this ring, and it never leaves her finger. Today, her granddaughter Tamar wears this ring.

My grandmother, German and practical, brings suitcases full of fabrics and wool with her. After all, Ilse learned haute couture sewing at Gerzon in Amsterdam, which now comes in handy. Haute couture may not be the most necessary thing in a country where only sailcloth and khaki fabrics are available, but Ilse can do a lot with my grandmother's fabrics. She can earn a few pennies with it, and so she sews beautiful dresses and knits beautiful sweaters. She has a few customers who can afford this luxury... For me, she sews and knits the most beautiful clothes and dresses me up like a mannequin. For many years, I stood there like a scarecrow in a field with my arms wide to the side, holding my breath in fear of being pricked by a pin.

In 1953, the Mandelbaums move again, this time to the 'Shikun,' an apartment complex built for the military. David and Ilse buy a small house there. The purchase is largely subsidized by the army. They consist of seven four-story buildings, each with three entrances, beautiful gardens between the houses, with sand, more sand and more sand around the houses. No road, access only in a command car, a military vehicle one could drive into the neighborhood.

The roofs of these seven beautiful buildings house the laundry rooms where the women meet every Sunday,
to do and hang laundry. White sheets would blow in the warm summer wind. The first sheet is already dry before the last sheet is hung. The atmosphere among all these women is a true celebration.

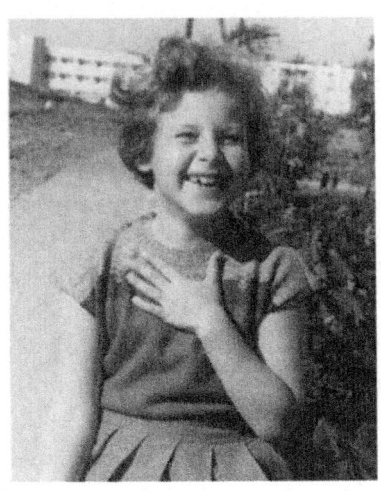

Joyful and happy in the Shikun, 1956

The population is homogeneous; everyone mostly has a lot of 'nothing.' A table, a few chairs and beds, some pans and plates. No one has a refrigerator, but they do have a cabinet with ice. So, very early every morning, all the men stand around the small, toothless, skinny man with his skinny donkey and his cart that is almost falling apart. They are dressed in a white undershirt, the hair on their chests blowing with the wind. With tongs specially designed for this sacred work, the sturdy men carry home the heavy ice block. We, little children, hovered around the ice vendor. Every now and then, a small piece of ice broke off, which was then 'the ice cream of the day' for us. This way, we had another 24 hours of ice in the refrigerator cabinet. On Friday, we buy a double portion because the skinny ice vendor doesn't come on the Sabbath.

Selling ice on the street, a big children's party, 1953.

For the first two years, there is no school in this neighborhood. We, about sixteen children, are stuffed into an ancient 'cab' and driven to a school in a neighborhood where there already is a school. After two years, our neighborhood gets its own school. Still, there are not enough classrooms, so we are taught in two shifts; a morning shift and an afternoon shift. This works out just fine.

The morning begins with a full hour of morning exercise each day. The school provides a hot meal every day, as well as all medical care. Every child is examined once a week by the school nurse. During these years, the government followed all the Bolshevik doctrines, which was not a bad policy at the time.

The food is much better, and the vomiting has lessened since the implementation of meals at school, where no one watches how much you do or do not eat, which definitely has a positive effect. However, that's also when the severe pneumonia epidemic starts, resulting in my not being allowed to play outside. For a child who only wants to play outside all the time, this is as bad as the death penalty. Whenever possible, I ran away from home to play outside with my friends, and when I came home with bright red cheeks, I got a few more sound slaps on the head, which made my cheeks blush even more.

And again, the motto echoed: 'Your father has suffered enough; you must not add to it!' (I was about 8 years old at the time.)

The years in the Shikun, when I was between six and eleven years old, were years of pure happiness. The Shikun was a paradise, an island of happiness for five years and the best years of my early childhood.

Top: With my friend Nechama. The Shikun in the background
Bottom: With my friend Uri.

Immigrating to the Netherlands

To this day, I don't know why my parents decided to leave Israel and move to the Netherlands.

My parents needed space to liquidate everything there was to liquidate, so on June 15, they put me on a plane to Amsterdam on my own.

Passport photo 1958.
How sad I was to leave my country

My Vati and Mutti embrace a crying, shivering child at Schiphol Airport. From a sunny, warm Israel to a chilly, gray Amsterdam. From a world full of friends to a lonely world without language and without freedom. Streetcar number 24 runs until eleven at night. The streetlights shine into the small room, and big raindrops hit the window. As I lean against the cold window crying, my Mutti comes in and says, 'Jetzt lebst du für immer in Holland, auch Holland ist ein gutes Land, du sollst nicht weinen, das hilft nicht' (Now you live in Holland forever. Holland is also a good country, so you shouldn't cry; crying doesn't help.) She didn't have a degree in psychology, but she meant well.

My parents won't arrive for three months. Why three months? I don't know, and I understand even less. Vacation? A vacation from me? I make do without my parents for three months; it is a lot to ask from an 11-year-old child who had to leave everything behind. After all, I never had a say in the decision to leave Israel! I was a pawn in a game that was moved around insensitively.

My Vati and Mutti, bad as they were with psychological issues, were wonderful grandparents. My Mutti never forced me to eat. She cooked whatever I wanted, and I loved 'Hammelfleisch mit grünen Bohnen,' mutton with green beans ... she cooked it for me daily for three months without any discussion. Perhaps my Mutti was not as bad at psychology after all. No unnecessary warfare...

After three months had passed, my parents finally arrived. They rented a very small apartment on Argonautenstraat on the corner of Olympiaplein. We shared this apartment with a nice, elderly, unmarried lady of German descent, Fraülein Schick. It was a disgusting apartment; my parents slept in the sitting room at the front, overlooking the street. I was given a dark, narrow, ugly back room that couldn't even hold a table.

Meanwhile, it is September, the beginning of autumn. It's gray outside, and the leaves are falling from the trees. My mood is also plummeting; without friends, it is depressing. I don't believe my parents were in a better situation, but unlike me, they chose this themselves.

Children are children, so after a few days, I meet the Busnach sisters. Now I hula hoop endlessly, from sunup to sundown. I am already learning my first Dutch words. Life becomes a bit lighter.

In September, I start school at the Rosj Pina School, although I still hardly speak a word of Dutch, let alone write or read. A kind Mr. Bolle, a teacher with heart and soul, voluntarily tutors me every day after school for half an hour. It works, and after six months, I can speak, write and read Dutch.

My very first best friend is Haya Hertzberger, who could already speak Hebrew. Haya and Haya, we are inseparable. She teaches me Dutch, and I teach her Hebrew – two sweet, fun and cheerful Hayas. My circle of friends grows: Dieuwke Themans, Saskia Themans, Rita Gunsberger, Gitta Meyers, Vonny Appelboom, and many more...

Meanwhile, the Mandelbaums move to Roerstraat 84, Amsterdam-Zuid. It's a nice house, and I get a nice room; life is on the up. The Rosj Pina School is quite close, so I walk to school; I don't need to take a streetcar or a bus. After a while, Haya takes me to the Haboniem youth movement. What an intelligent girl Haya Hertzberger is; she knows exactly what is right for me, and so the Haboniem youth movement becomes the compensation for the life I had to leave behind with great sorrow a few months earlier. I put my heart and soul into the movement. I make many new girlfriends and friends, and the De Groot sisters, Jolly and Bertie, become my dearest friends. They live in the Biesboschstraat, a small street next to the Roerstraat. The De Groot house became my house, and I still nostalgically think of Sunny and Sonja, the parents of Jolly and Bertie.

Haboniem becomes my lust and joy! I wear a blue blouse with a red ribbon, a 'Kaffia.' Meetings, madrichim (leaders), chanichim (students), shlichim (messengers), Ash Laila (bonfires), stencils. Fierce Zionist debates with only one theme: the moral duty to emigrate to Eretz Israel, which is a given for me.

I feel very good at Haboniem and at school, but my homesickness for Israel does not ease; quite the contrary. I miss my school, my neighborhood, my girlfriends, my cousins and my family. I miss the evening scent of Israel, and I miss the summer heat. I miss my little room, the big mulberry tree with its long and high branches in which we, children from all over the neighborhood, climbed to see the world from above. I miss the high sand hill that we clambered up to jump off of day in and day out. I miss the wild cacti with their thorns, I miss all that beauty across from our little home in the Shikun, and I miss the youth in my country that was taken from me, stolen from me – I am homesick. And yet, Haboniem is something very special.

The camps were always the highlight of Haboniem. For six months, the members lived in anticipation of the camp; for six months, they talked about how great the camp was. The tragedy before each camp was huge, as I was never allowed to go. Why? Concern? Fear? Was there a reasonable reason? No, not at all. The real reason was just selfish unwillingness to cause yourself unnecessary worry. Saying 'no' is easier than saying 'yes.' It was never clear to me who the 'culprit' was, my father or my mother. After all, surely she still remembered the situation in her childhood home! How is it possible that such behavior could be so precisely repeated?

And again, the motto echoes, 'Your father has suffered enough; you must not add to it!' (I was about 14 years old at the time.)

After a lot of crying and the efforts of many dear madrichim, many dear friends, and many dear parents of friends all doing their best to change my fate with my parents, it succeeds! I get to go to camp!

They were work camps, picking berries from a farmer, but also making love in the forest and eating hot food in the evening, which is a sticky mass somewhat reminiscent of 'pasta.' It tastes divine, although instead of salt, there is sand in it... I have never eaten anything this delicious at home.

A few years go by; camps are out, seminars are in. Seminars are very different, as they are much more mature. Intelligent lectures are given by very intelligent people,

all about Zionism, the State of Israel, Judaism, etc. A very serious business for very unserious youngsters full of healthy hormones. Seminars, staying in your room, having sex, while excruciatingly boring lectures are being held in the auditorium.

Wow, how wonderful it all was. I'm sure these Haboniem years played a very important role in my later life and may have defined the rest of my life. Haboniem was a mainstay, a kind of cast for all of us.

It was around this time that a beautiful, innocent love story began, my first love, tender yet real. Things were difficult at my home, but my boyfriend had no home at all; he wandered all over Amsterdam on his bicycle like a vagrant.

Pretty soon, my parents decided that he was not the right partner for me. Why my dear boyfriend was not right for me is a mystery to me, and thus, four years of lying to my parents began.

The lie became my other half; we saw each other daily, meaning I also lied daily.

Why? Is history repeating itself again? Is it a kind of revenge? I dare not think about it, but it certainly comes to mind. Every now and then, the lie fails. I get caught; we are a couple. A catastrophe: we are caught together. I have violated the strictest prohibition, which comes with severe punishment.

And once again, I have to listen to the motto: 'Your father has suffered enough; you must not add to it!' (I was around 16 or 20 years old.)

Four years go by with all the limitations and with all the lies that have long since stopped bothering us. Life is beautiful and sweet; we are beautiful and sweet. All of Amsterdam knows the story. Everyone, our friends and their parents are all collaborators, helping us with 'hiding places.' In fact, everyone is so sweet to the two of us! We were very ordinary, sweet teenagers in love... Yet this way of life at this age comes at a heavy price. A price that we, as two young, inexperienced, immature, naive, sweet children, cannot pay.

It is June 1967, and the Six-Day War breaks out. Before I understand what is happening, my boyfriend is on the first plane volunteering for Israel. It fits right in with our education, our upbringing, and our common goal. This unexpected opportunity just fell into his lap; it was an opportunity he would not pass up. My boyfriend stays away for four months; he is in the Kissufiem kibbutz, working himself half to death in the heat, but he is free, and he is happy... the lies are on vacation.

For four months, I think about my future, and then I decide: I am not staying in the Netherlands! After nine years in the Netherlands, I am going back to Israel.

I make this decision alone, without my boyfriend. I do not share my thoughts on this subject either with him or with my parents. However, I do share my plans with my boyfriend's dear mother. She understands, and we weep together.

Two years earlier, my father had said to me, 'You can leave home as soon as you have a trade and a driver's license.' I now meet the conditions. I am a dental technician, and I have a driver's license.

In early September 1967, my boyfriend came back from Israel, beautiful, happy and with a tan. We have about ten wonderful loving days and nights together, full of happiness and pure love, wild and tender, laughing, crying, shivering and trembling.

Farewell happiness? Does such a thing exist? No, there is no such thing. We were too young, too naive, too innocent, and lacked the necessary mental tools to make decisions substantiated with the required courage. I make my decision alone and leave him standing alone, crying, at streetcar stop number 4, Maasstraat. I walk into the Maasstraat, crying. We both know that we will never again have what we had.

And back again

On September 15, 1967, I leave the Netherlands. After nine wonderful years in the Netherlands, many wonderful friends and a fairytale romance. Holland has undoubtedly contributed to my personality, but to make it complete, I must leave my parental home, and that is what I am doing. I have never regretted it; I know I made the right decision for my parents and for me. My parents could not handle the responsibility of being my parents. By leaving, I relieve them of that responsibility. I am giving my parents back the peace and tranquility they need.

The motto 'Your father has suffered enough; you must not add to it!' no longer exists. No more lies, either. (I was 20 years old.)

Israel's blue sky is brimming with sunshine. Life after the Six-Day War is euphoric. The small country of Israel has grown nicely in the nineteen years it has been around, both in length and in width. New landscapes, new smells, new neighbors, and many excursions. The joy is unending, and our pleasure is unsatiable.

The world spoils me. My uncles, aunts, cousins, nieces, friends, and girlfriends are all nine years older. There are warm hugs, a warm welcome, lots of love, and all our hearts grow fond.

All my mother's (Ilse) friends also welcomed me with open arms, like Lore Pintus, who is now called Lore Herman. Lore paints beautifully, teaches art, and is successful. Lea Mikulinsky, now called Lilly Milstein, is a singer and performs a lot. Later, she also becomes a painter. Eshu Singer, now called Esther Yurman, is a nurse. All three of these women are in good contact with each other. The fourth part of the foursome, Ilse, is missing.

Lore has two children, Lilly (Lea) has two children, and Esther (Eshu) also has two children. One day, Judith, Lore's daughter, invites me over. She lives in a primitive artistic house filled with culture, good food and a nice atmosphere. After about an hour, an Apollo arrives. He can't stay long because his brother, who is studying veterinary medicine in Ghent, is leaving for Belgium again the next morning. Later on, I realized that Judith had invited the Apollo to meet the European Venus.

At the moment, I am not interested in a boyfriend, not even a Greek god.

The Apollo is still in the army and has been given the task of arranging something in the Sinai Desert for a week. He invites me to go along. A week (in uniform, me in uniform...) with him and with a few more soldiers in the Sinai Desert. How can I resist such a temptation? Of course I go with him. We spend a week crossing the whole magnificent Sinai Desert, Santa Catherine, Sharm-el-Sheikh, Abu Rhodes, the Suez Canal, A'tour, Ismaïlia, and more. The desert is beautiful by day but even more so by night, full of shining stars in a blue-gray sky and the howling of jackals in the distance.

Oded and Haya in the Sinaï, 1968

Oded Ravinsky (Apollo) and I are in touch from time to time. Oded is kind to me, and that is what I need during these first months in Israel. I need to heal, I need to recover, but most of all, I need to learn that normal people, in general, don't need to lie. Automatic lying is an addiction. You have to go through a rehabilitation process in order to get rid of it.

There is another thing that is very important to me: I need to be independent, not be directed or live someone else's life, and that means financial independence, of course. My father was right! Two things, a driver's license and a job. I don't have a car, but I do have a trade! I start working at a dental laboratory. There, I meet a very competent, 40-year-old dental technician from Romania, a great professional, but he can't read or write Hebrew. I can. Together, we open our own Dental Porcelain Laboratory in downtown Tel Aviv, on a side street just off the famous Dizengoff Street. At not even 21 years old, I have my own laboratory, the beginning of financial independence. Mental independence is still a long way away.

I often tell Oded about my boyfriend in Amsterdam. I say, 'If my boyfriend from Amsterdam comes here...' Oded replies, 'Yes, I know... if my girlfriend from Tel Aviv comes here...' My boyfriend intended to follow me, but I got scared because he had no profession or money, and Israel is a hard country. In the Netherlands, there are many open doors for him. I tell him, 'Don't do it, don't come here yet, go study, learn a trade and then we'll see...' Finally, this is how we slowly parted ways. Amsterdam-Tel Aviv, a great distance separates us.

Oded gradually becomes my pillar of support and strength, although I don't want to admit it. Oded is a very down-to-earth person. His parents did not experience World War II, so he had a normal childhood. Arguing with your parents ... that happens ... no catastrophe, no guilt.

Eleven months after I left Amsterdam, I hear that my boyfriend from Amsterdam, my first love, has married my classmate. She is a beautiful, cheerful, sociable girl with great parents, and my boyfriend, who basically had no home, now has a nice, beautiful wife with a sweet, warm, cozy home. Her parents embrace him with the love that he deserves. He found the stability and support he never knew until now. I understand, but it is very hard to accept.

Oded's shoulder is wet from my tears; I am happy to have this firm shoulder to cry on. Oded, always level-headed, immediately says: 'Right, this means that no one is waiting for us, and we are waiting for no one. Your boyfriend from Amsterdam is no longer coming, and neither is my girlfriend from Tel Aviv.'

Very slowly, my mental independence comes into view. The laboratory is doing very well, and the love between Oded and I unfolds very slowly, like a lotus flower. Roots sprout deep under the muddy water, and on top of the water, the beautiful lotus flower reveals strength, beauty, stability and security. Oded's strong arms work wonders, our love blossoms, we are happy, and we take life as if 'tomorrow' does not exist. As a side job, we work as photo models; our pictures are all over Tel Aviv. We are celebrities, we are VIPs, La Dolce Vita!

In the meantime, after three years of service, Oded is discharged from the army. A little while before university starts, Oded, who, until now, has never traveled by plane, wants to travel to Europe.

On Roerstraat 84 in Amsterdam, they welcome us politely. I sleep in my old little room, Oded sleeps in the dining room on a camping bed ... there is only one problem: the promenade at night across the creaking parquet floor ... how will the love-struck kitten get across the water ... to shore, to the strange camping bed inside Roerstraat 84.

Once back in Israel, I receive a long letter from Amsterdam. 'This boyfriend is not for you; this relationship must not continue.' Much explanation about 'why not' follows. Again, it is not good. Again, there is an attempt to control my happiness. This time, even remotely. How is it possible? Things are not the same anymore! It is different now. I live on another planet now, and I am less fragile, stronger, mentally and financially independent. I know how much my father suffered during the war, but I add nothing to the present suffering. I never added anything to it. Knowing this now, I no longer feel guilty. I owe that to my Oded.

Oded doesn't understand my problem at all. 'If I'm not good enough ... oh well ... they'll get used to it,' Oded says, and if not ... 'too bad ... what's it got to do with us?' He's right, that's how it is!

Slowly but surely, a great love develops. We get married in August 1969. The most beautiful couple in Tel Aviv gets married in the most beautiful garden in Tel Aviv. There are almost 500 guests, and it is a fairy tale wedding.

Haya and Oded's wedding, 1969

My father is surrounded by his brother, his sister, his cousins and his nieces, who survived the war. My mother is surrounded by her friends, Lore, Lilly (Lea) and Eshu, who survived the war. It is everyone's first big party after the war, and no one keeps a dry eye… tears of happiness.

Lilly (Lea) Milstein-Mikulinsky is one of the most moved guests. The son of her favorite cousin Aaron Ravinsky, dear Aaron, with whom she played for days in the hot sands of Tel Aviv in the years 1925-1930, is marrying the daughter of her favorite friend Ilse Mandelbaum-Birnbaum, with whom she played in the years 1938-1942 together in Maccabi Hatzair, the Zionist youth movement in Amsterdam.

Throughout the entire ceremony, Lea stood crying under the chuppah between Aaron and Ilse, her cousin from Tel Aviv and her friend from Amsterdam. Ilse Birnbaum and Lea Mikulinsky are now related; who could have imagined such a story?

Our laboratory is doing well. Oded is now a graduate economist. In 1971, our oldest daughter Efrat is born. In 1974, our second daughter Noa, and in 1979, our daughter Tamar. We have lived in a beautiful village in central Israel since 1975,

with green groves full of bright-colored oranges all around us. I sell the laboratory, and Oded leaves behind everything he is working on. We have a dream, an old dream: our daughters should grow up in a green, quiet, rural environment, and we should be farmers! We grow strawberries, melons, cucumbers, eggplants, zucchini, mushrooms and much more. Farming is not easy; there are many setbacks, such as freezing too hard, raining too much, a sudden heat wave occurring, and so on. Sowing does not guarantee a harvest yet. Agriculture has a lot in common with a casino.

In 1983, Oded and I quit farming after significant losses; we were basically bankrupt. Oded immediately finds a fantastic job, and I start working at a dental laboratory in Tel Aviv. The agricultural episode is over for good; we spend many years licking our wounds.

Finally, luck is on our side.

The seasons change, landscapes change, smells change, and our thoughts and insights change. I come to realize that I am not without fault myself. Slowly, I learn to understand my parents, especially my mother. I learn to accept and try to forgive.

I forgive them for leaving me alone in a hospital for nine months. I forgive them that I had to eat my own vomit. I forgive them the fact that they gave me no say in the decision to leave Israel. I forgive them for the decision to leave me alone for three months again, albeit with my grandparents, but still alone again.

I forgive them for sending me to a completely strange school with no help or tutoring. I forgive them for the fact that getting permission to go to summer or winter camp always had to be a battle. And I forgive them that I had to lie for four years to be allowed to see my boyfriend, my first true love.

My mother and I in my garden in Jarkona, 1995

I forgive, I must forgive, I must understand.
'Your father has suffered enough; you must not add anything to that!'

No, I don't add to it; I never added to it. Hitler and his Deutsche Reich added to it.

The second generation
The third generation
The fourth generation
It is now 2020, and they are still adding to it.

My reconciliation

The year 2020 is the year of the coronavirus: lockdown, home, time galore.

It is the day of Holocaust Remembrance, Tuesday, April 21, 2020. For the first time since 1988, a memorial service will not be held for the hundred thousand murdered saints of the Zaglebie District in Poland. The names of my grandparents, Haya and Ephraim Mandelbaum, are two of the one hundred thousand names engraved in the black granite. For the first time since 1988, I am absent.

My name is Haya. I was named after my grandmother; may her soul be bound up in the bond of eternal life. Efrat is my daughter's name. I named her after my grandfather Ephraim; may his soul be bound up in the bond of eternal life.

My parents often came to Israel to attend the memorial ceremony. My father was

In Auschwitz
In Brande
In Johannisdorf
In Paniow
In Direnfurt
In Bunzlau
In Groß-Rosen
And again in Auschwitz

In the Johannisdorf concentration camp, the Commander asked, 'Jude, wie alt bist du?' (Jew, how old are you) My father said, 'Ich bin 17 Jahren alt.' 'Du wirst das Alter von 20 nicht erreichen!' ('I'm 17 years old.' 'You won't reach the age of 20!') And he continued.

On February 11, 1945, the Death March from Auschwitz commenced. On February 20, after nine days of walking, the few survivors who remained were liberated by the Russians.

Since 2012, my father has not been with us.
My father was born on May 11, 1922.
On February 11, 1945, the Death March began.
On February 11, 2012, he passed away.
Does the number 11 mean anything? The number 11 probably protected him.

2020, coronavirus, home, time, no memorial. This time, I don't think about my father. Instead, I am lost in my thoughts and think: My father was stamped; the number 35215 was tattooed on his arm. His Holocaust was visible. My mother had no number tattooed on her arm. Her Holocaust was invisible. Does that mean she didn't have a Holocaust? Suddenly, it dawned on me. My mother had played second fiddle all her life.

'Your father has suffered enough; you must not add to it!'

Now, I suddenly understand. It was never about her. Her bucket was never emptied; she didn't stand a chance. Her fiancé, her friends, her war years, her fears, her memories. Suffering has no hierarchy, but my mother probably thought otherwise.

My mother did not have a stamp.

David and Ilse in 1990

In reality, both my parents were heavily stamped. The ink of the stamp fades with age. We, the children of stamped victims, have absorbed a lot of ink. I was no different from all my second-generation peers. For years, I was angry. For years, I didn't understand. For years, I always had a guilty conscience, although I was a good daughter; at least, I think I was. My flight to Israel was my salvation and their redemption. I could grow as a person, and my parents were finally no longer responsible for me. My mother just couldn't do it anymore. She once said, 'I need a lot of rest.'

My parents were wonderful grandparents to my three daughters, Efrat, Noa and Tamar. My daughters went to the Netherlands almost every summer vacation, often for up to two months. My daughters wistfully remember these times; they were so happy with their grandparents.

After more than forty years of silence, it was my daughter who first heard her grandfather's story. The children of Israel wandered through the desert for forty years to reach the Promised Land. It will probably take another forty years before a trusted peace emerges that allows them to share the horror. It takes a generation before the cast can be removed.

David and Ilse in 1982

On October 16, 1999, my beautiful, sweet, brave mother, after suffering while I stood beside her bed, passed away in Amsterdam.

Four rooms in her heart. One of the rooms was dark, black and locked. Erco's heart was tucked away in this room. She never overcame losing Erco. The love between my parents was great; they were in love with each other for 53 years. Her love for Erco did not stand in the way of her love for my father. The other three rooms in her heart were not empty either. Her wounded soul was blowing restlessly through these rooms.

Is she at peace now?

On October 18, my mother was buried peacefully, next to her parents, the Birnbaums, at the Liberal Jewish Cemetery Gan Hashalom in Amstelveen. My mother's stone reads:

Ilse Mandelbaum Birnbaum
Born 26-07-1921
Died 16-10-1999
Strikingly modest

In 2005, five years after he said goodbye to my mother, my brave father, aged eighty-three, sold everything in the Netherlands, packed up his memories and went alyah for the second time. Back to Israel. What a hero, what a Zionist. Overjoyed like a fish in water. The whole family spent seven more wonderful years together.

On February 11, 2012, while I was standing next to him, my beautiful, dear, brave father passed away in Kfar Saba. On February 12, my father, with the number 35215 tattooed in black on his arm, was buried peacefully in his home country. He rests in Ramat Hadar, a pastoral cemetery.

A light breeze blows caressingly among the field crops and across his black grave. My father's stone reads:

David Mandelbaum Nr. 35215
Born 11-05-1922
Freed from Auschwitz 11-02-1945
Died 11-02-2012

The year 2020 is the year of the coronavirus: lockdown, home, time galore.

April 2020, Memorial Day. For the first time in many years, there will be no memorial ceremony in the Zaglebie Forest, near the city of Modi'ien, the commemoration of the hundred thousand victims from the Zaglebie district in Poland. The names of my grandparents, Haya and Efraim Mandelbaum, are engraved on the black granite. My father had been in 11 concentration camps. For five years, Satan cast his gaze on him before releasing him in February 1945.

For more than twenty years, the copies of Erco's letters sat on a shelf in my bookcase. I had never read them. On this 2020 Memorial Day, I plunged myself into the letters.

There are not enough words to describe my feelings. Suddenly, after so many years, a window opened in my heart. The more I read, the clearer the picture became, the more I felt my mother.

My father had a stamp on his arm; his Shoah was visible. My mother had no stamp; her Shoah was invisible. The words 'Strikingly modest' are engraved on her tombstone. Ilse is buried next to David; she always played second fiddle.

My parents had to fight their way through thorns, snakes and across rocks and stones.

They still managed to pave beautiful paths and plant fragrant roses, even though those roses bore thorns. Now I understand the thorns that scratched and wounded me. My scratches are healed. My heart is open; there is room for understanding and forgiveness.

With Ilses' permission, Shlomo Samson once translated the letters from German into Hebrew. The original letters are kept at Yad Vashem in Jerusalem. Only the letters from Erco to Ilse. Ilse's letters to Erco, of course, are no longer there.

Because the whole story of the love that was not allowed to exist took place in the Netherlands, I understood that this story had to come back to the Netherlands and be written in Dutch.

We, the children of the 'second generation,' have a task. Our task is to convey our feelings with love, understanding and admiration to the third generation, telling it so it is never forgotten.

Dear Ima, Aba is the Violin, and you are the Piano. The music I suddenly hear after so many years sounds loving and gives me much strength. Two souls float between the clouds, giving me peace.

In reading the letters of Ernst (Erco) Cosmann, my mother's lover during the darkest years and the boy who did not survive Auschwitz, I found the comfort and the strength to forgive, to love, to accept, to understand and above all, to be so grateful for everything that DID survive.

Some of the people who feature in this book:

Werner Ahlfeld

Born in Nordhausen in 1911, and came to the Netherlands in 1939. He was a fruit farmer by profession. In Elden, he was one of the pacesetters and deputy director. Married in 1941 to Ella Cahen. When he lived in Elden, Ella had to stay in Amsterdam because of the new German rules. Only in Westerbork were they together. They were both in Bergen-Belsen and were liberated by the Russians on a train near Tröbitz. Died in Beit Yitzhak, Israel, in 1998.

Shlomo Samson

Born in Leipzig in 1923. He fled to the Netherlands after Kristallnacht, where his father already was. He stayed in Gouda and Elden and was sent to Westerbork with the other residents of Huize Voorburg. His father, who had lived there before the German invasion, had an influential position in the camp. Through his intervention, the Elden group was zurückgestellt (safeguarded) upon arrival from immediate deportation. Shlomo was on the extradition list for Palestine and was

deported to Bergen-Belsen. He was liberated by the Russians on a train near Tröbitz, the 'lost transport.' Emigrated to Palestine. Samson is the author of the book Zwischen Finsternis und Licht, in which he quotes heavily from Erco's letters. He translated Erco's letters into Hebrew. He lives in Israel.

Joachim 'Shushu' Simon

A German Palestine pioneer and resistance hero in the Netherlands. After Kristallnacht, he was incarcerated in the Buchenwald concentration camp. So he knew better than others what went on in those German camps. He was a youth leader in Loosdrecht and got the young residents there to go into hiding in time. He was also an important member of the resistance group of Joop Westerweel. To-  gether, they established an escape route to Switzerland in August 1942 to bring the Loosdrecht group and later also others to safety. In January 1943, he was arrested in Breda. He was given a sentence of 23 years. He committed suicide in his cell so that he would not betray his comrades under torture.

Lore Durlacher

Ilse worked closely with Lore Durlacher during her activities in the Resistance. In 1939, she came to the Netherlands as a refugee and ended up in the Werkdorp in Wieringen. After its evacuation in 1942, many Palestine pioneers from Wieringen were deported to Mauthausen, where they were murdered. Lore went to work in the Jewish psychiatric institution Het

Apeldoornsche Bosch. When it was evacuated by the Germans, she went into hiding and joined the underground. She became a member of the Westerweel group, was involved in the liberation of Jews from Westerbork, arranged hiding places and forged personal identity cards. Initially, she did so as Ilse Birnbaum, using Ilse's ID, but later, she became Els v.d. Bergh. She also obtained her nurse's degree under Ilse's name. After the war, Lore lived in Israel under the name Ora Goren. She died in 1992.

Hans and Ruth Stein

Edith Feuerstein (Vienna 1919) fled to the Netherlands in 1938 with her boyfriend Hans Stein (Olomouc, Czech Republic, 1917). They became good friends with Erco and Ilse. Ruth, as she was called, married Hans in 1940. They went to live in Deventer. Hans went into hiding in Wilp with Marcella de Vries and David Spitz.  He was arrested in June 1944 and sent via Westerbork and Bergen-Belsen to Auschwitz and murdered there. Ruth gave birth to a son, Michael, in 1943. She was very active in the Resistance and regularly worked with Ilse. She met her second husband, Erich Flegenheimer, near the end of the war. After the war, she and her son emigrated with Erich to the United States after staying in a kibbutz in Palestine. There, she founded a fashion empire that made her very wealthy. Edith Flagg, as she called herself in America, died in 2014.

Harmen and Antonia Oldenboom

The farmer family from Wilp, where Ernst worked and learned the farming trade. They always supported Erco, and through Ilse, they had sent a lot of fresh food to Westerbork when he was there. 'Super wonderful people' according to Ernst. Their farm was called the Barchel.

Marcella de Vries (Amersfoort 1924 – Auschwitz 1942)David Spitz (Hilversum 1918 – East-Europe 1942)

Marcella was a good friend of Erco. She was head of the household in Elden and got along very well with everyone. She was married to David Spitz. Ernst writes about their marriage in his letters. In 1942, they settled in Wilp and also went into hiding there. When they tried to flee to the south, they were arrested and ended up in Camp Mechelen. Marcella was murdered in Auschwitz on September 4, 1942.

David was among the group of most healthy people who were taken off the train 80 kilometers before Auschwitz-Birkenau and sent to a forced labor camp. His place and exact date of death is unknown.

Alfred 'Tzippi' Fränkel

He was born in 1920 in Breslau. He participated in training in the Working Village. He later became a courier and liaison between the Jewish Council and the camp institutions of Westerbork. He also participated in the underground Resistance of the Westerweel Group. After the Jewish Council was disbanded, he went into hiding and became active in France. The Germans caught him, and he remained in Buchenwald concentration camp until his liberation in August 1944. He passed away in Israel in the year 2000.

David Levison

He had a wholesale business in old metals, was treasurer of the Deventer Association and financially supported the Hechaloets movement. Ilse worked as a maid at his house in Zutphen until the Levison family was also rounded up. As a member of the Jewish Council, he only arrived in Westerbork much later, after a short stay with his family in the infamous Camp Vught. He survived the war.

Mau Reichenberger

According to Ernst, he was a 'Deventer hakhshara activist, who, as an official of the Jewish Council, was left unbothered for a long time. He was given permission to visit Westerbork in that capacity. He was 'our man' in Arnhem and thus also 'our man' in Elden. He was also a member of the board in Elden. Reichenberger was head of the Jewish Council in Gelderland. He spent thousands of guilders on packages for the Palestine pioneers from Elden until the Jewish Council forbade him to do so in August 1943. He ended up as an Austauschjude in Bergen-Belsen. He was liberated by the Russians on a train near Tröbitz on April 23, 1945. However, he died there the following day.

Kurt Reilinger

He was born in Stuttgart in 1917 and was a resistance fighter – one of the founders of the pioneer resistance movement. He was Ilse's main contact person during her illegal activities. His underground names were Nanno and Victor. He saved Jews by smuggling them to Spain. Unfortunately, he was betrayed and sent to Buchenwald. He survived but died in a car accident shortly after the war.

Miel Stranders

He was born in Amsterdam in 1917 and schooled at the Rabbinical Seminary in Amsterdam. Like Erco, he was a youth leader and teacher in Elden. He taught the Bible and Hebrew there. He was deported with Erco to Auschwitz on September 14, 1943, and died on the death march to Buchenwald

on February 2, 1945. He was married to Betty Baars, who oversaw clothing and laundry in Elden. In Westerbork, Betty and Miel worked as school teachers. Betty was part of that same deportation group to Auschwitz, fell into the hands of Mengele there, but survived. After the war, she remarried. She lived in Jerusalem.

Rudolf 'Ru' Cohen

He was a furniture dealer born in Deventer in 1889. Together with his wife, Eva Königsberger, he founded the Deventer Association for the Professional Training of Palestine Pioneers in 1918. He was the brother of David Cohen – chairman of the Jewish Council. He and his wife were sent to Westerbork in December 1943 and then to Bergen-Belsen in January. They both died there.

Selfried 'Fokki' Fuchs

He was born in Königshütte in 1913 and came to the Netherlands in 1938. He was a landscaper who specialized in creating rock gardens. In Westerbork, he made himself indispensable by caring for Commander Gemmeker's garden and was, therefore, not deported. He had to ensure there were fresh white carnations every day, Gemmeker's favorite flower. Fokki married the much younger Helena van Leeven (b. 1926), who worked in Gemmeker's household in Westerbork in 1943. On April 16, 1945, five days after the liberation of Camp Westerbork, their daughter Ruth was born at the camp.

David (Dudi) Rosenbaum

He was born in Cologne in 1925. He stayed at the Pavilion Loosdrechtse Rade and went into hiding like the other children that were there at the time.
He was betrayed and taken to Westerbork, where he became Erco's bunk buddy. According to Ilse, he managed to escape from the camp several times but was caught again each time. The last time he tried, Mirjam Waterman of the Westerweel
group brought him to Assen train station on the back of a bicycle. On the train, he was recognized and taken back to Westerbork, where he was put on punitive transport. He was murdered in Auschwitz on January 1, 1945. Dudi was the boyfriend of Ellen's friend Esther (Eshu) Singer, who survived the war.

Esther (Eshu) Singer

She was born in Ustrzyki, Poland, in 1924. She was with Erco in Elden and was deported to Theresienstadt via Westerbork. Eshu survived the war; her friend Dudi died. On her return to the Netherlands, she only knew one address where she could go, Stadionweg 117, to the Birnbaums. Eshu recovered there, but it took a long time. Together with Ilse, they went to the
south of France and, in March 1946, to Palestine via Marseille.

Albert Konrad Gemmeker

He was appointed camp commander of Polizeiliches Durchgangslager Westerbork in October 1942 with the rank of SS-Obersturmführer. He considered the deportations of the Jews 'kriegsnotwendig' (made necessary by the war) but left the drafting of the deportation lists largely up to the Jewish camp leaders. In January 1943, he personally attended the deportation of 1200 Jewish patients and their caretakers from the Apeldoornsche Bosch to Auschwitz.  After the liberation, he was sentenced to ten years in prison but was released after only six years due to good behavior. He settled in Düsseldorf again, where he died in 1982. He always denied having any knowledge of the mass murder of the Jews.

Tieke Jansma

Ilse mentions her during the interview in 1957. Tieke Jansma was a teacher and nurse. She cared for twelve people hiding in her upstairs apartment at 90 Nieuwe Prinsengracht in Amsterdam for many years. At one point, typhoid broke out in her home. Tieke was the only person who died from this disease; she was 31. All of her hiders survived the war. Jansma had ties to the Westerweel group, so her hiders were probably Palestine pioneers. Her name is on the Westerweel monument in Israel.

Arnold 'Effie' Koller and Hans 'Honki' Horwitz

Arnold Koller (Berlin, 1924) and Hans Horwitz (Berlin, 1923) fled to the Netherlands in 1939. They ended up in the Youth Alias Home in Mijnsheerenland and later in the Pavilion Loosdrechtse Rade. From September 1942, they lived in Huize Voorburg in Elden. From Westerbork, they were deported to Bergen-Belsen, where they were placed in the Sonderkommando. They had to burn the corpses in the crematorium after stripping them of all valuables, such as their jewelry and gold in their mouths. Because this work was to remain secret, they were put in a separate hut outside the camp, where they felt isolated from their comrades in Bergen-Belsen. 'Are we forever cut off from the other chawerim? Why?' they wrote in their very touching diary, some of which has been preserved. On November 23, 1944, Arnold and Honki were deported to Neuengamme. They were murdered on November 27, 1944.

With many thanks to:

Shlomo Samson

Dan Keren (the son of Werner, Ernst Cosmann's brother)

Hans Putman, Historische Kring Elden

Guido Abuys, Memorial Center Kamp Westerbork

The Het Joodse Schooltje museum in Leek

Bert and Ingrid Oldenboom

Ruth Kirschner-Fuchs (daughter of Helena and Selfried 'Fokki' Fuchs)

Acknowledgments

After translating all 105 letters from Hebrew into Dutch in June 2021, I wondered what the next step should be. I looked for someone who understood my story and also knew what I needed. Through a mediator, I received a number of names. All were nice, competent people, but I immediately knew who I had to have: Jan Torringa.
This was his first reaction:
'What an extraordinary possession, such a comprehensive correspondence, telling a personal story from the most horrific period of our history.
Combined with the life story of your mother, I can imagine that it must be possible to base a book on it that will be a valuable and interesting addition to all that has already been written about World War II.
A personal story like this always has value.'

Working with Jan was a pure pleasure from the very first moment.
A man with so much knowledge and yet so humble.
Always incredibly careful, so knowledgeable, so professional.
I translated the letters; Jan did the historical research.

My thanks to Jan Torringa, from the first moment I knew it had to be Jan!
I was right!
It could not have gone any better.

Consulted resources and literature:

Frans van der Straten: *Om nooit te vergeten; Palestina-pioniers in Nederland* 19391945 (Mijnsheerenland, n.y.)

Shlomo Samson: *Zwischen Finsternis und Licht. 50 Jahre nach Bergen-Belsen* (Jeruzalem 1995)

Paul Siegel: *Locomotieven trekken wagons* 1933-1945 (Westervoort 2000)

Hans Schippers: *De Westerweelgroep en de Palestinapioniers* (Hilversum 2015)

Hans Putman: *Palestina-pioniers in Elden*, in Kringbulletins of the Historische Kring Elden, 134 – 140 2018/2019

Heinz (Zwi) Durlacher: *Stationen des Weges* (manuscript n.y.)

Yigal Benjamin: *They were our friends*, Tel Aviv 1990

Willie Westerweel: *Verzet zonder geweld*: Joop Westerweel 1899-1944

J. Presser: *Ondergang; de vervolging en verdelging van het Nederlandse* Jodendom 1940-1945 ('s-Gravenhage 1965)

Philip Mechanicus: *In dêpot, dagboek uit Westerbork* (Amsterdam 1964)

Ad van Liempt: *Gemmeker; Commandant van Kamp Westerbork* (2019)

Willy Lindwer: *Getuigen van Westerbork; kamp van hoop en wanhoop*

Guido Abuys en Dirk Mulder: *Een gat in het prikkeldraad; Kamp Westerbork, ontsnappingen en verzet*

Harm van der Veen: Westerbork 1939 – 1945; *Het verhaal van vluchtelingenkamp en Durchgangslager Westerbork*, 2013

Raymond Schütz: *Vermoedelijk op transport*, (Master's thesis Archival Sciences, Leiden 2010)

Lisette Lewin: *Vorig jaar in Jeruzalem*, Amsterdam 2013

Dr. L. de Jong: *Het Koninkrijk der Nederlanden in de Tweede Wereldoorlog*

Mirjam Pinkhof: *De jeugdalijah van het Paviljoen Loosdrechtse Rade*, 1998

Nathan Mageen (Hans Mogendorff): *Zwischen Abend und Morgenrot*, Düsseldorf 2005

Jochewed Leuvenberg-Nathans: *Twee Palestina-pioniers in oorlogstijd*, Bedum 2000

Eli Wiesel: Nacht, 2006 Primo Levi: *Is dit een mens*, 1987

Online sources:

Yad Vashem Documents Archive: https://documents.yadvashem.org/
(Which includes the letters of Ernst Cosmann)

Ghetto Fighters House Archive, Lohamei Hageta'ot, Israel: https://www.infocenters.co.il
(In which testimonies, letters and documents, on which the above is based or from which is quoted, by Ilse Birnbaum, Lini de Bruin, Lore Durlacher, Werner Ahlfeld, Ygal Benjamin, Lotte Schnurmann, Betty Baars, Zwi and Ruth Durlacher, Lore Sieskind, Erica Blüth-Henschel and Jan Smit. The archives of the Association for Vocational Training Palestine Pioneers can also be found here.)

https://spurenimvest.de/2021/10/08/cosmann-ernst/

The Herinneringscentrum Westerbork website: https://www.kampwesterbork.nl/
https://arolsen-archives.org

Printed in Dunstable, United Kingdom

Printed in Dunstable, United Kingdom